Brendan DuBois is the author of *Resurrection Day*, *Six Days*, the Lewis Cole mysteries and numerous short stories, which have earned him two Shamus Awards and three Edgar Award nominations. He lives in Exeter, New Hampshire.

Visit the author's website at: www.BrendanDuBois.com

D03357819

BETRAYED

Brendan DuBois

timewarner
paperbacks

A *Time Warner* Paperback

First published in Great Britain in 2003 by
Time Warner Paperbacks

A CIP catalogue record for this book
is available from the British Library.

ISBN 0 7515 3418 8

Typeset in Goudy by M Rules
Printed and bound in Great Britain by
Clays Ltd, St Ives plc

Time Warner Paperbacks
An imprint of
Time Warner Books UK
Brettenham House
Lancaster Place
London WC2E 7EN

www.TimeWarnerBooks.co.uk

This book is dedicated to the memory of my uncle:

T/5 Leo M. Callaghan, Co. L, 325th Infantry Regiment,
35th Army Division
Born: June 26, 1925, Dover, N.H.
Killed in Action: November 20, 1944, Bermering, France

And to all those others who served
and never came home.

ACKNOWLEDGMENTS

The author wishes to express his thanks and appreciation to the following individuals and organizations:

John Clayton of the *Union Leader* newspaper, Manchester, N.H.; Jennifer Crompton and Jeff Bartlett, of WMUR television, Manchester, N.H., Capt. Chris Colitti and Lt. Mark Myrdek, N.H. State Police; Norm St. Hillaire of the New Hampshire Department of Safety; Detective Stephen DuBois, Portsmouth (N.H.) Police Department, and his fellow SWAT team members; the staff of the Exeter (N.H.) Public Library; Jed Mattes, Fred Morris, and Aaron Downey of the Jed Mattes Literary Agency; Isabel Kim; Ruth Cavin of St. Martin's Press; and Hilary Hale of Time Warner UK.

In addition, the author thanks his wife, Mona Pinette, for her keen editorial eye and unflagging encouragement; Dan and Blythe Brown, fellow travelers; and the members of the Sunset Shores Association of Conway Lake, N.H.

Any errors in depicting the activities of law enforcement and news agencies mentioned in this novel are the author's alone and not of those sources who so generously gave of their time and knowledge.

Equally frustrating were our discussions of the American soldiers and airmen who were prisoners of war or missing in action. We knew of at least eighty instances in which an American serviceman had been captured alive and had subsequently disappeared. The evidence consisted of either voice communications from the ground in advance of capture or photographs and names published by the Communists. Yet none of these men were on the list of POWs handed over after the Agreement. Why? Were they dead? How did they die? Were they missing? How was that possible after capture?

– Secretary of State Henry Kissinger
Years of Upheaval

BETRAYED

PROLOGUE

On Saturday, March 7, 1973, in a small red Cape Cod house in the Dover Point section of Dover, New Hampshire, twelve-year-old Jason Harper sat on the couch in the family's living room, watching the television with his parents, squeezing his arms tight against his chest, so tight he found it hard to breathe. The room was small, with a tile floor that was bitterly cold in the winter, and which was covered—mostly—by a braided rug his mother had made while watching television these past several months. His mother this Saturday evening wasn't braiding any kind of rug; she had a copy of *Time* magazine in her hands from last December, opened up to a certain page. On this Saturday Mother also hadn't found the time or energy to get dressed; she was still wearing her light blue housecoat over a red flannel nightgown, yellow slippers on her feet with the bottoms scuffed to gray from months of use. She was sitting in her chair, next to Father, who was sitting in his own chair. Between them was a narrow table that had piles of *Reader's Digest*, *Catholic Digest*, *Newsweek*, and even a few old *Life* magazines, the magazine having ceased its life back in December, about the same time Mother and Father thought that their own lives had ended.

Father had managed to get dressed in an old gray sweatshirt

1

and green chino workpants, but the fly was down on his pants. Any other time, Jason would have thought about teasing his father about the open fly, but the look on Dad's face, made even more haunted by the gray stubble from his having skipped shaving that morning, silenced Jason. His mother and father continued staring at the television set, and Jason joined them, watching the flickering picture on the old Zenith. The program was coming from Clark Air Force Base in the Philippines, and as it aired, Mother would occasionally sigh loudly. It scared Jason, scared him so much that he wanted to go upstairs to his bedroom and close the door, but he knew he couldn't leave.

'Tom,' his mother said to his father. 'Tom, what do you think? I think he might be there. What do you think?'

'Grace,' his father said patiently. 'You know what the Air Force said. All right? You know just as well as I do.'

'Still,' she said, holding the *Time* magazine close to her. 'This has to be him in the magazine, right? How can the magazine be wrong?'

Jason's dad said nothing, kept on staring at the television screen, where an Air Force plane was taxiing down a runway. Jason took a breath, tried to ease the tension in his chest. On top of the television was a framed photo of a young man wearing an Air Force uniform. His older brother, Roy. Next to the large photo was a smaller one, of Roy standing before his plane. A B-52, stationed in Guam. The B-52 that Roy piloted. The B-52 that went down over North Vietnam last December, the B-52 that had magically transported his brother—his smart, demanding, strong, older brother—from a pilot in the Air Force to something else.

MIA. Missing In Action.

The plane on the television set was coming to a halt.

2

People were waving signs and flags and banners, and were straining against rope barriers. From the newspapers and news reports, Jason knew what was going on over there, half a world away. Operation Homecoming, the return of the last POWs from North Vietnam after the recently signed Paris Peace Accords. Peace. It had come just a month ago, and if only Roy had been back in the United States on a training mission, or hadn't gone on that last bombing run, or if he had been laid up with a broken leg or some damn thing . . .

Weeks. A matter of weeks for a stupid war to end and for him to lose his brother.

On the television there were lots of Air Force personnel, smiling and laughing. Sure, he thought. Laugh all you want, you jerks. It's not your brother who's gone. Jason remembered back in December, when the doorbell had rung, early that Sunday morning. An Air Force officer and a chaplain had come up from Pease Air Force Base in Newington, to pass on the news. Even before they could say a word, Mom had been wailing, almost screeching, and he had tumbled downstairs, pulling a brown flannel robe on over his pajamas. It had been awful, nothing like he could ever imagine, in their tiny living room, with the Christmas tree and wrapped gifts on the floor, the two Air Force guys looking red-faced and embarrassed, Mom on the couch, one slipper on, Dad next to her, saying, 'Just let them speak, all right, Grace? Just let them speak.'

And Mom had gone on and on, wailing and mentioning Roy's name, over and over again. Finally, the Air Force guys had managed to get the story out. Roy's B-52 had been shot down near Hanoi. The plane had crashed. Two members of the crew managed to get rescued, the tail gunner and radar-navigator. The others—including Roy—were listed as missing in action, but his parachute had been seen by the rescued tail

3

gunner. The chaplain, a plump red-faced man in his Air Force uniform whom Jason instantly disliked, had grasped his mother's hand and had said, 'Time, Mrs. Harper. Just give it time. Your son's a strong boy. Chances are he's been captured, and the war will be over soon. Quite soon. Chances are you'll be seeing your boy in a couple of months.'

Chances. Jason picked up a pillow from the couch and wrapped his arms around it, squeezed it tight. A sleet storm was banging against the windows outside. Well, Officer Chaplain, he thought, it's been a couple of months and chances are my parents and I will never see my brother, ever again. What do you think about that? And what are you doing this winter evening? Drinking it up at the officers' club?

The door to the airplane on the television opened. A mobile stairway was brought up, and cheers began to sound out from the crowd. Jason had to wipe at his moist eyes. His mom was now on the floor, the copy of *Time* magazine open in her shaking hands. He had to look away for a second, for he could not stand seeing his mom acting like this. But he knew what she was looking for. Her son. That's all. Jason knew the page of *Time* magazine by heart. There were photos of some of the captured B-52 crews that had been shot down during the December bombing raids. One photo showed an Air Force officer, knee-deep in some rice paddy, hands held high, his parachute draped about his shoulders and the ground, face partially obscured by his helmet. North Vietnamese soldiers were angrily pointing Russian-made rifles at him. The photo said the officer was 'currently unidentified,' but Mom knew better. That was her boy. Had to be. And despite her calls, letters, and even visits to the local congressman's office having not led to anybody else believing in her, she still believed. That was her boy. And he

4

wasn't missing in action. He was captured. He was a prisoner of war.

And today, this Saturday in March, the last prisoners of war were to be returned.

Including Roy.

Jason looked over at Father, whose hand kept on rubbing at the stubble on his face. His hand was shaking, as well, and Jason guessed what was going on: Dad was just trying to keep it together, trying to agree with Mom if possible, but knowing in his heart of hearts that his boy wasn't coming home. He would always be an MIA. Always. And right now, the newspapers and television news were equating MIAs with being dead.

Still, there was a look in Father's eyes, a look that wanted to believe so much that his wife and the mother of their oldest boy was right.

'They're coming down!' Mom announced. 'They're coming down!'

And so they were, streaming down the stairway, their faces wide with happiness and joy, even the ones with crutches waving at the crowds. Some wore uniforms while others had on blue jeans and light blue shirts, and then his view was blocked, as Mom put her face close up to the television screen, examining each returning POW as he exited the jet. She kept the *Time* magazine close at hand, sometimes looking down at it, but only for a moment, as if she was afraid that by looking away, she would miss her boy on the television screen.

Jason sat stock-still, arms tight against the pillow, blinking back the tears again. Bad enough if Roy had been killed. Jesus, never to see him again, never to get patches and old flight manuals and postcards from places like Thailand or Hong Kong or Hawaii. Never again to look up to the tall guy and

5

know that his brother was one who knew how to fly a jet. His brother. Missing. Not dead, not alive. Missing.

Then the line of POWs stopped coming out of the aircraft. The open door was empty. Mom turned back to Dad. 'Is that it? Is that it?'

Dad nodded, his eyes filled with tears as well.

Mom wailed, started touching the television screen with her free hand. 'That can't be! That can't be! Roy must still be there, he must still be there somewhere. Tom, we've got to fly out there. We've got to! We have to meet those prisoners, see if any of them have seen Roy. We should leave tomorrow!'

Dad looked at Jason with such a look of anguish that Jason had to turn away. Dad cleared his throat and said, 'We'll talk about it later, Grace. We'll talk about it later.'

Mom said nothing, weeping on the floor, the *Time* magazine opened up to that magic page. Even from the couch Jason could see the photo of the pilot, helmet obscuring most of his head, hands held up high. Maybe it was Roy. Maybe it wasn't. Jason wanted to believe his mom, but he couldn't be sure.

But he was sure of one thing, looking at the smiling faces of the returning POWs and their Air Force officers, slapping them on the back and shaking hands. He would never forget, not once, how his brother had been lost, in a stupid, bloody, and long war. For no good reason, he would never see his brother again. Not because of the North Vietnamese. No, it wasn't them who put Roy over their airspace. It was those jerks in Washington like Nixon and Kissinger. They had done it. Not the North Vietnamese.

He squeezed the pillow hard, one more time. That he would never forget.

ONE

Nearly thirty years after seeing his brother's photograph on top of a Zenith television set, Jason Harper looked at it again, in his tiny office at his home in Berwick, Maine, about ten miles north of Dover. A small desk, a chair, an Apple iMac, and bookshelves crowded the room, which also had a window overlooking a small yard that bordered the Salmon Falls River. He touched the photo, whose colors had faded away in the intervening years, making Roy look like one of those Civil War soldiers standing fierce and proud across the ages. Almost three decades. It and a number of other framed items cluttered the top of the room's sole bookcase. He looked over to another, larger photo. His mom and dad, bravely smiling at the camera during their fiftieth wedding anniversary. Now they were in Florida, having decided five years ago that New England winters were no longer something to be endured. Still, it had taken some convincing from Dad to get Mom to move.

'Suppose,' she had said. 'Just suppose the phone rings and, well, you know . . .'

And Dad, without complaining or arguing, had just gone ahead and ensured that the current congressman, the local newspapers, and the tenth (or eleventh) liaison officer with the

7

POW-MIA office at the Pentagon were notified of their new address. Jason frowned, remembering all the vacation trips postponed, truncated, or never taken, because Mom was terrified that if they were gone from the house, they would miss the Call.

At first, Jason had thought it made sense, especially since the status of Roy's case had been so iffy, right from the start. It was very likely that he had arrived on the ground of North Vietnam alive, and it was even possible that some faction in North Vietnam was holding him and other MIAs for some sort of hostage deal. He remembered reading a newspaper story in high school in the late seventies, about how the North Vietnamese felt betrayed that subsequent administrations after Nixon's had never supplied the promised billions of dollars in rebuilding aid.

There had been another story as well, and he remembered clipping it out of *Newsweek* and showing it to Dad. (He didn't want to get Mom's hopes up, after all that time.) This article had mentioned that years after the French got kicked out of Vietnam, some French POWs—many thought dead—had been released, even five or ten years after the peace treaty had been signed.

So. A chance. Slim, but a chance, for some of those hundreds of American MIAs to find their way home.

But as he got older, he found his thoughts of Roy returning less and less to the possibility his older brother was still alive. He had read other stories through college and afterward, as MIA investigations were finally allowed in Vietnam, and he came to the conclusion that most investigators had reached: a certain percentage of downed airmen had been executed, right after landing on the ground, by enraged villagers or militiamen. And as much as he hated to admit it, even though it concerned his brother, there was a certain rough justice in those cases. How would he feel, being on the ground and seeing one's homeland, friends, and neighbors pulverized by 500-pound bombs? And to then see one of those responsible for all this death and destruction land in your backyard? Geneva Convention or no, he doubted he would have the self-control to turn a downed pilot or crewmen over to the local army unit.

'Hey, you in there!' came a voice from the kitchen. 'You ready to eat?'

'In a sec,' he said, looking to a third framed item. A miniature front page from the college newspaper of the University of New Hampshire, with his first bylined story. About the rise in parking fees at the college. Not earth-shattering, nothing worth noting, except it was his first, one of many more stories to come.

'Sorry, I didn't hear you,' came the voice again, and he turned, smiling, looking at his wife of ten years. The former Patricia Ann Sullivan, her brown hair trimmed short, wearing blue-jean coveralls. She was wiping her hands on a dish towel, and he said, 'Yes, dinner sounds fine.'

She came into the small office, put her arm around him, nudged her lips against a bearded cheek. 'Still think about him much?'

He enjoyed her touch, which still made him tingle, years after first meeting her. He said, 'Some, now and then. He was quite the guy. You hear about big brothers always picking on little brothers. But not Roy. Not that he was perfect, but he was a good guy. Taught me how to ride a bike, how to fish. Let me drink my first beer when I was twelve, the last time I saw him before he went to Guam. Always wanted to fly, always wanted to travel. Got appointed to the Air Force Academy and when he became captain, was assigned to a B-52 . . . but you already knew that.'

9

She gave him a squeeze with her arm. 'Always glad to hear it still.'

From the kitchen came a young boy's voice: 'Mom! Dad! Caleb's trying to get up on the table.'

Patty kissed him on his cheek. 'Come along, sport, before our son and dog demolish dinner.'

'All right,' he said, leaving the office and switching off the light. The last thing he saw as the room darkened was the framed photo of his long-lost brother.

He parked the stolen car in a spot of woods near the target house, his hands cold, just as the engine rattled and finally died. Made it. Jesus. He thought about everything that was ahead of him and felt that dagger of despair twist inside, but he pushed it away. He remembered a few years back seeing a video of the movie *Apollo 13*. A fight had broken out among the three astronauts in the damaged capsule, and the mission commander, James Lovell, had pointed out that for all of them to live, there were about 800 steps to finish, in correct sequence, to guarantee that outcome. And that they were only on step eighteen.

And us? he thought, stepping out of the car, holding on to a dirty gray knapsack. We are on step three, and there's a hell of a lot more steps ahead of us, much more dangerous than being in a crippled spacecraft, thousands of miles away from earth.

He pocketed the keys, opened the door—having earlier switched off the dome light—and softly closed it behind him.

Jason tried to smile gamely as he ate Patty's dinner, which was a traditional Sunday evening feast, a New England boiled dinner, which he couldn't stand. Ham, boiled potatoes, turnip, carrots, and cabbage. Except for the ham, everything else tasted to him like salty sludge. Yet he ate all of it, for he didn't want to hurt Patty's feelings—during their initial courtship, when he was trying to think of everything and anything to keep her interested in him, he had lied and said her boiled dinner was the best he had ever eaten—and he was also trying to be an example to their six-year-old, Paul R., who was deciding lately that he would only eat bread and cheese.

But tonight, Caleb—a perpetually drooling black Labrador retriever, who thought Paul was his older sibling—was distracting the boy enough with rolling around on the floor that he ate with no objections. The kitchen was small, like the rest of the house, and with the stove, refrigerator, and countertops was almost overwhelmed by the dining room set, a gift from one of Patty's rich uncles. From the kitchen Jason could see the living room and the stairs that led upstairs to the bathroom and three bedrooms: theirs, Paul's, and soon—he hoped—a nursery for a future sister or brother. For ever since 1972, Jason had been an only child, and he'd hated it, hated the solitude, hated the loneliness. Now he was part of a family, and he didn't want Paul to grow up as alone as he had.

He smiled at Patty as he put a piece of yellow something—turnip?—into his mouth and started chewing. 'Great, hon,' he said, lying with the ease that came from years of practice. 'Delicious.'

He moved down the dirt driveway, to the small house, letting patience be his guide. The early summer evening was cool and he shivered, though it was nothing like the cold he had experienced during those long years. He went among the

11

shadows, only moving when the wind came up and rustled the tree branches and brush, masking his approach. Lights were on at the house, and through a small window he could see people inside, eating. He squatted down by a woodpile. He saw a pleasant-looking young woman, smiling at somebody at the other end of the table. He could barely make out the top of what was a child, a boy or a girl, he couldn't tell. He waited, just waited, hoping to see if the third person would be there.

He let his hand drift to his left pocket, where there was a folding knife, ready to come out at the right time.

As he washed the dishes—and Patty dried—Paul R. came over, yawning. He had on a pair of Oshkosh B'Gosh jeans and a Mickey Mouse sweatshirt, and he leaned forward and wrapped his arms around Jason's upper leg.

'Daddy?' he murmured.

'Yeah, tiger, what is it,' Jason said, scrubbing at a plate. Next year, he thought, maybe next year we could spring for a dishwasher. But, truth be told, sometimes he liked washing dishes. It was a little family ceremony that all of them shared, and he knew he would hate to see it disappear. With so many families scattering to soccer practice, flute practice, school meetings, and whatever, it was nice to hold on to these precious few minutes with everyone.

Paul yawned. 'Do you think I could go with you tomorrow night?'

'Monday? To the town selectmen's meeting? Why?'

"Cause you're working, right? And I wanna see you when you're working.'

Patty tried hard to stifle a smile. 'Six years old and you've already corrupted him.'

He reached down with the moist towel and made a point of rubbing Paul's face vigorously. The boy made a funny sound of disgust and pulled away. 'Tell you what, we'll see how sleepy you are after supper.'

'Why?' Paul said, now on the floor, rubbing the belly of Caleb, who had rolled over on his back.

'Because those meetings are so boring, you'll be asleep in five minutes, and that will be way before your bedtime,' Jason said. 'And then how could I do my job if I have to bring you back to bed?'

'Oh, okay,' Paul said, now entranced with Caleb's tongue, which was hanging over his sagging jowls. Patty gently bumped hips with Jason, and he returned to the dishes, and then froze, looking out into the darkness of their front yard. Patty noticed it instantly.

'What's wrong?'

He was surprised at how dry his mouth was. 'I thought I saw something move out there.'

Patty looked to see if Paul had been listening, but he was now playing with Caleb's hind legs. She lowered her voice. 'Something or someone?' she asked.

'I don't know,' he said, picking up a wet sponge. 'Just a quick movement. Maybe a deer or something.'

Another soft bump of the hips. 'Or maybe a disgruntled subscriber.'

Jason smiled and passed a wet plate over to her. 'Does that mean the majority of our subscribers are gruntled?'

He chastised himself for what had just happened, for he had been startled and felt himself jerk involuntarily as he saw the man through the kitchen window. Pudgy-looking fellow in his late thirties, wearing a blue Oxford shirt, no tie, khakis.

Receding hairline, close-cropped beard. Smiling a lot as he did the dishes, and who could blame him for smiling so much, with a beautiful young wife at his side, and no doubt an attractive child as well? Still, he thought, touching the shape of the knife in his pants, he still looked soft. Could he be hard enough for what was going to happen, what had to occur? Could he?

In the darkness he sighed, knapsack in his hand, and then shifted quietly as the shapes moved away from the lit kitchen window.

In a while Paul had been put to bed, after three requests were filled: a small drink of water, Caleb lying down next to him on the floor, and one of the *Curious George* books read to him. Patty had kissed the top of Jason's head—'Hey, hon, my lips are starting to touch bare flesh up there; maybe it's time for a pharmacist visit'—and he had gamely gone through the book that he had no doubt read about twenty or thirty times.

When Caleb was snoring and Paul's eyes were getting droopy, he closed the book and leaned over to kiss his son's forehead. The eyes fluttered open and Paul whispered, 'Dad?'

'Yes, Paul.'

'Dad . . . Mommy sometimes says that one of these days you're going to write a book. Is that true?'

He nodded. 'Yes. One of these days.'

'Oh. Will there be pictures in it?'

'Maybe.'

'Will . . . will you let me draw 'em?'

Jason didn't have the heart to tell his boy that any pictures in this particular book would be photographs, so he kissed him again on the forehead. 'We'll talk about it later, okay?'

14

''Kay.'

'Now, get to sleep.'

He got up from the small chair, put the book back in the low bookshelf, and, on the way out, stopped to rub Caleb on his furry belly. The Lab stretched and yawned, and as he went out the door, Jason left it ajar, in case the dog needed to get out for a drink.

He let himself relax for a few minutes, as the lights inside the house began to be turned off. He touched the pine trees and birches, then knelt down, felt the moist dirt in his hands, sniffed at the richness of spring. A sudden urge came to him, to leave this place and everything else, to set off by himself and just to . . . live. Nothing extraordinary. Nothing demanding. Just exist, day to day. He could do it. He had been alone plenty of times these past years. Why not? Hadn't he been through enough? Hadn't he?

He waited. There was the whisper of a jet going overhead, and he looked up into the sky, saw the running lights.

No, he wouldn't leave. He couldn't. Not after all this time.

There was a small television at the foot of their bed, placed on a bureau, and the sound was turned down so low he could hardly make out what was going on. But that was all right. The boy's bedroom was right next to theirs, and they had learned a year or two ago that he got to sleep quicker when he could hear that murmuring sound of a television, the comforting noise that meant Mom and Dad were still awake.

Plus, Jason thought, smiling to himself, the television could also mask other noises coming from this room, noises that they didn't want to explain quite yet to curious little Paul.

He looked over at Patty, who was rolled on her side toward him, reading a folded-over copy of that day's edition of the Berwick *Banner*, the only newspaper that covered Berwick, North Berwick, and South Berwick, Maine. It wasn't much of a newspaper, but it had grown over the past five years, the years when he and Patty had made the great leap into the unknown and had started it up by themselves. Earlier he had been an assistant editor and she the accounts manager at the York County *Coast Star*, and decided in a flurry of decisions to go into business themselves. She handled business and he handled the editorial side, and it had grown from just the two of them—he covering police, fire and politics in the three towns, she juggling the books and trying to sell advertising space to the tightfisted Mainers who lived here— to a paper that subscribed to the Associated Press wire service, had three part-time reporters, an assistant editor, and a full-time ad agent.

The newspaper was still owned by the local branch of Fleet Bank, but each month a little more of it belonged to them. And when they had started the newspaper, it had just been a weekly. Now it came out three times a week, and if God, the economy and local advertisers all smiled in their direction, they planned to make it a daily next year, just in time for the new millennium.

Patty looked up at him. 'Nice editorial on the district school budget,' she said.

'Thanks.'

Then she wrinkled her nose, as if Caleb had been in the room and just had a noxious release. 'But I'm not too sure about the other editorial. About the Defense Department budget.'

'Why?' he asked. 'Are you in favor of a larger budget for those clowns at the Pentagon?'

Another wrinkle of her nose. 'You don't have to convince me, stud. I'm just thinking about our readers.'

'What about our readers?'

'Well, we know they like the local coverage. I don't know if running editorials and the occasional wire service piece on the evils of the military-industrial complex suits their needs. They can get that stuff from the Boston *Globe* or the Portland *Press Herald*.'

He moved his bare foot to her equally bare leg, stroked up and down. 'I don't overtrumpet things, and you know that. It's just that if we're going to change things in this country, you know how it's going to happen. Not from the state capitals, or the lobbyists, or the well-connected. It's going to be the grass-roots, the people in the towns like these. And if they're going to make these kinds of decisions, they'll need information. And that's our job.'

Patty smiled over at him, leaned up and kissed him on the cheek. 'All right, Jason. You can put away your Rotary Club speech. Lord knows I've heard it plenty of times before. I just want you to keep aware of how many times you climb up on that particular soapbox. Some parts of this county are still pretty conservative. And if you're going to pay for this soap-box, you can't irritate those nice people who pay our bills.'

He stopped stroking her leg. 'You getting any push-back?'

She turned the newspaper around, folded over another page. 'Nope, not yet. But I can sense it's going to happen.'

'Unh-hunh,' he said, rolling over so he was now on his side, looking into those light brown eyes. 'I thought all good newspapers keep the editorial and business side apart.'

Patty kept on reading the newspaper. 'Looks like this paper's editor and business side are already in bed together. So much for integrity.'

He reached over, stroked a cheek. 'I suppose . . . since we're in bed already, that it wouldn't matter much to the newspaper's integrity if we took things . . . to another level. Would it?'

She whapped him on the end of his nose with the newspaper. 'For an editor, you can be pretty dense. Should I have sent up a flare?'

He grabbed the newspaper, tossed it to the floor. 'No,' he said, leaning in to kiss her. 'You should have taken out an advertisement.'

Now, he thought. Time. He got up, felt his knees pop with old age, and walked across the dirt driveway, to the small porch. His heart was thumping so hard he thought it was impossible that the people inside the house couldn't hear a thing. It was time for the next step, the most important one of all, and he walked up the porch and hesitated, looking at the little illuminated round button that was the doorbell. A little light switch. Sure looked familiar, like he hadn't seen these kinds of switches, many times before, years ago . . .

Knock it off, he thought angrily. You're getting stir crazy. It's time.

He leaned his thumb into the doorbell, heard the chime, heard a dog start barking, and to make sure he was heard, he rang the bell again and again.

Jason sat up, hands and feet chilled. Patty rolled over, looked at the clock. 'Christ, it's ten o'clock. Who in hell . . .'

He swung his feet to the floor, wearing shorts that only a few seconds earlier he had planned to toss aside while being delightfully engaged in crawling on top of his happy and inviting wife. The doorbell rang again, Caleb was barking, and young Paul was calling out. Jason went to the closet, pulled out a blue terry-cloth robe.

'Jason,' Patty said, following him with her own robe.

'Look,' he said. 'Calm Paul down, grab Caleb. I'll go see who it is.'

He went into the hallway, just as the doorbell rang again. Patty called out, 'Paul, it's okay, it's okay. Daddy's going to check.'

Sure, he thought, one scared daddy is going to make everything right, little boy. He flipped on the stairway lights and started going down. Patty called out, 'I'll be right down.'

'No,' he said. 'Stay with Paul. I'll take care of it.'

'The hell you will by yourself,' she said. 'I'm grabbing the phone and calling the cops. Maybe it's someone who hated your editorial today.'

He stopped at the foot of the stairs, looked up to his wife, who was holding back a frantic Caleb. 'Look,' he said. 'You'll see. It'll be somebody lost or somebody drunk. It'll just take a sec. Hold on.'

But as he went through the living room, he could hear the footsteps of his wife and dog, following him.

He blinked hard as the porch light came on, took a step back. His heart rate even went up another notch, and he had a dark, amusing thought, that right now, at this important point, he would drop dead of a heart attack before saying a single word.

Jason turned on the light, snuck a peek outside, felt his hands and feet again get chilled. He had been hoping for a couple of teenagers, maybe drunk, looking for a party somewhere, but there was only one guy out there. Dressed in jeans and filthy sweatshirt, red-gray beard, hair pulled back in a ponytail. Drifter, maybe, looking for a buck or a handout, and suddenly he was quite glad that Patty and Caleb were out in the living room, backing him up.

Patty said, 'Who's there?'

'I don't know,' he said, stepping away from the window. 'Look, you've got the phone?'

'Yes,' she said.

'Okay, I'll just open the door a bit. Anything weird goes on, call the cops.'

'Jason,' she said, 'don't open the door.'

'Hunh?'

Her voice was sharper. 'Just step back, don't open the door. Maybe he'll go away.'

He tried to give her a reassuring smile as he walked to the front door. 'Hon, it'll be okay. Honest.'

And twenty-four hours later, he wished he had listened to her.

He took another step back, as the door was unlocked. The man of the house slowly opened the door, just a notch, so he could look out, his pudgy face concerned, a robe around his body.

'Yes?' the man said.

'Sorry to bother you, but are you Jason Harper?'

'Yes, I am. Look, it's late and—'

'Jason Harper, editor of the Berwick *Banner*?'

'Yes,' he said, his voice growing annoyed. 'That I am. Look, this is going on—'

'Just one more question, please,' he said.

Jason kept his foot on the edge of the door, knowing he would slam it shut in an instant if things went to the shits pretty quick. This ratty old man—late fifties, early sixties?—looked like his place of residence was a shack back in the woods, and his drink of choice was Thunderbird. There was a filthy knapsack at his feet. Patty whispered to him, 'Should I? Jason, should I?'

'Hold on,' he whispered back, and louder he said, 'Okay. One more question, and that's it. We're calling the police.'

The man smiled, revealing teeth that obviously hadn't been touched by a dentist in years. 'All right, that's fair. One more question. Are you the Jason Harper who grew up in Dover, New Hampshire, and whose parents are Tom and Grace?'

It was as if all other sounds had been muted, from Patty's voice to the harsh breathing of Caleb to the calls from Paul upstairs, wondering if everything was all right.

'Yes,' he said slowly. 'I am. And how in hell do you know that?'

The old man suddenly grinned, wiped at his eyes. 'Jesus, Jason. It's me.'

'Me? What do you mean, me?'

The grin was still there. Tears were now rolling down the man's cheeks, into his scraggly beard, and Jason had to lean into the door so he wouldn't fall down, as the old man said that one simple sentence: 'Jason, it's me, Roy, your brother.'

TWO

In Portsmouth, New Hampshire, about twenty miles south of Berwick, Maine, a man whose Massachusetts driver's license identified him as Conrad Sinclair of Newton—and who had never set foot in Newton in his entire life—sat in a dark blue van, engine idling, in the parking lot of an adult bookstore near the main Interstate, I-95, which went from Maine to Florida. His companion this shift, a man called Gary Buelling, had gone into the bookstore over a half-hour ago, a roll of quarters in his eager hand. Conrad idly tuned the radio, listening to the different stations available in this part of the world on a Sunday night. So much trash, so much yak-yak!

He looked to the entrance of the bookstore, a glass door obscured by brown paper, taped up. He got a kick out of watching the men as they streamed in and out of the store. They would depart their cars and trucks, walking to the store at quick step, shoulders hunched up, like they were trying to hide their identity from the world. Then, after a while, they would emerge. They would walk fast, fisted hands in their pockets, or carrying packages in plain brown paper bags, hidden under their arms. Then, into their vehicles they would go, and in seconds they would

22

be part of the anonymous stream of traffic going by about six meters away.

The door opened up again, and a man strode out, bulky, wearing a short leather jacket and jeans, pager and cell phone clipped to his side, his fleshy head barely covered with a thin stubble of black hair. He didn't seem ashamed. He didn't move too fast. He was grinning as he came by the front of the van, thumping the front of the hood with his thick hands. Conrad kept his face impassive, watched as his companion jumped in the passenger's seat.

'Well,' Gary said. 'That was great.'

'I'm sure,' Conrad said, backing out of the lot. 'Do you have any quarters left?'

A snort of laughter. 'Nope. Used them all up. Some good stuff in there, in the back booths. Have to bribe the store manager to see it. I mean it, stuff like we got back home, where—'

'Stow it,' he said.

'Hey, I was just saying—'

'Stow it,' Conrad said, stopping before the entrance to Route 1-A. Time for another roundabout trip. New Hampshire to Maine to Vermont and back again, with a pig as a companion. What a life. A well-paid life, to be sure, but straining sometimes. Like right now.

His companion folded his arms, muttered something, and Conrad said, 'Hey, you know the rules. English only.'

'Well, sometimes I like to fuck the rules. Okay?'

Conrad eased the van out into traffic, spared a glance at Gary. 'You fuck the rules, and somebody's going to fuck you over.'

Another sharp laugh. 'Who, you?'

Conrad said, 'You're here to do a job, you're here to follow my lead, and that's . . . ah, shit.'

23

Gary said, 'What?' He looked out his side-view mirror, and said something again, not in English, as he saw what Conrad had just seen: the blue lights of a police cruiser, said cruiser right on their ass.

Conrad turned on the directional and started to pull over, near a bridge overpass. Gary said, 'What the fuck are you doing?'

'What the fuck can I do, idiot? Outrun him in this over-loaded piece of crap?'

Gary kept an eye on the side-view mirror. 'And what are you going to do if he starts poking around back there?'

He slowed down, put the van in park, switched off the engine. That's what cops around here liked to see happen. But a good point from Gary, as much as he hated to admit it. The sliding metal door hanging behind both of their seats was just the thing cops liked to ask questions about.

'He's not going to do anything like that,' Conrad said. 'I'm going to talk our way out of it.'

'You are, are you?'

'Yes,' he said, 'and don't you try anything else.'

Gary looked at him, thick eyebrows furrowed. 'If that pig decides to do something, I'm not going to wait around with a thumb up my ass,' he said. And with that, he popped open the glove box, removed a leather holster, and quickly released a 7.65 mm Tokarev. There was already a round in the chamber. He snapped back the hammer and put the automatic pistol between his thighs, clenching them tight, then folded his arms and looked over in defiance.

Conrad looked in the side-view mirror, saw the cop approaching. He started rolling down the window, said in a low voice, 'You don't do anything without my say-so.'

Gary said in a low voice, 'That cop asks you to open up the

rear door of the van, lean back, 'cause I'm gonna blow his ass into the next state. And I don't think you want his brains on your face, do you?'

'Don't,' Conrad said.

'Watch me.'

And then Conrad kept quiet, as the glare of a flashlight beam lit up the van's interior.

On the small porch of the house in Berwick, his legs were quivering as he watched Jason take in the news, and he could not believe what the guy said next.

'Bullshit,' he said, looking right at him.

'Excuse me?'

Jason's voice got louder. 'Bullshit,' he said. 'You're not my brother, and if you don't get your ass off this porch, right now, I'm calling the cops. Understood?'

He couldn't help it. He started grinning. This was unbelievable!

The smile on the older man's face was starting to infuriate him, and Jason turned to his wife and said, 'Hon, you got the phone ready?'

'Yes, yes, of course. Who is he?'

'I don't know, some nut trying something. Give me another thirty seconds, and then call the cops.' Jason turned back to the slightly open door and raised his voice. 'It's really pathetic, honest to God, what you folks try to do.'

'What do you mean, you folks?' the older man asked.

'Shit, the whole POW-MIA business. You know how many times creeps like you contact me or my parents? Do you? Every three or four months, that's how often. You call or write or sometimes visit, though never at this late

25

hour, thanks a whole hell of a lot. You're trying to sell us dog tags or blurry photos or some statement from some rice farmer in Laos, all saying my brother is alive. There's never anything solid, nothing reliable. And you know what the bottom line is? Do you?'

'Tell me, and then I'll stop bothering you,' he said.

'Okay, it's money,' Jason said, feeling that old burning anger coming back, remembering the times these people had bothered poor Mom and Dad, especially making Mom's life miserable. 'That's all. You miserable creeps keep on coming back, reopening old wounds, picking at scabs, not letting the dead rest in piece, nearly thirty years later. You come by with your fantasy stories about survivors, and you ask for donations—secretly, of course, not to raise any publicity—to fund some outlandish rescue mission with over-the-hill vets who are still fighting the Vietnam war. Well, forget it, pal. I don't know what you're peddling, but this is the worst, the absolute fucking worst. Saying you're my brother. Jesus, you don't even look like him.'

The man self-consciously rubbed at his face, and then his eyes. 'Yeah. You're right, Jason. I guess I don't. Tell me, the paper route on Dover Point Road. You took it over when I got older, didn't you? Mrs. Pearson, she was the first customer, wasn't she.'

Patty was saying something and Jason couldn't hear her. He had to grab the door again.

'Go on.'

He grinned at Jason's expression, decided to let it all loose. 'Your first grade teacher at St. Mary's Academy, in Dover. Sister Fatima, right? And your first day at school, you missed the bus and tried to walk the five miles home, all by yourself.'

Jason's voice suddenly became weak. 'That's . . . that could be public knowledge. That's no secret.'

He stepped closer to the partially open door. 'Sure. Like Dad working at Clarostat in Dover as a senior buyer, Mom working out of the basement with her own little beauty salon. Dover Point Beauty Walk, right? I could find that out, do that kind of research, all to scam you into something. Right? Tell me this, little brother. Tell me who might know this, who you've told. My last leave home, before I went back to Guam, before I got shot down. It was spring of '72. I had picked up the bathing suit issue of *Sports Illustrated*. Couldn't find it. And I walked into the bathroom and there you were, my twelve-year-old brother, the *Sports Illustrated* on the back of the toilet and you with your pants and underwear around your ankles, fisting your little—'

And the door flew open and the man started yelling, 'Roy! Roy! Roy!' over and over again, and he fell back as the man hugged him and grabbed him and tumbled him down the short steps to the ground, and despite the shock and the air being knocked out of him, Roy Harper started blubbering as well, holding on to his younger brother for dear life, hating what he was about to put him through.

The police officer was young, polite, and insistent. 'Driver's license and registration, please.'

Conrad's training clicked in automatically. 'Absolutely, officer. Hold on.' He dug out his wallet, pulled the license free, passed it over. He leaned over to the side, opened up the glove box, noting with professional admiration how the cop stepped back as his hand went into the open compartment. Nicely trained, he thought. Let's just try not to test that training tonight.

He passed both items over to the cop, who examined them by flashlight. Traffic slowed down on the two-lane highway, everybody heading up to the bridge that spanned the river that separated New Hampshire from Maine. Just another sixty seconds, he thought ruefully, we would be in Maine by now. And if my pig companion hadn't needed to drain his instrument back at that adult store, we would have been in Maine over an hour ago.

'Mister Sinclair?' the cop asked. 'Is this your correct address, in Newton?'

'Yes, it is.'

The flashlight came up, examined the interior again, spent a second or two on Gary's unsmiling face. 'What are you gentlemen up to tonight?'

'We're making a delivery,' he said. 'To an electronics supply store in Portland.'

'Unh-hunh,' the cop replied. 'And why did you just depart the Portsmouth Adult Emporium? Dropping off something there?'

Gary said something under his breath and Conrad desperately hoped the cop hadn't heard the sound. 'Ah, you know how it is,' he said. 'On the road for a while, you need some entertainment.'

'Sure,' the cop said. 'Thing is, I pulled you over because you have a burnt-out taillight. On the left-hand side.'

'Really?' Conrad asked. 'Gee, thanks for pointing it out.'

'No problem,' he said. 'Just a verbal warning this time. Hold on and let me do a records check, and you'll be on your way in a sec.'

'Sure,' Conrad said.

'By the way, you seem to have an accent. Where are you from? Germany?'

28

Conrad nodded. 'As a child. My parents, they emigrated to America, years ago.'

'Thought so,' the cop said, and when he strolled back to the cruiser, Gary swore and said, 'German. What a fool.'

'I don't care what he thinks,' Conrad said. 'Dutch, German, Bulgarian, as long as we're polite to him.'

'Your lips all brown now, from kissing his ass?'

Conrad kept both hands on the steering wheel, but he let his voice loose. 'Shut up,' he said. 'You forget who's lead on this case, and it's not you. If you don't shut up, do as I say, you'll be on the next plane home. Maybe you'll go somewhere else to work, someplace where you have to shit on the side of the road and get your balls cut off and stuffed down your throat when you do something wrong. Understood?'

Gary scowled. 'Sure. Understood. And understand this. That cop wants to look inside the van, he's a dead man.'

Conrad looked at the side-view mirror, saw the cop approaching, flashlight in hand. 'All right, then. He's a dead man. But only when I say he is.'

'Good,' Gary said, his hand going to the pistol hidden between his legs.

Jason could not sit down, could not rest, could not do anything else but bounce around the kitchen, laughing and crying, feeling the hysteria of happiness crawl up his throat. Caleb was underfoot and a frightened Paul was sitting in his chair, sucking on his thumb for the first time in months, and Roy was at the head of the table, and Patty, her face impassive, was rustling up a meal for Roy. God, Roy's back! Roy's alive!

'Mom and Dad,' Jason said, sitting right next to his brother, hand on a thin, muscular wrist. 'We've got to call them, right now. Right now, my God—'

Roy shook his head, picked up a steaming mug of coffee. 'Jason, relax. All right? We'll call them tomorrow. Not now. It's getting late. Let them sleep and we'll call them tomorrow. Okay?'

Jason nodded. 'Then we'll fly down. All of us. Fly down to Tampa to see them. Tomorrow.'

Patty slammed the refrigerator door as she brought out a covered bowl. 'The paper.'

'Hunh?' Jason asked. Patty shook her head, opened up a cupboard, pulled out a plate, and said, 'Newspaper. The Berwick *Banner*. Our newspaper, in case you've forgotten it. Who's going to get it out while we're away?'

Jason laughed. 'Jack can.'

'Jack? He can barely edit his own copy. And you're going to let him run the paper?'

'Hon, it'll be fine. Jesus, I mean, look. Roy! My brother!'

Patty turned and Jason noticed right away the forced smile on her face, the way she was going about the kitchen, and he knew things were going on behind that steely smile, but Mother of God, he thought, Roy! Alive! Imagine the front page he'd put on it before they left! Local man thought missing and presumed dead for almost thirty years turns up alive!

He looked to his brother, looked beyond the beard and puffy eyes and leathery skin, and like a slowly developing photo it started to come together, the facial structure, the shape of the head, the look in the eyes. No doubt. No doubt at all.

'Roy, how in hell did you get here?'

'A car. Before that, a bus.'

'The Air Force . . . do they know?'

Another slurp from the coffee cup. 'Nope.'

Jason nodded. 'A secret deal, with the Vietnamese. Right? Is that how you were sprung? Is that it?'

Roy slowly shook his head. 'It's a long story, brother. Quite a long story and forgive me, but I'm terribly hungry. Can I just eat, please? Just have some food?'

There was a *beep* from the microwave and Patty removed a plate, and Roy looked down and smiled. 'Looks good. But ma'am, you'll forgive me if I don't touch the cabbage. I've had enough cabbage these past years to choke an elephant.'

Patty nodded, her lips pursed. 'Sure. You're forgiven. For that. More coffee?'

'Please,' Roy said, picking up a knife and fork, and Jason felt something jolt him as he noticed the old, round scars on the back of his hands. Burn marks, it looked like. Torture. My God, the years of torture that his poor brother had been put through. He suddenly felt nauseous and had to look away, and saw his son, his young boy, looking at Roy with wide-eyed curiosity.

'Mister?' Paul asked, thumb now pressed against a cheek.

'Yes, young fella?' Roy replied.

'Are you really my daddy's brother?'

'I sure am,' he said, working with the knife and fork.

'You were in a war, weren't you?'

'Yep,' he said, picking up a piece of ham. 'A long time ago.'

'Were you scared?'

'Lots of times,' Roy said.

'Paul,' Patty said, filling up a tan coffee cup and putting it back in front of Roy. 'It's about time you headed upstairs, don't you think?'

'One more thing,' he said, adding, 'If you're my daddy's brother, that makes you my uncle, is that right?'

Roy's eyes seemed to fill up, and he just nodded. Paul said, 'Cool. All I got is aunts. I'd like to have an uncle.'

Jason found that he had to rub at his eyes, as well, when Roy said, 'Good. 'Cause I'd like to have a nephew just like you.'

The cop came back to the van and said, 'Everything's clear. Just make sure you get that taillight fixed tomorrow. Next time, it'll be a ticket.'

Conrad felt a smile go across his face as he took the license and registration back. 'Thanks, officer, I appreciate it.'

'Sure,' he said, making to turn. 'Oh, one more thing.'

Conrad froze, reaching over to the glove compartment. 'Yes?'

There was a motion with the flashlight. 'The back of the van. I'd like to take a look at it.'

Conrad moved back into his seat, sensed Gary getting into position. Oh, fuck.

'Why, is there a problem?'

The cop moved some, too, and said, 'I don't know. Is there a problem? Look, open up the rear of the van. Now.'

Gary whispered something, and Conrad was going to sit back suddenly in his seat and let it all happen, when the radio at the cop's side crackled into life. With a free hand he toggled the microphone, fastened to a shoulder epaulet, and said, 'Unit fifteen responding.' There was a crackled broadcast and he looked up and said, 'Go on, get the hell out of my town. And get that damn light fixed.'

Conrad swallowed as the cop half-trotted back to his cruiser, got in, and pulled out into traffic, lights still flashing, the siren now sounding. He put the registration back into the glove box and his license back in his wallet. Gary laughed and put the Tokarev back into its place.

'Man, that cop . . . he came about five seconds away from getting his ass blown across two lanes of traffic. I wonder if he knows how lucky he was.'

'Who cares,' Conrad said. 'We're late. We've got to get into Maine, meet our schedule.'

'Oh, fuck our schedule,' Gary said. 'And you're lucky too, you know.'

'How's that?'

Gary folded his arms, looked out the window as they crossed the bridge that took them into Maine. 'I know you don't have any clean shirts left, and I don't know what you'd wear if you had blood and brains over that one.'

Conrad kept the speed right at the legal limit. 'I'm sure I would have figured something out.'

When Roy had finished eating and Paul had gone up to bed, accompanied by Caleb, he started yawning and then reached over and squeezed Jason's hand. 'Brother, I know I owe you a lot of answers to a lot of questions, but I can't do it right now. I've got to get to sleep. Got to. I've been on the road for days, weeks it seems like.'

'Sure,' Jason said. 'We've got a spare room upstairs. C'mon, I'll show it to you.'

Roy backed up from the table, picked up his plate and looked at the leftover cabbage and a bit of potato. Something about the look in his eyes haunted Jason. Roy softly said, 'In my first prison, this would have been considered a feast. You know? A feast. Now . . . it's just scraps. Tossed out.' He looked up at Patty, leaning back against the kitchen counter. 'Of course, ma'am, wonderful

33

scraps. I can't tell you how long it's been since I've eaten this well.'

Jason took the plate from his hands, put it in the sink. 'You'll tell us everything tomorrow, right? A big breakfast, anything you want. Anything.'

Roy yawned again, and again Jason noticed the poor state of his teeth. My God, nearly three decades . . . How did he survive? Roy said, 'Excuse that last yawn. Jesus, I'm tired, and I'm sorry, can I ask a favor?'

'Anything,' Jason said.

Roy glanced at Patty and then looked back at him. 'It's just that . . . well, I'd like to keep this all quiet. If you don't mind not telling anybody. Family, friends, neighbors. No phone calls, all right?'

Patty asked, 'Why? What are you hiding?'

Roy looked down at his feet. 'A good point, ma'am. It's just right now, it's not really what I'm hiding. It's what I'm trying to keep, which is my privacy. Just for now. I know I've got questions to answer and stories to tell, and I'm ready to do that. Tomorrow, if that's fine. But in the meantime . . . well, one phone call to somebody means a couple of people will know. And one of those people will call somebody else, and somebody else will be called, and pretty soon, there'll be a television crew knocking at your door in a few hours. And, please, I really need to sleep.'

Jason said, 'Not a problem, Roy, not a problem. No phone calls, no contact. We'll take your lead.'

Roy smiled. 'Thanks, brother. I'm glad to hear that. Now, how about showing me that spare bedroom you've been promising?'

Jason said, 'Follow me, right upstairs.'

'Sure,' he said. 'Patty, by the by, thanks for the meal and the hospitality.'

Patty, back turned, was scrubbing at the dinner dish, and if she said something in reply, Jason didn't hear it.

Roy was surprised at how tired he was, how much he needed to crawl into bed. He had earlier thought that the joy and fear of the reunion would keep him up for days, but he was crashing, and crashing hard. He followed his younger brother upstairs and down the hallway, to a room at the end of the house. There were two windows, overlooking the rear yard. The bed was small and Jason made a production of laying out spare blankets, showing him where the light switches were, and which door in the hallway belonged to the bathroom. Roy just half-heard his brother talking, thinking about what he had to do tomorrow, and wondering how his younger brother would react when he gave him the news. Well, Jason would have to make do. Have to.

Jason stopped, eyes bright, breathing hard. 'Well. That's that.'

'Thanks, Jason,' Roy said. 'My God, thanks.'

His brother brought his hands up to his eyes, wiped at them. 'I was thinking about our house back on Dover Point. Our bedrooms there. And Christmas Eve. Remember the broken lightbulb trick you pulled on me? God, it must have been three or four years before I figured that one out.'

Roy remembered, too, the snowy nights in New Hampshire, crawling out of bed on Christmas Eve, a burnt-out lightbulb in one hand. He'd go to the door of his younger brother's room and gently shake the lightbulb behind his back, the broken filament making a ringing noise. And he would say, 'Sleigh bells . . . hear that, Jason? Santa Claus is in the neighborhood. Better get to sleep!'

Aloud, he said, 'Yeah, those were good times, Jason. Good times.'

Then his brother moved on him, threw his arms around him and gave him a rib-crushing hug. He hugged him in return, patting him on the back, and Jason was blubbering some. 'God, Roy, it's so good to see you. God, we've got so much to catch up on, so much to tell each other. Jesus, Roy, welcome home. Welcome home.'

Roy touched the hair on his brother's head, knowing he couldn't say what he really felt, that he wasn't home. Not yet, and not by a long shot. Instead, he whispered, 'Thanks, brother. Thanks for bringing me in.'

When Patty finished drying the dishes, she slapped them back into the cabinet over the sink, and then slammed the door shut. Men! Jesus, what in God's name was Jason thinking? Inviting this bum into their house, their home, risking who knows what with her son!

She wiped her hands on a towel and stayed in the kitchen, fuming. She loved Jason dearly, but he had a soft and mushy way of looking at things, like hoping everything would work out for the best. He couldn't go toe-to-toe with suppliers, with advertisers who owed them money, with people who wanted free subscriptions for the asking. Which is where she came in. She knew her strengths, knew how her mind worked, and one of those strengths was an inherent suspicion of anything new, anything different, anybody who was trying to pull a scam.

Like a ghost showing up on your doorstep. That was pretty friggin' different. She sighed, rubbed one cold foot against the other. If only she'd had a moment or two alone with Jason, she could have put a stop to it. Sure, maybe it was his brother. Maybe he did make a dramatic escape. But she had doubts. If he had really been cooped up in a Vietnamese prison all these years, why end up on Jason's doorstep? Why not walk into an American embassy in Thailand or Burma or Malaysia? And if you do get back to the United States, do you bus your way across the country, all the way to Maine?

Or do you report back to the nearest Air Force base, salute smartly, and report your miraculous story?

Hunh, she thought. Some frigging miracle. If the story was legit, Roy wouldn't be here. He'd be at some Air Force base, getting seriously debriefed, or he'd be on *Larry King Live*, telling his fantastic tale. The fact he hadn't done both had triggered all of her alarms. She knew Jason wouldn't like what she was thinking, but some sort of scam had to be going on. She wasn't sure what kind of scam, but she had an idea it would involve a loan of some money—hell, a lot of money—and she was going to be damned if that was going to happen. The fact he had been gone for almost thirty years . . . hell, it meant he had done something wrong, something illegal. Maybe he had gone over to the other side. Maybe he had been living freely in Vietnam all these years, got bored or tired and decided to hit up his younger and more innocent brother. Sure. That made sense. A derring-do escape, something for a made-for-TV movie? Not likely. And she knew that would tear up Jason, having Roy showing up suddenly, not part of some dramatic rescue but something more base, like scamming him for some money.

And that would not happen. Patty had grown up in Lewiston, Maine, a scraggly mill town, and she knew the value of a quarter, of a buck. She had gotten through Colby on scholarships, working waitressing jobs and eating lots of rice and beans, and with her administrative science degree —business administration to everybody else—she planned to go far and not let anybody at her money. Especially a ghost brother-in-law who looked like he had spent the previous night sleeping under a bridge.

Well. She put the dish towel away, looked about her small and neat kitchen. All hers, all paid for, except for a mortgage that they could handle well, every month. She and Jason and little Paul and even that drooly dog were making a warm, special, and safe life here in Berwick, and she was damned if some clown was going to disturb it.

By the counter. Near the coffee maker. The telephone. She looked at the stairs, knew what Roy had said, what he had warned just a while ago. No phone calls. No contacts. Like an NBC news crew was out there in the countryside, roaming around, just waiting to jump on such a strange story.

She went over and picked up the phone, dialed her sister Marie's number by memory. She needed to talk to somebody about what had just gone on, and Marie—who lived in Omaha with her husband, Art, and who taught sociology at the University of Nebraska—would do just nicely. It was too late to call her other sister, Denise, who lived in Portland.

The phone rang once, twice, and then went straight to voicemail. She waited until the cheery voice of her sister asked her to leave a message, debated what to say, and then said: 'Hey, Marie. It's your younger sister. Give me a call. There's something strange going on back here in Maine. I know it sounds crazy, but it's about Jason's brother, Roy, the pilot who went missing during the Vietnam War. You won't believe it, but he's just shown up on our doorstep. Alive and in need of a bath. Call me when you can, but if Jason answers the phone, don't say a word. It's supposed to be a big secret or something. Love to Art. Hope he gets his tenure this year. Bye.'

38

She hung up the phone. Men and their secrets and their wars.

Both Conrad and Gary felt the same thing at the same time, and Gary swore—again in his native language—but Conrad let that breach of training go by, as the pager at his side started vibrating, knowing Gary's was doing the same. From the rear of the van, there was a high-pitched beeping signal. Conrad felt his armpits get itchy, hoped Gary would never know that particular weakness of his, and Gary said, '*Bojemoi*, a real one. Do you think it's a real one?'

'Don't overreact,' Conrad said, blessing all gods, past and present, that a rest stop was coming up ahead on this stretch of I-95. 'I had two false signals last year. It'll only take a moment.'

He slowed the van down, put on the right-hand directional, and pulled into the rest stop, which had a large parking lot, fenced in along the sides, and nothing else. Not even a toilet. Some rest stop. With the van in park and the engine idling, he got out of the seat and with a set of keys unlocked the sliding metal door to the rear of the van. Gary joined him, and when Conrad drew the door back, red-dimmed lights automatically came on. There were banks of electronic gear on each side of the van, black gym bags held to the floor by bungee cords, and padded swivel stools fastened to the floor. A computer screen was up and running, with a blood-red message scrolling across the screen:

A LIVE INTERCEPT HAS BEEN RECORDED. PRESS CTRL-D TO CONTINUE. A LIVE INTERCEPT HAS BEEN RECORDED. PRESS CTRL-D TO CONTINUE.

Gary took the far stool and Conrad took the one in front of the computer screen. At Gary's feet was a small metal safe, and for once in this lousy stretch of work, he was at least following orders. He bent over—grunting with the exertion—and spun the combination dial with a quickness that surprised Conrad, considering how thick the man's fingers were. When the safe popped open, Gary reached in and took out four thick manila envelopes, each sealed at the top with wax and string. A man's name was printed on each envelope.

'Ready,' Gary said.

'Good,' Conrad said. He pressed the Control-D key combination, and a password screen flickered into life. He punched in the password, the screen went blank again, and there was a tiny loudspeaker logo, centered in the screen. He double-clicked on the logo, and then a woman's voice came over the computer's speakers:

Hey, Marie. It's your younger sister. Give me a call. There's something strange going on back here in Maine. I know it sounds crazy but it's about Jason's brother, Roy, the pilot who went missing during the Vietnam War. You won't believe it, but he's just shown up on our doorstep. Alive and in need of a bath. Call me when you can, but if Jason answers the phone, don't say a word. It's supposed to be a big secret or something. Love to Art. Hope he gets his tenure this year. Bye.

Gary said, 'Shit, sounds pretty fucking real to me.'

Conrad licked his dry lips, thinking about the technology that could sift through so many phone messages every day and kick in an alarm with the right keywords. 'Sure does. Hold on, let's nail it down.'

From the sparse menu on the screen after the message, he clicked on a SEARCH DATABASE icon, and typed in: Jason, Roy,

Maine. He waited less than a heartbeat, then the icon clicked up and reported: AF CAPT. ROY HARPER.

'Okay,' Conrad said. 'A positive match. You got it there?'

Gary flipped through the envelope, pulled out the right one. He carefully replaced the other envelopes in the safe, slammed the door shut, and spun the dial. With the envelope marked ROY HARPER now on a small counter, he ripped through the wax and string, started pulling out a thick file, photographs, and maps.

'Where?' Conrad asked.

'Small town called Berwick. Not far away. Maybe a half-hour, maybe less.'

'Good. What do we have?'

'Husband. Wife. Small boy. Dog.'

'Oh,' Conrad said. 'Kid. You sure?'

Gary said, 'Yeah, I'm fucking sure. Why?'

Conrad shrugged, went back to the computer, decided to replay the intercept message one more time. 'Don't like killing kids, that's all.'

Gary laughed. 'Man, that's okay. I'll take care of it. Stuff we did in Chechnya . . . It'll be fine.'

For the first time this day, Conrad felt warm feelings for his comrade.

'Thanks,' he said.

'Don't mention it.'

THREE

When Jason finally left, the shakes started, and Roy sat on the soft bed and let them pass through. He got up and switched off the lights, and then lay out on the bed, tired, staring up at the ceiling. Lots of thoughts and memories and scents and sounds were crowding in about him, and he forced them all away, forced them away through the discipline he had learned generations ago, at the academy in Colorado Springs. That discipline, that training, though, had been a Boy Scout campout compared to what he had been put through since that night in December, nearly thirty years ago, in Bonny 02, part of a three-plane cell going into Hanoi airspace, the tracers from the triple-A lighting up the sky like long streamers of Christmas tree lights, the brighter flares from the SAM missiles corkscrewing their way up to you and your mates, the copilot on the horn, 'Pilot, pilot, break left, break left . . .'

The shakes came back. He clenched his fists. The bed was too soft and the room was too warm. He got up and opened both windows, listened to the peepers at work out there by the riverbank. It was nice to hear something familiar, something homey like that. It had been such a long, long, long time. He yawned and went back to the bed, took his shoes off and lay down. A breeze came in, bringing with it the night sounds of birds and other animals out there, hunting each other in the darkness.

There were other noises as well. He strained his ears, focused on hearing what was going on. Something was snoring, the next room over. Not the boy—his nephew!—no, probably the dog, that slobbering and friendly black Lab. Other sounds, a murmuring. He tensed up and then relaxed. Voices in the master bedroom, between his brother and his pretty yet hard-edged wife. He could tell right from the start that she didn't like him, didn't want him in her home, didn't buy a single thing he was saying.

He put his hands behind his head, wondered if he would ever get used to sleeping in a soft bed, ever. He also wondered if that pretty woman down the hallway would ever forgive him for what he was about to do.

Roy closed his eyes, and then opened them again, as the wind did its work.

In his years with Patty they had gone through some dust-ups, some serious discussions and arguments. Patty was one to pull any problem, any misunderstanding, out in the open, to poke and prod and pry, whether it was buying a house or deciding which way the toilet paper in the bathroom was hung. He was exactly the opposite—thereby once again proving the maxim of who gets married to whom—and preferred to think that most problems took care of themselves, and that you should focus on the real ones that crop up. Yet he took her seriously enough when she was upset, figuring that these discussions were just a safety valve, blowing off some steam, clearing the air.

But tonight was different.

She was lying in bed, covers pulled up, and he was sitting at the foot of the bed, still wearing his blue terry-cloth bathrobe. She was viciously flipping through the pages of a *Newsweek* magazine and said, 'I still can't believe you let him in our house without discussing it first!'

He pressed his knees together, somehow finding the pressure comforting. 'Really? And discuss how? Tell my brother, my own brother I haven't seen in nearly thirty years and have always thought was dead, tell him to cool his heels out on the porch? Is that what you wanted?'

A fast flip of the page. 'Or send him to a motel. It would have made sense.'

'Made sense?' he said, trying to keep his voice down, knowing he didn't want to quite let Paul into the awful secret that sometimes mommys and daddys fought, used sharp words at each other. 'The last time I saw him I was twelve years old, Patty. Twelve! And you expect me to turn my back on him?'

'Hunh,' she said. 'And how do you know that's your brother? He looks like a bum.'

'He is my brother,' he shot back. 'First of all, he looks like a picture I've seen of my grandad, when he had a beard. And he knows things about me and Mom and Dad that nobody else would know.'

Another sharp turn of the page. 'You mean, more than your young masturbation habits?'

He kept quiet, just breathing, watching her pretend to read her magazine, her face quite red. She looked up at him and said, 'So. Enjoying the conversation you're having with yourself?'

'No, I'm not,' he said. 'And he knows other things as well. My paper route customers. The name of Mom's beautician business. Patty, that man down the hallway is my brother. I'm convinced of it. And I'm convinced of something else, too.'

He got up and took off his robe, climbed into his side of the bed, and Patty said, 'Yes? And what are you convinced of?'

'I haven't seen my brother in almost thirty years,' he said, his voice low, choosing the words carefully. 'If you go thirty days without seeing or hearing from your two sisters, you get moody and cranky. I would have thought you'd understand. And I'm sorry to find out that I'm wrong. I've been an only child for most of my life, Patty, and instead of being happy for me, you're being pissy. And I don't like it.'

He reached up, turned off his light and pulled the blankets up.

Conrad slowed the van as they went past the driveway with the black mailbox on the end that said HARPER in white letters. He went a few more meters and pulled over to the side of the road, put the engine in park. Gary had a detailed street map that he had pulled from the envelope marked with Harper's name, illuminated by a small lamp from the glove box. He checked the map, then a photo that showed the mailbox.

'Perfect match,' Gary said.

'What's the house like?' Conrad said.

'Straightforward. Two-story. Basement, then living room, kitchen on the first floor. Upstairs, three bedrooms and a bathroom. Pretty small quarters.'

'Security or alarm system?'

'None indicated,' Gary said.

'What kind of dog?'

'Says here a Labrador retriever.'

'Good,' Conrad said, switching off the engine. 'I hate going up against Rottweilers or Dobermans. Let's get started.'

Gary followed him into the rear of the van, and Conrad pulled a slim black binder from a tiny bookshelf, set in among the computers and communications gear. He noted the date and switched on the transmitter, adjusting the frequency. He leaned into a small microphone, depressed the switch.

'Control, control, control, this is Ebony Three, Ebony Three. How do you copy?'

There was a hiss of static from the speakers. Nothing else.

Conrad cleared his throat, talked louder into the microphone: 'Control, control, control, this is Ebony Three, Ebony Three. How do you copy?'

Gary shook his head. 'Lazy fucks must be sleeping.'

'Maybe,' Conrad said. 'Let me do a diagnostics check.'

He turned to the computer, went through the menu, trying to keep his hands and head steady. There was a job to do and he wasn't going to screw it up. He brought up the diagnostics section of the menu, ran a quick check. Things seemed fine with the communications equipment on his end. So where was the problem?

At the other end, and there was nothing he could do about it. Nothing.

'Looks okay from here,' Conrad said. 'I'll try one more time.' He leaned into the microphone again, talking even louder, though he knew the level of his voice wouldn't make a damn difference. 'Control, control, this is Ebony Three, Ebony Three, Ebony Three. Do you copy, over? Control, control, control, Ebony Three is calling.'

The hiss of static. Gary started unzipping some of the black duffel bags and said, 'You know we don't have time to fuck around with the comm gear. We've got a clear go order, am I right?'

'Yeah, you're right,' Conrad said, switching off the radio with disgust, and returned to the checklist binder. 'Procedures say, loud and clear, that if we can't contact control, we're to proceed. And that's what we're going to do.'

Gary grinned. 'Perfect. It's been a long time since I've had some wet work. And what do our precious procedures say we're to do in this little house tonight?'

'You know what they say,' Conrad said.

Gary pulled out a 9-mm Uzi semiautomatic rifle, started working the bolt. 'I know. I just like to hear it from your pretty little mouth, that's all.'

Conrad slapped the cover shut on the binder and went to his own duffel bag. 'Secure the site. Locate the subject. Place him in custody, kill all witnesses.'

Gary started pulling out full magazines of 9-mm rounds, passed one of the rectangular objects over to Conrad, who took it. The metal was smooth and cool to the touch.

'Nicest thing I've heard all night,' Gary said.

In the dim light of the bedroom, Patty listened to her husband breathe, knew he was awake. Sometimes he liked to fake going to sleep, especially after having one of these kinds of discussions, and most times she let it go by. But not tonight. Usually arguments with Jason meant eventually bringing him around to her point of view, but something he had said had really gotten to her. It was the sharp little comment about her sisters. She hated to admit it, but Jason was right.

She and her sisters were tight. She talked to Marie at least once a week and kept up a steady e-mail correspondence, complete with digital photos of Paul attached so his aunt

17

could see his growth. Her other sister, Denise—the youngest of the bunch—was single. She was an attorney in Portland, and they got together at least once every other week. She remembered the times living in a dirty apartment, sharing one bedroom, listening to Dad stumble home Friday and Saturday nights, drunk, and how Mom and he would go at it, sometimes even before he got the key into the door. The three of them would sometimes huddle together in one bed, blankets pulled over their heads, and Marie would tell stories, about princes and horses and cowboys, about anything, anything so that they could get their minds off the screaming and dishes breaking and doors slamming that was going on in the next room.

Her sisters. They chatted, they gossiped, but most of all they were there. The safety net, the place to go to with a problem, the women you could talk to who knew everything about you, your hopes and dreams and fears.

But what about her husband? What about the man in her life? She suddenly felt cold and bleak at the thought that, almost thirty years ago, her sisters might suddenly have disappeared. What would it have been like growing up alone? Not even having a body to mourn, a cemetery grave site to visit once a year and place flowers upon? What would that have been like?

Patty shivered and rolled over in bed, gently touched the back of Jason's neck. 'Hey,' she said.

'Hey, yourself,' he said, his voice quiet.

'I'm sorry,' she said. 'You're right, I should be happy for you, glad that Roy's come back. It's just that . . . well, it was so sudden.'

'Unh-hunh.'

'And I went into defense mode, automatically. You know

48

how that is. I love you and our boy and this place and our little newspaper, and I was threatened, all right? Having this scary-looking guy show up on our doorstep . . . well, I overreacted. I felt like something bad was happening to us tonight, that's all. You know what my family life was like, growing up in Lewiston. It was scary and awful and terrifying, and I didn't want anything bad to happen to you or me or Paul. Especially Paul.'

Jason kept on breathing, and she wondered if he had fallen asleep or if he was being stubborn, and then he sighed. 'Patty, this evening . . . this night has been one of the best nights of my life. One of the best. And you can't see that. All you can see is trouble, or the potential for trouble. Nothing good. That's . . . that's hurtful.'

She touched his ear again. 'I'm just thinking of all of us, that's all.'

He shifted in the bed. 'I know. That's what you always say. Thinking about all of us. But I wish you would have seen yourself tonight, Patty. My brother . . . He's supposed to be dead and he shows up alive, after all these years, and you treated him like a criminal.'

She said it instantly and regretted it. 'What makes you think he isn't?'

'What makes you think he is?' he shot back.

Patty moved, cuddled up close to him. 'I don't want to fight with you, hon. I just want you to look at the facts. Look, he probably is your brother. But he just shows up like this, out of the blue? Why did he come here? If he's been a POW all these years, shouldn't he have reported back to the Air Force? Or an American embassy? Why here? And where has he been all this time, and how did he get here?'

Jason again took the time to answer, and said reluctantly: 'He said he needed sleep. He said he would tell us all tomorrow. I have to trust him, all right? I have to. He's my brother.'

Patty touched her husband's hair again. It was time to finish this. 'Yes, he's your brother, and you missed him terribly, and I'm sorry for the way I acted. It'll be better in the morning, promise.'

A pause. 'Okay.'

She reached up, kissed his ear, and whispered, 'I do love you dearly.'

'And I love you, too.'

Conrad set the pace, going down the side of the gravel driveway, Gary behind him and covering his rear. Earlier they had taken care of the phone line and the cable TV line—some of those lines carried alarm signals, no use leaving anything to chance. They had on black fatigues, soft leather boots, black gloves, and ski masks. Waist belts carried flashlights, plastic restraints, Mace canisters, and extra clips for their Uzis. Earlier Conrad had removed the body armor inside the back of the van and Gary had sniffed at the offering. 'No fucking way. Too hot, makes me move too slow, and besides, what are they going to get us with, forks?'

'You forget, lots of people in these towns have firearms,' Conrad pointed out.

'Sure,' he had sneered. 'And lots of people in these towns have experience in facing snatch and grabs. Right?'

So, without wanting to look foolish in front of somebody who was supposed to be his inferior, Conrad had let it slide. Now they were just outside of the house. Small, two-story. One-car garage, unattached, to the right. Lights off downstairs, a bit of a glow upstairs. Maybe a night-light or something.

Gary came up next to him, his breath sour. 'Looks like everybody's gone to bed.'

'Yeah,' Conrad said. 'Chances are, that's where we'll find 'em. Sacked out and sleeping.'

'Good,' Gary said, hefting his Uzi up, the sound suppressor at the muzzle end looking fat and bulbous in the moonlight. 'You know, I never liked Yids that much, but you've gotta give them credit. They sure know how to make a good weapon.'

Conrad looked about the yard, wondering why his armpits were getting itchy again. This was something he and Gary had trained for, over and over again. It should be easy, not a problem. Husband and wife and kid and some poor guy who was probably exhausted, hungry, and scared of his own shadow. Conrad didn't know all the particulars and didn't care to know. All he had been doing since he had been hired was to drive around in a big loop, and respond when necessary if a certain call came in.

Gary said, 'You still there?'

Conrad felt the tension start to ease. Just prejob jitters, that's all. He leaned into Gary and said, 'Yeah, I'm still here. This is what we're going to do. Nothing too sneaky, nothing too fancy. Just a straight blitz in and do the job. Find the old guy, secure him, and we'll take care of everything else. But leave the everything else for last. If the old guy's gone to town to get a smoke, we want to know that before we start greasing witnesses.'

Gary grunted. 'All right, sounds good.'

At that, Conrad's tension really eased. Gary was on board, Gary was listening to him, and this should be so easy that they would be out of here in minutes.

'Fine,' Conrad said, heading to the porch steps. 'Let's do it.'

*

Jason stirred, opened his eyes, listened to the regular and slow breathing of his wife. He hadn't yet fallen asleep and rarely did after one of their set-tos. Tonight was no exception, and what was really making him angry was that Patty was making a lot of sense. He remembered once, as a college student, learning the basics of journalism. His professor—a man named Winslow who had worked at the Boston *Globe* and *Wall Street Journal*—had said, 'If someone tells you that he loves his mother, check it out. Don't take anything for granted.'

So. Tonight. He had taken everything for granted, everything. Oh, he had no doubt that the man down at the other end of the hallway was in fact his brother—the resemblance was there, once you got past the lines in the face and the beard, and the man knew details of Jason's life that nobody else would know. Nobody.

All right then, he thought. What about everything else? Patty was right: if Roy had been held captive these long years—almost three decades!—would he skulk into his home at night, without any announcement, without going to the Air Force or the Pentagon first? Would he? And how in hell did he get from Southeast Asia to Maine? Walk?

So Patty was on target. He rolled over in bed, stared up in the darkness, listened to the regular sound of Patty breathing, a sound that always comforted him, but not tonight. Let's look at the facts, Mister Editor. Your brother Roy shows up unannounced on your doorstep, late at night. He's reluctant to say anything about where he's been, or how he got to Maine. He even goes to the level of asking you to keep quiet. No phone call to Mom and Dad. No phone calls period. So. What do these facts mean, Mister Editor?

Roy was on the run. Roy was involved in something illegal. And Jason doubted very much that he had been stuck in the modern version of the Hanoi Hilton since 1973. Hell, the past ten years or so, American MIA investigators had been crawling up and down that miserably hot and wet country, excavating crash sites, sifting through dusty documents, and talking to villagers who had been alive when the shot-down Americans had come floating down at night from their destroyed aircraft.

And not one MIA had been found alive. Not one.

But now, one of them was supposedly asleep in his spare bedroom.

Jason slowly rolled out of bed, trying not to wake Patty. It was time for some answers, and now was as good a time as ever. He put on his robe, slowly opened the bedroom door, and went down the hallway. The door to Paul's room was open, and in there Caleb was flopped on his side, snoring gently. The bathroom door was open as well and the room was empty. Then he came to the last bedroom, the one that would some-day, God and the mechanics of reproduction willing, be a nursery.

He softly tapped on the door. 'Roy? Are you awake? Can I come in?'

There was no answer.

He tapped again, louder. 'Roy?'

Jason sighed, knowing that all Roy had asked for was a good night's sleep, and he was about to disturb it. Well, what the hell. This had turned out to be one weird evening, and he wanted some answers.

He opened the door, stepped in.

The room was empty, the wind gently disturbing the cur-tains.

'Roy?' he said, louder. He looked in the closet, under the bed. Nothing.

His brother was gone.

Jason shook his head, left the empty room. Okay, don't panic. He's probably restless, probably downstairs, getting something to eat. That's all. He quickly retraced his steps back down the hallway, then went downstairs. It took just a minute. Kitchen empty. Living room empty. He even flicked on the lights to the cellar and checked out the tiny space under their house. Boxes and dust and a bicycle on flat tires.

No brother. Nothing. In an instant he was back upstairs, his fist against his mouth. The front door that led outside was still locked, from the inside.

So where in hell did he go? A soft groan came from his mouth. No, this cannot be, he thought. His brother couldn't just show up after all these years, show up alive, show up on his doorstep, and then disappear!

It couldn't be happening!

And as he turned, to go back upstairs, the front door to his house blew in.

FOUR

In Cambridge, Massachusetts, the phone in an upstairs bedroom of a Victorian house on Brattle Street began to ring. The large man in the bed blinked open his eyes, rubbed at the crust gathering at the corners. A woman's voice said, 'Whass . . . whass going on . . .' and he said, 'Quiet, it's okay, go back to sleep,' and as he sat up and reached over for the phone, he tried to remember what the woman's name was. Not that it mattered much.

'Sloan Woodbury,' he said, remembering for a quick second all those disturbed nights over the years, with phone calls coming in from all parts of the globe, at all times of the night. Even after his official retirement, he thought the goddamn things would eventually end, but no, not ever. Not ever.

'Mister Secretary,' the young man's voice said. 'I have a Nolan-level message for you. Can you receive it?'

'No, hold on,' he said. 'Call back in sixty seconds. I'll take the message then.'

'Very well, sir,' the young man said, hanging up. He hung up the phone as well. The woman stirred and he said, 'I'll be down the hallway. Don't pick up the phone. Understood?'

''Kay,' came the voice, and she snuggled deeper into the blankets. Woodbury ran both hands across his face, felt the

55

stubble on his cheeks and chin. He eased his bulk over the side of the bed, slipped his feet into open-back slippers, put on a black silk dressing gown, and went out into the hallway.

In his office he switched on just one lamp, illuminating the large oak desk, leather chair, a few of the bookcases, and just part of his ego wall. He sat his bulk down in the leather chair, looked at the phone, and waited. Sixty seconds had never seemed so long. He moved the chair and looked out the window, out at the lights of Cambridge, and he imagined he could see some of the lights on in some of the brick-and-ivy buildings where he spent most of his time now, lecturing to eager young things who thought diplomacy and negotiations were all glamor and champagne receptions. Not bloody likely, and if they only knew what he was up to at this ungodly hour, they would demand their tuition refunded and transfer to UMass-Boston.

The phone rang and he snapped it up. 'Woodbury.'

'Mister Secretary—'

'Please don't call me that,' he interrupted, looking quickly at the ego wall, filled with plaques, framed certificates, and photos of him with popes, presidents, prime ministers, and a few unindicted war criminals. 'I've been retired for a number of years now. Just get on with it. What's the message?'

The young man said, 'It's a Nolan-level message, sir. One of the field units did not report in at midnight, per its schedule.'

'Why?' Woodbury asked.

'We're not sure. It could be something like . . . Well, there's a solar storm going on right now.'

'A solar what?'

'Storm. High-energy particles being emitted from the sun. It can shut down communications satellites, play havoc with frequencies. Cops in a town can't talk to dispatch, but they can talk to taxi drivers a time zone away.'

Woodbury rubbed at his forehead. 'So you woke me up because of a fucking solar storm?'

The young man instantly became apologetic. 'No, sir. I woke you up because of the strict protocol. If a field unit is out of touch for more than an hour, you are to be contacted.'

'Well, I'm going to change that little protocol. Same thing happened last year, and it turned out the unit was having a drink with some college girls in Seattle. I don't like having my sleep disturbed for no good reason. Where was this unit assigned?'

'Maine, Vermont, New Hampshire.'

'Were they in response?'

'Sir?'

'Were they going anywhere in particular? Had they been activated? Do you know that at least?'

Again, the kicked-puppy tone to the man's voice. 'That's another thing we're trying to track down, sir. That solar storm has interfered with—'

'Look. Take the solar storm and put it where the sun don't shine, all right? Jesus!' He looked at the clock, remembered that breakfast seminar he had agreed to do at the Copley Plaza at nine A.M., less than a handful of hours away. All those nameless chattering mobs out there, demanding his attention, demanding his time, demanding his presence. Why in hell couldn't they all just leave him alone?

'One more thing,' Woodbury said. 'Get a hold of Clay Goodwin. You know who he is, right?'

'He's on the contact list as well.'

'Good. Tell him that I want to see him at my home at seven A.M.'

57

'Today, sir?'

'No, during the next fucking leap year. Of course I mean today!'

'It might be hard to locate him—'

'Then get to work on it, all right? Seven A.M., or you're done doing whatever it is that you're being paid for.'

And just as he was hanging up the phone, there was a click, and then another click. It seemed as if two phones—not one—had been hung up. He replaced the receiver in the cradle, turned again and looked out the window. He wished he was in his other office, over there at Harvard, or as the local wags called it WGU—the World's Greatest University. Playing with political theories could be a hell of a lot more fun and satisfying than dealing with this reality crap being slung his way.

He got out of his chair and went back down the hallway, and then into his bedroom. The scent in there was of sweat, perfume, and old exertions, and that scent had a tinge of foulness to it. The woman was awake, looking at him, long red hair lying across the big white pillow. Annie. That was her name. Annie from Southie. Atrocious accent but a nice bod, one that would last her for a few years before she married a fellow knucklehead from South Boston, raised a brood of five or six kids, increased her drinking habits and decreased her dentist visits.

'You picked up the phone, didn't you?' he said.

'Uh, I couldn't help it,' she said. 'It rang and it was automatic.'

'Even though I told you to leave it alone?'

Her bare shoulders moved in a shrug. 'I told ya, it was automatic.'

He took off the dressing gown, put it on the bed, not minding at all when she averted her eyes as he crawled back under the covers. 'Did you listen in to what was going on?'

'No, of course not!' she protested.

'Are you lying?'

'Look, mister,' she said, sitting up, revealing an impressive chest that hadn't met a plastic surgeon's knife, which he had enjoyed playing with earlier. 'Why don't I just head out and—'

He grabbed her wrist. 'No, please. Stay. I believe you.' Right, he thought, as much as I believed every initial Chinese diplomatic note. 'I'll pay you extra, spend the night?'

She stopped trying to pull her wrist away. 'How much?'

'Double.'

She seemed to ponder that for all of a second or two. ''Kay. Double it is.' She crawled back in, and as if her mind had slipped back into service mode, she was resting on his chest, playing with his sparse hair. 'Do you have anything else in mind?'

Well, that was a thought. Keep his mind off a few things. 'Sure. One more round. The whole show.'

He could sense her frown. 'Do we need . . . the sheets back? Do we?'

His mouth seemed a bit dry. It had been a long time since he had done this, twice in one evening, but after that phone call, he needed the diversion. 'I'm sure they're dry. They're good-quality rubber.'

'But they smell.'

'Is that a problem?'

She forced a laugh, a nasal Southie laugh. 'Nah. I can handle it. I'll just need a couple more beers.' She bent down and placed a chaste kiss on his chest. 'By the way, how much longer do you want me to stay?'

Woodbury thought of the request he had just made. 'Just after seven A.M. All right?'

'Sure,' she said. 'That gives me plenty of time.'

He shook his head, almost whispered. 'Me too.'

Patty woke with a start of sheer terror, hoping she was in a dream or nightmare, knowing with a quick sense of horror that no, everything was real. There was a loud *bang* that shook the bed, followed by things downstairs breaking and men shouting and yelling. She rolled and turned on the light and then picked up the phone, dialed 911, got nothing in reply, not a hiss, not a dial tone. Nothing. 'Jason!' she screamed, and she got out of bed, switching on the hallway light, and there was Paul R., crying, his face red, eyes screwed tight in terror, clutching a teddy bear, and there was this . . . creature, alien apparition, running up the stairs, carrying a weapon of some sort. All she saw was this monstrous shape in black, yelling at her, yelling something about Roy.

And then Caleb, brave Caleb, came running around Paul, growling, teeth bared, and the creature moved so fast, so damn fast, and the weapon coughed three times. Caleb yelped and spun and tumbled down the stairs.

Paul's screaming was louder now, and Patty rushed forward to get to him, but the man with the gun came to her, throwing an elbow into her chin, throwing her back against the wall, knocking a framed print of a lighthouse to the floor. A gloved hand grabbed at her throat and the man yelled with a thick voice, 'Where is Roy Harper? Tell us right now or your boy is dead! Where is Roy Harper?'

She freed her throat from his grasp, pointed down at the end of the hallway. 'There! That room! Get him, kill him, do anything you want! Just don't hurt my boy!'

The man then moved again, down the hallway, and when he got past Paul she crawled over, her chin and throat aching, her knees cut by the broken glass from the shattered print. She grabbed Paul and hugged him close, tried to ease his screaming, but no matter what she said or did, his screaming went on and on and on.

The door down at the end of the hallway slammed open, and the man ducked in. She grabbed Paul tight against her and rocked him back and forth, and then picked him up and headed for the stairs.

The noise of the door bursting open deafened Jason and the flash from whatever was used to break open the door blinded him. He fell back and tripped over a coffee table, and a quick thought came to him of running back upstairs, to go to the rear closet in the bedroom and grab the only weapon in the house, an old .20-gauge shotgun that had belonged to Dad. But as his mind was just completing that thought, a man had kicked him and turned him over.

'Roy!' the man yelled, his voice muffled by the black ski mask. 'Where is Roy Harper?'

From upstairs Jason could make out the screaming of Patty and the cries of their boy, and he swallowed and said, 'He was upstairs a while ago, but I don't know—'

The man yelled at a second man, 'Move, upstairs!' and then the second man bounded up the stairs. Jason started to get up and the guy kicked him again and threw him against the couch, and in another confused handful of seconds his arms were bound behind him by some sort of plastic string. Jason looked up at the man as he stepped back, weapon slung at his side, flashlight beam shooting out, and said, 'Who . . . who the hell are you?'

The man kicked him again. 'Shut up.'

From upstairs, more screaming, a loud growl from Caleb, a

succession of three pops and the sound of brass hitting the floor, and then, oh sweet Jesus, no, not that, Jason thought, as poor Caleb yelped and then tumbled down the stairs. More yells, more screams, and Jason closed his eyes, tried to push everything away, and then he opened them again, tried to stand up. Someone came running down the stairs and he yelled, 'Patty, no!'

And the man with the weapon spun around, aiming it right at his wife, holding their terrified six-year-old boy at her side.

The man whose driver's license identified him as Gary Buelling was grinning as he popped open the bedroom door. So far this had been as slick as goose shit, much smoother than some of the dirty jobs he had done in Armenia and Chechnya. That woman back there gave Roy Harper up as easy as a whore opening her legs after seeing a hundred-dollar bill, and if things went right, they could have this wrapped up and be back on the road in five minutes.

His flashlight illuminated the room, which was empty. He scanned it, and then kicked off the mattress and box spring. Nothing hiding underneath except for a knapsack. Then he spotted a closet door, closed. He was tempted to hose down the door but recalled the quite specific orders he and that fresh young whelp worked under, so he maneuvered to the wall and popped the doorknob open with one quick move. Nothing. The closet was empty, just wire hangers dangling overhead.

Shit. So much for having this thing wrapped up in five minutes. He'd have to go back after that woman, start talking to her, start playing some games with that kid of hers, to find out where Roy Harper was hiding out. He moved to the other side of the room, where there were two closed windows.

'Hey!' came Conrad's voice. 'What's going on up there?'

Gary turned around and was about to say something in reply.

Patty froze as another man came at her with a gun, and she spun about so that if he was to shoot, at least her body might protect Paul a little, but the man lowered the weapon and said, 'There. By your husband. Now.'

She went over and sat down next to Jason on the floor, trying to say something through the tears and the terror. 'Jason . . . what is . . .'

'Shut up,' the man said. He went back to the stairs. She looked around the living room, their safe, warm, inviting living room, now broken and in pieces, the door outside hanging by one hinge, a haze of smoke up by the ceiling, and Caleb, oh, dear lord, poor sweet Caleb, lying dead on the floor. She pulled Paul close to her chest, grabbed his head to make sure he couldn't see what was going on, and wished mightily that she could be transported back in time to when she was six, when she was utterly confident that Mom and Dad—as drunk as he was—could protect her from everything.

Through it all, Jason was feeling the burning shame of humiliation, of being so weak that he could not protect his wife, his son, their house, and even their dog. He had always thought of himself as being fairly competent at his job and his life, and reckoned that if he kept his nose clean, kept things going in this rural part of Maine, everything would be fine, everything would be safe, forever.

No more. Not ever.

He looked up at the man with the black fatigues, the utility belt with gear hanging off it, the weapon. No insignia. No badges. He couldn't imagine the Maine State Police or the FBI or any other federal police agency barreling in like this, killing a family dog, not identifying themselves or even presenting a warrant. So these guys weren't legit. They were something else. And they were focused on one thing: where was Roy Harper?

Then the anger started. Roy, showing up on his doorstep after nearly thirty years, without even the courtesy of a fucking phone call. Not even a letter, a postcard, nothing. Not a single bit of warning. Just a late-night ring of the doorbell, hey ho, here I am, after three bloody decades. Where have I been? How did I get to Maine? What's going on?

Jeezum, I need to sleep. All will be explained tomorrow.

Oh, and by the way, if two maniacs come bursting in and kill your dog and threaten you and your family, don't worry about it. I'll be long gone by then . . .

The armed man went to the foot of the stairs, yelled up. 'Hey! What's going on up there?'

There was a shattering noise, like glass breaking. The man quickly unslung his weapon. 'Gary! What's going on? Talk to me!'

No answer. The man looked over at Jason and Patty, still whimpering next to him, holding Paul tight. There was a voice from upstairs, speaking in a language Jason didn't recognize. The man on the stairs looked over and said, 'You move, we kill the boy,' and then he yelled upstairs in the foreign language, and bounded up.

Conrad took the stairs, two steps at a time. Damn that Gary, for slipping up again, in the heat of an action. The training had been specific, from minute one of day one: always use English, always, no matter what was going on. And Gary had screwed up, in the excitement, no doubt, yelling down, 'I've got him, I've got him!'

He called out again as he got to the top of the stairs. 'Gary, which room?'

'Here!' came the voice at the end of the hallway, in English, at least. Conrad turned and trotted down the hallway, booted feet crunching on broken glass, until he reached the bedroom at the end. He entered the room, froze, just for a second. Gary was there, but he was on the floor, staring up. His ski mask had been torn off and his throat was a bloody mess. A gaunt man with a beard was standing over him, holding Gary's Uzi in his hands. He was staring right at Conrad, and the last thing Conrad heard was the man's raspy voice, '*Dos vidanya.*'

And then the muzzle flash erupted from the end of the silencer.

When the man disappeared from the top of the stairs, Jason turned and said, 'Patty, get the hell out of here, now!'

She turned to him in a fury, her eyes teary, cheeks bright crimson. 'The hell I will.'

He pulled at his bonds, felt the sharp plastic cut through his skin. 'Don't worry about me, just get the hell out!'

'Who said I was worrying about you?' she said, cradling Paul's head against her right shoulder. 'You heard what that asshole said. If I move, they kill Paul. Did you hear that? They'll kill Paul! I could start running and they could catch me outside!'

He tugged again, swore, wondered if he could get up and kick her or propel her or do something, because he couldn't believe what he was about to say, couldn't believe it had come to this in just ten minutes, ten minutes since he was in this living room looking for his brother, but it had to be said.

65

'Patty, they're going to kill us, no matter what. Can't you see that?'

She turned to him again. 'What are you, the fucking expert? They want your criminal brother, that's what they want. Maybe they'll just leave after they find him. But they told us, straight out, that if we moved, then . . . I can't stand even saying it. You know what he said, and I'm not going to risk it.'

Something thudded on the floor above, and Jason looked up. 'Something just happened.'

'Shhh,' Patty said, whispered to Paul, who was whimpering into her shoulder, face pressed tight against her. 'Shhh, honey, it'll be all right. The bad men will go away. Just you wait. Just you see. Shhh, honey.'

The humiliation and anger and rage churned inside of Jason, and part of him knew that Patty was right: Roy had done something terribly wrong over there in Vietnam, wrong enough to bring down this terrible shitstorm upon his family and his home.

Roy stood still in the room that was supposed to be just a guest room, not a charnel house. He looked at the two dead men on the floor and felt bad for what had just happened to his brother and family. Their safe little world had been tossed up and shattered into a hundred pieces, and he knew that it was his fault. If he had stayed away, if he had done things differently, but . . . shit. There was a task to be completed, a holy task if you wanted to look at it that way, and he wasn't about to back out of it. Not now.

He looked at his hands, which were bleeding, and then to the first of the two windows, shattered. Something had disturbed him earlier, resting on the bed, and when he got up and looked out the window, being careful not to be back-lighted or to let anything show, he had seen movement on the ground, shadows out there, and heard the whisper of voices. Hunters, on the prowl, and he knew that eventually they would get up to this room. So he had gently closed one window and slipped out through the other one, pulling himself up on to the roof, and with great exertion had managed to close it behind him.

Then the wait. Hearing the loud entrance, the yells, the screams, not knowing what was happening, only knowing that it was bad and he was sorry for Jason and his family, but it was all he could do. And then the first gunman came in, and he swung in through the window like a friggin' circus acrobat, shattering the glass, catching the guy right in the back, and in a few bloody seconds his knife had come out and he had made quick work of him. Then an answer back to the other gunman, and there you go.

He wiped his hands on his shirt, stepped over the bodies, not sparing them a second glance or thought. They were dead and he was alive and there was work to be done, places to go. He was just sorry that this had to happen to Jason. But he was also certain he knew why these two men had suddenly arrived, and that was something he had to confirm.

Roy went out to the hallway, walking slowly, holding the Uzi in his hands, admiring the feel and weight. What he would have paid or done these past years to have such a weapon available to him . . . My God, all those lost years, lost time, lost opportunities, think of what he could have done . . .

Stop it, he thought furiously. Getting stir crazy and there's no time, no time at all.

He got to the stairs, walked slowly down, saw Jason sitting on the floor, by a couch, with Patty and the boy next to him. The dog, Caleb, that was his name, was dead, blood matting his fur, the poor creature lying stiff on the floor. Jason and Patty and even Paul started talking to him, yammering, their faces confused and angry and shocked, but the heavy weight that had been in him lifted a bit. They were all alive.

'Quiet,' he said, raising a hand. 'I need to know something, and I need to know it right now.'

They stopped talking, Jason now clumsily getting to his feet, Patty as well, and Jason said, 'I don't think we owe you a fucking thing, Roy. Where are those two men?'

'Upstairs.'

'Are they . . . Are they tied up or something?'

Roy looked at the expression on his brother's face, wondered again if he had the stones to do what needed to be done. He said softly, 'Yes. Or something. They won't bother you again.'

Jason took a deep breath. 'Roy, what in hell is going on?'

'I'll tell you, right after you or Patty tell me this,' he said, looking at each of them, trying to gauge what was being hidden there. 'I need to know this: who called?'

Jason looked confused, but there, Patty, he could tell his words had found the mark. He turned to her and said, 'Patty, who did you call, and what did you say?'

Patty held Paul tighter, now feeling the harsh looks of both Roy and Jason upon her, and she said quickly, 'I don't know what you mean.'

The man's eyes seemed to lock right on to her. 'I'm sorry, but you're lying. Patty, look, I will tell you what's going on, I'll tell you everything I can, but I need to know what additional risks are out there. Who did you call?'

She turned to Jason, standing with his arms bound behind him, and she could not bear to see the look on his face. Paul whimpered again and she rubbed at his hair. 'Oh, all right, I called my sister, okay? But she wasn't home. So I left a message. Big deal.'

It looked like the bones in Roy's body had slowly turned into something soft and malleable, since he seemed to sag, right there. 'Where does your sister live?'

'Nebraska.'

'Is she married? Does she have children?'

'Yes, she's married. No, she doesn't have any goddamn children. What is this, a family history?'

Patty watched as Roy came over, weapon slung over his shoulder, and took out a folding knife. He grabbed hold of Jason's shoulders and turned him about, and then slit the plastic ties holding his wrists together. Jason gasped, with relief it seemed like, and started rubbing at his wrists.

Roy then looked her way, his gaze chilling her. He said, 'Then I'm quite sorry, for they are in terrible danger. You'll have to warn them to leave their house, their place of work, immediately.'

Jason said, 'Roy, what in hell is going on here?'

'Just a second,' Roy said, and he picked up an afghan throw on the back of the couch and placed it gently over the body of Caleb. Patty's throat thickened at the sight, and she said, 'Jason. The police, right now.'

Roy said, 'Hold on,' and Jason said, 'No, Roy, I'm sorry, we've got to.' He picked up the phone and then Patty remembered what had happened upstairs, and started walking toward the door, getting away from this horrid scene.

'The phone is . . . Patty, where are you going?'

She turned, holding Paul, who was shaking in her arms.

'I'm going to the Picards, next door. I'm going to call the police from there, and Jason, if you had any sense, you'd come right along.'

She was pleased to see what her husband did, for he looked at Roy and said, 'I don't know what you're involved with, Roy, and I don't really give a shit. All I know is . . . all I know is that my family almost got killed tonight, by people who were looking for you. I don't know what your story is, and I don't care. Patty, let's go.'

And just as they were heading out, Roy said, 'You're a shitty newspaperman, then.'

Jason held Patty's arm, turned back to look at his brother. 'What the hell do you mean by that?'

'I'm ready to tell you what you want to know,' Roy said calmly. 'Everything you want to know. The biggest story of your career, the biggest story of the century. And you're going to walk out?'

Patty was trying to pull him along but Jason stood there. 'Yeah. I'm going to walk out. And after I call the cops, maybe I'll come back and talk to you.'

Roy shook his head. 'I won't be here.'

'What do you mean, you won't be here?'

Roy shrugged. 'There are things going on, Jason, quite important things, and I'm not going to waste a single second trying to explain to your local constable about what just happened here. And trust me when I tell you this, even if you go to the police, you will still be in danger, terrible danger. The people who sent those two men have quite a wide range of talents. Arranging for a traffic accident or a house fire for the three of you, and Patty's sister as well, would be quite easy. Your precious police—do you think they could protect you

70

from what you just went through? They would have been dead within seconds.'

Jason shook his head. 'You're nuts.'

Roy said, 'Look at what just happened, and you call me nuts? Come along, Jason. You've been a newspaper reporter, now an editor. You even had a piece in *USA Today* a few years back, didn't you? About the influence of lobbyists on the American defense budget.'

Patty said, 'Jason. We've got to go, right now.'

Jason pulled his arm away from her. 'That *USA Today* article, how did you know about that?'

'Where I was being held, newspapers and magazines—usually a few weeks or months old—found their way to me. Through the good graces of the people who sent those men.'

'Those men . . .' Jason began. 'Jesus, who are they? I heard them speak something else, something besides English. Roy, who are they?'

'Professionals, ex-military,' he said.

'I could see that,' he said impatiently. 'Damn it, where did they come from?'

Something about the look he was getting from his brother began to chill him. It was almost as terrifying as when the door blew open, not more than ten minutes ago.

Roy said, 'Fair enough. You asked. I'll tell you.'

Patty said, 'Jason, don't listen to what he has to say. Come on, we've got to call the cops. We've got to.'

Jason looked at Roy, felt that tickle of curiosity that had been a curse ever since he decided to become a newspaperman, back in college. 'Go ahead,' he said.

Roy paused, just for a moment, and said, 'Russia, Jason. Those men were from Russia.'

FIVE

Along a stretch of the border between Vermont and Canada, at about 3 A.M., Clay Goodwin was in a hunting blind, talking to a shivering man who was from Colombia and who wore a heavy down parka and had a wool blanket across his legs. Clay didn't think it was that damn cold, but the Colombian was shivering so much that you'd think he was up by Baffin Island or something.

'How much longer, then?' the Colombian asked.

'Ten, fifteen minutes,' Clay said.

'This is a very long border, between your country and Canada. How do you know he will end up here?'

Clay picked up a pair of night-vision goggles, pressed them against his eyes. The landscape in front of him—trees, a creek, a well-worn path—came into ghostly green focus. He said, 'Sure. Longest undefended border in the world and all that. But lots of it is wilderness. Your typical courier don't like wilderness. He likes to go through trails, and you can narrow it down so that he ends up on the right one.'

'Yes,' the Colombian said. 'But how do you know this is the right trail?'

Clay lowered the night-vision goggles, looked over at the

shape of his visitor sitting next to him. 'Easy. Enough money greased enough people to get him to go through here.'

'Oh. Well, why didn't you say so in the first place?'

Clay said, 'Because I like to fucking hear myself talk, okay?'

There was a pause, and Clay imagined he could feel the crackle of energy increase as the man next to him decided what to do. Colombians were good business people—had to be, considering the rough market they had cornered—but they sure were prickly sons of bitches.

'As you wish,' the other man eventually said. 'Still, even if this goes well, I am not sure if it is worth the price and the effort.'

Clay couldn't resist. 'Very well, as you wish. But let me tell you a story. When I was younger and a hell of a lot more innocent, I went to parochial school.'

'Excuse? What is parochial?'

'Catholic school. Nuns and priests and crucifixes on the wall and rulers against the knuckles if you fooled around. And you know what? One of the first lies they taught me was that love is the strongest emotion. Love is what rules the world, love is what will conquer all. And it wasn't until I joined the Army that I knew they were wrong. It wasn't love. It was fear. Fear makes the world go around.'

The Colombian grunted, put up his own night-vision goggles to his face. 'I think I see movement coming down the trail.'

'Sure, you probably do,' Clay said, wanting to make his point before the courier arrived. 'Thing is, and I'm sure you'll agree, there's fear and there's fear. The guys you work with, the guys you hire to mule your crap around the world, they're in fear of you and what you can do. But that's a kind of fear they're used to. Fear of being beaten up, cut, shot, strangled.

73

Stuff they're familiar with, stuff they can put behind them as they decide to work for you or not.'

'I see him approaching,' the Colombian said. 'He's about four or five meters from the border.'

'See? Told you he'd come.'

'He's coming closer.'

Clay leaned over to the Colombian. 'Listen to me, or this whole little demonstration ain't going to mean shit. The thing is, guys can work around those kind of fears. They're real. They've seen it. They've heard about it. And however fearful they might be, at least it's a fear of something real, something known.'

'He's getting closer now, quite close.'

Clay said, 'All right already. Stop yapping or he might turn around.' He picked up his goggles again, pressed them up against his face, his muscle memory recalling all the times he had used gear like this, both in the service and out, on fast boats, helicopters, or on headgear, breaking into somebody's home. The power of the night, all opened up to him through the grace of technology. God may be good, but He's always on the side of the heavier firepower.

Okay. Like the guy said, here was the courier, head moving back and forth as he listened to the night sounds. Poor bastard had probably never seen a tree before except in a park or a jungle somewhere. He was dressed in jeans and a sweatshirt, wearing muddy sneakers, and his face was dark and had a mustache. A flashlight was cupped in his hands, barely illuminating the trail ahead of him. A long fucking way from home, Clay thought, and in a few seconds you're going to be even further away. On his back he carried a knapsack, and Clay was certain what was in there: clothes, maybe some food, a blanket, nothing illegal. Maybe a Bible or something. But what the guy was bringing across the border—and which might explain the pained expression on his face—was wrapped up in little balloons or condoms, riding in his guts.

'How soon?' the Colombian whispered.

'Right about now.'

The courier kept on moving and Clay looked at his feet, left foot, right foot, left foot now going from Canada to the blessed ground of the United States, and before the right foot could touch down, the courier's face grimaced and he blew up. There was a flare of light and it was like he was a puppet, all its strings cut at once, as he crumpled in a bloody and violent spray of light. The Colombian murmured, '*Madre de Dios . . .*' as the flames flickered up and burned brightly and then faded.

Clay nudged him. 'C'mon, let's go check it out.' He got out of the blind, pulled a penlight out of his coat pocket, went up to the trail, the air now filled with the odors of blood, viscera, and things burning. What was once the courier smoldered on the trail, his sneakered feet about the only recognizable item that identified him as being human.

'It worked,' the Colombian said, standing there like a refugee, the wool blanket wrapped about his head.

'Surely did,' Clay said, pulling another item from out of his pocket, tossing it over to the Colombian, who managed to catch it. It was about the size of a small thimble and the Colombian examined it and said, 'This is it?'

'Surely is, partner,' Clay said, playing the beam from the penlight across the burnt flesh and organs. 'Little expanded thermite bomb. Slipped into one of those condoms he swallowed, back in Medellín or Bogotá or Mexico City. Whatever. Comes up here to the border, crosses a transmission beam we've set up. Beam sets off the charge. Bloop and burn, there's nothing left except a barbecued mess. Work like this, and with the feds here cracking down on the major shipments, can really take care of your business rivals. Imagine a transmission system at every port, every border crossing, every airport.'

The Colombian seemed to ponder that for a moment. 'A lot of effort, and a lot of expense. We could merely just capture the couriers, if it came to that, and send their heads back home.'

'Sure,' Clay said, 'but remember what I said earlier? Fear, my friend. Fear is what rules. Your typical courier knows the odds, knows the chances. Figures, hey, won't happen to me, right? But if an occasional courier trying to get here or anywhere else starts burning up and melting . . . well, how many couriers will your rivals have at month's end?'

The Colombian reached forward with a foot, gently kicked one of the sneakers on the ground. Clay could sense his smile. 'Good. Very good. I am sure we can do some business, your group and mine?'

'Without a doubt,' Clay said. 'Without a doubt.' And, he thought, in about six months I'll go avisiting to your rivals, and we'll see what kind of countermeasures we can offer to them, to level the playing field once again. Fear, plus money, equaled quite a comfortable lifestyle.

A couple of minutes later, walking back to his rental car, the Colombian huffing and puffing next to him, his pager started vibrating. He pulled the object from his belt and toggled the button that illuminated the screen. He read the message and whistled. The Colombian seemed interested.

'Something going on?'

'You could say that.'

'What's wrong?'

Clay put the pager back on his belt. 'Nothing. Just another part of my job description.'

'Excuse me?'

He slapped the Colombian on the back, knowing the guy wouldn't like the gesture and not giving a shit. 'Job description. Besides demonstrating little fun items like this, I get to do other things as well. Like cleaning up.'

The Colombian laughed. 'Like a maid?'

Clay wasn't angered. 'Sure. Like the baddest-ass maid you ever did see.'

Roy felt that awful pressure of time start closing in about his head, but he knew he had to start supplying some answers, or the plans that had carefully been drawn together during those long years would fall apart, like trying to rescue a sand castle from the approaching tide with your bare hands.

Jason looked numb. 'Russians?'

'Yeah, Russians,' Roy said. 'Look, I'm an escapee, all right? And this was what they call an H/K squad. Hunter-killer. Sent to bring me back in and to kill all witnesses.' He looked to Patty. 'No time for blame, no time to argue, Patty, but your phone call is what set it off. It's easy enough to tap phone lines to catch a certain phrase. Like a long-dead MIA showing up and knocking on the door. Which is why we've got to get out of here, now, before there's a follow-up visit, and which is why you've got to call your sister and tell her to leave.'

Patty said, 'Leave? For how long?'

Roy shrugged. 'Two, maybe three days. Then it'll be safe.'

Jason rubbed at his wrists again. 'Why will it be safe then?'

The pressure increased around Roy's head, like a steel band, slowly constricting. Jesus, would these people stop yapping and asking questions? he thought, but he restrained himself, forced himself to pull back, tried to stay cool. If this was going to work, he was going to need their cooperation, and fast.

'And why not call the police?' Patty demanded. 'Look what they did here, look what they did to poor Caleb.'

'I can't waste the time,' Roy said, feeling the sharpness creep into his voice. Couldn't they see what was going on? 'Jason, I need your help, right now. Brother to brother.'

Patty interrupted Jason, and Roy thought, she's a sharp one. 'Jason, don't even think of it. This man . . . what kind of brother is he, to come here and bring all this into our home?' She stroked the hair of Paul, who was still whimpering. 'Who almost got us killed? Are you really going to try to help him? Do you really believe anything he says?'

Roy broke in, knowing she wasn't coming over to his side, knowing she had to be neutralized. 'A good point, Patty. But the question is to Jason.' He took a breath, looked into that man's face, tried to remember the boy's face he had last seen so long ago. 'I have to get moving, brother, to get things done. I'm asking you, as a brother, for your help. If you don't want to do anything because of our relationship or because of what I brought down on you, fine. But I'm also offering you the biggest story of your career, Jason. Something that will be the story of the century, beating everything before it, from World War II to the JFK assassination. Something to make you and your newspaper famous. All right?'

Jason looked to his wife, and then back to Roy. 'Get moving, you said. Where?'

'To meet someone, someone who can help me and some friends.' There, that should get his attention. Patty was too angry and too busy with the child to pick up on it, but Jason did, and for a moment Roy felt like maybe it would start working. The pressure about his head eased, just a little.

78

'Friends? Roy, are you telling me there are others out there?'

Roy allowed himself a smile. 'Yeah. There's only thirty-six of us left. All Air Force and Navy aviators, reported missing in action, forgotten and thought dead. I managed to get out and get here. And brother, I mean to get them out, and get them out alive, and nothing is going to get in my way.'

Patty stopped caressing her boy, looked over in disbelief. Even Jason seemed taken aback. Roy decided it was time to stop fooling around, time to go for broke. 'I mean that. To get them out alive, even if it means going at it alone. By myself, I might fail. With you, Jason, I know I won't. Now. I'm done arguing, discussing, debating. I just need to know one thing: are you with me, or not?'

Never in his life had he ever felt so scared, so exposed, so torn. Patty was looking at him with fire in her eyes, and Roy . . . my God, just a few hours ago there was such joy and happiness in this house, so much pleasure and life at seeing Roy show up after so many long and empty years. And now? There was the unmoving shape of poor Caleb over there, under an afghan, and the blown-in door and damaged house and Patty with her pale face and red-rimmed eyes, and poor little Paul, and upstairs . . . From the way Roy was handling himself and not saying anything more about what had happened, Jason could guess about those two Russians. Dead, upstairs in his house. His dream house with his dream family and dream job . . . all gone. All that was left was an angry wife and a weeping child and a long-lost brother, asking for an impossible favor.

'How can I possibly help?'

'I don't have time to tell you. Just trust me that I know you can.'

He took a breath, looked at his brother's calm gaze. 'Roy, I'm sorry. I can't.'

A crisp nod, the eyes looking sorrowful. 'All right. I've got to get going. You three should get away from here, right now. Don't go to the newspaper, don't go anywhere you usually would, like a favorite resort or hotel. Just stay away. No credit cards. Just use cash. Patty, somehow, get the same news out to your sister and brother-in-law. In two days, it should be safe.'

Patty said, 'Why two days?'

'Because that's all the time I have. Either I'll succeed or I'll fail. If I succeed, great. If I fail . . . well, I'll be back in prison. And you should be all right, if you keep your heads low over the next couple of days.'

'What are you going to do?'

Roy said, 'Sorry. You gave up the right to ask that question by saying you won't help. And time is wasting. In the meantime, don't say anything about what happened here. Not a word. I'll clean up the best I can, if you can give me a hand here.'

Jason swallowed, shuffled his feet, said, 'Roy, look, I can help by—'

'No, no favors,' Roy said. 'And no more time. All right?'

Jason pressed on, the guilt starting to make him nauseous. 'Roy, have you thought this through, about what—'

Roy's voice was scornful. 'Yes, little brother. I've thought it through. For nearly thirty years, I've thought it through quite thoroughly. And as the expression goes, either help or get out of the fucking way, all right? You've already chosen not to help. So get out of the way.'

In the large kitchen of his Cambridge home, Sloan Woodbury sipped at his second cup of coffee of the morning, an unread copy of the New York *Times* and Boston *Globe* at his elbow. From upstairs came the sound of a shower, as his overnight guest readied herself before leaving, taking the third shower of her visit. He frowned at the memories of the hours they had shared. There was a deep aching sense of humiliation, that he had to pay for his pleasures, as strange as they were. Take Kissinger, he thought morbidly. Looked like a hairy gnome with big ears and thick glasses, and he had movie stars chasing after him all his years in Washington. Power being the ultimate aphrodisiac and all that crap. But Sloan Woodbury? Sure, he was heavyset—the word *fat* was not in his vocabulary—but except for one or two women who shared his unusual tastes, his physical satisfaction came from hurried contacts and folded wads of hundred-dollar bills. He knew the humiliation would eventually fade away, to be replaced by a sense of emptiness, and then, after a few weeks, a gnawing physical hunger that would cause the whole cycle to flip through one more time.

He delicately traced the rim of the coffee cup with a chubby finger. Ah yes, the whole cycle, and too bad that he wouldn't ride that cycle with Annie from Southie, ever again.

He looked up at a clock near the stainless-steel refrigerator. Seven A.M. And as if it were timed by some atomic clock in Geneva, there was a knock at the rear kitchen door.

'Come in!' he called out. 'It's open.'

A man dressed in jeans and leather jacket came in, the jacket not quite hiding the bulk of his shoulders and upper arms. His head was shaved and he had a thick black mustache, and a fine network of lines about his eyes, as if he had spent a lot of time outdoors, squinting under a hot sun while hunting and killing things.

Clay Goodwin came over, said, 'Mister Secretary,' and then

81

made a beeline to the coffeemaker. He poured himself a cup, black, and came over to the round oak kitchen table and sat down, sprawling his legs out. 'So,' he said. 'What's the situation?'

Woodbury hated being in this man's presence, hated the thought that this kind of man even existed, but still . . . jobs had to be accomplished, no matter what. 'There was an incident last night. Involving one of the Ebony teams operating in this area. It missed its check-in time.'

Clay slurped noisily from his cup. 'So? Why me? There're protocols in place, aren't there?'

'Sure, the protocols are in place,' Woodbury said. 'But read the newspapers. It's a delicate time. I may not want the protocols enacted, if you know what I mean.'

'Ah, it's always a delicate time. So what?'

Woodbury turned his cup around, so that the curved handle pointed in Clay's direction. 'I want somebody to look into it. I want you, Clay. You contact whomever you have to contact, but I want a delay in the protocols. Go see if you can't find this Ebony crew, and report back to me. It shouldn't take more than a day.'

Clay took another slurp. 'I might have to get Mister Pickering's approval for this.'

'Do it, then. I don't care. But I want the protocols delayed. This Ebony crew might be on a drunk or something. I don't trust you for much of anything, but I do trust that you can get the job done quickly, before questions get raised, before something is done that might hurt a lot of things, including Mister Pickering.'

Another noisy slurp. 'All right. A day, maybe two.'

From upstairs came the sound of Annie singing, off-key. Clay winced and said, 'Who the hell is that?'

'That's Annie,' Woodbury said, explaining without an ounce of embarrassment. 'An overnight guest. And I would take it as a great personal favor if you would give her a ride. And take care of things.'

There was the sound of young and eager feet on the main staircase, and Annie came in, hair still wet from the shower, wearing tight white slacks and a sleeveless light blue blouse that accented her two best charms, small leather purse over her left shoulder. 'Oh. Sorry to disturb you and all that,' she said. 'Um, I guess I'll be going . . .'

Woodbury stood up, put on his best soothing face, which he usually pulled out for the Sunday morning TV talk shows and the occasional Senate committee. 'M'dear, this gentleman works for me. I'd be so grateful if you allowed him to give you a ride home. I'd feel so much better if that happened, instead of having you try to catch a cab or the T at this hour.'

Annie shrugged, shifted her purse to the other shoulder. 'Sure. Whatever. What's your name?'

His guest stood up, smiling. 'Clay.'

Annie laughed. 'Clay. Like dirt, hunh?'

Clay's eyes narrowed. 'Yeah. Like dirt. Mister Woodbury. I'll take care of that first matter, and . . . Annie. If that's your wish.'

The young girl started to go through her purse, looking for God knows what. Woodbury looked at Clay, who was staring right back, and that melancholy feeling he had earlier was gone. There was a sharp buzzing sensation in his chest, knowing that this young lady from Southie had no idea what was being decided in front of her. Woodbury wished he could extend the sensation, and a pleasurable one it was, but he didn't want her to get suspicious.

'Yes,' he finally said. 'That's my wish. For both items to be taken care of.'

Clay smiled, like a young boy being presented with a large wrapped gift box for his birthday.

'Thanks,' he said. 'I'll call you later.'

Woodbury sighed. 'Please do.'

Patty sat in their old Volvo in the single-car garage, Paul at her side, while the men did their thing inside the house. Paul was starting to crash, his poor little body feeling tired and sleepy, even after all the trauma his small eyes had seen in the previous hours. She had grabbed some clothes and toys for Paul and cash—and Roy had said something strange, about cash. 'There are machines now, that can dispense cash. Am I right?'

And Jason had said, 'Yes, ATMs. Automatic teller machines.'

And Roy had said, 'I don't know how they operate, but stay away from them. I understand if you use one your location can be instantly spotted. So just use whatever cash you have on hand. Don't use those machines.'

So here she sat. Jesus. She wiped at her eyes and thought the minute she and Jason got out of here they were going straight to the police station and to Chief Malone. No matter what kind of crap and nonsense Roy was peddling, she wasn't going to let this slide by. This place of theirs was so homey, so reassuring, and she had looked forward to years of a happy life here, growing old with Jason and with Paul and maybe another brother or sister for him.

But now? Dead men upstairs, a dead dog in the living room, blood and bullets and death everywhere. She squeezed Paul and he murmured, 'Mommy?'

She bent down, kissed the top of his head. 'Yes, hon.'

'The bad men, they've gone away?'

'Yes, the bad men, they've gone away. And we're going for

a little trip in a little while, to make sure no more bad men come this way.'

He shifted in her arms, and she squeezed him again. 'Mommy?'

'Right here, babe.'

'Caleb . . . he's not waking up, ever, is he?'

'I'm afraid not, love.'

'He was a brave dog, though.'

'The bravest.'

'He was trying to get the bad men, wasn't he.'

The damn tears and the fresh hate she had for Jason's brother came right back, making her choke out a 'yes, Paul' before she realized she couldn't continue.

Paul reached up and stroked her wrist. 'If we get another dog, can we call him Caleb too?'

'Yes,' she whispered, kissing her boy's head. 'Yes, of course.'

Jason felt himself get woozy at what they had just done. The two bodies were now in the kitchen, wrapped in old sheets and thick chain from the cellar, and cinder blocks—which had once held up a bookcase when he was in college—were tied to their feet. Upstairs the two of them had scrubbed and scrubbed the hardwood floor with bleach, until Roy had said, 'Okay, that's fine. Let's get a move on.'

The broken window in the spare bedroom and the shattered door were also a problem, and Roy had explained, 'It'd take a day or two to make your house look untouched. This way, though, questions will be raised. The two Russians will be gone, you'll be gone, and while it'll look like something violent has happened here, there'll be more questions than answers. And it'll take time for them to look for the answers, which helps me.'

Now Roy opened the rear door to the kitchen, nodded to Jason and said, 'Okay, let's do it, before it gets too busy around here.'

Jason bent over, grabbed the cinder block and the end of the wrapped sheet, thankful that Roy had taken the other end, the one splotchy and stained with blood. They stumbled through the door and outside, where birds were chirping and the sound of the river rushing past would normally make him feel safe and secure. Hah. Safe and secure. Two words he doubted he would ever use again.

Roy moved quickly, and Jason found it hard to keep up with him, and then they were at the river's edge, where there was a tiny knee-high white picket fence, more for decoration than anything else. Roy moved around so they were parallel and said, 'Okay, on three,' and after swinging the body back and forth, twice, they let go. The river in this part of town was relatively fast-moving, and Jason rubbed at his hands, watching the body bob up once before sinking down.

Roy stood next to him, breathing hard, his lungs sounding raspy. 'One more to go.'

'Yeah. Remember the Bellamy River?'

'Sure,' Roy said. 'About a ten-minute walk from the house.'

'Remember how we used to go down there, walking along, beachcombing?'

Roy folded his arms. 'Yep. Took home a few horseshoe crab shells, which Mom didn't like stinking up the house.'

Jason thought for a moment, and said, 'Remember how we used to borrow old man Piper's rowboat, and go fishing? Man, I hated putting those worms on the hooks.'

Roy kept on staring out at the river. 'Fishing?'

'Yeah, fishing?'

Roy said, his voice flat, 'I don't remember anybody called

Piper living on the river. And I don't ever remember fishing from a rowboat in that river with you. The only time we fished—and maybe it was twice, maybe it was three times—was on the Durham bridge, at the south end of the river, with Dad.'

Jason kicked at a piece of grass, humiliated. 'Oh. Okay.'

Roy turned, eyes hard. 'Still have doubts I'm your brother?'

Jason looked back, flinching. 'No.'

'Good. Let's go fetch the other one, and then I'll get out of here.'

Roy watched with some sense of satisfaction as the second body went into the river. In a day or two, it would probably be found, but so what? Right now he felt better than he should, feeling like finally, finally, oh lord, he had struck back at the other side, had popped them twice. A very tiny victory, hardly worth matching up against what was ahead of him, but he had struck back. Jesus, that was a good feeling.

He saw his younger brother tremble, could barely imagine what was going on inside that mind of his. He gently tapped him on the shoulder and said, 'Look, thanks for your help. Go in and take a shower or something. Five minutes won't make much of a difference.'

Tears seemed to form around the man's eyes. 'Will you . . . will you still be here?'

Another gentle tap. 'Sure I will. I won't leave without saying goodbye. But take your shower and get ready. I've got one more thing to do.'

And he waited, standing by the peaceful river in this peaceful state in this allegedly peaceful country, and when Jason went into the house, he walked around to the left, across the carefully mown lawn, until he reached the garage. A dark gray

Volvo was parked inside, and sitting in the front seat of the car was Patty, holding her boy—his nephew!—in her arms. Roy stared at that tender moment, remembered Stacy Burke, a girl he had written to, back on Guam. My God, where would she be now? Married, no doubt, with children and grandchildren. He tried for a moment to resurrect a thought of what she looked like, but failed.

He moved quietly into the garage, pulled down a shovel, and then backed out. He was glad that his brother's wife hadn't seen him, for he couldn't think of a single thing to say to her.

When he got out of the shower, the trembling came back again, and Jason got down on his knees and vomited up bile into the toilet. He had thrown up twice already—once while helping Roy bag up the corpses of the two dead Russians, and once just a while ago in the shower. He refused to think anymore of what had just happened, how he had gone from the happiest guy in Maine with the best and safest family imaginable, to this point, where he was so scared of the bad men out there and what might happen to Patty and Paul.

After getting dressed, he went back downstairs, hurrying to be with Patty and Paul. He stopped for a moment in the living room. Something was wrong, something was missing, and then he went outside and there was Roy, leaning on a shovel, his sweatshirt off, sleeves rolled up, knapsack at his feet. A mound of dirt had been smoothed out at the base of a young maple tree.

'I tossed the weapons into the river,' Roy explained. 'Where I'm going, I don't want a suspicious cop pulling me over and finding fully automatic rifles with their serial numbers filed off. And while you were showering, I buried your dog. Said some words over him. Not enough to make up for what happened, but I figured I'd take care of it.' Roy gazed about the small yard and said, 'Thought this'd be a good spot. Was I right?'

Jason's hands felt itchy, like they should be doing something. 'Yes, that was a good spot.'

'Good,' Roy said, tamping down the shovel blade against the dirt. 'Sometime later this summer, it would look nice with some flowers planted over it.'

Jason said, 'I'm not sure that we'll ever come back here.'

Roy leaned on the shovel handle again, sweat trickling along his thin wrists. 'Oh, you should come back, really, when this is all through. You let those two bastards chase you out of here, because of what they did to you, then they win. They may be dead and their bosses may eventually be dead, but they'll still win.'

Jason thought his brother was raving, and he looked again at Roy's hands and wrists, at the old round scars on his brother's hands, and other scars on his wrists as well, long scars that ran up along the side of each arm. Roy noticed his look and said, 'Admiring my war trophies?'

'What happened?'

Roy started putting his sweatshirt over his head and said, 'Ones on the hands, that comes from cigarettes. French cigarettes, if you can believe it, 'cause that's what a lot of the North Vietnamese smoked. They held your hands down flat and touched 'em up with the butt end of a cigarette. The other scars—' Roy's head poked through the top of the sweatshirt, and he smoothed it down, 'those other scars came from a little trick they had, called weightlifting. They'd put you on your knees and then tie your wrists together back there, letting the thin ropes dig in, nice and tight, and then they'd yank you up, try to lift you up as high as they could.'

'Jesus,' Jason said.

'Yeah, not a pretty story, hunh? Most times it didn't stop until you fainted or until your arms got pulled out from the sockets. Got to be so that you could tell what was happening to other guys in the cells by how much they screamed. Well.' Roy took the shovel, carefully leaned it against the maple tree. He held out his hand. 'This is it, Jason. Thanks for the meal, thanks for the bed, and I'm sorry for what happened here. But I've got to get going. If I make it, I'll try to get back here. That is, if your wife lets me.'

Jason looked at the outstretched hand, then up to the face of his brother.

His brother.

'I'm going with you,' he said.

Roy grinned, shook his head. 'No you're not.'

'Yes I am,' Jason said, feeling the nausea and weakness in his gut start to disappear. 'It's the right thing to do. Roy, I'm coming with you. I'll help you any way I can. Just let me know what I can do.'

Roy lowered his hand. 'It's going to be tough. We're going to be breaking a few laws along the way.'

Now Jason was smiling at his brother. 'I don't care. Let's go.'

'Your wife isn't going to like it.'

His smile wavered, but still, damn it, this was the right thing to do. 'I can take care of Patty.'

Roy grabbed his hand, shook it. 'Damn it, I don't know if you will or not, but let's get going.'

And then Jason walked out of the yard with Roy, and halfway to the garage he put his arm around his older brother's shoulder.

SIX

After she had given him directions, and about twenty minutes into their trip, the young girl called Annie said, 'This isn't the way to my apartment.'

Clay turned to her and said, 'How much was that fat guy paying you?'

She seemed to shudder. 'I don't even like thinking about what I had to do for him. Four bills for the night, and I still feel like taking another shower. Quite gross.'

'Because he's fat?' Clay asked.

She shook her head. 'No, because . . . ugh. I had to drink a lot of beers. You figure it out.'

How charming, Clay thought. Aloud he said, 'How about something vanilla, for one bill?'

She opened up her purse, took out a breath mint, and popped it in her mouth. 'For real? Right now?'

'Sure, why not? Top off your morning.'

Annie giggled. 'Sure. Why not, dirt man.'

He reached over, caressed her thigh. 'Sure. Why not.'

He drove on, eventually going into an industrial part of Chelsea, a place he was familiar with from an earlier job, a couple of months back. He backed the Excursion up a brick-lined alley in a district of abandoned warehouses, making sure nobody and nothing was around. He took out his wallet, peeled off a Ben Franklin, and passed it over, and within seconds this fine specimen of South Boston womanhood had unzipped his jeans and gone to work with what he immediately detected was an enthusiastic though somewhat amateur mouth.

After about ten minutes of her ministrations, he sighed and leaned forward some, gently inserting his right thumb into her mouth, causing her to gag for just a second. He moved his thumb so it was rubbing against her rear molars. She started to struggle, and he took a breath and with his free hand clenched her nose tight, as the free fingers on his first hand started pressing against her windpipe. She coughed, gagged, struggled, and tried to bite down, but his thumb—his poor, bleeding thumb—prevented any collateral damage. In about two minutes she was done, about thirty seconds ahead of him. He rested, caught his breath, and then got out of the Ford. Toward the rear of the alleyway—which he had fortunately found on his last trip—was a rusting manhole cover that led to God knows what. He pried it open, went back to the Excursion, pulled out her limp body, retrieved his hundred-dollar bill and the four bills from Woodbury, and in a matter of seconds had accomplished the first part of the day's events.

He went back to the Excursion, gently sucked on his bleeding thumb, and sniffed the morning salt air.

'God,' he said to no one in particular, 'what a beautiful day.'

Sloan Woodbury lay in the now-tepid water of his morning bath, a wet washcloth over his forehead. The bathtub was extra-large, to accommodate his bulk, and he never felt like looking at himself while he bathed. He moved his legs about, knew he should get moving in a second or two if he was going to make that damn event over at the Copley Plaza. He was thinking about the phone call last night, the one that had woken him up. Over the past few years, he had gotten two similar phone calls, and each time, within a few hours, things had straightened out. Nothing untoward had happened, and life had rolled merrily along. Outside, the traffic noise had increased some, as Cambridge bestirred itself and those who thought they should be running things instead of those clowns down in D.C. were on their way to their lecture halls, book-lined offices, and think tanks. If only they knew, he thought, if only they knew . . . and then he found himself smiling. Jesus. In war there were casualties, and if some of those casualties were for the greater good, well, why not?

Patty looked up at him from the driver's seat of the Volvo, stopped at the end of their driveway. Her hands gripped the steering wheel, making the knuckles a stark white, and their boy was huddled on the other side, a blanket covering him. Jason looked in, miserable, hands feeling useless at his side.

'So,' she said, 'this is it.'

'Yes, for now,' he said. 'I've got to help Roy. I just have to.'

'After all that happened, after all that he brought into our house? Forget it, I don't want to start that again. Look, you do what you have to do. Don't expect things to be the same when you get back.'

'What do you mean?'

'Not in front of the boy,' she said. 'Jesus, now let me go . . .'

'Hold on,' came a voice, and Jason stepped aside as Roy came up, hands soiled from work, his face still sweaty. Roy said, 'It'll only be for two days, Patty. And then I'll make it up to you.'

She murmured something, and Roy said, 'I'm sorry, I didn't hear you.'

'I said,' she responded, loudly, and then she lowered her voice, 'I said, if you're still alive, you mean.'

Then she put the car in drive, pulled out, and turned left. Jason stood there and watched the Volvo disappear beyond the trees along the side of the road. Roy said, 'I'm sorry, Jason.'

Jason folded his arms, rubbed his biceps. He felt cold. 'You should be.'

'Yeah, you're right.'

Jason tried to gauge what was going on beyond those cautious eyes, that grizzled face. Tried to peel away in his own mind what three decades of imprisonment had placed upon this man standing next to him, this man who had taught him how to shoot a .22, start a fire in the damp woods, and who had taught him the constellations of the night sky. He felt a stab of fear, that Patty was right, that this man next to him was no longer his brother, but a crazed man, on some doomed mission, on some quest that would kill him or destroy his family.

He said, 'There are thirty-six, you said, back there, still being held prisoner?'

'Yep. Just like me.'

'And this will be my story, right? Story of the century?'

'All yours,' he said.

'Okay,' Jason said, looking back at his house, knowing with a sick certainty that this was the last time he would ever see this place. 'Let's get going. But not just for the story, Roy. I'm doing it for you, and for Mom and Dad, and . . . well, me, too. Don't let me down.'

'I won't,' the older man said.

Along Interstate 95 in Saugus, Massachusetts, just north of

Boston, the roadway is lined with restaurants, malls, muffler repair shops, cocktail lounges, adult bookstores, two strip joints, and stores selling everything from pool supplies to masonry. Roads leading out from the exits along this stretch of highway support a number of industrial and office parks. Clay Goodwin, still playing with the wound on his thumb, found his way to one of them, Murray Office Estates. The place had cubed steel and glass buildings that looked like they had been designed by architects about an hour after they had gotten their licenses, and he found a parking spot in one office building that supported a medical supply company, a communications software company, and something called J.P. Security Services, which was on the first floor. A larger sign outside the door showed the logo of the company—a high-tech version of the U.S. marshal's badge from the Old West—and a smaller sentence indicated that it was 'A Pickering Industries Company.'

Clay blew through the receptionist and got to see the man he wanted about ninety seconds after displaying his ID. In one field or another, Clay had been working for Pickering Industries ever since he was discharged from the Army, and never in his life had he been so happy. Most of the time, he worked for the security end of the company, where he had started out as a bounty hunter. That had been some real fun, back when he was younger. When some idiot jumped bail, his ass belonged to a bail bondsman, which meant that a bounty hunter could pretty much do anything, go anywhere, and bust down any doors to get the criminal back. His talents had gotten the eye of some industrious folks at JPSS, as it was known, and after a year of doing contract work for them, he had been asked to do some highly irregular bounty hunting work. This kind of work was contracted out by certain aggrieved—and mostly wealthy—individuals who had been wronged by members of the criminal class, and instead of grabbing the fugitive and bringing him back to whatever passed for justice nowadays, he would bring him to an empty field (amazing how many empty fields there were in this increasingly crowded United States) and introduce him to a previously dug hole. Two taps to the back of the head later, it was time for the next assignment.

When this particular job had first been described to him by an older member of the firm, with all the dignity and foot-dragging that reminded him of a certain nun in eighth grade who was trying to explain human reproduction, he had just one question: When do I start?

Now, though, as he shook the hand of the Saugus office manager, he missed the simplicity of those days. Old man Pickering had been giving him more and more exotic assignments, and this particular one was about as exotic as it got.

The office manager led him to a private elevator that operated with a keypad. The manager's name was Budlong and he wore the Pickering Industries uniform of black slacks, white shirt, and necktie. His black hair was cut short, and the back of his neck was quite red, as if he were nervous about sharing a confined space like an elevator with Clay. In Dallas, at the company headquarters, the neckties were always red or blue. Here in Massachusetts, on the East Coast of the Pickering empire, this manager flirted with danger by wearing a striped number, and Clay decided to let him live.

The door opened up to a small room with computer consoles and radio equipment and a solitary office chair. Clay stepped forward and took the chair without asking, and Budlong came up right behind him, lecturing on what had happened the previous night, when he had eventually made a phone call to Sloan Woodbury, waking him from a sound sleep.

'After I contacted the secretary, only then did I realize that Ebony Three had received a call-out,' Budlong said, his voice a bit breathless, as if he had just come in that morning from a marathon. 'You see, my initial call to the secretary was after the field unit had missed a scheduled communications check.'

'What kind of call-out? Was it real, or a false alarm?'

Budlong looked miserable, like a young man who had forgotten to bring in his homework. 'The problem is that, under the security arrangements, once a call-out is made to a field unit, it's kept in memory for an hour, and then automatically erased. So there's no archive, no record of what the message was, except for the field unit. The security procedures are quite tight.'

Clay said, 'That's a hell of a fix, ain't it?'

Budlong nodded quickly. 'That it is. All I can tell from here is that the unit, Ebony Three, received an initiation signal. I don't know what was on the signal, and even then, we should have received a follow-up message from Ebony Three, but we didn't.'

Clay let his eyes wander around the consoles, not really watching what was going on, just letting this drone prattle on and on. 'And why didn't you receive a follow-up message?'

'Solar storms,' he said, a defensive tone in his voice, as if he were refusing to take blame for something originating more than 93 million miles away. 'Blanketed this portion of the hemisphere with interference. Mister Goodwin, our night person was on duty, all night long. She didn't hear a thing.'

Clay moved the chair, side to side. No squeaks. Good. It wouldn't be appropriate for a chair within Pickering Industries, even in this lonely outpost of the military-industrial complex, to squeak. 'All right, then. I take it there's been no successful communication with Ebony Three?'

'No.'

Clay let his hands move across the smooth metal of the counter in front of the comm gear. 'Do you have any idea where Ebony Three is located?'

'Oh, of course we do,' Budlong said simply.

Clay slowly turned the chair around, moving it deliberately with the aid of his left foot. 'You do?'

'Yes. It's in Maine. The GPS signal is now coming in loud and clear, and—'

Clay folded his arms, enjoyed the terrified look of this man, who no doubt knew that his career was up for grabs in the next few seconds. 'And when were you going to tell me this little bit of news? While we were having lunch later today? Hmmm?'

Budlong shook his head. 'Sir, I wanted to bring you up to speed as to what happened. Then I was going to tell you where Ebony Three was located. You just got ahead of me, that's all.'

Clay looked into that scared little face, decided squashing him was going to take too much effort. 'All right, then. Ebony Three's surveillance area. What is it?'

'New Hampshire, Maine, and Vermont.'

'How many targets in Maine?'

'Two. Berwick and Portland.'

'And where is Ebony Three located?'

'Berwick.'

Clay thought about the geography, figured a drive of just over an hour. 'All right. You have the files on the Berwick target?'

'Of course,' Budlong said. 'Upstairs in my office safe. I have all of Ebony Three's target files.'

Clay thought about something else. 'You ever look into those files? Have you?'

Budlong now looked like he was being accused of embezzlement. 'Sir, absolutely not! All I know is that those files are of the highest security, and they are only to be transferred to someone with your access authorization. I don't even know the target name. I just know the community involved.'

Clay leaned a bit in the chair, pleased again at how oiled the mechanism was. 'You ever wonder what might be in those files, young man?'

The office manager tried to smile, which looked awful on his pale face. 'Somebody the firm wants to keep track of. Maybe ex-employees. Or criminals. I don't think it's my place to try to figure it out.'

Clay stood up, and gently tapped Budlong on the cheek. 'You keep on thinking like that, son, and I guarantee you'll have a long and healthy career with the company. Come along, now, let's get back to your office.'

He could sense the relief in Budlong's demeanor as he ushered him back to the elevator, where the young man again punched in the access code. He glanced shyly over at Clay, and then looked away again. Clay said, 'Something on your mind?'

'Well,' Budlong said, stammering slightly. 'Just wondering . . . by the way . . . what in heck happened to your thumb.'

Clay smiled at him, making sure to reveal lots of teeth. 'Some teenage whore chewed on it this morning while I strangled her.'

Roy stood with his brother on Linden Street, where Jason's home was located. He looked about, carrying a knapsack over his shoulder. 'Tell me, Jason. What's the nearest highway or state road?'

'Route Four.'

'If you were coming here from Route Four, which way would you come.'

Jason pointed to the left. 'From there.'

'Okay,' Roy said, walking to the right. 'We'll start looking in this direction.'

Jason fell in with him and said, 'What are you looking for?'

'Wheels,' he said.

'What kind of wheels?'

Roy looked up and down the wood-lined street. Such a peaceful place, and so many trees. He wondered what it would be like to live in a place with so many beautiful trees.

'The wheels those Russian characters were using. We've got to find them.'

'Why?' Jason asked.

Roy resumed walking. 'Two reasons. First, it might tell us something useful. Second, we're going to need to use them. The car I used to get here died on me.'

Jason stayed silent for a moment, and said, 'That highway question. You figured the Russians came from Route Four, spotted the house, and—'

'And drove on for a bit, before pulling over and coming out to see us.' There. On the right, in a small turnoff. Black van, tinted windows. Massachusetts plates. He turned to his brother and said, 'So far, so good. Let's see what we can find.'

Roy looked around the van, sitting there quiet and deadly. Like a bomber, he thought. Or a fighter aircraft. Designed for killing, that's all. He reached up to the driver's door, opened it. The keys were hanging from the ignition. Jason crowded in behind him and said, 'Doors unlocked? Keys out there in the open? Sure looks sloppy.'

Roy shrugged off the knapsack, tossed it in. 'No, brother.

Not sloppy at all. It's very smart. Speed is of the essence in the kind of mission they were on last night. They meant to snatch me and . . . well, snatch me and bring me back here. They didn't want to fumble around in the dark, trying to unlock doors, trying to find keys. Nope. They wanted to come back here and get the hell out. Which is what we're about to do.'

He sat in the van, while Jason came in on the other side and then looked past a sliding metal door. 'Holy shit, Roy, you ought to take a look at this. Computer gear, gym bags, radios . . . it's a goddamn spookville back there.'

'Unh-hunh,' Roy said. He turned the key, the engine roared into life, and he carefully maneuvered the van out on to the pavement. 'Okay, geography question. Which is bigger now, Dover or Portsmouth?'

'Both are about the same.'

'Okay, next question. Which one is livelier, more bars, young kids, transients, stuff like that.'

'Portsmouth, without a doubt.'

'Great,' Roy said, enjoying the sensation of the steering wheel under his hands again. 'It's time to revert back to my flying days, Jason. I'm the pilot and you're the navigator. Tell me how best to get to Portsmouth from here.'

'All right, I will, but I want something in exchange,' Jason said.

Roy kept the speed right at thirty miles an hour. No time to get pulled over for speeding. 'Sure,' he said. 'And I can guess at what you want. Questions answered, right?'

'That's right,' his brother said. 'Questions answered.'

'Fair enough,' Roy said.

Patty drove for all of five minutes before ending up in the center of town, which, for Berwick, wasn't that large. A town square—actually, the damn thing was round and had a statue stuck in the center, but why be picky—and a couple of blocks of stores and offices in small brick buildings, and nearby as well were the offices for their newspaper, the Berwick *Banner*. A bridge spanned the Salmon Falls River, and across the river was New Hampshire and the small city of Somersworth. The Berwick town hall was also made of brick, with white columns out front, and in the basement of the town hall was the police station. She parked the Volvo and savagely tossed the gear shift into park, making the car jerk.

She reached over and touched the face of her strong little boy. Paul had a yellow toy dump truck in his pudgy hands and said, 'What are we doing?'

'We're going in to see the police chief, hon,' she said.

He scratched his nose. 'I thought Daddy and Uncle Roy said we shouldn't go to the police.'

She kissed his forehead. 'Well, Mommy thinks we should. We should tell them about the bad men.'

Now tears were forming in his eyes. ''Cause of Caleb?'

'Unh-hunh,' she said. ''Cause of Caleb.'

She got out and let Paul scoot out after her, feeling the buzz of energy about her when she was doing something that she knew was one hundred percent right. She had put up a good face back there at her house, with Roy and Jason demanding that she not talk to the cops, and she had nodded in all the right places and said the right things, and she had made up her mind about two yards away from the house. She was going to do things by the book, straight and narrow, and that meant going in to the Berwick Police Department and revealing all.

The interior of the police station was cool and old, with worn wooden benches—looking like they had been salvaged from a Baptist church—and a waist-high wooden railing. A woman about the age of Patty's mother was hesitantly tapping on a computer keyboard at a metal desk, peering over her glasses, and the door behind her—marked CHIEF—was closed. She looked up and said, 'Well, good morning, Patty. What are you doing over here so early? Getting the overnight log for your husband?'

Patty smiled in return, thinking furiously. Nadine. That was her name. Nadine Sheldon. The newspaper covered three towns, and it was hard keeping track of those people—mostly older men and women—who ran things, including administrative assistants and secretaries and office managers. The gatekeepers for the elected or appointed officials, like Jed Malone, the chief of police.

'No, Nadine, actually I was hoping to see the chief. Is he in?'

Nadine smiled and shook her head. 'Sorry, Patty. He's up in Springvale, had to go to court this morning. I don't expect him back for an hour. Is there a message you'd like to leave him?'

Patty wondered, just for a second, what this nice older Maine woman would say if she knew what had happened in her quiet little town the previous night. Boy, she thought, that would be one hell of a message. 'Who's on duty?'

Nadine's demeanor changed. 'Carl Connor is,' she said. 'Do you want me to call him in? Is there something going on?'

Carl Connor, and she suddenly remembered who he was. Came in last month to get his picture taken. Newest officer on the force. All of twenty-one years old. And she was going to tell this child about what had happened at her house? No, she'd wait for the chief. She and Jason were friendly with the chief—as friendly as you could be when you were the local newspaper and sometimes had to squeeze him for information—but she trusted him well enough.

'Mommy,' Paul said. 'I have to go pee.'

There. That decided it. She squeezed Paul's hand and said, 'No, it's fine, Nadine. Look, if Chief Malone calls in, tell him I need to talk to him. I'll be over at the newspaper.'

Nadine's smile looked forced. 'All right, then. You go on and take care of your little boy.'

Patty turned and headed out the door. 'You can believe that.'

Outside the sun seemed brighter. She squinted at the glare and started walking to the offices of the *Banner*. There she would take care of Paul, and then . . . what? Sit and wait for the chief to call in? No, she thought. She'd do something else. If she was lucky, Jack Schweitzer was in, the young guy who was the assistant editor—a glorified reporter and copy editor, but he took some of the load off of Jason and, for the title, agreed to get paid less—and she'd talk to him. Maybe he knew somebody in the Maine State Police, if the chief hadn't called back in a while. That might be the ticket. And shit, look, if the chief doesn't call, then contact Nadine and have her page him. What was going on was worth pulling him out of court for, that was for damn sure.

'Are we going to the paper, Mommy?' Paul said, patiently walking with her on the sidewalk, as Patty nodded and smiled at the locals out doing their morning errands.

'That's right, hon.'

'Will Daddy and Uncle Roy be there?'

'No, I'm afraid not. They're on . . . a trip. They should be back in a while.'

'Oh. Can we go look for a new dog then?'

Damn it, here came those tears again. She squeezed his

hand. 'Of course. We can go look for a new dog then. A dog just as brave as Caleb.'

At the corner of Route 4 and Pope Street, she started to head right, to the wood-frame building that served as the offices for the Berwick *Banner*, an accountant, and a dental supply office, but something made her stop.

'Mommy, I have to go pee really bad.'

'Just a sec, Paul. Just a sec.'

She moved back to the corner, at the edge of a Fleet Bank, and then looked around again, down the street. There, in front of the Berwick *Banner*. A black Ford Excursion, with Connecticut plates. Sure looked out of place. And a man was there, leaning against the front fender. From what she saw, he was tall, muscular looking, with a bald head and a mustache. He was just leaning there, looking at something . . . what? A file? Photos?

Sure. Photos. He was looking at photos. Like he was comparing what was in the photos to what was before him.

Like he was making sure he was in the right place. She saw his head moving, like he was going to look up here, and she felt a cold tongue of fear race up her back, like something awful and bad was about to happen.

She ducked back round the corner again, her breathing quickening. Paul said, 'Mommy, you're hurting my hand.'

'Okay, Paul, hold on. Look, Mommy's changed her mind, okay? Just be a brave boy and hold things in, just for a few more minutes, and I'll give you something nice. Maybe an ice cream cone.'

'Really? Before lunch?'

She started walking fast, back to the car, not daring to look behind her. 'Sure. Before lunch. No problem.'

And ten minutes later—after a successful pee in the woods

and a stop at a Cumberland Farms convenience store—Paul was in the front seat of the Volvo, chocolate ice cream smearing his face, while she was at a pay phone, punching in quarters and trying to think of a direct and pleasant way to tell her sister in Omaha that she and her husband were in terrible danger.

Jason said, 'Okay, question one. What happened after you were shot down? Who captured you, the North Vietnamese?'

'Sure, it was the North Vietnamese. Okay, this is where you want to start? The beginning?'

'Good a place as any.'

Roy looked over at his brother, slapped him on the knee. 'Sure. The beginning. Here we go.'

SEVEN

North Vietnamese Airspace, December 23, 1972

In his earphones, Air Force Captain Roy Harper heard the warning message from his Electronic Warfare Officer, Lieutenant Tom Grissom, seated at the rear of the cockpit. 'Pilot, EWO. We got SAM activity, coming up ahead. Maybe twelve, fifteen miles.'

'EWO, you just keep letting me know how we're doing.'

'Roger, sir.'

His copilot, First Lieutenant Scott Campbell, murmured something that only Harper heard: 'It's gonna be a hot time in the old town tonight.'

Harper nodded. Ain't that the truth. His fingers on the control yoke were cramping up, after the five-hour flight over the Pacific from Anderson Air Force Base on Guam, which included two aerial refuelings from KC-135s: once over the Philippines, the second time off the coast of South Vietnam, as his B-52 and dozens of others lined up for the evening's run on targets above the DMZ, the Demilitarized Zone that marked the border between North and South Vietnam.

He was Bonny 02, part of a three-jet cell, coming in to bomb the living shit out of the North Vietnamese in Hanoi and surrounding bases. Bonny 01 was a mile ahead and five hundred feet below him, and Bonny 03 was a mile behind and five hundred feet above. This was his third flight over North Vietnam, and he sure hoped it would be his last. Earlier in the year he and the other flight crews had joked about how easy it would be, to cruise in over Hanoi—hell, a friggin' third-world capital, that's all it was—but these rice farmers and peasants were getting the best triple-A and SAM air defense systems from their buddies in Moscow, and after the first B-52 had been shot down—Charcoal 01, just five days ago—nobody was laughing any more. Especially since this pissant war was supposed to be winding down, not escalating with bombing crap like this.

Man, wasn't that the fucking truth. Tonight's mission was standard, carrying eight 750-pound bombs and four 500-pound bombs, nothing like the 'special packages' he and the other crews had trained for. That kind of flying, going into the heart of the Soviet Union, meant a lot of ass-puckering, surface-terrain flying, nothing like this aerial screw-up taking place here.

He flexed his fingers again. Focus, he thought, focus on the mission. Let everything else take care of everything else. In the darkened interior of the cockpit, lit by comforting red lights, it was easy enough to see the activity up ahead, the twirling tracers of the antiaircraft artillery blossoming up into the sky, the hard white lights of the SA-7 surface-to-air-missiles rising up through the cloud cover. He could make out the chatter from the cell leader, Bonny 01, as they got closer to their target, a set of railroad marshaling yards north of Hanoi.

Hanoi. That deceptively simple-sounding city, which down there was holding several hundred, maybe even more than a thousand, prisoners of war. Their tales of punishment and torture had been spread around the ready rooms back at

Anderson AFB, and it gave him and the other crews pleasure to know that those poor bastards at least had a front row seat at the largest bombing campaign this bloody and useless war had ever seen.

'Pilot, R/N,' came the voice of Simpson, the radar-navigator. 'Target approaching, ten miles out.'

'Ten miles out, roger,' Harper replied, and his copilot glanced over, gave him a thumbs-up, which he returned. Close, so damn close, and there was a rumor of a Christmas truce, for at least a day or two off, and wouldn't that be a—

'Pilot, EWO! SAM lock-on, four miles out! SAM lock-on, three miles out!'

His copilot yelled, 'Pilot, SAM, two o'clock! Break left, break left, break left!'

Harper responded automatically, grabbing the control yoke, breaking left, forgetting just for a moment the target up ahead, the target they had flown so many hours to reach and—

'Pilot, EWO, we're gonna get hit—'

BANG!

He had a flash of memory, riding in a car back in high school, on Spur Road, Carl Dennis was driving too fast, they missed the curve, flew about a yard or two, struck a tree, thank God he was wearing his seatbelt, never in his life had he been so pounded, bouncing around like that, Jesus Christ, look at all those fucking red lights . . .

Harper shook his head, the control yoke now soft and mushy in his hands. Bright white emergency lights filled the cockpit. Sparks were shooting out from the instrument panel. There was an orange glow to the right, visible through the side windscreen, and the aircraft was beginning to pitch to the left. He and Campbell pulled and pulled at their control yokes, but Harper could feel the aircraft slipping away from his control. Red warning lights were popping up everywhere, four starboard engines were dead, the orange glow off to the right was getting brighter, and Harper coldly looked at the situation and abandoned any fantasy of nursing Bonny 02 back to safe territory, like South Vietnam or Thailand. Time for facts. He and his crew were now riding an aerial bomb, consisting of more than a hundred tons of JP-4 aviation fuel and thirty tons of ordinance.

Harper slapped the abandon-ship alarm and spoke into the intercom. 'Pilot to crew, bail out, bail out, bail out!'

There was a thump, and another thump, and Harper knew that the crew members down below weren't wasting any time. Shit. What a way to end the mission. He looked over at his copilot, and again, the thumbs-up signal, which he returned. Harper assumed the ejection position, rotated the seat-arming handles, exposing the ejection triggers. He took a deep breath, tightened up his gut, and squeezed the handles.

Darkness. Cold air. Stars. His oxygen mask was still attached and he realized he couldn't breathe. Harper reached down, pulled the green apple to trigger the emergency oxygen, which started blasting through his mask. He splayed open his arms and legs, trying to orient himself. Below him he could see a tremendous display of fireworks, and if he wasn't so terrified and disorientated, he thought he could at least enjoy the lights of the triple-A, and the damn bright white lights of the rising SAMs, coming up through the clouds. There. To the left. Bonny 02, heading down in a death spiral, sheets of flame rolling up the right wing. A pang of regret, seeing a good aircraft he had trained on and flown these past two years. Gone.

Harper was wondering if he would have to open the chute manually when he felt a jerk on his shoulders, and then above him, blossoming open and filling out well, was his parachute.

He tugged at a strap on his leg, letting his survival gear drop on a long strap, and automatically opening up his life raft. Next he ripped off his patches, tossed out any ID from his pockets, letting it fly out from his gloved hands. Get to the ground safe, he thought. Dump the gear and head into the woods. Trigger the survival beacon. Out there in the dark night were SAR—search-and-rescue—units, and if he could get hidden before daybreak, there was a good chance he could be picked up. Anything to avoid becoming a guest at the Hanoi Hilton.

He went through some low cloud cover, lost orientation, felt the parachute lanyards in his hands vibrate. There. He was through the cloud cover and, damn it, the ground was coming up pretty fast, pretty damn fast. It was a rice paddy, flat and wide and without a tree to be seen. He hit the ground, sank in the soft soil, and stumbled, amazed that he was still standing. He started pulling in the parachute, his legs trembling, trying to get that damn flapping piece of nylon hidden away.

A shout. The low stammer of an AK-47 being fired. He turned, felt his knees weaken as he saw the line of men coming toward him, illuminated by a searchlight on the back of a truck, parked on a dirt road. The men were followed by a crowd of what looked like civilians. More shouts. The parachute was partially draped over his shoulders. He raised his arms. There was a semicircle of men with AK-47s about him, yelling and screaming at him. Harper raised his arms higher.

There was a bright flash and he flinched. Was he being shot at?

Another bright flash, and he almost giggled in relief. No, it was some clown, holding a camera almost as big as he was, taking a picture of the brave North Vietnamese Army capturing an American air pirate. That's all.

111

Then the photographer moved back, as did the line of armed men. He shifted some in the wet soil, wondering what in hell was going on.

Then the crowd moved through the soldiers, shouting, their faces twisted in anger, holding bamboo staves, rakes, and hoes. They swarmed about him as he backpedaled and tripped and fell, and the blows started hitting him, as somebody tugged off his helmet, and he curled up in a ball, as the blows rained down upon him, and the pain started blossoming in ugly flashes, about his head and ribs and hands and feet.

There would be no rescue tonight.

Roy Harper sat on his thin mattress on the concrete floor of his cell staring at his sandaled feet. It sure as hell had been a long time since that night back in December, when the local NVA militia had let the villagers take out their rage and frustrations on him. The beating hadn't gone on that long, before the militia came back in and took him out. Bound and tied, he had been dumped in the back of a truck and taken to what seemed to be a local police or militia station. The first interrogations had been the easiest, since the poor guys talking to him seemed to be reading from some sort of script, and what little English they had escaped them whenever they left the script. They had asked him what kind of aircraft he flew, and he lied, saying he was a Navy pilot, flying a single-seat A-4. That way, the locals wouldn't be alerted that other crew members from Bonny 02 were out in the countryside.

After a single night in a smelly cell that felt like it had once served as a home for pigs, a series of rides in the back of a truck began, blindfolded and bound, interrupted only by visits to villages, where he had been forced to stand up with the blindfold off in front of a gathering of civilians. The squad leader would say something in a long speech—Harper had a pretty good idea of what was being said—and invite the villagers to shout and toss rocks at him. One time in a village somebody had led them in an oddly accented cheer: 'Nixon eats shit! Nixon eats shit! Nixon eats shit!' and he remembered with pleasure the shocked look on everyone's faces when he smiled and nodded in agreement and chanted right along with them.

Pleasure. That had been the last real pleasurable moment he could remember.

After the long ride in the back of the truck, he was brought here, to this prison, still blindfolded. All that existed in the world was this concrete room with a dirty tile floor, ten feet by ten feet, with the thin mattress and single wool blanket, the honeypot in the corner with a wooden cover, and a single basin. There was a wooden and metal door with a sliding peephole, but he had no idea what was beyond the door, since he was blindfolded each time he was let out. A long corridor of some sort, he knew, and another room, which had been used for interrogations.

His possessions consisted of the maroon and gray prison pajamas, a wooden spoon, and a single washcloth, now gray after weeks of use. High above his mattress was a solitary barred window, with three bars. Every now and then he would jump up and grab the bars and look around. He could make out a high wall, and that was it. Most days he was pleased to see blue sky, and most nights he was equally pleased to make out a few stars. But what depressed him the most at night was the silence. Where was he? Near Hanoi or Haiphong or Nam Dinh, but where were the nightly bombing raids? The whine of the air raid sirens? Was there a truce? An armistice?

And were there other Americans here as well? Sometimes he would hear muffled voices in the distance, voices that sounded like English. On a couple of terrifying occasions, he could hear the sounds of men screaming, and once, just once—though he wished he had never heard it—somebody was dragged by his door and the man said, in desperate-sounding English, 'For the love of God, please, no, I've told you everything.'

He rubbed at his thin arms, looked at the angry red scars on the backs of his hands. Cigarette burns, and he knew if he raised his pajama sleeves, he would make out the long thin scars on his wrists. Coming into this prison, he had still clung to the romantic notion of holding out, to resist until the very end, to tell the enemy nothing of who he was or what kind of aircraft he had flown. Well, a few days and nights of torture had taken care of that, had shattered that resolve like a dainty blown-glass vase. Within the very first day, his interrogator—a squat, ugly little man with yellow teeth whom he had privately nicknamed Frogger—had pointed out that Harper was not in fact an A-4 pilot, but a B-52 pilot. Harper tried to keep up the charade, but the vile little fuck seemed to have a crew manifest, and named every member on Bonny 02. Still, there was that resolve of his, which lasted until the fourth or fifth beating, the fourth or fifth encounter with the guards who bound his wrists together and tried to raise him up, to either snap his wrists or pull his arms out of their sockets. Then he had talked. He had tried to rationalize it, over and over again, and for the most part, he had succeeded, though there was a tiny part of him that whispered 'traitor' each time he went for another round of questions.

Harper got up, started pacing about the cell, counting off the yards. He had decided a while ago that to occupy his mind, he would walk across the United States, starting up in the far reaches of Maine and then going through New England and

New York State, and head right out. He figured that he was probably somewhere in Kansas by now, and as he walked, he closed his eyes and tried to place himself there, out on the side of the road, trying to imagine he was far, far away from this smelly and cold cell, far, far away from the men who questioned and beat him. And as he walked, a little gnawing of fear would sometimes start in his belly, about what he would do when his imaginary walk took him to the Santa Monica pier in California. What then? And the easy answer was a plan to keep on walking, to circumnavigate the whole damn country, go up the West Coast, follow the Canadian border back to Maine, head down the East Coast.

Jesus, he thought, stopping and opening his eyes. Would he still be here that long? What had happened to Nixon and Kissinger, and peace being at hand and all that crap?

There was a rattle at the door that made him jump. Shit, it wasn't time for that watery rice crap that passed for soup. An interrogation? His mouth was dry. It had been a couple of weeks since his last meeting with Frogger. He backed away from the door, which swung open. And then, another mattress was tossed in, followed by an American, dressed like him, in the same pajamas, carrying a bowl and a blanket. His face was lumpy from old bruises, and as the two NVA guards slammed the door behind him, he grinned, revealing that a tooth had been knocked out.

'Captain Harper, it sure is nice to make your acquaintance again,' the man said, and Harper came forward with a whoop and a holler, to hug his EWO, Lieutenant Tom Grissom.

That turned out to be the first surprise of the day, for lunch was a bowl of thick vegetable soup, with chunks of bread, and dinner was even better, rice and vegetables and pieces of brown meat that looked to be like pork and were the biggest pieces of meat Harper had eaten since being taken prisoner. Between meals they had sat across from each other, on their respective mattresses, and talked and talked and talked. Grissom told of his own experience, ejecting just a few seconds before Harper and seeing a lot more than Harper did. 'Man, that was one crazy experience, rising up and looking down and seeing all those flames on the starboard wing.' He described his own capture, landing near some type of military depot, where soldiers had been waiting patiently, pointing their AK-47s at him.

'And you know what, Cap?' Grissom had said. 'If I had been better with those parachute lanyards, I could have dumped myself in the back of a truck. Saved those gooks on the ground having to kick me and drag me up there.'

They talked long into the night as well, and before falling asleep Harper said, 'And you're sure you didn't see anybody else from the crew?'

Grissom sighed. 'Sorry, Cap. I haven't seen another American since I got picked up. You're the first. I sure as hell hope you're not the last.'

'Me, too,' he said, falling asleep with a smile on his face for the first time in a very long time.

The surprises kept on coming in the morning, when they exchanged their full honeypot for an empty one, and a real breakfast tray was handed in by the two blank-faced and silent guards. 'Jesus, Cap,' Grissom whispered in awe. 'Take a look at that.'

'That' was four hard-boiled eggs, some kind of French croissants, orange juice, and strong black coffee in chipped white mugs. They sat down and ate everything—including the shells

116

of the eggs—and when they were finished, Grissom said, 'Care to hear an analysis of what's going on?'

'I'm afraid to guess, but go ahead.'

Grissom motioned to the empty tray. 'Clear as day. They're fattening us up. Makes me think that we're getting ready to be released. Maybe the damn war's over after all. What's the date, anyway?'

Harper went over to the base of the wall, near the door, where he had kept a series of scratches. He counted them off once, and then twice. He looked back at his EWO. 'April the third,' he said. 'I think.'

Grissom nodded. 'That jibes with what I've been keeping track of. Yeah, April third.' He folded his arms and said, 'Jesus, you'd think the war would be over by now.'

'You'd think,' Harper said.

Along with another vegetable stew for lunch came new clothing, as well as a pail of hot water, a shaving brush, soap, and a double-edged razor. Harper examined the clothing: badly made blue jeans with no identifying marks or labels, as well as light blue shirts. Thick wool socks. They spent a few giddy minutes out of their striped pajamas, trying on the clothes, and Harper was quietly shocked at how prominent Grissom's ribs were. Christ, he thought, do I look that bad, too? Then they both shaved, and Grissom said, 'I tell you, Cap, I've got a good feeling. I think it's going to be time to head out of here.'

Harper rubbed at his face, feeling the strange smoothness of his skin. 'Maybe so, but don't get too excited. They might just be getting ready to show us off to the foreign press, like a French or Polish TV crew.'

Grissom took his washcloth and carefully washed each toe of his dirty feet. 'Even that would be an improvement, to see another face that's not Vietnamese. You know, I wonder what our families are thinking.'

'How's that?'

Grissom finished his left foot, and started on his right. 'I've asked dozens of times for paper to write letters home. Refused. Asked to see a representative of the Red Cross. Refused. Demanded my rights under the Geneva Convention. And you know what they said?'

Harper nodded, remembering his own attempts at doing exactly what Grissom had done, speaking to a hostile Frogger. 'Sure. The Geneva Convention is for prisoners captured while two nations are at war. And since our Congress did not declare war against the People's Republic of Vietnam, we are not officially prisoners of war. We are air pirates. Criminals. Usually I got stomped on a few times by a couple of the guards after debating the finer points of prisoners' rights.'

'Unh-hunh, Cap. So that brings me back to the original question. What about our families? What do they know about us?'

Harper made to speak, and then froze for a moment. Shit. Grissom was making sense, as scary as it was. 'They don't know shit. We're either dead or MIA.'

Grissom nodded and pulled on a pair of the thick socks, wiggled his toes inside the coarse wool. 'That's right. These clowns haven't given us any indication that they've notified the government that we're POWs. So we're either dead or MIA. Which is why I'm hoping that if we're not getting released, at least we're being paraded before the cameras. It's easy to turn an MIA into a POW; after your photo's been on the front page of *Paris-Match* magazine, it's hard to reverse the process.'

'Grissom?'

'Sir?'

'What in hell were you doing in the Air Force, anyway?'

'What do you mean?'

'You don't sound like any EWO I've ever met.'

Grissom grinned. 'Air Force ROTC, Indiana University. Majored in history. Was promised a slot with the Air Force Historians' Project after graduation and my commissioning. Air Force had other ideas, turned me into an EWO. There you go, sir.'

They both turned at the sound of the door being unlocked. Two guards were there, one carrying lightweight jackets in his arms. He tossed them on the floor. 'Get dressed now. You leave soon.'

The door slammed shut. Harper got up and retrieved one of the tan jackets, which he passed over to Grissom. They both got dressed and Roy felt something rushing back into him, something he had hidden and repressed all these months: hope. His mind was racing, thinking that Grissom was right: they were being fattened up, cleaned, shaved, and dressed. A bit too fancy for an interview with a sympathetic press corps from France or Eastern Europe. Nope, this was something more. This had to be it: Freedom Day. Harper thought ahead, about what it would be like to get back in the world. Hot showers, ice cream, cheeseburgers, clean sheets, being able to sleep an entire night without being afraid of being woken up for another torture session. He looked about the tiny cell and said, 'I never thought I'd say it, but I just might miss this little shithole.'

'Really?' Grissom asked, his voice filled with amazement.

'Sure,' Harper said. 'In about fifty years or so.'

He and Grissom sat back down on the mattresses, Harper thinking this could be it. The last time he'd ever sit on one of these mattresses, the last time he'd ever see the dirty tile floor, the last time he'd ever have to look out that barred window. He felt at the corner of his mattress, peeled back a bit of the cloth, removed a chalky stone, then went to the wall where the hash marks had been placed, all those long days. He started writing, making the letters large. He wanted to write R. HARPER CAPT USAF WAS HERE 12/72/4/73, but by the time he reached the last R in his name, the door opened up and two clean black cloth blindfolds were tossed in. The guard was smiling, another first.

'Blindfolds on. Then you leave.'

Grissom looked at Harper, grinning. 'You heard the man. Let's leave.'

Before Harper put on his blindfold, he put his washcloth and wooden spoon in his pocket. Souvenirs, he thought. When he covered his eyes, he could hear men entering the tiny cell. 'Up, up, up,' came a voice. He stood up and Grissom's voice came out. 'You there, Cap?'

'I'm here,' he said.

'Quiet,' said a guard. 'You leave now.'

He and Grissom were led out into the hallway, and Harper felt a brief flash of panic. It took twenty-five paces to reach the interrogation room, and he wondered if this had all been a big charade, get them weakened to think that they were leaving, wear down their resolve. But after twenty-five paces, they kept on walking. With each additional step, the pressure in his chest continued to increase, like a tire being overinflated. He stumbled a bit as he went down a step, and then he felt sunshine on his face. They were outside.

'Cap?' came the voice.

'No talking!' came the reply, but Harper smiled. Just a

quick signal from his EWO, indicating he was right behind him.

They walked along a courtyard of some sort, the guard's hands firm on his right elbow. He found he had lost track of the paces and didn't particularly care. Something good was happening, he thought. Something very good indeed.

'Step up,' came the voice. 'Bus.'

And sure enough, that's what it was. Other hands helped him up, sat him down on a wooden seat. The engine was running. 'Hey, Cap,' came the whisper, as Grissom sat down next to him. Harper pressed his leg against Grissom's, to let him know he had heard him. There were other footsteps, whispers, and Harper felt like other POWs were coming in as well. Some murmurs, and a couple of times 'No talking! You talk, you stay!' managed to quiet the murmur. Then came the sound of a door closing, and another Vietnamese voice started talking: 'You are now leaving our facility. We wish you luck in your new lives. Perhaps you will come back in peace.'

Somebody from the rear of the bus blew a raspberry, and there was a brief moment of laughter. The tone of the voice grew harsh. 'You stay quiet. You keep your blindfolds on. Or you may stay here longer. That is all.'

Harper felt a bump and a jostle, as the engine revved up, and he wasn't sure but it sounded like other buses were being driven near them. More bumps, more jostles, and the bus swayed from side to side, and steadied some, as it came out on a fairly well-paved road. As the bus gained speed, a male voice: 'Navy eats shit!'

And a quick reply: 'Air Force eats shit!'

More laughter, and even Harper couldn't help himself. A bus full of Americans, heading home. What a gorgeous, gorgeous day.

'Quiet! Quiet back there!'

Another wet raspberry, and Harper stayed quiet. Why not. It'd be over soon.

The bus ride seemed to take about a half-hour or so, and then the engine slowed down and there were turns and one long stretch where they seemed to go in a straight line. Grissom whispered, 'Listen. Here that?'

Harper surely did. 'Aircraft. Must be close to an airport.'

The bus slowed and made a wide turn and then stopped. The same voice as before, that had told them not to speak: 'You will leave now and board an aircraft. Good luck to all of you.'

And then, oddly enough, it seemed like the guy snickered. The door opened up and hands reached down, grabbing Harper at his shoulder and elbow. He walked awkwardly off the bus, wondering why this rigmarole was going on. He could smell aviation fuel again, a scent that actually made him hungry. The floor he was on seemed like concrete, and there were no voices now, just the impersonal hands, helping him up a gangway. Then, an aircraft interior of some sort. He could feel the upholstery on the seats. He was pushed down in a seat and Grissom was with him again, and Grissom said, 'Cap, things don't seem right.'

Harper said, 'I get that feeling, too.'

Some low voices, more people going by. He could sense that people were sitting down, and heard the click of seatbelts being attached. He felt around, found the seatbelt and put it on snug, remembering with sharp clarity how many months ago it had been, buckling up in Bonny 02, back at Anderson AFB. He wondered if the Air Force would give him another crew, another B-52, and he wondered if he would want to stay in. Right now, he wanted some serious R&R, back home in New Hampshire with Mom and Dad and Jason, and to think of nothing, nothing at all.

The aircraft's engines started up, the aircraft started moving. Harper sat there, waiting, wondering what was going to be said, who was there. The wait seemed intolerable, as the aircraft started taxiing, and he raised his hand and lifted a corner of the blindfold. In front of him was a swatch of dark red upholstery, dirty and patched in one corner by black thread. There were no threatening voices, nobody shouting at him. He lifted the blindfold up higher, saw the back of a man's head in front of him. Red hair. American. Harper was sitting in an aisle seat, leaned out, and saw another man, six or seven seats forward, doing the same thing. The man looked back, grinned, and waved. Harper waved back. Jesus! He undid the seatbelt, raised himself up. The plane held maybe a hundred or so passengers, and all—as far as he could see—were Americans. There were no Vietnamese at all.

'Hey!' he yelled. 'Harper here, 509th Bomb Group, Anderson! Take your blindfolds off, guys, we're going home!'

Whoops, yells, and shouts, and the aircraft gained speed and blindfolds were tossed in the air, as the jet took off, landing gear and flaps rumbling beneath them. Grissom was saying something, but Roy couldn't hear him at first, over the yells and shouts, as names and units were exchanged, as some flight crews were reunited.

'Cap!' Grissom yelled, leaning into his ear. 'Check this out.'

'What's that?' Harper said, looking back to him.

Grissom made a quick and simple demonstration, a demonstration that stopped Harper, and his part of the celebration, right in his tracks.

The window at Grissom's elbow was sealed shut.

Just like every other window in the aircraft.

And, as they learned in a very few minutes, so was the door to the cockpit.

The flight took three hours, and by the time the jet started descending for a landing, an Air Force colonel named Jackson was found to be the senior officer on board, and had taken command. Paper and a pencil stub were produced, a census was taken of the ninety-eight aviators aboard, and the piece of paper was given to Jackson, a silver-haired man who walked up and down the aisle using a crutch.

Harper was in his seat, belted in, as the wheels squealed on touchdown. Grissom's face was white, and his hands seemed to shake. 'Grissom, what's going on?' Roy said.

Grissom shook his head. 'This is all wrong. This is all very, very wrong, sir.'

The jet taxied for just a short time before it came to a stop. There was a clanking sound as what seemed like a stairway was being pushed up against the plane. Then the door swung open and into the fuselage, and there was silence, as the men up forward, led by Colonel Jackson, left the aircraft first. Harper looked to Grissom, who was still shaking. 'Hey, EWO, stick with me. I'll get you through all right.'

Grissom managed a sickly grin. 'No offense, sir, last time I stuck with you I got shot down and stuck in a POW camp.'

When it was Harper's turn to leave the aircraft, a childish fear came over him, and he wanted to run back and hide in the aft lavatory. Maybe this jet would go somewhere else. Maybe something bad was waiting for them. He shook off the fear, thinking of his EWO behind him, still his responsibility. He exited the jet, went down the stairway. They were in a large hangar, and the jet—painted gray with no identifying marks except for a series of red numerals on the tail—was the only aircraft inside. There were no windows, just the bare concrete floor, and beyond a white rope barrier there were piles of . . . junk, it looked like—piles of parts, debris, engines. Harper quickly recognized what was there—aircraft wreckage. American aircraft wreckage. By the near wall was a door, and in front of the door was a simple wooden platform.

'Line up, line up,' an officer standing next to Jackson announced, and that's what they did, lining up in formation, as if they were back on base. He made sure he was still with Grissom, who said, 'Sir, I think we're—'

The door opened up, and men came out, some in uniform, some in suits. Murmuring started and there were a few gasps, and Harper felt his feet and hands go cold, ice cold. A stocky man in a suit came up on the platform, flanked by a skinnier guy in a suit. The suits were black and the men had white shirts, skinny black ties, and poor-looking shoes. But he kept his eyes on the guards, who, while they looked somewhat Asian, were definitely not Vietnamese.

The stocky man started talking in a loud voice, pausing every few seconds to allow the skinny man to translate, and with every phrase Harper felt the chills travel up his arms and legs.

'You are now here . . . in the Soviet Union . . . as detainees of the GRU . . . the Soviet military intelligence agency . . . Your country, your families, your military . . . they think you are all dead . . . and this is a misconception . . . we intend not to correct . . . All of you have been tried as war criminals . . . for war crimes against the peace-loving Vietnamese people . . . You will serve out your sentences here . . . forever . . . for we can keep you forever . . . and intend to do so . . .'

Harper could not find his voice, nor, apparently, could any of his fellow aviators. The large man coughed, and the translator waited patiently, and then continued. 'Beyond this base . . . are hundreds of kilometers . . . of snow and steppe . . . You will never escape . . . never . . . but your time here . . . need not be arduous . . . We will feed you well . . . give you drink, drugs if you prefer . . . even female companionship . . . but we require cooperation . . . your willing cooperation . . .'

The Russian speaker pointed to the piles of wreckage. 'Here are just some of your aircraft . . . we have salvaged . . . from your brutal war . . . against our fraternal socialist comrades . . . You will teach us the secrets of these aircraft . . . you will teach us the tactics . . . you will give us everything we need to know . . . if your stay here is to be a pleasant one.'

'Sir!' From the front lines, Colonel Jackson hobbled forward, going up to the platform. The Russian looked down at him and said something, and the translator said, 'And who are you?'

'Colonel Ralph Jackson, senior officer of this contingent. I demand to see a representative of my government, immediately.'

The Russian's voice was harsher. 'Does this mean . . . no cooperation?'

'I demand to see a representative of the American embassy.'

The translator was having problems keeping up. 'Colonel . . . does this mean . . . no cooperation?'

Even with the crutch, Colonel Jackson seemed to stand more erect. 'You are correct! There will be no cooperation! None! I demand to see a representative of—'

The stocky man stepped off the platform, struck Jackson across the face, kicked the crutch away from him. The colonel fell down and Harper craned to see what happened next, and was suddenly grateful that he couldn't see everything. The Russian reached under his coat for something and then there were two shots, the sound of the report echoing in the hangar. Shouts and yells from the Americans, and the Russian guards lowered their AK-47s as some of the men in the front rows surged forward. The Russian came back up to the platform, face red, breathing hard. He reholstered his pistol under his coat, and then delicately buttoned the coat up the front, like a banker getting ready to leave his office for lunch.

His voice was slower, even seemed more apologetic. The translator nodded and said, 'I would now like to see . . . the senior American officer . . . whoever he is . . . at the moment.'

Next to him, Grissom started trembling, and Harper reached over and put his arm over his EWO's shoulder.

EIGHT

In Berwick, Maine, Clay Goodwin first stopped at the house that belonged to the target's family, one Jason Harper, his wife, Patricia, and their son, Paul R. Harper. He pulled right up to the driveway, noted the empty garage. Not good. He got out, stretching, thinking of the high-speed drive he had just completed, from Saugus through New Hampshire and now here. He had cut it pretty close, just before the New Hampshire border, when a Massachusetts State Police cruiser had roared up after him, lights flashing. But the Statie had been after some other speeder, so Clay had gotten here in good time.

He took his time, walked around the house. My oh my, he thought. Some serious things have definitely gone on at this house. There was a broken window on the second floor, and as he made his way back to the front of the house, he noted the damaged front door as well. He kicked away chunks of broken glass as he maneuvered his way up the porch, and then gave the door a closer look. Entry cord, it looked like. Wrap it around the doorknob, the hinges, and a tug of the detonator, you're in the house in seconds. He pushed the door aside. Whoever had been here hadn't bothered trying to repair things, had just propped it up. Which meant something bad had happened to the Ebony Three crew. They wouldn't even have bothered doing that.

'Hello?' he called out to the empty living room. 'Anybody home?'

No answer, nor did he expect one. Still, it was good to keep one's image up. Suppose a neighbor was in here, snooping as well? Didn't need to waste time explaining why you came in unannounced. He sniffed the air in the living room. Spent gunpowder. A firefight of some sort had taken place here, and not so long ago.

A mess, a real mess.

So. Where was the target? And what had happened here?

Clay went back outside, sat down on the porch, let his legs dangle over the edge. He reached into his coat pocket, took out his cell phone—encrypted signal, of course—and dialed Budlong's direct line, down there in Saugus. But the receptionist answered the line instead, and when he identified himself, she sounded quite apologetic. 'I'm sorry, Mister Goodwin, but he's just left to go to the rest room.'

'He has, has he?'

'Yes, he has.'

He thought about having the dim bulb go in and drag him out, and thought, no, there was still plenty to do. He put on his best voice and said, 'Miss?'

'Yes, Mister Goodwin?'

'When Mister Budlong gets out and his bum is nicely patted dry and powdered, please do have him call me. All right?'

'Certainly,' she said, and if she had been ticked off by his tone, she kept it secret. Not a bad worker. Somebody he'd have to remember.

He snapped the cell phone shut and looked up, as a young

girl on a bicycle came down the driveway, her blond pigtails bouncing as the bike wheels bumped along the dirt. She came to a stop and frowned. She had on little white and pink sneakers, overalls, and a white T-shirt.

'Hi,' she said.

'Hi there, young lady.'

She scrunched up her nose, as if she were going to sneeze, and then said, 'I'm looking for Paul. Do you know where he is?'

He snapped back to the folder he had read, back in Saugus. 'No, I don't,' he said. 'The thing is, I'm looking for his mommy and daddy, too. Do you know where they might be?'

She rubbed at her nose and said, 'Mommy doesn't want me talking to strangers.'

Clay nodded. 'You have a very smart mommy. Tell you what . . .' He pulled a leather wallet from another jacket pocket and flipped it open. 'See that badge? I'm a police officer. Mommy's told you to trust police officers, hasn't she?'

A solemn nod from the girl on the bicycle.

'Good,' he said. 'Tell me, do you live next door?'

'Unh-hunh.'

'And did you hear anything funny last night? Like firecrackers or fireworks?'

She shook her head. 'Nope. But I did hear Caleb barking real loud, in the middle of the night.'

The dog, then. No doubt reacting to a forced entry. 'Very good. And anything else?'

'Nope.'

'Okay,' he said, getting up. Time for a business visit. He removed his wallet, took out a ten-dollar bill, passed it over to the girl. 'Here. This is for you, for being a big help. But I need you to do one more thing for me, okay?'

'Okay.'

'I want you to tell your mommy you found this money on the road. Don't tell her I gave it to you. Okay? Our secret.'

She scrunched up the ten-dollar bill and shoved it in a pocket. 'Unh-hunh. Our secret.'

He rubbed the top of her head. 'You're a sweet girl. You remind me of my sister, before she went to heaven with Jesus and the angels.'

She smiled and said, 'I think I'll wait here for Paul. We were supposed to go look for worms, to use when Daddy takes us fishing.'

Clay said, 'Okay, but don't wait too long. You don't want your mommy to worry.'

He got into the Ford, started it up and backed down the driveway, smiling at the sight of the little girl sitting there patiently on her bicycle, waiting.

Five minutes later Clay was parked on Pope Street, the home of the Berwick *Banner* newspaper, the business owned by Jason and Patricia Harper. He got out, enjoyed the feel of the morning air, and leaned against the fender of his Ford, examining the photos of the couple one more time. Newspaper types. If you were in a shitload of trouble and owned your own newspaper, where would you go?

Right to work, he thought. Put out a special edition or phone something in to the wire services.

The building was a two-story wood-frame. It held Mellon Dental Supply, and B. Lortie, CPA, up on the top floor, and the Berwick *Banner* had the entire first floor, with a separate entrance. A movement, out of the corner of his eye. He looked to the right, at the intersection, where a Fleet Bank was located. Funny, he thought somebody had just peeked around the corner or something. He was thinking of going over to check, when a chubby young man with a thick beard came down the sidewalk, used a key to the *Banner*'s door, and let himself in. Perfect. Clay put the photos back into the Excursion and then went in after the bearded man. The inside of the newspaper had a counter—no doubt for taking classified ads or whatever—and the bearded guy was in the center, where there were four metal desks, computer terminals, and an ungodly amount of old newspapers, envelopes, and other papers. He had on stained chinos and a dark blue sweatshirt, and said, 'Can I help you?'

'Yes, you can,' Clay said, using the police badge one more time. 'Clay Goodwin, with the Department of Justice. I'm looking for either Jason or Patricia Harper.'

The guy shook his head. 'They're not here.'

'Well,' he said, thinking, you dumb shit, no kidding. 'Do you expect them in later today?'

Another shake of the head. 'Nope.'

'And why's that?'

A shrug. 'I got a message on my voicemail, saying they wouldn't be in.'

'Oh. Are you an editor here as well, Mister . . .'

'Jack Schweitzer. I'm just a reporter, though I like to think I'm really the assistant editor. Hey, can I see that ID again?'

Clay smiled, came around the counter. 'Of course. Look, this is a rather sensitive topic I'm dealing with. Is there a room we can talk in?'

Jack scratched at his beard. 'I guess we can use Jason's office. Sure.'

Clay followed the guy into an office—after swiping a roll of duct tape from on top of a work desk—and was pleased to see the room had both a real door and a window with a shade.

132

Jack took a seat on the other side of a wooden desk, one of the advantages of being the editor, Clay guessed, and frowned when Clay closed the door.

'You don't have to close the door,' he said.

'Oh, sweetheart,' Clay said, coming around the desk, right to the chair. 'I most surely do.'

Clay stiffened the four fingers of his right hand and plowed it into the soft spot of Jack's belly, right below the sternum. Jack gasped and bent over double, started wheezing, holding himself with his arms. Clay closed the shade to the window, decided to give the guy a tap on the back of the head for good measure, which led to another outbreak of moaning and wheezing. He got to work quickly, taping the man's arms and legs to the office chair, and then slapping a piece of tape across his face. He was forced to be a bit sloppy—the man's damn beard got in the way—and Jack's face got quite red, and his eyes started bulging out. Clay started whistling some as he opened up the top drawer of the desk. Pens, pencils, stamps, scribbled-over Post-it notes, some coins, and ah . . . a nice sharp letter opener.

Clay took the letter opener out and held it up so that Jack could see it. Jack started shaking his head violently back and forth, and Clay was glad he had used double the tape around his face, for the scream was still fairly loud when he plunged the letter opener into the back of the man's left hand.

He popped it out, wiped the blood on the man's sweat-shirt, then leaned into him, smiling.

'Now that I've got your attention, let's talk, all right?' Clay asked.

The conference at the Copley Plaza was like so many he had attended before, with the registration area up forward—he knew it would be time to put a bullet in his head the day that Sloan Woodbury would ever need a nametag to identify himself—and the little buffet on white tablecloths, with coffee, tea, and orange juice and a half-dozen forms of pastry. Rows of chairs for the attendees and for the panelists, of which he was one, chairs in front of long tables with microphones and white tablecloths. The other panelists were a female Boston University professor of international relations, a male newspaper editor from the Boston *Globe*, and a somewhat male moderator from the Kennedy School of Government. He supposed after the events of this morning he should have canceled, but he didn't need a little story appearing in the next day's *Globe* or *Herald* gossip section speculating on what might have kept him from appearing.

Most of the attendees seemed to be graduate students from the outlandish number of colleges and universities that Boston supported—the city had lousy traffic, a balkanized political system that held grudges for generations and a perennially losing baseball team, but still, it had thousands of students—and their earnestness and eagerness reminded him of a litter of newborn puppies, all set to explore the world, confident and fearless. He sipped from his second cup of coffee of the morning as the *Globe* editor droned on about the current administration and its goals toward China and Russia, as the twentieth century drew to a close. He felt like interrupting the little bow-tied snot to tell him that the goal of any administration in the White House—Democrat or Republican—was to keep the peace so that its corporate contributors kept on making money and were able to peel off enough each year to keep each party flush with donations.

That was the way of the world, he thought, and the sooner these young pups knew about the wolves out there ready to rend them, limb from limb, the better. He could think of a half-dozen things he'd rather be doing this morning than to be in this stuffy ballroom, but he was here as a favor. He knew that Dean Woodall was getting pressure from the faculty about Woodbury's office space and workload and the amount of time he actually spent on campus, and when Dean Woodall had asked him to attend the conference, he had quickly said yes. A little favor like that went a long way. In fact, that was another lesson these puppies could afford to learn, about the way favors and trades greased a lot of agreements. But based on the current administration—constructed around a Southern governor who had no foreign policy experience and would probably choke on his morning grits if he knew what Sloan had done for his country in the last administration—they were still on a learning curve that—

'But it's not right!' said a voice, and he jerked himself out of his trance. He looked down at the audience and was surprised to see that the conference had already slipped into the question-and-answer phase. A young woman was at the microphone, wearing mostly black and with black lipstick—Goth, was that the style they now called it?—and she had a notebook clasped tight against her meager chest. Definitely not his type.

She went on, breathing quickly after each phrase. 'It's not right that power politics have to keep on being played! Country against country! Region against region! I've read about the cold war against the Soviet Union! Why should we have another one with China?'

There was some murmuring and a few chuckles, and Woodbury smiled, which was a mistake, since that slimy Kennedy School character tossed it right at him.

'Mister Woodbury? Perhaps you'd like to answer the young lady's question?'

Woodbury had two or three ideas of what he'd actually like to do to the young lady, but dusted off his Sunday-morning-talk-show concerned look, and said, 'Young lady, that indeed would be a beautiful world, where all nations could exist as friends. Perhaps someday, but, unfortunately, not this day. And as a diplomat in the service of Queen Victoria said, many, many years ago, nations don't have friends. They have interests. And our nation's interest—today, at this moment—requires that we contain the territorial ambitions of China. I wouldn't say it's like the cold war of the fifties and sixties. It's not that clear-cut. But what is clear-cut is that curbing China's ambitions—during this turbulent time, when their system is in turmoil—is the best approach for all of us.'

The young lady's face seemed to demand a follow-up, but the goo-goo moderator picked a young man this time, a kid who looked out of place with dress pants and a shirt and a necktie. Most likely a Boston College student, Woodbury thought.

'Mister Secretary? If I may?'

He motioned with his hand. 'Go ahead.'

'It's a personal question, if you don't mind.'

A thought, making him nauseous, of everything he had done and had done to him last night by that South Boston girlie. Could this questioner be a plant? Could his secret all these years be becoming public? Now? Here? He clasped his hands tightly, thinking of how so many times before he had come face to face with that fear of being found out. Paying for hookers was one thing. Being famous and paying them to do certain things was quite another.

'Go right ahead, young man,' he said, keeping his voice even.

'It's just that, well, it's been more than three years since you retired from the State Department. I was just wondering, do you miss it? Much?'

He guessed the relief on his face was pretty apparent, for the crowd laughed appreciatively at his look. Woodbury thought about what had just gone on this morning, and what might be going on over the next few days, and what had happened a long time ago that had brought him here. Oh God, if only he hadn't taken that trip.

He cleared his throat. 'There are many things I miss about working with the good people at the State Department. Their sense of devotion, their skills, their commitment to making this world a safer place, not only for their fellow Americans, but for the fellow citizens of the world. And I'd be lying if I said I didn't miss all that free air travel.' More laughter. There, Dean Woodall, he thought. You've got your fucking deal today—former Secretary of State Sloan Woodbury, performing for the peasants—so don't bug me anymore about my office hours.

Woodbury pressed on. 'But I will tell you what I don't miss. Secrets. I don't miss knowing the secrets of the world. Sometimes . . . sometimes that's a terrible burden.'

Jesus, he thought, sitting back in his chair. How in hell did that slip out? He rubbed his hands again, remembered a cold winter landscape, the small passenger jet he was on coming in, coming in hard, with nothing below him but snow, endless expanses of snow . . .

The moderator turned to him, curiosity now painted across his pretty little face. 'Mister Secretary, that was quite a statement. Would you care to expand upon it?'

He snapped forward to the microphone. 'No,' he said.

*

137

When Roy stopped talking, just as they crossed over the Memorial Bridge from Kittery to Portsmouth, Jason said, 'Jesus, Roy, you were MB!'

'MB? What do you mean, MB?'

Jason wished he had been taking notes during the long minutes when Roy had been telling him his incredible story. What a scoop! To hell with the Portland *Press Herald* or Boston *Globe* or even the frigging New York *Times*. Soon enough, he thought, with another sit-down session with Roy and some good reporting, it'd be the tiny Berwick *Banner* breaking this incredible story, a guaranteed Pulitzer winner, no doubt about it, just like that tiny newspaper in California that was awarded the prize in 1979.

'Jason,' Roy said sharply. 'What do you mean, MB?'

'MB,' he said. 'It means "Moscow Bound." There were always rumors and some reports that POWs were transported out of Vietnam to the Soviet Union, to be interrogated there about tactics and other secrets. Those prisoners were said to be Moscow Bound.'

Jason jerked forward against the seatbelt as Roy slammed on the brakes of the van, pulling them into a breakdown lane, just into New Hampshire. 'Jesus!' Jason said, trying to steady himself against the dashboard. 'What in hell was that?'

'Who knew?' Roy demanded, his eyes wide with anger. 'Who knew about this?'

Jason felt himself move to the side of the seat, away from his brother. 'I don't know, lots of people, I guess. There were some newspaper and magazine articles written about it, some chapters in books about POWs.'

'When?'

'A few years ago. I'm not sure of the exact date.'

Roy's eyes seemed to be tearing up, as both hands were

clenched on the steering wheel. 'And nobody did anything? Anything at all? Not a fucking thing?'

Jason swallowed. 'There were . . . investigations, in Russia, after the Soviet Union collapsed. Some archives were searched, old Soviet officials interviewed. A few hints here and there, Roy, but there was nothing substantial, nothing at all. It was just rumors and conjecture. There was no evidence.'

He could tell that his brother was breathing hard, trying to keep his anger under control. 'So. That was it? Rumors, conjecture, and we were all written off. Sent into the dustbin of history. No protests, no high-level delegations, nothing. Is that what happened?'

Traffic moved past them, heading south, heading into New Hampshire and Massachusetts and beyond, and Jason wished they were moving again. He didn't like being put under the spotlight like this. He wanted to say that it wasn't his fault, so don't get angry at me, big brother, but he couldn't. The haunted look on his brother's face seared him.

'Yes, Roy,' he said, 'that's what happened. There were stories and rumors and half-truths. And when it came to the POWs and MIAs, there were fakes, frauds, and unscrupulous types crowding up against the families, trying to raise their hopes and steal their money, all at the same time.'

'But people knew, people knew about—'

'Roy,' Jason said quickly, 'people wanted to know, wanted to believe, but there were no solid facts. Now there are facts. There's you. Look, I've got a suggestion.'

Roy looked to the side-view mirror, eased the van back out on the highway. 'All right, tell me.'

'Look, I know you said you're going to see someone, someone who can help you. But let me help, right now. Turn around and head back to Berwick. I'll get the newspaper ready, with a front page, reporting everything you've just said to me—'

'No,' Roy said.

'With the story out in the public like that, the news media attention will be—'

'Jason, no,' he said.

Jason pressed on, trying to figure out why his brother was being so stubborn. 'Okay, not the newspaper. Something else. Roy, I've got a friend who can help.'

'Little brother, for nearly the past thirty years we've been waiting for somebody to help us, somebody to remember us, somebody to give a shit,' Roy said, his tone flat and heavy. 'It never happened. I saw good men tortured to death, good men shot, good men die because they didn't have proper medical care. I've got a way to get the rest of them back, and that's what we're going to do. If you disagree, fine. Either keep quiet or leave the van at the next exit. All right?'

Jason felt his face flush while Roy was talking, and said, 'I was trying to help, to make suggestions. I'm not some subordinate in the Air Force or whatever, taking your orders. You asked for my help, after my family was almost killed, and I agreed. I didn't agree to be your whipping boy, or your servant.'

Roy stayed silent as he took an exit that led into downtown Portsmouth. They came to a stop sign, and then Roy reached his right hand over and slapped Jason on the knee. 'Good for you,' he said, his voice lighter. 'I've spent more than half of my life behind bars or a wire fence. I need to be reminded that things are different out here in the world, that you're not military or ex-military. Look, things are just starting to roll. I'm tending to be impatient, do you understand?'

'Yes,' Jason said, lying just a little. It was as if Roy had sensed what was going on in his mind, as he took a left, on to Harborview Road.

'No, you probably don't understand, but at least you're trying. I owe you some more information, but there's something we've got to do in Portsmouth, before we head out. And then you're in for another bout of story-telling, if you can handle it.'

'Sure,' Jason said. 'I can handle it.'

Roy slowed the van down as they approached a traffic light, turning red, and he said, 'Man, I can't stand it.'

'Stand what?'

Roy smiled, looked into the side-view mirror. 'The women! Jesus, I thought miniskirts and hotpants were something else, back in '72 . . . but what they're wearing nowadays . . . Jason, it's been too damn long a time.'

Jason looked out the windshield, at the old brick buildings and shops and restaurants of Portsmouth. 'Yeah, you can say that. A damn long time.'

At a phone stand at a Citgo service station outside of Sanford, Maine, Patty dialed a number from memory, pumping in lots of quarters, wondering if she would catch Marie in time. Please, please, please, she thought, let her be home, let her be home. She looked back at the Volvo, barely saw the top of Paul's little head, wondered how in God's name the little guy was holding up.

On the fifth ring the phone was picked up, the woman's voice almost out of breath. 'Hello?'

She felt herself lean in gratitude against the cement wall of the gas station. 'Marie . . . thank God, you're there.'

'Patty, what's wrong? Is it Mom? Dad? Jason? Paul?'

Tears again came to her eyes, making her think, damn it,

don't those ducts ever run out of fluid? 'Marie, please listen to me . . . just listen . . . There's trouble here, very bad trouble.'

Marie was quick. 'That message you left. The man who showed up. Was it really Jason's brother? Is that the trouble?'

'Yes, yes, that's what caused it. Look, you and Art. You've got to leave. You have to get away for a few days. I'm sorry, sis . . .' She sobbed and hid her face from customers going into the gas station.

'Sorry about what? And why in God's name do Art and I have to leave?'

'Because you're in danger, that's why, and it's my damn fault!'

She breathed hard, shifted the receiver to her other ear. Marie's voice was slow, full of concern. 'Patty, tell me what's wrong. Why are we in danger?'

A recorded voice came on the line. 'Please deposit another twenty-five cents for another two minutes.'

'Marie, I'm out of change and time. Jason is on the run, I'm in a gas station with Paul, and I'm scared, and there are men out there, dangerous men, who tried to kill us last night.'

'Patty, have you gone to the police?'

'Marie, please tell me you'll leave. Now! Tell me you'll leave and be safe. Please tell me you'll do it!'

'All right, all right, I'll do it, but I can't see how—'

Click. She was disconnected. Patty replaced the receiver, the plastic handle rattling as she hung up the phone, and she wiped her face against the sleeve of her jacket. Enough of tears, she thought. Enough. She had made her warning, now it was time to leave.

Patty walked back to the Volvo and froze as a Ford Excursion came up to the pumps. She watched as the vehicle slowed down, heading toward her, and closed her eyes in relief at what she saw.

The vehicle had Maine plates. Not Connecticut.

Clay's cell phone rang twice as he worked in the increasingly stuffy office, and he let it ring, not liking to be disturbed once he got going. For all his discourtesy when he had first met the man a while ago, Jack proved to be an eager interview subject once Clay got rolling. Twice he had given the guy a drink of water, and he only had to use the letter opener once more to refresh the man's memory. Jason Harper was an okay editor. Not a tough guy, no, a guy who liked to read and whose idea of extreme sports was paddling a canoe. Wife ran the business side of the newspaper. His parents lived in Florida. Her parents lived up in Maine. She had a sister in Omaha, and another sister somewhere else. If they were in trouble, where would they go? There, Jack had a few problems coming up with destinations or names. It seemed Jason and Patricia—or Patty, as she liked to be called—were pretty boring and liked to keep to themselves. Newspaper work and home life. A few town events, like the Memorial Day picnic and Old Home Days during the Fourth of July. How nauseatingly patriotic, how dull.

'Well?' Clay asked. 'Anything else you can offer?'

Jack's eyes were red-rimmed, moist with tears. 'Look, mister, I've told you everything, everything you've asked.' He started weeping again. 'Please don't hurt me anymore . . . please . . .'

Clay took the letter opener—a bit stained and bent at the end—and twirled it around the top of the desk. The room was starting to smell and he could hardly wait to get out of here. 'Okay, sport. Think one more time. Where else would they go if they were in trouble?'

Jack sniffed up some snot. 'That's all I can think of . . . besides the cops of course . . . I think they're friends with Chief Malone . . .'

Sure, Clay thought. I'll trot right over to the police station and ask for some help. That sure as hell would make lots of sense.

'Fine,' he said, sighing, still twirling the letter opener. 'Here's another question for you to ponder. Jason Harper.'

The bound man nodded, still sniffling. 'Okay.'

'Do you know if he has a brother?'

'No, he doesn't.'

Clay picked up the letter opener, just barely moved it toward the man's left hand, and Jack squealed and said, 'Wait! Wait! Wait! Do you mean a brother who's still alive? Is that what you mean?'

With the edge of the letter opener, Clay barely touched the bloody skin, causing Jack to flinch. 'You go on, sport, and tell me what I think.'

'Yes, a brother, he had a brother. But he's dead, been dead for years and years.'

'Really? Is that what Jason said about his brother? That he's dead?'

A series of quick nods, like an eager student, trying to avoid detention. 'His brother was in the Air Force. He was shot down in Vietnam. He's missing and presumed dead. That's all I know.'

Clay gently pressed the letter opener into the back of Jack's hand. 'You sure?'

'Yes, yes, yes.'

He pressed again. 'Jason hasn't spoken to you or come to you with some crazy story about his brother being alive, has he?'

Jack sniffed again. 'Shit, no, and he would.'

'Why?'

'Because that'd be a hell of a story, that's why, that his brother . . . oh, Jesus, look, mister, please . . . I've told you everything . . . I don't want to know anymore . . . please, just leave me alone . . . please, I beg you . . . I can't stand this . . .'

Clay got up, slapped some more tape across the man's drooling face. Interesting quandary, he thought. Ebony Three was missing, as was the family in question. Yet this poor bleeding and drooling hunk was right. The man ran a newspaper. If an older brother miraculously showed up and announced himself, he would logically move right into the office and start writing a front-page story.

So where was everybody? On their way to the *Today* show?

Of course, the whole damn mystery could be solved with a single phone call, but he didn't know the number, and Woodbury was on some sort of strange mission, ignoring the protocols. Clay couldn't figure that one out, but he knew that following Woodbury's lead wouldn't get him into any trouble. His own orders and protocols had been quite specific. Oh well. Time to get out of this place.

'Jack, old bean,' Clay said soothingly. 'You've been quite cooperative. Right now, I'm going to ask you to do me a little favor. I'm going to take the tape off your right hand and give you a pen. Then you're going to sign a blank piece of paper. That's all. Just your signature and I promise I'll stop torturing you. All right?'

More quick nods, and with a folding knife he undid the tape and Jack did just as he was told, signing his name. Clay said, 'Good, good, nicely done. You just hold on here for a sec.' He replaced the tape on the man's hand, and then, picking the paper up by its edges, went out to the empty main office and found an old IBM Selectric. Working quickly and carefully, he typed a note, all in capital letters: I'M SORRY. IT WAS ALL MY FAULT. He put the paper on the counter and went out back to see what he could find. There. Perfect. A door that said, 'Knock or you'll let all the dark out.' A photographic darkroom. Lots of nice chemicals. A couple of matches later, he went back to Jason Harper's office, where a frightened yet expectant Jack Schweitzer was waiting for him.

'Sorry, I had to run a couple of errands. But I always keep my promises.'

He went around to Jack's rear, gently grasped his head, and pinched the man's nose. The struggle went on for a couple of minutes and Jack soiled himself, but it was true, he had stopped torturing him. A haze of smoke was starting to develop in the office. He spared the room one last glance. Photos of Jason and his wife, in a canoe, climbing a mountain, holding a young boy's hands. A ribbon-cutting ceremony in front of this very same building, this building and dreams of theirs that were about to go up in flames.

Clay quickstepped himself out of the office, closed the door behind him, and headed briskly to his Excursion. As he maneuvered his way out of Berwick, going across a small bridge to New Hampshire and a town he had never heard of—Somersworth—his cell phone rang once again.

'Goodwin,' he said.

'Mister Goodwin, this is Peter Budlong calling, from—'

'Shit, I know who you are. What's going on?'

'I've been calling you for the past twenty minutes, returning your call.'

'Sorry, I was busy.' Up ahead was a crosswalk, where a young woman was waiting, a baby carriage in front of her. He slowed down and let the woman walk across. She waved, as did the young boy, secure in the carriage. Clay smiled and waved back.

'Oh,' and Clay could sense that the young pup back in Saugus in his air-conditioned office and corporate dress didn't really want to know any more than that. 'Well, Mister Goodwin, the moment I learned you had called, I tried calling you back.'

'You certainly did. What's going on?'

'The van, the one used by Ebony Three. It's moved.'

'Shit, I know that,' he said, letting a couple of kids scamper across the crosswalk. Traffic behind him was starting to back up and somebody blew a horn, but he ignored them all. 'It wasn't at the target location. Where is it now?'

'In Portsmouth, New Hampshire. And it's still moving.'

'Can you give me a real-time track of it? Let me know where it's going?'

'Sure, Mister Goodwin. A piece of cake.'

'Good. Start feeding me that info, right now, and don't even dare think of hanging up.'

'I won't,' Budlong said.

'Perfect.'

The last of the children had passed. The way ahead was clear, and Clay accelerated through the late morning air.

NINE

The morning nightmare continued as Sloan Woodbury tried his best to ease his way out after the seminar was over. But that damned bow-tied creep from the *Globe* had cornered him, just by the exit door, and Woodbury was forced to cool his heels for a while, as this particular representative of the Fourth Estate tried in vain to conduct some sort of interview with him.

'Mister Secretary,' he began, his voice all oily and unctuous. 'I was wondering if I could just have a moment of your time, to expand somewhat on your earlier comments.'

He made a show of peering at the creep's nametag. 'I'm sorry, ah, Mister Jordan. I really must be going.'

'Please, just a few questions.'

Woodbury looked to the ballroom for a moment, as the hired help started clearing away dishes and glassware and half-eaten pastries, and he wondered how much better his sleep would have been these past years if he had followed his father into the banking business. Just paper and numbers and long lunches. That's it. No negotiations, no diplomacies, no secret protocols, nothing to disturb one's slumber.

'Very well, just for a few minutes, but off the record.'

Jordan tried his own brand of negotiation. 'How about deep background? A former State Department official?'

Woodbury said, 'A former State Department official residing in Washington.'

The reporter nodded. 'Fair enough.'

'All right, go ahead. But make it quick.'

'Mister Secretary, you knew President Filipov when he was foreign minister.'

Woodbury smiled. 'Yes, I did. That's an easy one. What's next?'

'Since he's become president of Russia, how have you assessed his administration?'

A brief pause, but he saw the flicker of interest in the reporter's eyes, and he said, 'There are some areas of admiration, some areas of concern. Those areas of concern are the usual: the control of the media, the overtures to rebels in former Soviet Union republics, and the sale of certain technologies to Iran and Pakistan. But I do admire the crackdown on official corruption, the lead in trying to establish some form of legal system, and their assistance in certain foreign policy matters.'

'Like China?'

He nodded. 'Like China. It is in everyone's interest to have China emerge from its current troubles to become a nation that respects the rule of law, that respects human rights for her people, and that respects the territorial integrity of her neighbors. We have an interest in seeing this accomplished, as does Japan, India, Russia, and the two Koreas.'

'And Taiwan as well?'

Woodbury said, 'As I and my predecessors and successors have always said, the fate of Taiwan should be determined in a peaceful manner by the people of China and the people of Taiwan. No news there, I'm afraid.'

'Mister Secretary, just one more question.'

'All right,' he said, remembering fondly his time as secretary of state, when he could avoid morons like this by relying on his phalanx of security people to usher him out to his limo. 'One more, and then I really must leave.'

'There are certain reports that in the upcoming meeting this week between President Filipov and the current administration, the informal alliance between the United States and Russia may be formalized.'

Woodbury knew where this was going but was curious about what had leaked out. At least some of the groundwork he had set up in his term of office was being used by the current set of clowns down there at the State Department in Foggy Bottom. 'Formalized in what way?'

'Nomination of Russia to become an associate member of NATO. Joint US–Russia surveillance flights along the Manchurian and Mongolian borders. Joint US–Russia naval exercises in the Sea of Japan, and possibly the East China and South China seas. Possible basing of certain US forces in Vladivostok. And other areas as well.'

Woodbury waited until the reporter said, 'Well, Mister Secretary?'

'I'm sorry, I didn't hear a question there.'

'Oh.' There, Woodbury thought, got you, you little squirrely bastard. The reporter said, 'Don't you think these actions would be considered quite provocative by the government in Beijing?'

Woodbury shrugged. 'I'm no longer a member of the State Department, I have no say in this administration's foreign policy, and whatever reaction may or may not occur from Beijing, I suggest you contact their embassy in Washington. I understand they have quite a knowledgeable press office. Now, I really must go.'

He pushed past the little snot, smiled, and waved to a couple of college students who started trailing after him, like kids running behind some sort of circus parade or some damn thing, and then he got outside of the slick exterior of the Copley, saw his driver standing by the door of the Town Car, not a limo, but at least it would get him away from here and all these prying people and questions.

He breathed heavily as he eased himself into the rear of the Town Car, and the driver went forward and said, 'Sir?'

'Yes?'

'Where to?' he asked.

'Home,' Woodbury said. 'Nice, quiet home.'

And as they entered Boston traffic, Woodbury enjoyed about ten seconds of solitude before his cell phone started ringing.

As they got into the center of Portsmouth, traffic slowed and Roy allowed himself a few moments just to appreciate the sights. The buildings hadn't changed much in the last thirty years—hell, some of the buildings hadn't changed much in the last hundred years—and his head still ached at seeing the sheer number and quantity of cars and pickup trucks.

And the women . . . God, so many of them on this warm day were just wearing tight black slacks and white tanktops, and the self-assured and sexy way they moved made him want to stop the van for a while and sip a beer at a corner café with his brother, and watch the world go by. Christ, that was a good fantasy, wasn't it, and he had only allowed himself a few wasted seconds to think about it before getting back to the job at hand.

He looked over at Jason, who seemed to be holding up all

right. He still felt guilty at what he had done to his younger brother and his family, but that guilt was way overwhelmed by the responsibility he had to those still alive, those still back in those damn cold cells, where snow on some winters would drift through the cracks in the wall and make tiny little piles on the dirty concrete floor. Jason noticed his gaze and said, 'What's up?'

'Just curious,' he said. 'I've told you some stuff, now it's my turn.'

'All right.'

'Mom and Dad. How are they doing?'

'Pretty good, considering they're both closing in on eighty. Dad made the big move five years ago and went down to Florida. Longboat Key. He couldn't stand another New Hampshire winter, and Mom—reluctantly—went along.'

'Didn't want to move away from home?'

Jason said, 'More than just that. It was because of you.'

Roy knew how his voice sounded: 'Me? Why because of me?'

Jason shrugged. 'Mom . . . she never gave up hope, never gave up faith that there'd be a phone call some day, from the Pentagon, saying you'd been found. She thought that maybe you were injured—a head injury, she'd say sometimes—and that maybe you were in some remote hospital or clinic. Eventually, she thought you'd turn up.'

'So,' Roy said. 'That's what she thought. And what did Dad think? And you, for that matter?'

Jason's voice was somber. 'Roy, I'm sorry. We thought you were dead.'

Roy's chest felt heavy. 'Yeah. I can see why. Okay. Physically they're doing okay?'

'Sure,' Jason said. 'Mom had a hip replaced last year, and

Dad's back bothers him every now and then . . . Shit, Roy, are you sure we can't call them?'

Roy said flatly, 'You want another couple of Russians like those guys to visit them in Florida?'

'No.'

Roy shook his head. 'Sorry I snapped. Look. Your turn for question time. High school. Did you go to St. Thomas Aquinas?'

'Yeah, and after that, UNH in Durham.'

Roy laughed. 'Shit, you didn't go far, did you?'

Jason sounded just a bit defensive. 'I wasn't too sure what I wanted to do, and UNH seemed a safe choice. Plus, money was tight, as always, and my grades were so-so.'

'Okay, UNH it was. Good times?'

'Some. In freshman year, one of my English instructors, named Johnson, she said I had a bit of a writing talent. Sent me over to the college newspaper. They took what I wrote. Published my first story and, well . . . it was like a little flash-bulb going off in my head. I knew right then and there that's what I wanted to do. I wanted to report the news, get my name in the paper, be somebody in the community.'

'Unh-hunh,' Roy said. 'And when did you decide you wanted to own your own paper?'

'After college, I got a job in Kennebunkport, the *York County Coast Star*. Spent a couple of good years there, got promoted to news editor, and then assistant editor, and then . . . well, the door slammed on me. It was a family-owned paper, and one day, at a Christmas party, one of them was slightly drunk and told me that no matter how good a job I had, I would never be editor.'

'Why didn't you go someplace else?'

Jason rubbed his hands on top of his thighs. 'By then I had

met Patty. She was the business manager for the paper, and we were engaged, and she has a thing for Maine. Didn't want to move out of the state. We started nosing around, looking for newspaper jobs in Portland and Lewiston and Bangor, and then one of her uncles died. She was a favorite niece of his, and he left her some money. Not a whole hell of a lot, but at the same time this free shopper was for sale in the Berwick area. Six months later it was ours, and we started turning it into a real newspaper.'

Roy halted the van at a red light, watched the scurrying crowds go by, and felt terribly old and worn-down. How many, he thought, how many of those people going by knew anything about Vietnam, anything about his sacrifice and the sacrifice of so many others, over the years? How many? Maybe a handful, if he was lucky. We few, he thought, misquoting Shakespeare, we forgotten and lonely few. A wonderful country with a wonderful people, who often had very short memories of the men they had sent into harm's way.

'Patty seems to be a great woman.'

'She is. A great partner, a good friend, and a wonderful mother. I just wish . . . well, I just wish the two of you had met under better circumstances.'

Roy said, 'Me too, brother. Me too.'

'You know . . . well, do you know Paul's full name?'

'Your son? No, I don't know.'

Jason folded his arms, his voice choking a bit. 'Paul Roy Harper. I thought I'd let you know.'

Roy blinked a few times, his eyes now moist. 'Thanks. Thanks for telling me.'

Clay decided it was time to check in and told Budlong, 'I'm

going to hang up, but you better answer my callback in less than a single ring, or I'll have your ass.'

'I will.'

'Good. Where's the van?'

'Moving in downtown Portsmouth.'

'Okay.' He looked up at the passing highway sign. He was on Route 16, heading south, in a place called Dover, just a few miles north of Portsmouth. He clicked off with Budlong and then struck a speed dial, and the phone was picked up on the second ring.

'Woodbury here,' came the voice.

'This is Goodwin. I've been to the target house. Nobody's there. There's also nobody at their place of business, a newspaper in the same town.'

'Go on.' The voice was flat, emotionless.

'We've located the van used by the missing Ebony team. It's in Portsmouth, New Hampshire. I'm about ten, fifteen minutes away from intercepting it. But there's still a couple of loose ends I think need to be wrapped up.'

'Name them.'

He passed a minivan, checked his speed. Damn it, seventy-eight in a fifty-five zone. Sometimes when he was really working, he had a hard time keeping his lead foot in check. 'I still think you need to initiate the protocols. This has a chance of getting out of hand.'

'Duly noted. Go on.'

Shit, so that wasn't going to happen. Well, no blame would come his way, Clay was sure of that. He had made the suggestion and it was up to Woodbury to make the decision. Screw it, then.

'Okay. I need to contact someone in Mister Pickering's organization. We need to borrow some government assets, see if we can't track down the target family. Full electronic snoop and sweep. I think we need to cover all possibilities.'

'Sounds reasonable. I'll clear it through the organization. Anything else?'

'No, not for now,' Clay said, watching the speedometer back down as he raised his right foot. 'Once I find out what the hell is going on with Ebony Three, I'll let you know.'

Woodbury's voice suddenly sounded hopeful. 'It could just be a foul-up, right? Like a two-day drunk or something.'

'Possible, but not probable,' Clay said, slowing down as he approached a tollbooth. Damn state had no sales tax or income tax, had to pickpocket drivers to pay for their budget.

'Oh, well. And that other matter this morning?'

Clay couldn't think of what the old fat man was driving at until he glanced at his thumb, just as he was ready to toss two quarters in the tollbooth basket. 'Not a problem. In fact, it was kind of fun. Do you want a full debrief?'

'No,' came the reply, though the tone of the voice said otherwise.

Clay laughed. 'Signing off.'

He sped up as he went through the tollbooth and speed-dialed the other number. Budlong answered it right away and Clay said, 'Status?'

'The van is in downtown Portsmouth, moving slowly on Congress Street. It's made a right-hand turn. Now it's come to a full stop.'

'Okay,' Clay said. 'Just keep on feeding me info, sport, just keep on feeding me.'

His brother slowed the van and made a turn on to Fleet Street, between old brick buildings and stores. Up ahead was a small diner, set right next to a three-story parking garage.

Roy whispered, 'My God, it's still here. Gilley's. Still here. Remember?'

Jason found himself smiling. He surely did remember. Gilley's was a Portsmouth institution, a lunch and dinner wagon that had served generations of tourists and workers and residents in Portsmouth. Late at night, the place could be crowded with well-dressed couples, coming in after an evening at a local play, standing next to oil-stained and blue-jeaned workers just getting off shift from the Portsmouth Naval Shipyard, and mixed in with local rockers, punks, drug dealers, and runaways. Sometimes Dad, after taking them to a special treat—like a Red Sox game at Fenway Park—would take a very young Jason and not so young Roy here for a late-night dinner, before getting on to the Spaulding Turnpike and back home.

'Sure,' Jason said. 'I remember. Coming back from Fenway Park.'

'Or Hampton Beach.'

Roy suddenly swung the van over to the right, into a parking spot. 'Look. I'm hungry. How about a quick bite to eat?'

Jason took out his wallet, checked the bills. Sure. He had enough. 'You know, that'd be nice, Roy.'

Roy rubbed at his face. 'I've missed so much, Jason. You have no idea. Just look at how many presidents we've had since I was shot down—a movie star, a CIA director, a couple of Southern governors—and everything else. Oil embargoes. The space shuttle. The Berlin Wall coming down. Computers. Is it true computers are so cheap that people can actually own their own? I've read about it, but it still doesn't seem real.'

'Yes, it's true.'

His brother still seemed amazed. 'Really? Your own computer?'

Jason felt a pang of compassion, just now beginning to grasp the extent of the horrors Roy had been put through. My God, he thought, he's a real-life Rip Van Winkle. Imagine falling asleep in 1972 and waking up thirty years later . . . disco, polyester, leisure suits, gas shortages, X-rated videos, VCRs, CDs, MP3s, Palm Pilots, cell phones, ATM cards, 747 jets, Mars probes, pictures from Jupiter, Saturn, Uranus, Neptune, a presidential resignation, a presidential impeachment, an attempted presidential assassination, the space station, cocaine wars, rap, hip-hop, satellite television, voicemail, e-mail, the Internet . . . Poor Roy, he thought. No wonder he seems so blessed shell-shocked.

'Yes,' Jason said. 'We own a computer. And when this is all over, I'll get you one, too.'

Roy just shook his head. 'For now, cheeseburgers. I haven't had a decent cheeseburger in . . . well, a very long time. Plain cheeseburgers, fries, a Coke. The basic food groups. All right?'

'Sure,' Jason said. 'Sounds simple enough.'

He got out of the van and went up the sidewalk, up the short steps to the diner. A sliding door opened to the inside. He looked back, a twinge of fear coming to him that Roy would suddenly put the van into drive and leave him behind. But no. Roy was there, looking out at him, and he waved. Jason waved back and went into the tiny confines of the diner.

Patty felt herself to be in a fog, just driving along Route 4, hands fumbling as she got a Barney the Dinosaur cassette tape for Paul to listen to. She had delivered her warning to her sister and brother-in-law, she was on the road, she was using cash instead of her credit card, so she was doing what was right . . .

But shit, it wasn't right. She was running away, and Jason

was off on some adventure, leaving her alone with their boy, their house shattered, their loving pet killed. And what was to be done? Go to the police? Go to the authorities who were paid to put themselves between law-abiding citizens and criminals?

No. She was running scared, not doing anything, just lying low and hiding, while her husband had run off, her business was being abandoned.

Business. Shit, she hadn't thought of the *Banner* since she had left, and she wondered how in hell Jack was holding the fort. Up ahead was another service station, with a convenience store. 'Honey?' she asked.

'Unh-hunh,' Paul said, playing with a truck in his hand.

'Would you like a sandwich? Something to eat?'

'Sure. Ham "n" cheese?'

'Sure,' she said, slowing down. 'Ham and cheese.' And a few quarters, as well. Time to make that phone call, see what was going on at the newspaper. That shouldn't be a problem, should it?

Patty pulled the Volvo into an empty spot, thought about leaving Paul in the car and locking the door . . . but no, not after this morning. Her boy was going to be right at her side. 'Come along,' she said, and he went in with her, holding her hand. She went to the back of the store, where there were some deli sandwiches for sale. She got ham and cheese for them both, a bag of Tom's potato chips, a Diet Coke, and a fruit drink for Paul. She had Paul hold the little bag of groceries as they walked out—and her heart nearly broke as she saw how solemn he looked, fulfilling her request— and with a few quarters she dialed the number for the *Banner* from an outdoor phone stall.

Busy. She hung up, let the quarters rattle out and paused.

159

Paul stood by her, leaning into her leg. She patted his head and said, 'One more time, hon. One more time.'

She took the quarters, pumped them into the slot, punched in the numbers for the paper. Again, busy. There were three phone lines going into the *Banner*, and even if Jack was by himself, Claire Connelly should have been at work by now, answering the phone and taking ads.

What in hell was going on?

'Mommy,' came the plaintive voice, 'I'm really getting hungry.'

She hung up, retrieved the quarters, and grabbed his free hand. 'Okay. Let's go find someplace nice for a picnic and eat.'

They got back into the Volvo, and as she continued heading north, she looked at her young boy, the white plastic bag of groceries in his lap, and the music of that damn purple dinosaur, singing about love and family, made the tears come back again.

Roy looked at the crowd hanging around a few parked cars and the entrance to the diner. These were the citizens he had sworn to defend, all those years ago? He recalled the few sightings he had had, during leave when he came back home or at some of his overseas postings, of the strange creatures called hippies. With their long hair, beards, and patched clothes, they sure were a strange lot. But compared to what was out here now on the street, they seemed as straight as members of the Joint Chiefs of Staff. And what was out on the street was the strangest collection of humans he had ever seen: some of the young men, the sides of their heads were shaved, and the strip of hair running down the middle was teased up in some sort of mane. Some of the women

160

had hair that was dyed pink or green, and a couple were wearing black lipstick! Their jeans were tattered, barely held together, and they all wore short black leather jackets, decorated with studs and piercings.

My God, during these past few days, he thought, it was like he had been mysteriously transported from Earth to Mars.

The door to Gilley's slid open and Jason came out, carrying a brown paper bag. He didn't even spare a glance at the crew hovering outside. He came into the van and the smell seemed to go right through Roy's nose, past his saliva glands, and into his stomach.

'Jesus, I can't remember ever smelling anything this good,' he said, as Jason started opening up the bag.

'Hell, Roy, it's only Gilley's.'

With trembling hands, Roy received the wax-paper-wrapped cheeseburger, felt the warmth of the food in his fingers, even the sliminess of the grease oozing out.

'Jason, sure it's only Gilley's, but I'm a free man.' He unwrapped the cheeseburger, but before he took a bite he said, 'Fair warning. We need to eat quick, because there are miles that need to be burned off.'

Jason chewed and said, 'Will I get more of a debrief from you?'

Roy had to swallow twice, because of the saliva flooding through his mouth as he brought the cheeseburger up to it. 'Yes, another debrief. I promise.'

The man's whiny voice was beginning to bug him, but at least he was supplying the information he needed. Clay found himself in the city of Portsmouth, whose streets seemed to be a miniature of Boston's, with one-ways, multiple intersections, and dead-ends. Budlong said, 'All right, sir, they're moving again. They're heading west, it seems, trying to get on the interstate, I-95.'

'Okay. I'm on Congress Street. Where to?'

Budlong said, 'You'll come to a four-way intersection. Portsmouth Library across the way. Keep going straight. Van is about a half-mile ahead of you.'

Clay came to a stop, heart thumping, the bright copper taste of excitement in his mouth. All his life, ever since he could walk, he had been a hunter, a warrior. From squirrels and rabbits when he was not even a teenager, to deer and pheasant and turkey and bear, to longhorn sheep and even a frigging grizzly bear once. He had loved the hunt, until he had gotten bored matching wits against an animal. Then, while in the Army and beyond, he had slipped to the other side, hunting the most dangerous, intelligent, and nastiest creature on the planet: man. And nothing had ever been so much fun. Not ever. He knew one day that he'd run into a nastier creature than him, that it would end bloodily, but he had come to terms with that. To die like that would be the only way for a warrior to end his life. Not in bed, breathing through a tube, shitting in his pajamas.

The light turned green. Budlong was still on the phone. 'All right, it looks like they're not taking the highway. But they're still heading west.'

'West it is,' Clay said. 'Budlong, you keep me on track, 'till I'm right up their ass.'

'All right,' came the man's voice. 'Then what?'

Clay laughed. 'Pal, you really don't want to know.'

For a while, the two of them had been silent, the drone of the engine the only real noise. Jason leaned over to his brother and said, 'Debrief?'

162

Roy said, 'You sure sound hopeful.'

'Patient, you mean,' Jason said. 'I think I've been pretty damn patient, these past hours. I need to know, Roy. What the hell happened to you, and how did you end up here? And where are we going?'

'All stories need to be told in their own way,' Roy said quietly. 'But you deserve more. Okay, here we go. Debrief number two.'

Budlong's voice was triumphant. 'The van should be right ahead of you.'

'Yeah, it certainly is,' Clay said. 'Good job.'

'Thanks.'

They were on a rural road, somewhere west of Brentwood, about fifteen miles away from Portsmouth, lined on both sides by old stone walls and trees. Clay was working through options, choices, wondering what he could use in his toolboxes of tricks, back in the rear of his Excursion.

'And you've been trying to raise them on the radio? No answer, right?'

'That's right, sir. If Ebony Three is in there, they should have called me back a while ago.'

'Okay, I'm going off the air for a few minutes,' Clay said. 'In the meanwhile . . .' He fumbled for a moment on the passenger's seat, pulled over a printout. 'I'm going to need you to hook into the domestic ECHELON system, all right? Need a full snoop and sweep on one Patricia Harper, age thirty-eight, resident of Berwick, Maine . . . hold on, here's her Social Security, home phone number,' and he read those numbers off twice.

Budlong coughed. 'I . . . I've never worked through the ECHELON system.'

Clay said, 'Well, you better start. You'll find you have the necessary authorization. Gotta go.'

He clicked off the cell phone, saw there was room to pass the van, and made a quick choice. He speeded up and overtook it, and gave a quick glance in the rearview mirror as he moved away, leaving the van behind. Two subjects in the front. Hard to make out their faces through the tinted glass. No matter. He'd get to meet them quick enough. He kept on until he figured he was a few minutes ahead of them, then braked hard, slewed the Excursion to the right and jumped out. He went back to the rear of the Excursion, popped open the rear door, and went right to the box he needed, one of several tied down in the rear.

Move, move, move, a voice inside of him chanted, and he ran up the road carrying two items. One was a pump-action shotgun, barrel cut back so it was easy to carry, full magazine with .20-gauge shells. The other was a folded-up rumble strip. About a dozen feet away from the Excursion, he dropped the rumble strip, punched one end into the ground with his right foot. Grasping the other end, he ran across the narrow asphalt, the strip scissoring open, the sharp spikes pointing straight up. There. He punched the other end into the dirt, went up past a stone wall, sat on a tree stump, the shotgun across his lap. From somewhere a blue jay chattered at him. The sound of the van came to him, the four soon-to-be-punctured tires humming along on the road.

He smiled, quickly caressed the smooth metal. Sure was nice to be the hunter and not the hunted.

TEN

The First Decade

The left eye of Captain Roy Harper, USAF, was swollen shut, but the right eye was still functioning, as the man from Soviet military intelligence–the GRU—sat across from him, wiping his hands on a cloth towel stained rust red with Harper's blood. They were in a small, windowless interrogation room, cement cinder blocks that were white and cold to the touch. Between them was a wooden table, and Harper's hands were cuffed to a metal ring set in the table. A tape recorder was working on the other side of the table, its fat reels moving slowly. In one corner of the room was a smaller table. On this were a tray of sandwiches, an ice bucket with sweaty Budweiser beers, piles of Marlboro cigarettes, and what looked to be a collection of Hershey bars. Harper tried to keep his gaze away from that table and to keep it on the GRU man, who had worked up a bit of a sweat during these past several minutes. His black hair was cut short, and he was clean-shaven, and unlike the Eastern European cliché, his teeth were white and well ordered. He wore a black turtleneck sweater and Levi jeans, and even when he was beating the shit out of Harper, his accentless English-speaking voice was polite and almost apologetic.

'Captain Harper,' the GRU man said. 'I really do wish you'd start working with us, instead of against us. It would make everything so simple. All I need are some answers to some very simple questions. Please.'

Roy tried opening his left eye. No joy. 'Harper, Roy Earl. Captain, United States Air Force. Serial number 680912347.'

'Blah, blah, blah,' the GRU man said. 'We know lots about you, Captain Harper. You insult my intelligence, our intelligence, by sticking to your outdated script. We know you grew up in Dover, New Hampshire. A mill town in New England. Mother and father still alive, as well as one brother. Entered the Air Force Academy in 1964. Scored well enough on the aptitude tests to enter flight school. I won't bore you with the lists of schools and bases you either attended or were stationed at. Trust me, we know them all. We even know you were corresponding with a young lady from your hometown during the last few months of your service. A Miss Stacy Burke. Correct?'

Harper felt cold, so damn cold. The jeans and shirt that had been issued to him months ago in North Vietnam were soiled and starting to pull apart. 'It's not fair,' he said, ashamed at how weak his voice was.

'Fair? Of course it's not fair, in so many ways. But tell me, how do you think it's not fair?'

Harper tried to smile through the throbbing, burning pain in his face and along his arms. 'You know my name. I don't know yours.'

The GRU man laughed. 'Good, very good. Very well, you may call me Ivan. How is that?'

'Very good,' Harper said, shifting some in the hard plastic seat. 'How's this? Fuck you, Ivan.'

'All right, now we're communicating. And politely, too. Now, can we move on?'

166

Harper said, 'No. Fuck you, Ivan.'

Ivan shrugged, got up and went to the smaller table, came back and started munching on a sandwich. Even from where he sat, Harper could smell the fresh chicken. His stomach grumbled.

'Hungry?' Ivan asked.

'You know the answer to that.'

'Sure,' Ivan said, swallowing. 'And everything on that table can be yours, if you start cooperating. Come along, Captain. It's really a very simple question. What is your understanding and that of your crewmates of NATO's first-strike doctrine? Hmmm? Nothing too top secret about that, is there? Answer me that and everything on that table can belong to you.'

Harper swallowed, kept silent. Ivan took another bite and said, 'I know what you're thinking. That we are cruel, barbaric, uncivilized, for what we are doing to you and your comrades. Or compatriots, if you rather I not use that rather loaded word. Very well. Tell me this, Captain. Imagine the role is reversed. Let us say . . . Guatemala. All right? Guatemala. A civil war has erupted in Guatemala, in your own backyard. You support the government in the north, we support the government in the south. And in our support of this government we bring in our best pilots, our best weapons, our best everything. Oh, to the outside world we tell everyone that we are there to support our fraternal socialist comrades or some other fucking nonsense. But you're a professional. You know why we're there. Correct?'

Ivan stared at him, and said, 'Come along, Captain. That's a fair question, is it not? I'll tell you what. Half a chicken sandwich, for answering.'

Harper stared back at him. Ivan reached over, undid one wrist and then passed over the plate. 'There you go. Half a sandwich, answer or no. All right?'

Harper looked at the bread of the sandwich, the first white bread he had seen since Guam. His stomach grumbled even louder, and he was humiliated to think that Ivan could probably hear the noise. He looked up to the GRU man as he used his free hand to touch his swollen eye. 'Tactics,' Harper said. 'An intervention like that would be a perfect practice area to demonstrate your tactics in a real-life combat environment.'

'Exactly!' Ivan said, excitement in his voice. 'Very good. Yes, tactics. It's one thing to have practice bombing and gunnery missions going on in your western deserts. It's quite another thing to be using these very same tactics in very real missions, with a very real enemy shooting back at you. Enough of that military assistance nonsense. You finally have an opportunity to test your training, your tactics, and your weapons, and you do just that.'

Ivan picked up the cloth napkin, grimaced at the bloodstains, and dropped it and went back to the smaller table, where he picked up a fresh one. He wiped his fingers as he went on. 'So. There we are, the defenders of socialism, in your hemisphere, bringing in our very best weapons and pilots to assist our brethren in Guatemala. You're not particularly happy about that, but you don't want a nuclear conflict with us. But you can't just sit back and let us play in your territory without paying a price. So you rush in material and weapons support to your allies. The war continues for a while, and then you Americans, you quickly realize, what an intelligence bonanza—that's the right word, correct?—yes, a bonanza, is happening in your own backyard. The latest military hardware, aircraft, and trained personnel from your sworn enemies are dropping from the sky, to land on the surface of your close ally.'

Ivan picked up the sandwich, finished it with a satisfied look on his face as he chewed. 'Your CIA, your military intelligence, your Pentagon. If they sat on their asses and let this intelligence windfall drop, almost in their laps, and did not do anything about it, they should be shot for dereliction of duty. Correct?'

Harper started rubbing his wrist, just nodded. Ivan said, 'So. What we do, no doubt, you and your people would do if the circumstances were reversed.'

'Why . . . why now?'

Ivan's mood darkened. 'Ah, a good question. See, Captain Harper? Having an intelligent conversation with me is not so difficult, is it? And a good question: why now? And the answer is, because of the ignorant rice farmers that we had to deal with. Those little monkey bastards did not appreciate everything we did for them and continue to do for them. Since the mid-1960s, we have been attempting to interrogate crewmen and retrieve shot-down aircraft. And always, with the fucking Vietnamese, it was delay, talk, delay, and if we made any fuss they would smile sweetly and say that no doubt we knew they could get additional socialist assistance from their neighboring friends, the Chinese. Oh, they knew how to work us, they did. But we continued to press, here and there, and we found that—as in most areas of the world—the right amount of gold and trickery will get you anything you need. We retrieved you folks, just in time, and my word, what we're learning. Your FB-111s. Quite an extraordinary flying machine, with the most wonderful laser-guided ordinance, to destroy bridges and railroad trestles. Imagine what you and NATO could do at the right time during a conflict. Similar strikes to those you performed in Hanoi and Haiphong, performed in Prague or Dresden, could ruin any chance of needed resupply during

169

any NATO–Warsaw Pact conflict. In fact, we are learning quite a good deal from some FB-111 crew members.'

Harper still refused to look at the chicken sandwich. 'Then they will be taken care of, later.'

'Really? By whom?'

'By the senior officer, or the SROs, or a court-martial when . . .' And Harper couldn't finish the sentence.

Ivan smiled. 'I knew what you were going to say. A court-martial when you get home. My dear captain, our cousins the KGB, they have a phrase that they stamp on certain sensitive documents that are to be stored for a very long time. The stamp says "To Be Kept Forever."' Ivan lowered his voice. 'That is your fate, and that of your fellow Air Force and Navy fliers. You will be kept here forever. There will be no release. No parole. No escape. There is a phrase from one of your movies, where a prisoner is brought in. You can do easy time or hard time. That is your choice, Captain. Easy time or hard time, it does not matter to me, because you will be serving out that time here. Forever.'

Harper kept silent, and Ivan looked over at the still-moving reels on the tape recorder. 'Captain Harper,' he said, his voice more formal. 'Please tell me, what is your understanding and that of your crewmates of NATO's first-strike doctrine?'

Roy looked down at the sandwich, stomach now actually hurting, and pushed it back toward his interrogator, then refastened his own wrist to the metal ring in the table.

'Harper, Roy Earl,' he said slowly. 'Captain, United States Air Force. Serial number 680912347.'

Of course, it ended badly, for there are limits and there are limits, and each man has his own limits, including Roy

Harper, who did no better or no worse than most of his compatriots in the chilly prison that soon became known to them as the Siberian Sheraton. His limit was reached the day Ivan pulled out a butane torch, and it took two passes on Roy's bare back before he broke. After receiving medical attention from a silent GRU doctor, he was placed back in his cell, a concrete cube with metal cot, bucket, and single wool blanket. Later, though, he was taken out and led to the general quarters of the prison, where other officers who had broken as well were waiting for him. There wasn't much of a greeting when he arrived, for he saw in their faces their own shame at having broken before him.

Eventually he was placed in a two-man cell, and after some delicate and serious negotiations he managed to room with Tom Grissom, his EWO. The new cell was an improvement, with real beds with mattresses and blankets, a bookshelf, a sink with hot and cold water, and a window made of a thick glass that actually looked outside. A smelly toilet down the hallway served about a dozen fellow prisoners, and they had use of a large shower room.

Grissom came in the day the room negotiations were successfully completed and sat down on the bed, testing the mattress. 'Not bad, Cap, not bad. Better than our last lodgings.'

'You ever figure out where we were, back in North Vietnam?'

'Nope,' Grissom said. 'And I don't hold much hope we'll know where we are now.'

His EWO got off the bunk and went over to the window, which he cranked open. Harper joined him, looking out at the flat expanse before them. The prison camp was a square, surrounded by three separate wire fences, about twelve feet tall.

All three were topped with barbed wire and razor wire, and all three were electrified. Guard towers were at each corner, with searchlights and guards armed with scoped rifles and AK-47s. Grissom said, 'You know the layout that well, Cap?'

'No, not really.'

Grissom rubbed at his face, which was still clean-shaven. 'The whole place is a self-contained unit, best as I can tell. This building is concrete and steel. Holds us and the other POWs, plus the interrogation rooms. Power, water supply, barracks for the guards, the GRU bastards, they're all in a different building, maybe a half-mile or so on the other side. There's a road that connects the two, and word is, that place is as isolated as this one. No roads to that building, either. Just a landing strip and the occasional helicopter or small aircraft, in and out. No villages, no other towns, no rivers with boat traffic. Perfectly isolated. Look out there, will you?'

Harper shivered as he stared through the wire fence, out to . . . nothingness. Flat white. 'Siberia?'

'Probably, but who knows? Could be any part of their fucking empire. I mean, Jesus, goddamn country is so big it has eleven time zones. How hard would it be to hide a hundred or so Americans? Not hard at all. Plus, look at it out there . . . ice and snow and permafrost. Maybe a month or two when it melts and it's flat grassland. Let's say you get out. Where do you go? Who the fuck knows? We could be hundreds of miles from the nearest village, and you can believe the GRU will have folks in the surrounding villages who'll be instantly aware if a stranger wanders in who can't speak the language. And how do we get out?' Grissom stamped his feet on the concrete, flashed a tired smile.

'Pretty tough going,' Harper said.

'Yeah, you could say that, Cap,' Grissom said. 'Remember

172

those great World War II movies? *Stalag 17* and *The Great Escape*? They were in wooden shacks, in a temperate zone, over dirt and rock. They could make tunnels. They were also in a place where if you did get out, you could blend in with the right clothes and attitude. Cap, we're in concrete cubes, over permafrost. If you could dig down, maybe, just maybe, you'd get six or seven inches before you hit solid, frozen dirt. Not to mention who the natives might be, out there beyond the horizon.'

Harper said, 'You make it sound hopeless.'

Grissom made a tapping motion against both ears with his hands, and there was something odd about the gesture that Harper couldn't make out, until he realized that Grissom was indicating that the room—and no doubt every room in the facility—was bugged. Grissom said, 'I'm just describing what's there, Captain. That's all.'

Harper went back to his bunk, while Grissom stood there, still looking out. 'My interrogator . . . he said something about us being here forever. My God, Cap, I expect he's probably right.'

'Wallenberg,' Harper said, the name coming unbidden to his mind.

'What's that?'

'Wallenberg,' Harper said, the memory coming back. 'Raoul Wallenberg. A Swedish diplomat, working in Hungary during World War II. Managed to smuggle out or rescue thousands of Jews. He was captured by the Russians after the war, and disappeared. Shit, there's a guy, a diplomat, who the Russians took, and they deny any knowledge of his whereabouts.' Harper rubbed at the coarse wool of the blanket. 'And that's public information. And us? Missing in action. We don't exist. No matter what the Geneva Convention says.'

Grissom laughed and sat on his own bed, drawing his knees up with his hands. 'Funny you should mention that. That's where my first interrogation was going, round and round. I kept on demanding my rights under the Geneva Convention. Ivan said something that made sense, in a horrible, twisted way. The Geneva Convention, he said, was an anachronism, written at a time when war was conducted in a gentlemanly fashion. And besides, we weren't officially prisoners of war. We were charged with war crimes by the peace-loving people of the Democratic Republic of Vietnam, and since there was no official war declared between Vietnam and the United States . . . Well, I'm sure you know the drill.'

'I do,' Harper said.

'Well, so did I,' Grissom said. 'But I was an insistent little bastard, bringing that up again and again.'

Harper said, 'What happened?'

Grissom held up his right hand, wiggled it, and Harper realized, with a twist of nausea, why the motion earlier with his hands and ears had looked so odd.

'They managed to convince me,' Grissom said simply, showing off his right hand, where the first two joints of his little finger had been cut off.

Time passed, day after day, week after week. The POWs organized themselves into the Sixth Allied POW Wing, and their senior officer was Harmon Blake, a Navy captain who flew an F-4 off the USS *Constellation*, and whose shattered hip still kept him on crutches. He was the third senior officer since their arrival in the Soviet Union; the second, another Air Force colonel named Harrington, had joined his predecessor about two minutes after he had been shot at their arrival hangar. Harper was pleased that, so far, nobody in the POW contingent thought any less of Captain Blake for offering cooperation, limited as it was. They all knew the Code of Conduct by heart; sometimes, during the infrequent mass meetings in the dining hall, Captain Blake would lead them through a recitation, and Harper felt particularly morose whenever they got to Part Five: 'When questioned, should I become a prisoner of war, I am bound to give only name, rank, service number, and date of birth. I will evade answering further questions to the utmost of my ability. I will make no oral or written statements disloyal to my country and its allies or harmful to their cause.'

Utmost ability. Despite the memory that took less than a second to call up, of Ivan leaning over him, the hissing of the butane torch, the sizzling and white-hot pain that nearly doubled him over, he still felt guilty, and he knew, seeing the faces of the other POWs, that so did they.

The word came down from Blake to the SROs—senior reporting officers—from the Air Force and the Navy: Resist as much as you can, but be reasonable. There was no contact with the outside. There were no visits from the International Red Cross. There was no mail. They were on their own, and would be on their own if not forever, as the GRU personnel claimed, then certainly for a very long time to come.

Harper found the interrogations to be almost friendly, compared to what had gone on earlier. They were recorded, and at first the GRU moved slowly and methodically, filling in the few blanks in his personnel file concerning the training and the schools he had attended. To begin with he wondered what was going on, but then, late at night, it spooked him: The GRU felt they had all the time in the world, and they intended to use it.

The interrogations sometimes lasted all day, sometimes just

175

a few hours. Sometimes days and weeks would pass before a pilot or EWO or radar-navigator was chosen, and it meant lots of spare time. The POWs shared stories, put on amateur plays and musicals, played elaborate poker and cribbage tournaments from packs of cards supplied by the GRU, gave lectures on everything from birdwatching (pathetic, since there seemed to be no local birds) to astronomy (equally pathetic, since the bright lights in the Siberian Sheraton's compound washed out the night sky). Harper found himself participating in these activities, and while he enjoyed the comradeship and the fact that it made the time pass by, he would sometimes find himself staring at a far concrete wall, blanking everything out.

He was always reminded then of high school, and a certain science fair showing off trained mice, going round and round in a maze. That's what he—and the others—felt like: trained mice. And he would always feel his hands tremble at the memory of what that student had done, once the mice had finished being useful: they were killed and thrown away.

Using potatoes and sugar and God knows what else, a type of home brew was concocted in one of the POW cells. It was strictly rationed and was kept secret, at least for a while, until a Navy lieutenant named Tompkins—who had saved up his ration, week after week—got drunk one night and started screaming out his cell window: 'We're here, America! Damn you, we're still alive! We're not dead! Come and get us, you fuckers! We fought for you, we bled for you! We're still here! We're still here!'

The still was found, confiscated, and the four POWs who had serviced it were confined to the cooler, a plain concrete block cell with only a bucket for waste: no blankets, no mattresses, nothing.

176

Soon afterward, Captain Blake passed down the word: no more home brew.

While professional GRU officers performed the interrogations, guard duty—inside and outside the camp—was performed by silent, serious-looking Asians, in quilted uniforms and carrying AK-47s, chained to their waists. Rumors were passed and bets were made as to their nationality: Mongolian? Chinese? Manchurian? There were strict orders against fraternization from the GRU staff, which didn't have much of an impact, since none of the guards spoke English and they were rotated out every two months, before they could pick up any phrases or words from their charges. But during one winter, a number of Navy men had managed to get some sort of communication going with one of the guards, whom they named Charlie. They passed along Hershey bars and cigarettes to Charlie and started teaching him a few phrases. Yet the officers' goal wasn't to make a friend of him before he left. No, they had something more important going on: intelligence.

Inside the Siberian Sheraton was an escape committee, though Harper knew very little of who was on the committee or what they were planning. There were too many listening devices in the cells and common areas, and it was known that the committee conducted their meetings in the exercise yard, with bits of conversation passed along as the POWs walked in circles, or played soccer during the six or eight weeks when the weather was actually warm. But everyone knew that the committee's first priority was to find out where the Siberian Sheraton was. For what good was an escape if you didn't know which horizon to head out to?

Harper wasn't sure how much intelligence the Navy pilots were able to get from Charlie; one day, the entire camp was forced to stand out in the exercise yard while Charlie—dressed in soiled white underwear—was brought out by his fellow guards and forced to kneel down in front of the assembled POWs. A GRU officer came into the line of men and brusquely pulled out three POWs, whom Harper recognized as the Navy men who had befriended the guard.

Grissom said, 'Cap, this isn't going to end well.'

'No, it's not.'

The three pilots were forced to stand behind the kneeling Charlie. Words were said by the GRU, but a stiff breeze made them unintelligible to Harper. Three revolvers were produced and Harper felt something do a slow flip-flop in his gut, thinking he was about to see four men get killed.

Yet it didn't happen that way. The revolvers were forced into the hands of the Navy pilots. Other guards came behind them as well, their AK-47s pushing against their backs. More words, more yells, and then Charlie, kneeling on the ground, screamed out in a thick accent: 'No, John! No, Paulie! No, Pete! USA okay! USA okay!'

Harper closed his eyes, listening to the muffled pops of the revolvers as the Navy men were forced to shoot Charlie. They dropped the revolvers on the ground and stumbled back into the ranks of the other POWs, their faces ashen. Grissom whispered, 'Those bastards. Those rotten bastards.'

None of the guards ever came close to befriending anyone ever again.

But the escape committee did learn at least one thing: Charlie and the others were North Korean.

Sometimes the interrogations were unusual. Harper spent one morning describing all of the American mixed drinks he had ever consumed and what they were made of. Other interrogations went far afield. He spent one day with Ivan and another Russian whose name or identity he never knew. Ivan said simply, 'You grew up in Dover, New Hampshire. It is the city next to Portsmouth, New Hampshire. Your Navy has a shipyard there. Please tell us everything you know about the shipyard, its personnel, its location, the restaurants and bars nearby, lodgings, traffic patterns. Now.'

The GRU officer in charge of the camp called himself Yuri. Occasionally he would take over one of the interrogation rooms and meet with the SROs or dispense whatever high justice was available in this part of the Soviet empire. The GRU had been generous with some items—there were plenty of books and magazines, *Time* and *Newsweek* and *Playboy*, many months old, and Captain Blake's crutches were replaced by a wheelchair. But there were no radios, no television, nothing electronic, and Harper realized it made sense: with the EWO techs and everyone else with a highly technical background in the POW population, they wanted no chance for outside communication.

But the attempts went on just the same.

One day Harper was asked to assist Captain Blake to a meeting with Yuri. Blake was slowly losing weight, even though the GRU fed the POWs fairly well, and he had developed a shaking palsy in his hands, which he tried to keep firm in his lap. 'Captain Blake,' Harper said as he entered the captain's cell. Being the senior officer, Blake had a cell to himself, though Harper thought he would hate the isolation. Sometimes Grissom snored and other times, especially after eating cabbage, his gas was enough to make Harper's eyes water, but he was a companion, a link to the days of freedom, back there on Guam at Anderson.

'Thank you, Captain,' Blake said, his white hair a bit tangled, stubble on his chin where he had missed shaving. Harper took the wheelchair handles in his grasp and took Captain Blake to the interrogation room, where two unsmiling North Koreans stood guard outside. Inside the room, the heavyset Yuri—who didn't speak English as well as his subordinates—chain-smoked and sat behind a well-polished table. He was flanked by Ivan and another GRU officer, named Petr.

Harper made to leave but Yuri said, 'No, you. Stay. This will not take long.'

'Sir,' Captain Blake began, 'I once again must protest—'

Yuri dismissed him with a gesture of his hand. 'Please. I must meet my transport in ten minutes. For sake of brevity, we shall agree that we had the same conversation we have always had before. Geneva Convention. Detainees. War criminals. So forth, so on. There. We are done with that subject.'

Harper could feel Blake shift his weight in the wheelchair. Blake remained silent.

Yuri took a puff from a cigarette—Marlboro, of course—and slid over a glossy photo. Blake lifted one of his shaking hands but Harper got there before he did, picking up the photo and placing it in the captain's lap. The photo was an overhead shot—perhaps from an aircraft, perhaps from a satellite—that showed a small collection of buildings in a compound surrounded by fences. Along the bottom of the photo was a string of numbers and Cyrillic letters. To one side of the compound—which Harper recognized instantly as their prison—was the exercise yard. And there, in the yard, in ghost letters that took up almost the entire exercise compound, one letter and two numerals.

B52.

Harper looked up at Yuri, who was still smoking. Yuri shook his head, like a scoutmaster upset that his little boys had gone and done something bad.

'Did you think that we would not notice? Did you?'

Now Harper could hear equipment out there, moving around. A bulldozer, perhaps, scraping down the snow and ice in the exercise yard. Yuri said, 'Nicely done, to have your group walk in a pattern like that, pushing the snow down, the ice. Perhaps even sprinkling dirt or sweepings behind you, to make the letters stand out so much better. Imaginative. But trust me when I tell you this. We know the patterns of your surveillance satellites. A long time ago this particular area was denoted to be of no special interest to your intelligence community, which is why you are here. So your sign to the heavens was not seen, except, perhaps, by God. But since I do not believe in God, that does not anger me.'

Captain Blake said, 'It is our duty.'

Yuri nodded. 'Da. Perhaps it is. And it is my duty to tell you that there will be no more exercise outdoors. For two months. And if such a pattern returns, Captain Blake, you will be held personally responsible, and you will be shot before your men. Dismissed.'

Some months later, Harper was walking with another Air Force captain, Scott Whelan, who had been stationed at Anderson Air Force Base a few months before Harper, and was originally from Maine. Harper was sharing some stories about his home state, and Whelan was describing growing up in Portland, and it was just a pleasant way to spend a fucking winter afternoon in a fucking prison camp in fucking Siberia. They were in the exercise yard—now kept free of ice and snow—and were walking in a wide circle when Grissom came up to them, shivering, his arms folded. He joined them and listened as Whelan described a drunken evening where he consumed a six-pack of Narragansett beer and three lobsters. Then Grissom said quietly, 'Townsend's gone.'

Whelan paused, just as he was describing the melting butter running down the chin of his college girlfriend, and Harper said, 'For real?'

Grissom nodded. 'For real.'

Whelan said, 'How long?'

Grissom grinned, stamped his feet. 'Two weeks. Can you believe that? Two whole weeks.'

'And do the Ivans know?'

'Yeah. They just figured it out. They're going apeshit, tearing up the place. The escape committee's made the announcement, now that the Ivans got clued in.'

Whelan's voice was filled with marvel. 'How in hell did the goons not notice Townsend was gone?'

Harper started grinning too. 'We're mostly white men. We all look the same to them. During bed check, one guy would race ahead and take Townsend's place after his own cell was checked. Bed check in the morning and night matched. There you go.'

Out in the distance, helicopters were suddenly on the horizon. Harper's heart started thumping right along, almost matching the rhythm of the helicopter blades. Air Force Major Gary Townsend was a B-52 EWO from Anchorage, Alaska. A hunter, fisherman, and hiker who had spent many days and nights out in the Alaskan wilderness. 'Get me outside the fence, boys,' Townsend had said, 'and I'll fucking hike my way out of here and swim the Bering Strait, and I'll get you all home. Just you see.'

Whelan said, 'Jesus Christ, so he made it out. Jesus Christ.'

Later, Harper would find out how he had done it. The escape committee had been extraordinarily cautious in assisting Townsend, knowing that the first serious escape attempt had to succeed. They had supplied him with food, water, and a homemade compass. White sheets had been salvaged, to make a snow suit for him. The GRU never allowed heavy clothing for the POWs, so winter clothing had to be made from scraps of cloth. And the escape route . . . simple but something that could only be used once. During one of the late afternoon exercise periods, he had gone out and disappeared into a snowbank, camouflaged by the white sheets. He waited all afternoon, all night, and then into the next morning, when it was shift change for the guard force. A groaning truck—a half-ton Ford Army truck that looked like it had been part of the World War II lend-lease efforts—would come in with a new shift, and would bring out the old shift. And while the truck grumbled its way out, Townsend rolled underneath the slow-moving vehicle and grabbed on to the undercarriage. The North Koreans at the gate were supposed to stop the truck and examine every inch of it, but during the past couple of months they had gotten sloppy.

Sloppy enough that it had worked.

That night, after dinner, somebody started singing 'God Bless America,' and there were shouts and whoops of joy, and the North Koreans just stood there in the corner, faces as impassive as always.

A week later. Back out in the exercise yard, a helicopter again appeared on the horizon. But this one didn't stop at the buildings that held the guards and the GRU force and the supply facilities. It kept on flying and headed over to the exercise yard, and the POWs moved back from the wash of the blades, and Harper thought, shit, the damn thing is going to land, right here.

But it didn't land. A side door slid open, and something white fell out, landing with an audible thump on the concrete. The Soviet helicopter, with red star on the fuselage, lifted up and headed out, and before the sound of the engine was silent, they were all standing around the object that had fallen.

Before them, crusted with snow and ice crystals, was the frozen body of Major Gary Townsend, mostly wrapped in a white sheet.

Harper could feel the joy of the last week just melt away, like a snowflake held too long in his hands, and he could sense the sigh and murmurs of disappointment from the other POWs.

That night, all blankets and sheets were confiscated by the North Koreans, and they weren't returned for another month.

A week after Townsend's body was dumped, the first verifiable suicide occurred. An Air Force colonel Harper didn't know that well—Clarke, from Los Angeles—walked away from the exercise yard, went to the warning line, and, before his fellow officers could grab him, ran up and grabbed the first electrified fence.

Two more suicides happened, just like that, over the long winter.

Air Force Captain Roy Harper sat in the interrogation room before a GRU officer who identified himself as Ivan, but whom Harper identified as Ivan III, for he was the third officer to call himself that over time. He looked a bit like Ivan I, but was definitely thinner than Ivan II, and he smiled a lot more than either of them. Harper's stomach was bothering him, and he felt like he was getting a fever.

184

'Today, Captain Harper,' Ivan III said, 'I would like to get reacquainted with your training requirements for the dual-channel-code arming procedure for your tactical nuclear devices.'

Harper swallowed, his throat feeling even more sore than it did at breakfast. 'I'm sorry,' he whispered. 'I'm really not feeling well.'

'You're not fooling me, are you?'

'No,' Harper said.

Ivan III looked at him as if he were trying to gauge what was really going on. Then he shrugged and removed something from a small leather case at his feet. 'Oh, that is fine. Here. A gift for you, to keep you occupied. Perhaps you will feel better in the morning.'

He passed over a *Newsweek* magazine, which Harper picked up. It showed a smiling Ronald Reagan on the cover, waving. The headline said, 'A New Beginning.' The date was January 27, 1981.

Ivan III's smile was almost as wide as Reagan's. 'After all,' he said, 'you will be here tomorrow. And the day after that. And the day after that.'

Harper's fingers caressed the shiny paper, knowing that weeks ago this particular issue of this magazine had been produced by free hands, in a free country, his homeland, and had been transported thousands of miles, to end up here, in the hands of one of his nation's forgotten sons.

'Forever,' Ivan III said. 'Forever.'

ELEVEN

In Manchester, New Hampshire, Frank Burnett sat at a small, polished wooden table in his office at the ABC-TV affiliate for New Hampshire ('Channel 21—The One for N.H.!') and scribbled aimlessly on a yellow legal pad as his news anchor for the five P.M. news prattled on about how a fire at a condo complex in Bedford should get more play during 'her' hour than on the regular news broadcast at six P.M. Frank looked up at one of the many digital clocks visible in the news room through the glass walls of his office, knew that in a few hours he'd be meeting with the entire staff to go over their news budget for the less than twenty minutes they had to inform, entertain, and educate the hundred thousand or so people in New Hampshire, Maine, and Massachusetts who were regular viewers, and said, 'Kim?'

'Yes, Frank?' she said, breathlessly. Kim Briscoe was blond and pretty, and had on a red dress, cut conservatively—this was the New Hampshire market, of course, not Miami. She did have a nice pair of legs, but as news director Frank knew he should be concerned with what was between Kim's ears, not below her navel.

'Kim, you know what the standard philosophy is for our afternoon news cycles,' he said, trying to inject patience into his voice. 'From five P.M. to six P.M. is the light hour. From six to six-thirty is when we give the hard news the most play. You can do a brief on the Bedford fire at the top of the half-hour. Other than that, it belongs to the six P.M. shift.'

Kim frowned and said, 'Frank, just a little more. That's all I want. Just a bit more. I want to do more hard news . . . not keep on doing the throw-ins for the cooking demos and the sports!'

Another aimless doodle on his pad, recalling a time back in college when he had wanted so badly to be just a newspaper editor, that's all. But for whatever reason, his copy was always too short, too punchy, and he found himself drifting into television. Now he was news director for the state's largest—and, let's face it, the only real—television station, and most nights he stared up into nothing before going to sleep, still amazed that it had happened. He looked up at the nearest clock, realized that he had been at work for just twenty minutes and already felt behind schedule.

'Kim, I don't have time to go over this right now. You're doing a great job at the five P.M. and you know that. We'll see if we can't do some shuffling next month, get you on some more hard news assignments. But for tonight, the Bedford fire belongs to the six P.M. shift.'

With that, her face started matching the color of her outfit, and Frank felt a quick burst of sympathy for the poor girl . . . all right, young woman, he thought. She wanted desperately to get into the hard news side of the business, to get out in the field and do stand-ups in front of fires and boating accidents and tractor-trailer jackknifes on the Everett Turnpike. But her looks and the breathy way she did her news reading had already—though Kim didn't know it—doomed her to a soft career the rest of her life. Frank had no doubt that she would do well and go far, but he knew he'd never see her on one of the main networks, being a White House correspondent or some field reporter out in China or India. No, poor Kim—her legs flashing fast as she got up silently and exited his office—would end up on *Extra* or *Entertainment Tonight* or *E! television*. She would have a happy and fulfilling career talking to rock stars, silicon-modified actresses, and brooding movie directors, and late at night, over mixed drinks at some hideaway in Beverly Hills or Malibu, she would complain bitterly that she could have become the next Christiane Amanpour, if it hadn't been for some prick news director back in frozen New Hampshire.

Now his office belonged just to him. He took a number of breaths. He thought about his wife, Carol, and the twins, neither of whom was doing well this year. Their three-year-old daughters—Mary and Megan—were constantly beset with respiratory problems, which meant long drives either to Dartmouth-Hitchcock Hospital up in Lebanon, or MassGeneral in Boston, and thank God he had a good health plan, but that health plan was going to mean shit unless their viewership increased. Channel 21 was holding its own, but holding its own wasn't good enough for the corporate masters out in Los Angeles, and unless something changed during the next time their ratings were measured, he knew who was going to get shitcanned, and it wouldn't be his happy collection of news anchors and—

'Frank?' came a voice at his door.

'Yeah,' he said, sitting up, looking at one of his producers, Greg Flemming, a good kid two years out of Emerson College. Greg had a scared look on his face, which made sense, for Frank had a hard and fast rule, which Kim had already broken: ten minutes of isolation in his office when he got there, for he needed that solitude to get his head on straight, and according to the clock, he had only used up about one minute since he had gotten here.

'Sorry to disturb you Frank, but I thought you'd like to see this.' Greg passed over a sheet of paper, a printout from their Associated Press wire. 'There was a fire over at a newspaper in Berwick, Maine. Just over the border. Completely destroyed the building, killed one of its staff members.'

Frank scanned the copy quickly and brought his free hand up to his face, suddenly not wanting his young producer to see his expression. How many times, he thought, had he read copy like this, about some tragedy or disaster, bodies on the ground, dreams destroyed and sent up in smoke? How many times had what little sympathy he felt been crushed by his news-director fist. Get the story, no matter what. Just get the story, and leave the sympathy to Hallmark.

'Frank . . .'

'Yeah.'

'Didn't you go to college with the guy who owns that paper? Harper?'

Frank tried blinking his eyes quickly, to dispel the moisture gathering there, and it wasn't working. 'Yes,' he said, managing to get the words out and feeling proud that he could without his voice trembling. 'Yes, I did.'

In Raymond, New Hampshire, Steve Josephs, a trooper with the New Hampshire State Police, checked his gear one last time before heading out for the evening's swing shift. Uniform on and looking good, boots polished to the proper level of illumination, and Kevlar vest safe and secure under his shirt. Leather gear creaking right along, and 10-mm Glock safely holstered at his side. At the tiny entranceway heading outdoors, he paused, ready for his little ceremony, a ceremony that only his wife, Jill, knew about. On a table near the door were three framed photos: one of his mom, hanging on at a Catholic Charities retirement facility in Manchester; one of Jill, with their three-year-old boy Mike sitting on her lap; and the other of his dad, wearing a uniform similar to his, for in New Hampshire, traditions lived a very long time, and the state trooper uniform hadn't changed much, even after all these years. He gently touched the top of each framed photo, and when he was done he said softly, 'I promise.' That was it, for he didn't have to say aloud what he was thinking, which was 'I promise to do a good job and get my ass safely back home to my loved ones.'

For a moment, he touched his dad's photo one more time. He had tried, so many, many times, to bring up memories of his dad, but he had always failed. His father had been gone since Steve had been barely three years old, and the only real memory he had of him was sitting in his lap at some family function, over in Deerfield, at Grandfather's farm. He had skinned his knee or had been stung by something, and he was hurting, and all he remembered was a deep voice and a hug and the raspiness of beard bristles against his cheek. Mom had shown him dozens and dozens of photos over the years, of them all together, Dad and Mom and him and his older sister Terri, trying to jog his memory, but those attempts had always failed. Looking at the photos was like looking at strangers— had he really worn a T-shirt showing a lion when he was two years old—and he was only left with that sensation, of being held, of having those chin bristles rub up against him. Damn it, if only he could remember that face, remember that look . . . It would make all the difference.

After going to the closet and retrieving his orange raincoat—

rain was forecast for later in the evening—Steve headed to the door, idly scratching at an itch under his vest. He wondered whether such a vest would have made a difference for Dad, but he didn't know. Who ever would know?

Just before he touched the doorknob, the phone rang. Shit! He looked at his watch, saw that he had just a few minutes to spare, and quickly answered it. 'Hello?' he asked, knowing that whoever was on the other line had exactly two seconds to make a case before he hung up on them.

'Steve? Ben Tyson here.'

'Hey, Ben, how are you doing?' he said, looking at the clock again. Ben was a fellow trooper, but was assigned to the Troop B barracks, next county over. They only saw each other for special training sessions or when accidents or some other malfeasance caused them to work together.

'Look, I know you don't have much time, just wanted to let you know that the salesman from Excalibur Arms stopped by. He left off a case of practice rounds for us to pop off at our convenience. I'm going to swing by Troop A later tonight, drop off a box for you. Sound good?'

'Sure, Ben, sounds great.'

'Okay. Take care.'

Steve gathered up his raincoat, walked outside, and made sure both locks in the door were secure. Jill was due home from the elementary school in another hour—she worked there as a secretary to the principal—and one of her little ceremonies was to page him when she and Mike were home safe. Parked in the driveway was his cruiser, with the plate with red letters that marked him as State Police 203. In New Hampshire, all state troopers got to bring their cruisers home, which made some sort of sense—it sure did cut down on the speeders in the neighborhood and on the spring outbreaks of mailbox baseball from the local youths—but sometimes it could be a pain in the ass, especially when the local yokels kept a careful eye on him to make sure he didn't use state resources or state fuel to get milk or bread.

Steve popped open the trunk, draped his raincoat in it, gave a quick look at everything there. Accident gear, flares, flashlights, fire extinguishers, and a special double-locked hard black plastic box, bolted to the floor of the trunk, containing a camouflage jumpsuit, Kevlar helmet, additional body armor, and a scoped Remington .308 rifle.

For besides being a trooper, he—like Ben and several of the other troopers—was a part of the state police's SWAT team.

He slammed the trunk lid down and headed to work his shift, hoping it would be a quiet one.

In Brentwood, New Hampshire, Clay watched as the Ebony Three van rounded the corner, going way too fast for this rural stretch of road, and even over the roar of its engine he could make out the pleasant popping sounds of all four of its tires shredding as it went over the rumble strip. The van slewed to the left and right, tires squealing and smoking, and flew off the side of the road, rotating over to its right side before slamming into a stone wall with a satisfying smash and bang that blew out its windshield and crushed the front end.

Clay got off the tree stump, went over and retrieved the rumble strip, and then trotted up to the shattered van, holding the rumble strip in one hand, shotgun in the other, shaking his head in amazement. 'Jesus,' he whispered to no one in particular. 'Figure you used enough dynamite there, Butch?'

He scrambled over a weed-clogged drainage ditch, past some of the chunks of the windshield, got on his knees and peered in. A head of blue hair looked back at him.

'I'll be damned,' Clay said.

From inside the van came some groaning, and it took him a few seconds to make sense of it. The blue-haired driver was wearing a seatbelt—surprise!—and was curled up, hanging down a bit. His face was scraggly, with bad skin and tufts of hair. His T-shirt was a silkscreen of some rock band Clay never heard of, and it looked like he had on jeans. His companion was female and pudgy, and her hair was jet-black, as was her lipstick, offsetting a cream-white face. She was curled up and had on a similar kind of T-shirt, and no bra, Clay was careful to observe. She was breathing real fast, like a chipmunk frozen still under the gaze of a hungry cat.

'Hey, man,' the boy said. 'Get us the fuck out of here, will ya?'

Clay reached in with the barrel of the shotgun, nudged the boy's chin. 'You two wouldn't be in the employ of Pickering Industries or one of its subsidiaries, would you?'

The girl said, 'Please, mister, my legs hurt.'

Clay nudged the boy again. 'You stole this van, didn't you? Where did you steal it from? Maine? New Hampshire?'

'Fuck you,' the kid said. 'I don't have to say anything except get me a lawyer.'

Clay nudged harder, punctuating each word with another push from the end of the shotgun barrel. 'Where . . . did . . . you . . . steal . . . this . . . van?'

The kid tried to spit, missed. 'And I said, fuck you. I don't talk to cops. And neither does Carrie.'

'Okay, we'll see if you're right,' Clay said, moving the barrel down to the boy's scrawny chest, holding the shotgun firm with both hands, and pulling the trigger. The blast jostled the boy back, and he gurgled and coughed, and blood spatter sprayed over the dashboard, some of it flecking on to Carrie's cheek. Clay pumped the action, retrieved the still warm shell, and put it in his coat pocket.

He moved around to Carrie, who, he was pleased to see, hadn't dissolved into hysterics. Her white face was even whiter. 'Portsmouth,' she said, her voice even, but tears now trickling down her cheeks. 'We stole it in Portsmouth. Please, mister, my legs hurt really bad.'

'What part of Portsmouth?'

'Fleet Street, near Gilley's Lunchstand.'

'Why?'

She winced as she moved. 'It was Tony's idea . . . the keys were still in the ignition. We thought we'd drive out to Fremont, see his brother, maybe hawk some of the electronic stuff in the back.'

'He didn't hot-wire it, did he? Or do anything fancy?'

She shook her head. 'No, no, the keys were in it. Two guys parked it there walked away.'

Now Clay was quite interested. He moved in closer, the shotgun cradled in his arms. 'Really? What did they look like? Young or old?'

'Old . . . I guess. One guy was really old. Gray hair and a beard. The other guy had a beard, too, but he wasn't that old.'

'Where did they go?'

'I don't know, I don't know. They just walked down the street, went around the corner. That's it. Tony and me and a couple of others were watching, waiting. The van looked really hot . . . Tony looked in, saw the keys . . . that's when we took off. Honest. We didn't mean to steal it or nothing. We weren't going to strip it that much.'

Clay said, 'This is very important. Are you sure these men had beards?'

'Yes.'

194

Well, he thought, that tears it. Pickering Industries didn't allow its workers or contractors to have facial hair. And the photo in the information packet he got from Budlong back at Saugus clearly showed Jason Harper had facial hair. The crew of Ebony Three was no longer. This had definitely gone beyond the guess of a weekend drunk or bender. Time to let Woodbury know what was going on.

'Mister . . .' came the plaintive voice.

'Oh,' Clay said. 'I'm sorry. Is there anything else you can tell me about these two men? Did they walk funny? Dress funny? Say anything to each other that you might have heard?'

'No. Mister, are you going to hurt me?'

Clay nodded. 'I'm afraid I am.'

He pulled up the shotgun again, placed the end of the barrel between her young breasts, and pulled the trigger. Having not been belted in like her companion, she flopped around a bit, which was fine. He got up, picked up the rumble strip that had caused these two youths to fall into his lap, and walked out on to the road. There was a smell of gasoline, and he noted a puddle forming about the rear of the van. He went over to his Excursion, carefully replaced his gear, and then returned to the van and lit the gasoline with a match. The van caught fire with a satisfying *whoomph* and he went back to his own vehicle again. He yawned. Earlier today he had been in New York State. Since then, he had gone to Massachusetts, Maine, and New Hampshire, and in a little bit he would be heading back to Massachusetts again.

No matter how you sliced it, he thought, starting up the Excursion, it had been one hell of a full day.

The brakes of the Greyhound bus sighed as the bus slowed to a crawl, just outside of North Station in Boston, as the traffic

195

started backing up. Jason looked over at his brother, knowing his mouth was agape, just like some damn young kid finding out for the first time that Santa Claus did not exist.

'Roy,' he said, keeping his voice low, 'how in hell did you get out?'

'Well, I did, but that's not the important part of the story,' Roy said, staring over the rows of seats, as if he were trying to make the bus go faster. 'The important part is going to be the next twenty-four hours. Look, you still have enough cash, don't you? We're going to need to ride the T or take a cab. How are you set?'

'We're okay,' Jason said. 'I've got enough, but Roy, look, this isn't making sense. Why are we here?'

'To keep an appointment,' Roy said simply. 'That's why.'

'Shit,' Jason said, 'this doesn't make a lick of sense, not at all. When we get to North Station, we are about fifteen, maybe twenty minutes away from the Boston *Globe*, the Boston *Herald*, three major television stations . . . Okay, I can see why you didn't want to go to the *Banner*, it's such a small newspaper, but Roy . . . this is one of the biggest media markets in the country. You can get your story out to the world tonight!'

Roy turned to him, eyes sharp. 'I can, can I?'

'Of course you can.'

'You see stupid tattooed anywhere up there on my forehead?'

Jason felt confused, like the years had all passed away and his older brother was again taking him to task for some damn failing. 'No, of course not, but, Roy, it doesn't make any sense at all to go skulking around and—'

'Okay, smart guy. Let's say we walk into the lobby of the Boston *Globe*, hand in hand, and you say, hey everybody, here's my long-lost brother, shot down over Hanoi thirty years ago. What happens then?'

Jason said, 'Um, well, with my credentials from the *Banner* and such, I'm sure we'll get an interview right away, and we'll talk and the reporter will work on the story and—'

He stopped, just like that. It suddenly came to him, and yes, he did feel stupid, did feel small, did feel like a stumbling younger brother in front of his older, more mature, and much wiser brother, teaching him how to ride a bicycle, bat a ball, and now, how to handle a story that would rival Watergate or the Kennedy assassination. Jason said quickly, 'Okay, you're right. They would need to check into the story, Roy, need to do a background check and—'

'Right,' Roy interrupted. 'Because they're cautious. So you'll be checked, Jason. And so will I. Checked and double-checked. Phone calls will be made, people will be contacted, research will be done. And it will quickly become known in some quarters that I've flown the coop, that I'm free, and when that happens, Jason, thirty-six of the finest and bravest men I have ever known, people you and everybody else here have forgotten about, will be dead. Just like that. Dead. And evidence of their existence will be erased. And you know what? In a couple of days, the story won't check out. The official story will be that I was a deserter, that somebody else flew in my place on that mission, or something like that, and the story will be buried somewhere on page twelve or twenty. And during the time they're checking out the story, guaranteed, you and I and your wife and your boy will be dead. From a house fire, car crash, boating accident. Dead. Because you wanted to do it your way, tramp in nice and polite and announce, here's the story. Well, it's not going to happen. No, sir.'

The bus came into a brightly lit area of parking spots and brick buildings and taxicabs lining up. 'No, sir,' Roy repeated. 'What's going on tonight has been planned for years, Jason. Long, grueling years, and we're going to follow the plan. Tonight.'

Jason hated the feeling of humiliation, but he pressed on. 'What are we doing tonight? Who are we seeing?'

Roy started to get up from the seat as the bus sighed to a halt, and grabbed his gray knapsack. 'Right now, we're going to see a cab driver.'

Patty Harper walked from the office of the Wakefield Motor Inn on Route 16 feeling drained, as if every bit and piece of energy had been skillfully removed from her body. She could barely make out the top of Paul's head in their Volvo, sitting there patiently, waiting for her to return. The sight of her little boy waiting for whatever Mommy was doing, whatever Mommy had planned, made her knees buckle just for a moment. She had never been under any illusions about children, knowing the stresses that would come from dealing with a tired child, a child who wanted *Curious George* read to him for the sixtieth time, a child who would lie down on the floor of a Toys 'R' Us and make a fuss if he didn't get a special toy. But Paul was different. The little fella wasn't perfect, oh, not by a long shot, but he had a little reservoir of patience that Patty was sure was drained in her own young life, growing up in a millworker's household, where the beer budget often came to violent blows with the food budget.

She tapped on the glass of the car and then opened the door. 'Come along, sport. Time to meet our new room.'

Paul yawned, truck still in his hands. 'Will Daddy be coming by?'

She ruffled the hair at the top of his sweet head. 'Not tonight, hon. Maybe tomorrow we'll get to see your father.'

She took a look about the parking lot as she gathered up the duffel bags and Paul's bag of toys and snacks. Route 16, a two-lane highway that went straight up to the White Mountains, was well traveled. Earlier, reserving the room for the night, she had paid in cash, and the clerk—a matronly woman with a talent for asking about a dozen questions just by raising her eyebrows—hadn't made a fuss.

Paranoid, perhaps, but she imagined she could smell the stench of burnt gunpowder and the sourness of fear still on her skin and clothes. And maybe those scents could be washed out easily enough by a visit to the laundromat, but the memories? Sweet God, her perfect little house, shattered—poor Caleb, dead after trying to defend them all, and Jason, ignoring her and their boy, riding off on some strange quest with a man who claimed to be his brother.

'Mommy . . . is this our room?'

'Sure, babe, just hold on.'

She turned the key, opened the door, gave the place a quick inspection. Nothing fancy, not at all. Twin beds, sagging. Industrial-strength green carpet with cigarette burns by the entrance. Small television set, chained to the wall, and a bathroom that was at least clean. She dumped everything on the floor and stretched out on one of the beds, exhaustion suddenly storming at her. She felt that she could sleep for a week.

'Mommy?'

'Yes, love?'

'Can I put the television set on?'

'Sure, just a sec. Lt me close the door.'

She went to the open door, listened to the hum of the cars and trucks going by. Her stomach announced itself and she knew the dinner hour was approaching. There was a diner maybe a half-mile down the road. A nice, crowded, anonymous place for a mom and her boy to have dinner, and then to retreat back here.

And what about tomorrow? a voice demanded.

Tomorrow will have to take care of itself, she thought. She went back to the bed, stretched out again and found the remote, also chained to the nightstand, though the chain wasn't as thick as the one holding the television. 'Tell you what, Paul. I'll turn on the TV and keep it low, and I'll nap for a little while. Then we'll go have dinner.'

Paul asked, 'Can I have hotdogs for dinner?'

Ugh, little meat sausages that held God knows what sweepings from a butchering facility, but she let her normal instinct go away. 'Love, you can have anything you want. And ice cream for dessert, too.'

Forearm across her eyes, she aimed the remote at the television, switched on the power. It clicked right on to a news station, and the perky voice from the woman anchor started, 'And in a late-breaking story, a fire today claimed the life of a—'

Click, as she quickly switched the station. Jesus, more bad news. Wasn't the world full enough of it?

She clicked through the remote until she found Channel 11, the state's PBS station, and she quickly started dozing to the soothing sounds of Big Bird, Bert, and Ernie.

Roy got off the bus, knapsack over his shoulder, followed by his brother, his nerves jangling something awful. There were so many people, so many people jostling and bumping and shoving, the sounds of the engines, the honking horns, the constant hum of a large city in life and in action, and he could hardly remember being so young and hearing so many sounds, seeing so many people. The years in prison had turned down his resistance, made him sensitive to the slightest noise, the tiniest disturbance: the sound of a helicopter, off in the distance; the sound of the booted North Korean guards coming down a hallway; the clatter of pots and dishes as yet another dreary meal was delivered to the mess hall; the coughing of another American pilot, choking as lung cancer slowly killed him, for the GRU had neither the resources, interest, nor time to invest in trying to save him.

He walked quickly, found a concrete post to lean against, to close his eyes, letting the noises and the scents and the moving people just wash over and around him. He took a breath, thought again of that damn Code of Conduct, thought of Article One: 'I am an American fighting man. I serve in the forces which guard my country and our way of life. I am prepared to give my life in their defense.'

He opened his eyes. Yes, I was prepared, he thought, like so many others, to suffer wounds, to suffer captivity, and yes, even to give my life, if a SAM had found its mark. That was my job, that was my destiny, that was my life. He clenched his fists. But not what happened. Not this terrible waste, this terrible betrayal, seeing days and weeks and months and years of one's life frittered away and wasted, until he was here, finally free, with a terrible burden and even worse memories driving him, with aching bones and bad teeth and old wounds, finally back in his home country, broken and barely moving. That was not the fucking deal.

Roy tightened his fists even harder, and then let them go. Time to relax, he thought. Come on, let's get Jason and get going. Grab a taxicab, get on the subway or whatever, and soon enough we can start the next phase.

He looked around. Jason. There was no Jason.

'What the . . .' he said, and then there was a disturbance, over by the bus. Some voices raised, and movement of people. Then Jason came out of the small crowd, walking fast, face bright red. Roy came up to him and said, 'Jason—'

'Roy, shit,' Jason said. 'I just got fucking pickpocketed. Can you believe that? My wallet just got picked. Look, we've got to get a cop, report this and—'

Roy grabbed his brother's upper arm. 'The hell we are. We've got to get going. What did you lose?'

Jason now looked at him, his face scarlet and fearful. 'Roy, hold on.' He started fumbling about in his pockets, moving things about, then said, 'They took my wallet, right when I was getting off the bus. Hold on, I've got . . . Shit, that's just a receipt . . . Oh, Roy, I'm sorry, shit, I'm sorry . . .'

Roy said, 'Money. How much money do you have?'

Jason looked miserable. 'Roy, I don't even have a penny.'

TWELVE

Still in his office in the Channel 21 studios, the AP printout on his desk, Frank Burnett pawed through his Rolodex—he didn't trust having his phone numbers on one of those computer organizers that could often crash and scramble your data—and dialed a Maine number. He was startled when it was picked up on the first ring, and a male voice said, 'Hello?'

He leaned over his desk, hoping against hope. 'Hello, Jason, is that you?'

'No, it's not. Who's calling, please?'

'It's Frank Burnett. I'm a friend of Jason's. Who's this?'

'This is Malcolm Gray. I'm with the Maine State Police. Where are you calling from, Mister Burnett?'

'Manchester, New Hampshire. I saw the news about the fire and I was wondering—'

'I'm sorry, sir, I can't say anything else. Can you please give me a phone number where you can be reached?'

Frank did just that—giving him his private office line that didn't go through the switchboard—and then said, 'Look, can you tell me if Jason and Patty are all right? I saw the news about the fire and—'

'Somebody will be in touch with you later today, sir. Thank you.'

And the state police officer hung up.

Frank did the same, rubbing at his chin, then punched the intercom, got hold of his assistant, Greg Flemming. Greg came in, notebook in hand, and Frank said, 'Remind me again what's going on with our crew in Portsmouth.'

'The mayor's having a press conference at Prescott Park in an hour. Something about state money going to a clean water study for the harbor.'

Frank made a few notes, passed the piece of paper over to his assistant. 'Pull 'em off. I want that crew up in Berwick, Maine, to get something for the six-thirty.'

Greg didn't look happy. 'The mayor won't like it. It's the second time in a row we've stood her up, and this time it's for a story in Maine.'

'Right,' Frank shot back, 'but it's right over the border from New Hampshire, it's a newspaper that burned to the ground and its owners—one of whom is a New Hampshire native— happen to be missing. Give my compliments to the mayor but tell her she's not the fucking news director, I am, and if she's so hard and fast about the rules, we'll start talking about whether we should cover what goes on at the shipyard. Goddamn Maine thinks it belongs to them, don't they?'

His assistant avoided the question, just got out of the office after saying, 'I'll make the call.'

Frank rubbed at his head, remembered his days in college. He and Jason, working together on the college newspaper. Looking back, it sounded so silly and childish—the college newspaper!—but they subscribed to the AP wire service, they had a budget of almost a quarter-million dollars, and dozens of their stories each year—from asbestos in the ceiling tiles of campus buildings to the new college president who spent three hundred dollars on a new toilet seat after refurbishing her official household—were picked up by the news media in the state.

Jason. Even back then he was struggling with a beard, but he was a good writer, a damn good writer who always claimed there was a best-selling book hidden away back there. They both took as many writing courses as they could—news reporting, magazine writing, fiction writing—and there were always late-night writing sessions at the college newspaper office, pounding out their stories on Olympia typewriters (My God, he thought, did that poor company still exist? Did anyone make typewriters anymore?) and using the cheap light-brown copy paper, typing fast because they were young and there were so many stories to tell. Jason had drunk beer, had experimented with the same green leafy vegetative matter that most college students had, but there was always a bit of a shadow on his demeanor, as if when he was having fun, some little ghost inside of him whispered to take notice. Frank had gotten a bit of the story later, after graduation, something about an older brother who had died or something years earlier, but never the full story.

Stories. They had both made a pledge that before they were thirty they would have at least three books published. What was the big deal? From graduation to when you were thirty was about nine years. A book every three years? Piece of cake!

Well, Frank's own three aborted efforts rested in a cardboard box in the bottom of a closet at his home office. And Jason? Well, last time they had met, during some New England Press Association dinner in Boston, they had shared drinks at the hotel bar and he had said, 'I've decided to write nonfiction, Frank. Fiction is just too wispy for me. I like something real, something I can sink my teeth into.'

'Like what?' Frank had asked, working on his second scotch of the evening.

'Like I don't know yet,' Jason had replied. 'Something controversial, something big. Something that will cause people to sit up and take notice.'

Now Frank looked up at the clocks, then over through the glass at the newsroom, where his assistant was on the phone with someone. By the way Greg was leaning back in the chair, staring up at the exposed ceiling with lights and supports, he knew his assistant was listening to the mayor over in Portsmouth scream about having a film crew stolen from her to go up to Maine.

Frank decided it was time to stop brooding. Poor Jason. He had wanted to write something or do something to make people take notice, and he sure as hell had been successful at that.

Steve Josephs was traveling eastbound on Route 125 in Epping in his cruiser, heading for the Troop A barracks, which was a pretty fancy name for a dispatch center and a place to fuel up one's cruiser, when up ahead a black Ford Excursion whipped out in the oncoming lane and blew by him, missing his front fender by yards. 'Shit,' he muttered, slowing down and flipping on the blues. He didn't have radar running, so he didn't have a firm read on how fast the son-of-a-bitch was going, but he was still going to pull the guy over for a serious meeting of the minds. With his blues on, the traffic up ahead pulled over—in both lanes, thank you very much—and he flipped a tight U-turn, his right-side tires crunching a bit in the gravel. When he straightened out, he tromped on the accelerator and the souped-up engine of the Ford Crown Victoria made him feel like he was strapped to the top of the damn space shuttle or something.

It took only a moment or two to reach the black Ford—the few cars behind the Excursion peeling away promptly when he came up their ass—and so, too, did the Ford. The driver politely put on his right-side directional and pulled over, coming to a full stop. Steve pulled up behind him—pulling off to the left to give him a few feet of protection when he finally walked up to the driver for a 'Hello, what the hell do you think you're doing?' talk.

When he stopped, he pulled up the Motorola radio mike and said, 'Dispatch, this is 203, M/V stop on 125 . . . near Percy's Motel.'

'Two-oh-three, copy,' said the dispatcher, sitting not less than a half-mile away.

From inside the cruiser, the sound of the strobes made a *click-click-click* sound that was fairly loud, and he got his campaign hat—or Smokey the Bear hat, depending on your point of view—and stepped out on the roadway. Route 125 was a state highway, two lanes wide, and in this stretch of Epping was lined with stores, service stations, motels, hotels, bait shops, and a couple of general stores. He walked up to the Excursion, which had Connecticut plates. The windows were tinted and that caused the little alarm bells in the back of his head to jangle some. Then the engine on the Excursion switched off and the front window came down and he could make out the driver, both hands on the steering wheel, and he relaxed.

Just a bit.

Hand on his holstered Glock 10-mm, he approached the driver. So far, the driver was doing everything right.

When Clay Goodwin saw that he had just missed a head-on with a New Hampshire State Police trooper on his high-speed run back to Massachusetts, he swore and cursed his heavy foot. Goddamn thing got him good, he thought. He even slowed it down to give the trooper back there a fair chance of catching up with him quickly, and he gave the interior of the Excursion a quick glance to see if anything unusual was in plain view. No, nothing, but there sure as hell were a lot of interesting things back in the rear area, and he started playing through his choices, options, weapon opportunities, as he turned the engine off—keeping the battery power on from the key—powered down the window and put both hands on the steering wheel.

Steve walked up toward the driver's rear, so that any weapon the driver tried to pull on him would mean an awkward attempt to shoot or stab over his left shoulder. But both hands were still on the steering wheel as Steve came up and said, 'License and registration, please.'

'Absolutely, sir,' the man said, as he slowly went to the glove compartment, popped it open, and removed the registration, which was in a clear plastic sleeve. The driver—about ten years older than Steve, with a fleshy face, full mustache, and black stubble for hair—raised himself up a bit to remove his wallet. He took out a driver's license and passed that over as well. Steve glanced at both documents, made sure the guy's hands were back on the steering wheel, and looked down at his hand again. The license was Connecticut. Clay Goodwin. Hartford. The registration showed that the Excursion was registered to a company in Connecticut, as well. J.P. Security Services. The name sounded vaguely familiar.

'Sir,' Goodwin said, his voice pleasant, 'let me right off apologize for passing like that. I misjudged the distance, and I know I came awfully close to you. I sure am sorry.'

'You sure were speeding, too,' Steve said, keeping his trooper's voice low and formal. 'Do you know the speed limit on this road?'

'I'm sure whatever it is I was going over it, officer,' Goodwin said, his head cocked around, hands still on the steering wheel. 'See, the thing is, I'm running late for an important meeting down in Connecticut, and I was hoping I could make up some time. I know that's not a good excuse, but I sure am sorry.'

'Hold on, Mister Goodwin,' Steve said.

The man nodded. 'You bet.'

Back in the cruiser, Steve waited while dispatch ran both the registration and license through the NCIC system. He jotted down the information in his own log book, then looked up at the Excursion. The driver was still there, waiting patiently. Oftentimes drivers who had something to hide, something to worry about, would constantly check their side-view mirror to see what he was doing back here in the cruiser, but not this character. He was sitting there, nice and cool. Routine, Steve thought, as the dispatch radioed him back: all clear, no wants or warrants.

But as he got out of his cruiser and walked back to the Excursion, he recalled his training at the New Hampshire Police Academy, up in Concord. All traffic stops that end with the death of an officer always start out as routine stops. Always. So remember, there's no such thing as a routine traffic stop.

One of his hands held the guy's registration and license. And his other hand was still there, on top of his holstered pistol.

*

As Clay watched the state trooper approach, he suddenly felt quite tired. He had hoped to be back in Boston within an hour, and then to find someplace to coop up and catch some sleep, but this damn traffic stop sure as hell was playing havoc with his schedule. Just as the trooper came up to the window, his pager started vibrating, and he sure was glad that damn thing wasn't making any sounds.

'Here you go,' the trooper said, passing over his paperwork.

'Thanks,' Clay said, putting his license and registration back down on the seat.

The trooper said, 'Sir, I'm letting you go with a warning today, all right? Keep your speed at the limit, and we'll both end the day happy. All right?'

'Yes, sir, no problem,' Clay said.

Then the trooper surprised him. 'Tell me, Mister Goodwin. What exactly does your company do?'

'J.P. Security?' Clay asked. 'We're a security firm, specializing in industrial accounts. Shrinkage problems, background checks, building and perimeter security, some asset protection. The whole nine yards. Hold on, I'll give you my card,' and Clay did just that, reaching back in his wallet, passing over the card. The trooper pocketed it, and Clay looked at his nametag and said, 'Tell you what, Trooper . . . Josephs, if you ever decide to leave law enforcement, give me a call. I'm sure we could find something for you.'

Steve managed a wry smile. 'Tell you what, just keep it slow. All right?'

'Sure,' Clay said, and when the trooper went back to his cruiser, Clay smiled and carefully replaced his license in his wallet, and put his registration back in the glove compartment. There. Wasted eight, maybe ten minutes. Could probably pick that up on the Interstate, once he got there. He looked back at the side-view mirror, checked the traffic. Clear. And the last thing he saw there, as he got back on the road, was the trooper, head bowed, writing something down.

Cops. He loved 'em, loved 'em all, and he was so happy he was able to slip out of this one that he kept right at the speed limit, all the way to the Massachusetts border.

Steve looked up as the Excursion slowly went out into traffic and then headed south. He finished his log and then, surprisingly, he shivered. He couldn't figure out why. The stop was routine. The guy was polite. Had even offered him a job, if you could believe it. And if he had had his radar up and running, no doubt he would have given the guy a ticket, and Steve also had no doubt that Goodwin would have cheerfully taken it without complaint.

So what was the problem?

He suddenly remembered something two years ago, helping a couple of U.S. marshals escort a prisoner through Manchester airport. The prisoner had been a slim guy, wearing glasses, who had a ready smile and was unerringly polite as they moved him through the terminal, his hands and feet both shackled to a chain wrapped around his waist. The prisoner had seemed to be a church deacon on vacation, and as he was taken away, finally, to his flight to D.C., Steve couldn't fathom how this polite young man had taken an illegal modified semiautomatic rifle and had shot up an abortion clinic in Atlanta, killing three and wounding a half-dozen.

That was the problem. Goodwin had seemed polite, cheerful, and remorseful about almost causing an accident, yet there was something there, floating like the faint scent of gunmetal to a hiding deer during hunting season, something there that

211

told Steve he was lucky he had not ended up bleeding to death on the pavement of Route 125 this fine afternoon.

He picked up the radio mike. 'Two-oh-three is clear,' he said, and eased the cruiser back out into traffic. Time to get back to work.

Sloan Woodbury stood in the entranceway by the door to his house in Cambridge. Elaborate Victorian stained glass bordered the frame, and sometimes the afternoon light would blaze through the glass, casting colored shadows on the polished hardwood floor. A phone call had come to him a half-hour ago, surprising him no end, and he had agreed to see his visitor, a man he had not seen in person for years.

He shifted his weight from one foot to the other, feeling again that little taste of humiliation when he had told his visitor the keypad combination that would open up the gate at the sidewalk that led to a brick path, up here to the door. He sighed as he noticed the shadows through the stained glass. He thought about opening the door before the bell was rung, but no, that wouldn't be right. He didn't want to give them the impression, as true as it was, that he had been here cooling his heels, waiting.

After the doorbell rang, he counted off ten seconds to himself, and went forward to open the door. Out there in the Cambridge late afternoon, three men were clustered on the small porch. Two were young and hard-bodied, wearing dark blue suits tailored to carefully conceal whatever weaponry they were carrying. The third man was small and slim, and his skin was the color and consistency of old leather that had been left out in the Oklahoma sun for quite a long time. His thin hair was turning white and was cut in some sort of a crew cut, and the skin about his cheeks and jaw was drawn back, as if he had been dehydrated at an earlier age and had never quite got enough water back.

'Sloan,' he said, his voice still showing the western twang from having grown up at a very early age, wildcatting oil rigs across the Dakota Badlands, before founding an energy, defense, and security service empire that had offices in nearly every continent on the planet. 'You're looking . . . fit.'

Sloan didn't offer a hand, which his visitor didn't seem to mind. 'Hiram. You're looking as mean and pissed-off as always. Care to come in?'

'Sure, sure,' the man said, 'but my fellas will stay out here, if you don't mind. You and me got things to discuss, won't take long, I'm sure.'

Sloan went back inside, followed by Hiram Pickering, who still looked like the kind of guy who, when entering a clean house, always checked his boots to make sure horse or cow shit wasn't stuck in the tread. But Hiram hadn't had to worry about any kind of shit sticking to his feet for a very long time.

Sloan took his visitor to his first-floor library, which was just for show. They both sat down in leather chairs, Sloan sprawling back, letting his aching back lean against the soft comfort, Hiram sitting up straight, his gnarled hands resting on his legs.

'Let's get right to it,' Hiram said.

'All right, let's.'

'I've gotten reports about a situation developing up here,' Hiram said, looking around at the books rising up in shelves more than ten feet tall. 'A situation involving a Nolan-class signal being received last night. Am I right?'

'Yes. Do you want to know more?'

Hiram held up his hand. 'No, I don't. I just want to know if the . . . protocols, such as they are, need to be engaged.'

'Not yet.'

Hiram looked at him sharply. 'Why?'

Because I'm tired of it all, Sloan thought. Aloud he said, 'Because I want more information. Your man Clay Goodwin is up there right now. Once I get solid information, then I'll decide whether to engage the protocols or not.'

Hiram kept his beady little eyes right on him, and Sloan did his best to stare back. The old man said, 'You won't dilly-dally, will you?'

'Not for a second.'

'Good,' Hiram said. 'Because I don't have to tell you what we have coming up in the next few days. Your buddy Filipov is coming to D.C. to wrangle a number of agreements with that boneheaded administration. You know where I stand on this. It's gonna be an important session, one that's gotta go smoothly. A lot of contracts and side deals are riding on this summit going well. So if the protocols need to be engaged, if whatever's going on up here needs to be resolved, then do it.'

Banking, Sloan thought. He really should have followed Father's lead and gone into banking. Then all these agreements and protocols and understandings that continued to haunt him, years later and to this very day, would never have happened. Oh, he probably would have ended up dealing with lunatics like Hiram Pickering sitting over there, looking like a guy who was proud of an ancestor who scalped Native American children for sport, but at least he would have had room to maneuver, to get rid of them.

But not now. His room to maneuver could be measured in millimeters, all because of that damn time . . . and shit, it was like the old bastard was reading his mind when he said, 'This meeting comin' up . . . it's almost as important as the very first one we had with Filipov. Remember?'

Sloan said dryly, 'I doubt that I will ever forget, Hiram.'

A quick nod, like a hawk spotting a meal from miles away. 'That meeting got us where we are now. You did well, and if I may be immodest'—he grinned, a really terrifying sight, the rictus smile of a decades-old corpse—'so did I. We've got new friends over there, friends who need what we have to offer, and who are going to be in the front line, keepin' those Chinese bastards inside their own borders. We can't let this summit get screwed up, Sloan. I'm sure you can see that.'

'You're correct.'

'Fine, then I'm done.' He slapped both hands on his legs, stood up, and headed for the door. Sloan followed, feeling exhausted again. The early morning phone call, the bullshit session at the Copley, and now this. He asked, 'What in hell are you doing in Cambridge anyway? Getting an honorary degree at Harvard?'

That comment caused a barking laugh from Hiram, who made it to the door. 'Hardly. I just like to keep a close eye on things, Sloan. That's how Pickering Industries got to be where it is today. And when I heard about the Nolan-class signal, and when Clay gets authorization from me to access ECHE-LON through one of my security subsidiaries . . . well, I flew right up here to see what's what. And in however long it takes for my boys to bring me back to Logan, I intend to fly right out of this shitty city and get on down to D.C.'

Sloan nodded. 'Sounds like a busy day.'

'Still dealin', still breathin'. It's a good life. Tell you what, I'll give you a ring tonight, see what's up. I'm sure Clay will be in touch with you by then.'

'I'm sure.'

'That is, if you're not out somewhere, raising hell on the

town. Tell me' —Hiram reached out and opened the door—
'you still not married, right?'

Sloan's mouth got just a bit dry. 'No, I'm not.'

Hiram said, 'Guess you haven't found the right girl yet, hunh?'

'You could say that.'

Hiram grinned, showing off yellowed teeth. 'Or the right girl who'd stay for more than just money. You be careful, now.'

Sloan watched the old man saunter out of his house, flanked by his two security guards. While he was tempted to slam the door, he didn't want to give the old bastard any satisfaction, so he closed it gently. Then he went back to the library, opened up the windows, and listened for a bit to the traffic on Brattle Street, letting the late afternoon air clean out whatever scents or smells Hiram Pickering had brought into his home.

Then he went out and made a phone call.

Jason Harper thought his brother was going to collapse, right there and then in the main concourse of North Station. After he told him of the mugging, Roy brought his fists up to his cheeks and dug them in, moaning, 'Noooo, Jason. Please tell me you're wrong.'

Again Jason felt the sickening nausea of having been stripped of his wallet. 'No, I'm sorry, Roy . . . he moved too fast . . . I couldn't do anything.'

Roy dropped his fists, grabbed Jason by both shoulders, and drew him in close. 'You could have fought back!' he hissed. 'You sorry sack of shit, you could have put up a fight instead of letting him get away with— Ah, shit.' He pushed his brother away and spun around to look at the pillar, then put a hand up and leaned against the concrete as if he were trying to gain strength from it. Jason looked around at the crowd, to see whether anyone was watching this little minidrama take place, but nope, everybody was doing their urban best to mind their own business and not get involved.

He still couldn't believe it had happened. Coming off the bus, there was a jostle of bodies against him, and then he felt a tug. That was it. A simple tug and somebody running away, and he had slapped his hand against his empty pants pocket. Wallet gone.

Jason looked at Roy, feeling angry at the words he had just said, and then . . . hell, he just let it go. He reached up and touched his brother's shoulder.

'Roy, I'm sorry. Look. Let me get to a cop or traveler's aid or something, maybe I could bum a few dollars and—'

Roy turned, gently shaking his head, the fearful anger in his voice and his eyes now gone. 'Sorry, that won't do. We can't afford to be delayed or noticed by someone officially. We've got to keep moving.'

'You mean walk?'

Roy nodded, looked around the concourse, at all the people moving about. 'Unless you can sprout wings and fly, yeah, we've got to walk.'

'Where?'

It seemed Roy thought for a moment, and then he said, 'West. We head west. And oh, one more thing.'

Then Roy gently, almost lovingly, touched the side of his brother's face. Jason looked at him and Roy said, 'I didn't mean to yell at you. It's just . . . I'm getting close to doing something I've dreamed about . . . for very long years. I'm sorry.'

'Apology accepted.'

'Okay,' Roy said, finally stepping away from the concrete post. 'Time for a walk.'

Jason touched his own face as he fell in with his brother. He said, 'Going to be a long walk?'

'I'm afraid so.'

'Then why don't we pass the time?'

They reached the glass doors leading outside. 'All right,' Roy said. 'What do you suggest?'

'Tell me a story,' Jason said.

Roy said, 'All right, but stick close. I don't want the whole world to hear what I've got to say.'

THIRTEEN

The Second Decade

Thankfully, on this day, the winds had subsided some, so that the words being spoken out in public, in the exercise yard, could be heard in the farthest ranks. Roy Harper, Captain, U.S. Air Force, tried to stand at attention as best he could on the cold concrete. He was in the second line of POWs, staring forward at the quick ceremony that was taking place. An Air Force major named Reeves—a devout Mormon from Salt Lake City—was reading from the Bible, while another Air Force major—named Colson—stood next to him, holding a small metal container. Harper shivered and was glad that Reeves was speeding up the ceremony, for others that had taken place in the short summer had tended to drone on, since everyone wanted to stay outdoors as much as possible. But not on this day.

Next to him was his cellmate and EWO, Grissom, who whispered to him, 'Ashes to ashes, dust to dust, you'd think Reeves would have the damn thing memorized by now.'

Harper kept his mouth shut, just nodded. Reeves finished off the prayer and closed the Bible. He looked at his country-men and managed a smile. 'I wish I knew my poets better, for there is a poem that someone wrote during a period of great struggle, more than seventy years ago, about a time when British soldiers were being interred in the soil that they had fought to defend, the soil of Flanders in Europe. The poet said something like, wherever the poppies grow, in Flanders field, a part of that soil will always be a part of England.'

Reeves bowed his head for a moment, then pressed on. 'I wish I knew that poem better, or who wrote it. For his words have just as much meaning now as they did all those years ago.'

From far in the rear ranks, there was some murmuring. Harper remembered a time when an assembly of the officers and pilots, no matter the weather, no matter the time, would always be sharp and professional and quiet. But no longer. Things were changing, were changing for the worse, and sometimes that scared him more than the Ivans and their North Korean guards.

Reeves raised his voice. 'For now, we are consecrating this atheist soil, this hated place, with the ashes of an American, a man born and raised in freedom, a man sworn to defend freedom and liberty, a man who volunteered to serve. And as his ashes return to the earth, there will always be a part of this soil, this tortured land, that will remain American.'

With that, Colson handed the round container to Reeves. The Ivans were gracious in passing over the cremated remains of deceased POWs, but they allowed no interment or gravestones. No evidence for whatever visitors may troop through here during the next century. Reeves lifted the container and gauged it well, when the wind came up. He made a tossing motion with the container, and the wind caught the ashes and bits of bone that were once an American aviator, and carried them out and through the wire fencing, out beyond to the snow and the steppes and the endless waste-land, and Harper quickly lost sight of the tiny cloud. Something ached inside of him, and then—without a word from anyone—the line of POWs just fell apart, as they headed back to the buildings at their own speed. Some guys—those mostly in the rear—started laughing and gossiping.

'Well,' Harper heard someone saying, 'at least that poor son-of-a-bitch got outside the compound.'

Harper turned to see who would say such a thing, but the faces of his fellow POWs seemed blank as they walked by. Grissom waited for him, but Harper looked out beyond the fence in vain, to see if he could again see the mortal remains of Captain Harmon Blake, U.S. Navy, the commander of the Sixth Allied POW Wing.

One night Grissom was sewing a pair of socks. He had once helped out his mother, a seamstress back home in Indiana, and now it served him well, especially in doing repairs and such for the other POWs. There was an underground economy—which was fairly humorous, considering they were now residing in the largest command economy in the world—and Grissom earned extra cigarettes or Hershey's candy bars for his efforts. Harper was rereading a year-old issue of *National Geographic* when Grissom casually said, 'I hear that Colonel Miller doesn't want the job.'

Harper lowered the magazine. 'What do you mean, doesn't want the job? He's now the senior-ranking officer.'

'Yeah,' Grissom said, looking intently at a stitch. 'But he still doesn't want to do it. I hear he'll claim he's not physically fit or something.'

'You know the real reason?'

'Of course,' Grissom said, tying off the end of a thread, breaking it with his teeth. 'Thing is, Colonel Miller is married. Has kids. He's afraid that if and when we ever get out of here, he'll get court-martialed for whatever he did as SRO. Which would mean additional prison time, away from his family. The good colonel can't stand the thought of that. So he's going to decline the offer of command.'

Harper put the magazine down on his bunk. 'Doesn't he realize . . . I mean, doesn't he know that—'

'You mean the great unmentionable? That we'll never get out of here? Sure, I'm sure he knows that. But maybe he remembers that story from Herodotus, the old Greek historian. About a thief sentenced to death by the king. The man asks for a reprieve of one year, to teach the king's horse how to sing.'

Harper said, 'Yeah, I remember that. He was asked later why he did that, and he shrugged. He now had a year. Maybe the king would die. Maybe he would die. And maybe, just maybe, in the end, he'd teach the horse how to sing.'

'Unh-hunh,' Grissom said. 'I think Colonel Miller is just waiting, like the rest of us. A small chance, but still a chance. Maybe the GRU will tire of us and send us someplace else. Maybe Reagan will do something so that whoever's in the Kremlin will want to curry favor with that old cowboy and set us free. And maybe, somehow, we'll be discovered by the CIA or the National Security Agency or National Reconnaissance Office.'

Harper said, 'And maybe that horse will sing after all.'

'Maybe,' Grissom said.

The interrogations came in waves. Sometimes weeks or months built up, and then there was a flurry of questions, as if somewhere in the great GRU bureaucracy some sort of effort had to be made to justify the expense and work that went into keeping the American aviators alive.

During one such interrogation, Harper was asked, over and over again, which brands of American beer were popular in which parts of the country. The interrogation should have lasted just a half-hour or so, but he managed to stretch it out for a day, getting two pairs of wool socks, a *Playboy* magazine, and a very cold and congealed Big Mac hamburger for his cooperation. He gave one pair of socks to Grissom, kept the magazine to himself for a week, and that night, both of them ate the hamburger slowly, as cold and greasy as it was, not saying a word, knowing that this piece of free American food had traveled so very far to get into their hands.

So very far. And despite its cold condition, they both decided it was the best thing they had eaten in years and the worst thing the GRU could have done to them—give them a taste of both freedom and home.

Women were brought in occasionally, frightened women who couldn't speak English, whose rough hands and rough faces bespoke a life behind barbed wire as well, somewhere in the great prison system of the Soviet Union. The first time they were brought in, the women sat at one end of the mess hall, the men sat uncomfortably in the other. The women were outnumbered thirty to one, but nothing much happened, except for some crude attempts at communication.

The second time, one, and then another, and yet another American pilot got up, blushing furiously, and went over to the group of women. Chocolate bars and soap were offered. Harper couldn't stand it anymore and left, and went back to his cell, where he was soon joined by Grissom. 'Nice slave trade going on out there, don't you think?'

Harper tried not to think at all, and went into the faded pages of an old *Playboy* magazine, where smooth-skinned and full-bosomed California girls offered themselves in his dreams at night, offered themselves in such a variety of poses and postures. For a while, the Hugh Hefner-supplied fantasy kept him going.

For a while. One day the pressure and desire were just too much and he went to the mess hall. In his pocket he had a bar of French soap. The women were brought in, scared and trembling like the other groups—they were never brought back for a return visit—and in the corner of the mess hall, two of the North Korean guards, now called the 'Kims', Korean slang, to separate them from the Russian 'Ivans', were laughing at the sight. Harper watched them, feeling like a fucking zoo monkey being watched by the overseers, but something else was going on. One North Korean made a motion, a finger cocked to the side of his head, and spoke two words of English: 'Whores. Boom. Whores. Boom.'

The soap now felt like it was lead. No wonder the faces never repeated themselves, for Harper was as sure as that it would snow tomorrow that each Russian or Ukrainian or Estonian woman who was brought here was taken away and shot when her task had been fulfilled, and what little payment they had received would be seized by the North Koreans.

Harper left the mess hall, told Grissom, who told somebody else, who told somebody else, and within a month or so the visits from the women stopped when the pilots refused to step forward anymore.

It was one of the few times during the long years that Harper felt proud of the entire prison population.

*

One morning he was outside, walking around in a circle, remembering the innocent time, years ago, when he was pacing the inside of his cell in North Vietnam. Back then the goal had been to walk across the United States. Go from Maine to the Santa Monica pier. When he had arrived at the Siberian Sheraton, he had tried to do the same thing, to regain the same fantasy trip as before, but it never worked. Reality here was just too sharp to allow anything like a walking fantasy to intrude.

Around him were other prisoners, walking, talking, smoking. Some of them were letting their hair grow long, others had mustaches and beards. The SRO was an Air Force major named Cooper, and he spent most of his time in his own cell, writing out reports about who was a discipline problem, who was cooperating more than he should with the Soviets, and so forth and so on, for the inevitable court-martials he believed were going to occur one day.

Grissom joined in with him and said, 'Morning, Cap.'

'Morning.'

'Where you planning on going after this?'

Harper dug his hands further into his coat, which was starting to fall apart, no matter how many times Grissom had tried to repair it. 'Well, I was figuring on going up to the gate and asking the nice Kim there if I could stroll into town for a Coke, but instead I was thinking of taking a shower.'

Grissom barely moved his head. 'No, I wouldn't do that.'

'Why?'

'Because something bad is going to happen there shortly, that's why.'

Harper turned to him, kept his voice low. 'What the hell is going on?'

Grissom said, 'Just hold on, sir. Just for another minute or so.'

Harper looked over to the main building, and even from outside in the exercise yard he could make out the yell and the sharp scream. A couple of Kims, followed by a uniformed Ivan, suddenly appeared and trotted towards the building. Whistles started blowing, which meant for the prisoners in the yard to freeze, which Harper did. Grissom watched what was going on as well, but Harper had the sudden thought that what was happening was not a surprise to him.

The Kims came back out, escorted by an Ivan, as a truck came grumbling through the gate from the far compound. They were carrying a limp shape, wrapped in a white sheet that was splattered rust red. When the truck came in, their burden was dumped in the rear, and then the guards all went back in. But the all clear to move hadn't occurred, and so the prisoners stood as the afternoon wore on.

Harper said wearily, 'Who got shanked?'

Grissom said, 'Navy guy named Tyler.'

'You know why?'

'Well, there's rumors.'

'Pass on the rumor, then.'

Grissom shifted his weight from one foot to the other. 'Escape committee got themselves dumped into the cooler last week, right?'

'Yeah.'

'Story is, the escape committee was more like a rat committee. Guys volunteered to set themselves up in a way to smoke out the rats in the population. Story is, there were four or five suspects, guys who might have been cooperating with the Ivans. Shit, we've all cooperated with the Ivans, one way or another, but they were looking for guys who'd turn any of us in for a can of Spam.'

'Fake escape attempts?'

Grissom nodded. 'The same. The committee went to each guy with a fake story about what was going to happen next. A plot to grab some of the machine guns from the Kims, take some Ivan hostages. A plot to make a hot-air balloon, if you can believe that. And a suicide plot, really, to burn down the compound, though there's no shit in there to burn.'

'And the escape committee got bounced, right?'

'Right,' Grissom said. 'And they started asking questions about a fire. And the only guy who knew about the fire was Tyler. There you go. We lose a rat and any potential rats out there get a clear message.'

'Hell of a rumor you got there, Tom.'

'Thanks, Cap,' he said.

They both winced as a guard up in one of the towers let loose a burst of fire over the head of one of the POWs who sat down on the ground. The aviator quickly got back up.

'You want to hear one of mine?' Harper asked, eyeing his EWO.

'Sure.'

'Rumor is, my EWO belongs to the escape committee. The real, honest-to-God, secret escape committee. How's that for a rumor?'

'Not bad, Cap,' he said. 'But I've heard better.'

And Grissom turned away, smiling.

An FB-111 pilot named Kendricks, from Mississippi, was reading a two-month-old New York *Times* after lunch in the mess hall when he started laughing after coming across a story in the inside section. Aloud, he said, '"Reagan administration officials said today they were continuing to press Hanoi for a full and complete accounting of the more than two thousand servicemen reported missing in action during the Vietnam

227

war.'" Kendricks crumpled up the paper and said, 'You're pressing the wrong place! You're pressing the wrong place! Don't go to Hanoi, go to Moscow! Go to Moscow! We're here, you stupid shits! We're here! You've forgotten us! All of us! Oh God, Monica, Monica, I miss you so much, so very much, and Tommy and Eric and . . .'

By then he was screaming, his face white, and a number of the men in the mess hall wrestled him to the ground, before the Kims came over to take care of the situation. Kendricks writhed on the floor for a while until he calmed down, with great racking sobs.

Harper got out of there as quickly as he could, and he was joined by an A-7 pilot named Smithson. 'That's a scary thing, seeing Kendricks snap like that. I thought he was one of the strong ones.'

Harper said, 'You know what's even scarier?'

'What's that?'

'I thought he was stronger than me, that's what.'

Discipline problems began, with one, then three, and then several Air Force and Navy officers refusing to take orders any more from Major Cooper, or any other senior-ranking officer. They started growing their hair long, grew mustaches and beards, and after their morning breakfast of oatmeal and cold tea, one of them—a B-52 pilot named Wesson, from Seattle—stood up on the table and said, 'You listen, and listen good! My term went up a month ago, and I'm not re-upping! Screw that! I'm a civilian, and so are these guys behind me! Got it? Civilians!'

A voice from the rear of the mess hall. 'What are you going to do? Ask the Ivans to send you home 'cause you're a hippie now?'

'No,' Wesson shot back. 'But enough of this chickenshit military crap about keeping your quarters in order, appearance tidy, and all that. What did the Air Force ever do for me? They dumped me here in Siberia, and they sure as hell haven't gotten me out. Nobody cares anymore in the States. You've all read the papers and magazines, right? Nobody gives a shit unless it's Memorial Day or Veterans Day, and even then all they think about us is that we're bones somewhere, in a swamp or a rice paddy in Vietnam. Well, screw them, and screw you.'

For a while there was real tension, with some scrapes and fights in the exercise yard and other facilities. Major Cooper wanted extended court-martials, wanted the GRU to assist in disciplining those who no longer considered themselves servicemen, but Harper and others knew that would fracture their world even more. So a smart Navy flier from Pennsylvania came up with a solution from his Amish neighbors: shunning.

So those who considered themselves outside of the chain of command, who considered themselves civilians, sat by themselves in one corner of the mess hall, exercised by themselves in part of the yard, and weren't allowed to join the very few amateur plays and musical productions that some of the more dedicated officers kept going through all the years. Every few months their number would grow, by one or two, and sometimes the silence between the two groups was deafening.

Some nights, Harper and Grissom just drifted off to sleep, and other times they talked and talked and talked the night through, about women and sports and science and history and anything else that came to mind. One night Grissom said in the darkness, 'Your term is coming up, isn't it?'

'Yeah.' Harper stared up in the darkness.

'You figured what you're going to do then?'

'Nope.'

Silence, for a while, and Harper could hear the incessant wind beating against the windows and walls of their prison.

'Well, I'll tell you this, then.'

'What's that?'

'You become a civvie, I'll become a civvie, right behind you. Okay, Cap?'

'Sure,' he said, still looking up into the darkness.

Now his interrogator was Ivan V. He and Grissom often wondered what happened to the earlier Ivans. Were they promoted and transferred somewhere else, with an Order of Lenin pinned to their uniform, or were they thanked for their service to the Motherland, taken downstairs to a basement, and shot in the back of the head? Harper guessed that the GRU folks got promoted; after all, they had to be among the best to be assigned to this particular task. Grissom argued that the opposite was true: they had to be executed after being let in on such a secret, for how else could security be maintained?

The day he met Ivan V for the second time, the GRU officer was late. Harper sat alone in the interrogation room, noting again the white concrete blocks, the metal table, the unmoving chairs. There was a ring of metal set in the top of the table, and he remembered those first interrogations, a long time ago, from the GRU officer who had first called himself Ivan. He folded his hands, looked down at them. Noticed the wrinkles, the rough edges along the fingers, the age spots starting to appear. He thought about Mom and Dad. Were they still alive? Did they still grieve for him? And Jason. Poor young Jason, now growing up as an only child. And Stacy Burke, the young UNH girl he had been dating, all those years back. He could hardly remember her embraces, her kisses, the few sweet times that they had actually made love, her body underneath him, her hands upon his shoulders, encouraging him, whispering to him, squeezing him with those soft and moist muscles.

The door opened up. Ivan V was there, chatting with another GRU officer, accompanied by the usual contingent of guards. Ivan V was rattling along in Russian, and by now Harper and the others had picked up some words, some phrases. Ivan V was apparently leaving in a while, leaving this shitty place with the shitty Americans, and would soon go on holiday with his girlfriend to Yalta, where he intended to fuck her like a bunny. The other GRU officer laughed, and Ivan V strolled into the room carrying a large folder that Harper recognized as his own.

Ivan V sat down. He was tall, well-built, wearing blue jeans and an open-necked flannel shirt that looked like it could have come from L. L. Bean's up in Freeport, Maine. His blond hair was just a bit long, and Harper wondered if the youth revolution that had been well underway in the United States had made its way to the Soviet Union. Ivan opened up the file folder, took out an enormous fountain pen, and said, 'Captain Harper.'

'Yes.'

'You attended an introductory B-52 Stratofortress training course with a certain Air Force Major Glen Roundell. Please tell me everything you know about Major Roundell. His political opinions. His taste in music, drink, women. No detail is too small that it should be left out. Do you understand?'

Harper tightened the grip of his hands, looked at Ivan V, who was staring down at a blank sheet of paper, fountain pen in his hand, waiting expectantly. Harper kept quiet. Ivan V looked up and said, 'Captain Harper. Please answer the question. What do you know about Major Roundell?'

Harper waited, breathed in, breathed out. Listened to the wind out there, doing its incessant work. God, he wanted to go home. That's all. Just go home, away from this place, this place of so much hate and evil and solitude and despair and all bad things.

'Captain Harper. I must insist. What do you know about Major Glen Roundell, of Buffalo, New York?'

Harper took another breath. Looked Ivan V right in the eye.

'Harper, Roy Earl,' he said, keeping his voice even. 'Captain, United States Air Force. Serial number 680912347.'

After a while, Grissom managed to stop the worst of the bleeding from his ears and forehead. Harper blinked some more blood out of his eyes and Grissom said, 'I don't know where you've come from, trying to piss off the Ivans. Eventually they'll get it, you know. Eventually they will.'

'But not tonight,' Harper whispered, suddenly feeling the best he ever had, though so many of his joints and bones ached, and blood was still trickling down his face. 'Not tonight, Tom.'

'Sure,' Grissom said, rewetting the cloth from the sink. 'A tiny victory, but one nonetheless, right?'

'That's right,' he whispered, and then he winced as he sat up on his bunk, swung around so his feet were on the concrete floor. The room seemed to spin around some, and Grissom came back to him, concerned. 'Just what in hell do you think you're doing?'

'I'm off to see Major Cooper, that's where.'

'The hell you are!'

'The hell I'm not, and you're going to help me, Lieutenant. Understood?'

Grissom looked at him for a moment, nodded, and carefully spread out the wet washcloth on the edge of the sink. Taking Harper's arm, he helped him out into the cold corridor, and walked down to the last door on the left. Grissom knocked twice on the door, and a man's voice said, 'Enter!'

The two of them walked into the cell. Major John Cooper, USAF, sat behind a tiny wooden desk, working on some sort of paperwork, near a carefully made bunk. The entire cell was clean and neat, as if this were back in Colorado Springs, at the Air Force Academy, ready for inspection. Cooper's face was red, his eyes exhausted, and his hair had gone completely white. Harper felt a sudden flash of sympathy for the old man, and recalled that phrase 'the burden of command.' Cooper might be old, forgetful, and entirely too focused on keeping track of disciplinary functions, but he was the senior officer, the Man. Harper recalled Part IV of the Code of Conduct for prisoners of war: 'If I am senior, I will take command. If not, I will obey the lawful orders of those appointed over me and will back them up in every way.'

His sympathy was suddenly replaced by shame, remembering all the times he had griped and bitched and moaned about Cooper's leadership, or lack of leadership.

Cooper looked up at them. 'Yes?'

Harper tried to come to some semblance of attention. 'Sir, it's time.'

Cooper was confused. 'What do you mean, it's time?'

'Sir, my term of service is up. I'd like to reenlist in the Air Force.'

Cooper put his pen down and rubbed at his cracked and reddened hands. 'Are you certain?'

'Yes, sir. Quite certain.'

The major stood up. 'Very well, Captain. Raise your right hand.'

Which is what he did, even though it did hurt so much.

FOURTEEN

When the six P.M. newscast ended and they went into broadcasting the national news feed, Frank Burnett found a free phone and made a call to his crew out in Maine. New Hampshire television being New Hampshire television, there was no crew producer; just the correspondent, a young pup named Mike McKenna, and his camerawoman and van driver, Josie Sinclair. The story had been third up on the six P.M. newscast, and Mike had done a decent stand-up in front of the burnt wreckage of the building that had contained the Berwick *Banner* and a couple of other businesses.

Frank said, 'Not bad on the report. What do you have going for the eleven?'

Mike said, 'Ah, there's a couple of things we could look at, Frank, but . . .'

'But what?'

'The Portsmouth mayor was pushing on us coming back and talking to her. I sort of said we'd give it a try, if there was nothing else here for a follow-up.'

'Oh.'

'No offense, Frank, but she can put the clamp down on information coming from all the city departments if she's pissed enough, and trust me, she's pissed enough already.'

Frank said, 'You let me worry about her. You worry about the story. What's going on up there?'

'Cops and fire marshal's crew said it was definitely set, some sort of accelerant was used in the rear. By the time the firefighters got here—it's a volunteer department, so it takes a couple of minutes—most of the first floor was in flames. The assistant editor was found in one of the offices, apparently asphyxiated. And this was off the record but . . . a suicide note, slightly charred, was found near the front door. But the owners, Jason and Patty Harper, they are not around, though the cops aren't officially calling them missing.'

Frank waited for his reporter to continue and, when he didn't, said, 'Okay, what's really going on?'

'Whole thing stinks,' Mike said simply. 'Josie and I stopped at the owners' house for a sec, before heading over to where the newspaper was, and that place is sealed down even tighter than the fire scene. That's where I think the real story is. Back at the house. Something odd is going on over there, and I'd like to go check on it.'

Frank smiled. Mike might be young but he grew up in the West Side of Manchester, a tough place for a young kid and one that had trained him well to look suspiciously at almost everything. He'd go far, and there would be no Hollywood television gossip show in his future.

'Okay,' he said. 'You got it. I want a live shot set up for the eleven P.M. Okay? I'll take care of the mayor. Don't you worry about a thing. Just get a good story. And Mike?'

'Yeah?'

He hesitated for a moment before continuing, because he always wanted every single correspondent to at least think that he was made of stern stuff, with ice water in his veins and

236

a steel pump for a heart, but this was different. 'Mike, I know the family. It's personal. Get everything you can, even if it's off the record or just rumors. And I'll call you at eleven-thirty-five. Okay?'

'Sure, Frank.'

Frank hung up. 'Jason, old man,' he whispered. 'What in hell did you get caught up in?'

There was a light knock at the door. His assistant Greg was there. 'Sorry, Frank,' he said. 'The mayor's on the line, from Portsmouth. I think she's pissed.'

He sighed, reached for the phone. 'Tell me something newsworthy, why don't you.'

Clay Goodwin walked up to the small stairway that led to the open cabin of the Learjet parked on the runway at Lawrence Airport, a small airport for an old mill city that was dead and didn't have the decency to do something about it. Earlier Sloan Woodbury had rung him up, seeking a meet back at his home in Cambridge, but a follow-up phone call from somebody else had detoured him to Lawrence.

Inside the cabin Clay went right, where an old man was sitting on a padded couch, a glass of amber liquor in his wrinkled hand. Clay nodded. 'Mister Pickering.'

'Have a seat, son.'

Clay looked around, saw that the old man's boys weren't visible, knew something heavy was going to be slung his way. Besides working for Mister Pickering's vast holding of companies, he had also done some dark tasks for the old man before, and while Sloan might have his attention, Pickering signed his paycheck.

He took a padded swivel chair across from Pickering, noticed he wasn't offered a drink. It didn't offend him. He knew he was hired help. Pickering cleared his throat. 'This thing you've got going on with Woodbury, you satisfied?'

'No, not at all. It seems like—'

The old man lifted a hand. 'You're not going to tell me any more about that, okay?'

Clay nodded, knowing the cabin was no doubt wired for sight and sound, so if a heavy shitstorm ever did occur, Pickering could rightly claim he had no knowledge of what Clay had been up to. Traditional way of doing business at Pickering Industries.

'All right, I understand,' Clay said.

'Fine. Now look here, you're on the way back to see Woodbury, correct?'

'That's right, sir.'

Pickering took a noisy sip from his glass, sighed in contentment. 'Good. When you get there, I want you to have a quick little chat with that nice man. There are agreements in place, protocols, correct? Do you believe it's time for Mister Woodbury to engage them?'

Clay nodded. 'I may not have all the facts necessary, but it sure does point in that direction, sir.'

Another sip from the glass. 'Fine. When you see him tonight, I want you to find out from him his intentions about the damn thing, all right? If he's gonna engage the protocol tonight, you stand right there by his side and make sure it gets done. Okay? Clear enough?'

'Sure, but I need to make sure I understand. What if he doesn't intend to do it? What then?'

'Well,' Pickering said, his eyes wide in fake astonishment, 'I suppose then it would be your job to encourage him, wouldn't it? Encourage him in every way possible to make sure that he does it.'

'It might get messy.'

Pickering said, 'That's what I pay you for. To make sure things get cleared up.'

Clay nodded, started to get up, and then Pickering's mood changed and he said quietly, 'You know, the world sure has turned itself upside down these last years. When I was your age, startin' out, the big, bad Soviet Union was our sworn enemy. We were locked in a twilight struggle with Russia, or so the story went. And China . . . If they weren't our deep friends, they sure were fine acquaintances. We gave 'em help and assistance, all to piss off the Russians and keep 'em tied down for a while. Now we're only a year away from startin' a whole new century and there ain't no more Soviet Union . . . It's all broken up and the pieces are just lyin' there, waitin' for us and others to pick 'em up and make some decent money. Now it's the Chinese we've got to worry about. If they just stuck to their own rice bowls and minded their own business, we'd all get along. But they're squabblin' among themselves, scaring off their neighbors and Taiwan and such, and now we're helpin' the Russians to piss off the Chinese and keep 'em boxed up. A hell of a thing.'

'Yes, sir.'

Pickering eyed him. 'You read the newspapers, don't you?'

'Most every day.'

'Somethin' important's happenin' in a few days, down in D.C. We sure don't want anything to get in the way of that meeting, understood?'

'Clear,' Clay said.

'Good boy,' Pickering said. 'Now go take care of it.'

'I surely will,' Clay said, and as he made a quick exit of the aircraft, he thought, Sloan Woodbury, there is one heavy hammer right over your head right now, and I'm the one controlling it.

And that thought made him smile all the while he walked back to his Ford Excursion.

In his office on the second floor of his Victorian home, Sloan Woodbury sipped from his after-dinner cognac, sitting at his desk, most of the lights off. Dinner had been good, as always. A lobster fettucine dish with a lovely Bordeaux, followed by a millefeuille and a strong cup of Jamaican Blue coffee. His cook and part-time housekeeper—she came in for lunch and dinner, and no other time—was named Margaret. She was in her late fifties and was rotund and had a dark mustache over her lip. She was one of the most unattractive women he had ever hired, and she was perfect for what he needed: a good cook and house cleaner, who was discreet, and who didn't cause a single flicker of interest in him.

He moved his chair back, looked down at the bottom drawer of the old wooden desk. There, shiny and as out of place as a Porsche race car at the Kentucky Derby, was a round combination lock dial, right in the center of the mahogany. He sighed and put his glass down, and then reached down and undid the lock. The drawer slid out silently and with no problem. Nestled in the center of the drawer, in gray foam padding, was a telephone with no dial or keypad. None was necessary. The phone line was secured, hardened, and was a direct line to a place a long, long way from the gentle breezes and lights of Cambridge. All he had to do was pick up the phone and he would be instantly connected to someone he had never met, someone whose name he did not know, but someone who would instantly do whatever he asked him to do.

The phone was black and shiny. Just pick it up, and it would be done. That's all. Pick it up and a few words would be said, and that's it. And it would be over. And then . . .

Well, then what? That question suddenly terrified him. Then what?

He slid the drawer back, spun the combination lock and picked up his brandy glass. Took a healthy sip and suddenly remembered a cold night, a cold night in a small jet aircraft, flying low over a flat and dreary landscape of snow, snow, and snow . . .

Jason's feet hurt and his mouth tasted of diesel and other exhaust. It would have been nice if Boston had been more of a walking city, but that sure as hell wasn't the case around North Station. The last set of long minutes had been a nightmare landscape of tunnels, bridges, and crowded roads with barely inches of clearance as they walked toward the west. As they walked, he looked longingly at the taxicabs roaring by, knowing that if he had just been a bit more on the ball, a bit more sharp, they could have been in one of those cabs, riding comfortably to wherever the hell Roy wanted to get to.

Now they were on the Boston side of the Charles River. Roy stood there, arms crossed against his chest, looking out to the buildings and lights on the north bank of the river. There were hotels and office buildings and condo complexes, and even here they could make out the buildings of MIT. Beyond, too, were the buildings of Harvard and other colleges in Cambridge, and under a street lamp near the Boston Museum of Science, they rested. Jason looked again at his brother, noticed the gauntness of his features, the sharp nose, the unsparing eyes. Roy's story had been incredible, fantastic, and

Jason wished again he had some way of taking notes, for this was a story for the ages. Roy reminded him of something, something that nudged his memory, and then it came to him. He had recalled reading stories of knights in the Middle Ages, of how they had ridden off to the Crusades, and how they would often disappear, thought to be dead. Then they would return unexpectedly, old and bent, filled with wild tales of terror and hauntings, of great battles and conflicts, of meeting demons and witches and warlocks.

Roy reminded him of that, of a warrior gone far afield and returning with years of horrid memories, memories that would haunt anyone who heard them.

Roy started speaking, and Jason had to come close to hear him. 'There it is, Jason, the place that sent so many of us off to Vietnam, to bleed and die and disappear, all for nothing.'

Jason looked at the peaceful city lights and said, 'Don't you mean the Pentagon?'

'Hah,' Roy said. 'No, I certainly don't mean the Pentagon. Oh, the generals and planners there have their responsibility, their guilt for what happened. But they were merely the tool. The ones that sent us over there—they came from this place, and places like it in Stanford, Yale, Princeton. The best and the brightest, am I correct? Sure. They went to Washington filled with ideas, with plans, with the certainty that they could do anything and everything. So they did. They killed about fifty-eight thousand of us, and millions of the Vietnamese. And the bastards who did it all . . . they retired to write books, lecture, and sometimes even stay within the government. And they and their own . . . the blessed elite of this country, they didn't pay a price. Not one penny.'

Roy raised an arm, pointed across the river. 'Lookee there,

brother. Just a little ways out there is Harvard University. You want to know how many students there fought in Vietnam and died? Here. I'll tell you. Nineteen.' Roy shook his head. 'Nineteen.'

Quickly, he spun around and pointed back to where they'd come from, toward the confusing mass of buildings and roadways and parks and elevated highways. 'Back there, over beyond that mess, is South Boston. Old Southie. Working-class, beer-drinking, poor and proud neighborhood. They sacrificed nearly thirty. Tells you something, doesn't it. So don't go on about the Pentagon and the evil generals, Jason. The evil came from someplace else.'

'But the generals and admirals have some responsibility,' Jason said.

'Sure,' his brother replied. 'They should have never forgotten us. They should have never betrayed us.'

'And they should have never done it in the first place,' Jason replied.

Roy started walking. 'What makes you think they had a choice?'

Jason called out after his brother: 'The generals at the Pentagon had a choice! They could have refused the orders, retired, quit . . . done anything to stop the war.'

Roy turned back. 'Duty is an onerous thing, brother. Even when you want to quit, want to lie down, want to give it all up, that old four-letter word hauls you up on your ass and gets you going. Come along, we're getting closer. And once we're there, all will be revealed. I promise.'

Jason hesitated for just a moment, and then started moving. And as he resumed walking with his brother, he remembered something else about those knights from the Middle Ages: oftentimes they would go on foolish quests,

quests for the Holy Grail or pieces of the True Cross, quests that invariably ended in death.

An hour late, Trooper Steve Josephs drove into the driveway of his house, tired yet still a bit jumpy from the shift he had just completed. As he got out of the front of the cruiser, he saw a cardboard box sitting on the seat, with a bright red logo showing a sword stuck in a stone. Excalibur Arms, and he remembered picking up the test ammunition from fellow trooper and SWAT team member Ben Tyson, at the Troop A barracks. Sure, and just as he got to the barracks, all hell had broken loose over in Brentwood. He reached in and grabbed the box of test ammunition and stuck it in his pocket. Maybe this weekend he could try it out. The salesman had been quite enthusiastic about its properties, the special casing around the paraffin cartridge, its relatively low muzzle velocity. Steve yawned and walked as quietly as he could, not wanting to wake up Jill or Mike or any of the neighbors.

He unlocked the front door and walked slowly into the foyer of his house then stopped, just enjoying the quiet, the smell of his home. Steve smiled at himself in slight disgust as he hung up his raincoat in the closet—the promised rains had never come—and recalled how he had wished his shift was going to be an easy one. Well, in some ways it had been easy. For most of the last six hours he had been on traffic duty, directing traffic away from a certain stretch of road on Brentwood, about six or eight miles away. But that had been long duty, seeing the lights in the distance as detectives from the state police's Major Crimes Unit tried to decipher what in hell had happened to two persons inside a van that had crashed and incinerated on a country road.

The first unit in had been a Brentwood cop, who had called

in backup—and in these small towns, backup meant cruisers from nearby towns like Exeter and Kingston and Raymond— and then the state police. The van had been on its side, a burnt-out shell, with two bodies up forward. The intensity of the heat had made it a problem deciphering whether they were male or female. At first it had looked like a horrible accident, but then one of the cops noticed all the shredded rubber, stretching back to a point in the road. It looked like the van had crashed because of something in the road that had caused all four tires to come apart.

An accident? Doubtful. On purpose, then? Probably. But why?

The van had Massachusetts plates, registered to an electronics supplies firm in Boston. Phone calls to the company went straight to a voicemail system, and the Boston Police Department—responding in their usual glacial manner when assisting their brethren up north—had still not gotten to the place to see if somebody could get rousted out to check whether a van had been stolen or if two of their employees were missing. Any other accident scene like this that looked suspicious, he and other responding troopers would have assisted in a canvass of the neighborhood, to see if anybody had heard or seen anything. But this particular neighborhood was inhabited by chipmunks, squirrels, and three Morgan horses, about a hundred yards away. And they weren't talking.

He closed the closet door, went back to the table with the collection of photos, touched them all briefly. 'Made it back,' he whispered, and then he saw the note. It was a small piece of paper, in his wife's handwriting, and he held it up to the hallway lamp. 'Welcome home,' it said, in her familiar handwriting. 'Mike's fast asleep, but I don't want to be when you come in. Love, J.'

Steve smiled and carefully folded the note up, then went upstairs, taking off his jacket as he went to their small bedroom. Before going into the bedroom, he took off his belt and boots and other gear, and then went inside. The bedroom closet was slightly ajar and he smiled again. Jill had been busy. Inside he hung up the gear, put his service pistol in the lockbox on the top shelf, put the box of test ammo in his SWAT utility uniform, and then draped his clothes over a chair. After gently closing the door he walked across to the bed, where he could smell the delightful scent that Jill used. The television set was on mute and Jay Leno was interviewing some movie star, and he clicked it off before crawling into bed. Jill sighed and rolled over and he went up to her, gently kissing the top of her forehead. 'Mmmm,' she whispered. 'Do hurry up, babe, my husband's due home any second.'

He kissed her lips and murmured against her, 'But I do love to drag it out as much as I can.'

She giggled and threw her arms around his shoulders, pulled him down. She kissed him again and her voice was a bit louder. 'Okay shift?'

He stroked her side, cheerfully noting a lack of a nightgown, T-shirt, or any other piece of clothing. 'Okay shift,' he said. 'Bad van accident, two got themselves killed. MCU's there, but I got to come home. Lucky, lucky me.'

Jill kissed him again. 'Ain't that the truth.'

'And you?'

'Mmmm,' she said. 'Quiet. Mike was running a bit of fever but it went down 'fore I put him to bed. He was quite the question man tonight.'

'Really? About what?'

Her hands tightened some on his shoulders. 'Oh, he was

246

asking about your dad, Steve. His "other grandpa" as he said. Just asking lots of questions. I told him he should talk to you in the morning. But I said what I could.'

'Which was what?'

'That he was a brave man, just like Daddy, and one day he went off to fight some bad men, and he never came back. And that it was sad, but Daddy still loved him and missed him a lot.'

'Unh-hunh,' he said, thinking again about that long-ago, teasing memory of whiskers scraping against him. 'Anything else?'

Another longer, deeper kiss from Jill. 'I told him that his grandpa was a big man, just like Daddy.'

'You did, did you?' he asked, rolling on top of her. She giggled and squeezed him tight, and whispered in his ear, 'And Daddy's growing bigger by the second, I'm pleased to see.'

Patty Harper woke up with a start, thinking somebody had called out her name. She rubbed at her eyes, looked about her, feeling queasy at all the memories that were now storming their way back into her mind. Little dumpy motel room and there was Paul, curled up in a ball, gently snoring through a runny nose that she really should wipe, but she didn't want to wake the little fella.

Jesus, so what had woken her up?

She glanced at the television set, still on; she must have fallen asleep with it on, half watching a UNH hockey game that went into overtime and—

Oh Jesus!

She stumbled out of the bed, almost fell on the floor when the sheets and blankets wrapped around her legs, and got over to the television and toggled up the sound, looking at what she was seeing, not believing in a million years what was there, what existed on that tiny screen with the color tint a bit off, everything looking a bit green, but oh God, there it was, there it was . . .

Their office building. Their business. Their dreams and hopes and all they had worked for, all those years . . .

A charred pile of rubble. She pushed the sound up and the voiceover said: 'Schweitzer, twenty-nine, was believed to have died of smoke inhalation. The Maine State Fire Marshal's Office is still investigating. Reporting from Berwick, Maine, this is Mike McKenna.'

She turned the sound back down, thinking dimly of Paul. Can't wake him up. Not yet. Not yet. She touched the screen, as the newscast went into a mattress commercial, tears coming up again. Jack. Poor Jack. Dead. Oh God, Jack . . . He with the cranky attitude that the only reporting worth doing was the kind that pissed people off. Who hated having his copy edited but usually came around about an hour later to agree that yes, it certainly did need to be tightened up. Who had started at a daily newspaper in Dover, New Hampshire, and given it up when he realized his output was being measured in column inches, and it was the length of the story that meant you were doing a good job, not the story itself.

Jack Schweitzer. Rock climber. In love with a geology grad student from UNH. Tried and failed a half-dozen times to learn how to play the guitar . . .

She touched the screen again, felt the coldness of the glass, and then stood up. That's it, she thought. Time to do the right thing, and that didn't mean hiding out in a cheap motel while her husband and his brother were out doing God knows what. First their house was broken into, their lives threatened, poor Caleb executed, and now this . . . Jesus, now this. Jack dead, the Berwick *Banner* and the office building burned down. She had no idea who had done it, but she had a good guess who was ultimately responsible: that shitass brother of Jason's, popping up after thirty years and destroying everything he touched or saw. Patty wiped at her eyes and went over to the nightstand.

No phone.

Of course. Place this small couldn't afford a telephone for each room. Which meant that she had to find a pay phone, and fast, for she intended to call the Berwick Police, the Maine State Police, and even the friggin' governor himself, for she wasn't playing the good wife anymore, she wasn't playing at hide and seek. Time to pull things out into the open, and right now.

She wiped at her eyes again and bent down over the bed. 'Paul, hon, it's time to wake up.'

Roy kept up the pace, the knapsack bouncing comfortably off his shoulder, trying to hide the uneasiness that was rippling through him with every step. Soon enough the next phase would click in, and he wondered if Jason would stick by him. If so, great. That increased the chances of success. If not, well, if things went to the shits and Jason survived, at least the story would get out eventually. He had a flash of memory, of reading about the Vietnam Memorial in Washington. Besides listing the names of the dead, the Wall also listed the MIAs as well, and that caused some great laughter back at the compound, when the story had come out. Their names, the names of MIAs who were still prisoners and still alive, were listed on the Wall. And each time a set of remains had been recovered, a little cross had been cut into the stone, next to the name, to mark another MIA identified.

Well, he thought, if nothing else comes out of this, at least some stonecutters in D.C. might be busy in the next few weeks.

He turned and looked back at the lights of Boston, seeing, too, the lights of aircraft coming in to Logan Airport. He tried to remember again that special ecstasy that came from being up forward in the cockpit of a Stratofortress, the old BUFF (bowdlerized in Air Force PR to stand for Big Ugly Fat Fellow, but everybody knew that the last word stood for something much more obscene), and feeling the power, the surge, as the eight Pratt & Whitney jet engines started propelling the large, impossibly heavy shape down the runway. Feeling the vibration in your arms and legs, as the B-52—fully fueled and full of ordinance—struggled to come off the deck and climb into the air. My God, had he ever been that young, that strong, that confident? After all those years in prison, sometimes he could imagine, late at night, just before falling asleep, that it was all a terrible nightmare, a terrible dream that he had once flown bombers, had been trained to kill people from a distance, without ever seeing their faces.

Not like those Russian bastards back at Jason's home. That had been close and personal, and he was still delighted that the memory of killing them both hadn't disturbed him a bit.

He looked back, at his younger brother, trudging along with him, and a sudden surge of sympathy and love just rock-eted through him. Through the years of thought and planning and replanning, the one wild card had been his brother. The arguments had gone on, late into the night, as the plans were made, but with the odds so stacked against them, the only reasonable alternative was to rely on one Jason Harper. He had come around, he had stuck with him, and Roy felt the love he had for this man replaced almost instantly with a sour melancholy, of all the years missed, of seeing him grow old, go from a boy to a man, and as he was thinking this through, his steps took him off the bridge and on to land that marked the north side of the Charles River.

Jason came up next to him, breathing hard, looking exhausted. Roy reached over, squeezed his hand. 'Making progress,' he said. 'And now I'm going to tell you some more. And it's going to get real interesting.'

FIFTEEN

The Last Decade

It started off small at first. Little things. Like no new toothbrushes for months. The quality of the food starting to decline, going from adequate to awful, with lots of meals of soup and stews and stale bread. The lights flickering off and on, and the creaky heating system sometimes failing for weeks at a time. Then for a couple of months, no newspapers, no magazines, no visits from any of the Ivans. Just the bad food, poor laundry, and the rotation of the impassive Kims. There was speculation on what was going on, from bad economic times all over the Soviet Union, finally coming home to roost in this remote shithole, to thinking that somewhere, in the great bureaucracy that was the GRU, maybe they had been forgotten.

It was March when the word came out, when one of the Ivans came over and dropped off a bundle of old newspapers and magazines. The pages were read and reread, with fascination that the story might be true, with horror that it might be an elaborate hoax, designed by the Ivans for some cruel purpose. Harper wasn't sure what the truth was, only that he agreed with everyone that the story was simply fantastic. The

Soviet Union was no longer. Their enemy for almost a half-century was gone, and amazingly, unbelievably so, the Communist Party had been outlawed. The photographs were even more amazing, showing a coup attempt that had happened months earlier, against Gorbachev, tanks rolling through the streets of Moscow, statues of Lenin and Stalin being toppled. A hoax, perhaps . . . but those photos seemed so real, so damn real.

The talking and laughing had gone on all day in the mess hall, and even the civvies—or the traitors, as some called them—joined in the celebration. The Soviet Union was dead. It had to be good news. Had to. And for a while, the shunning between the aviators and the civvies collapsed, as they started thinking the impossible. Maybe, just maybe, they would be going home.

But Harper wouldn't join in the talking, the speculation, the dreams. He sat there, carefully looking through each newspaper and magazine, taking it all in.

That evening, in their cell, Grissom said, 'You didn't seem particularly happy today, Cap.'

'What's there to be happy about?' Harper said, curled over on his side, shivering slightly.

Grissom was quiet for a while, and Harper wondered if he would have to repeat what he had just said, when his EWO said slowly, 'If you didn't notice today, Cap, there was a bit of good news that got dumped in our lap.'

'Really? And how does the Soviet Union breaking up mean good news?'

'Oh, come on, Cap. No more Soviet Union? No more missiles aimed at New York or Chicago or Seattle? No more funding of terrorist groups. You don't think that's good news?'

Harper tried tucking in the blanket even more firmly under

his chin. 'Yeah, so what. That might be good news for the rest of the world, but how does it help us? Hunh?'

'It can help us a lot. I mean . . .' Grissom's words trailed off.

'Sure. Think it through. We've been held prisoners of the Soviet Union all these years. Then, one day, no more Soviet Union. Hey, I guess that means the cell doors will magically open up, right? Wrong. There're still agencies and organizations that know about us, and you can bet the people in charge have suddenly resigned from the Communist Party and are now catching up on their Jefferson and Madison. But we're still here. We're history. We're embarrassments. And sometimes embarrassments get tossed away.'

Harper rolled over, tried not to let his feet dislodge the blanket. 'Maybe the world will be safer without the Soviet Union. Probably. But fuck the world. I'm here and so are you and everybody else, and it was a lot safer for us with a Soviet Union. That's all I've got to say.'

And though Harper waited for it, Grissom said nothing else the rest of the long night.

Over the years, news would come in about family members and loved ones, and always purely by accident. One pilot saw a younger brother become a congressman, and he got some teasing about that, about whether his influential brother could actually do something or find some way to get them out. Another pilot saw that his own son—his own son!—had joined up and had gotten the Air Force Medal of Valor, for missions over Iraq during the Gulf War. That pilot had a silly-ass grin on his face for weeks. And Harper was shocked one day to read a letter to the editor in the New York Times, from one Jason Harper of York, Maine, chastising a Times columnist for saying something silly about New England politics. He had torn that piece of paper out and had read and reread those words, savoring each syllable, feeling that in a way Jason had actually been writing to him, to show him that he had gotten out of school and seemed to be doing all right.

But the one that really struck home was another B-52 pilot from Alabama, Greer, who saw a small article about his wife in the back pages of the Washington *Post*. She had recently been named director of Families United, an advocacy group for families of those missing in action during the Vietnam War. All these years later, she was still going to Capitol Hill, lecturing and writing opinion columns for newspapers, trying to move the bureaucracy to do something to get a clear and final accounting of every MIA from Vietnam.

Greer saw the article and sat for a long time in the mess hall, just touching the small piece of paper with the article and a photo of his wife standing before a podium at the National Press Club. And to everyone who came by, he said the same thing: 'Good old Doris. Keepin' the faith. Good old Doris. Keepin' the faith.'

One of the very worst days happened during a cold winter morning, when those in the exercise yard—including Harper and Grissom—looked up as the sound of engines approached them. They stood still, watching the line of trucks come up the short roadway between the prison and the administrative compound. As the trucks came closer, the words started rippling through the crowd. This is it. A deal's been reached. We're going home. Guys, Jesus, we're going home! Other POWs started coming out of the compound, active duty and civvies both, and there was laughing and clapping, and Harper found he was squeezing Grissom's hand. Grissom was sobbing, no tears but he was sobbing, saying, 'God, Cap, this could be it. Mom and Dad . . . all these years . . . my sisters . . . oh Jesus, Cap, please let it be true . . . please let it be true . . .'

They clustered around the trucks, which made a wide circle into the compound, and then the Americans moved back, as the canvas flaps at the rear of the trucks flew open. Each truck had two or three Kims inside it, Kims with AK-47s slung over their backs, and they leapt out to the hard concrete. There were uniformed GRUs there as well, speaking in Korean, holding out pistols, and Grissom said, 'Cap, this is bad.'

A thought came to Harper as he watched the armed men line up. 'It's Malmédy all over again.'

'What?'

'Malmédy. I'm sorry, Tom, it's when the SS soldiers shot some American soldiers they captured during the Battle of the Bulge. I guess—'

But his guess was wrong. The GRU and the Kims went through the crowd, separating out the aviators and the civvies, the ones who'd stayed in the service and those who had abandoned it. There was a low groan, as though the entire assembly could not believe what was going on, and any shouts or yells or signs of displeasure were met by a rifle butt to the gut or to the chin. Soon enough, there were two groups of Americans in the exercise yard, and the civvies were directed to climb into the rear of the trucks. The servicemen surged forward, but the Kims were there, bayonets at the end of their automatic rifles. The civvies helped each other up into the rear of the trucks, their faces set under the beards and long hair and mustaches. Harper looked at them and could not believe the dark hate that was coursing through him. He thought about grabbing an automatic rifle from one of the Kims and hosing down those lucky, traitorous bastards, but he knew it would be futile.

The rifles were chained to their waists and there were too many of the Kims. He would be shot down in an instant.

'Oh, shit, Cap, they're letting them go . . . they're letting them go,' Grissom said, voice quavering.

There were shouts from the aviators being left behind. A couple shouted, 'Traitors!' but there were others who yelled, 'Remember us!'

'Don't forget us!'

'Call my wife!'

'Call my dad!'

'Tell them we're alive!'

Some of the civvies were sobbing, hands reaching out, begging the Kims or the GRU officers to let others come along, but the line of armed North Koreans stayed firm. More shouts and pleas, and then the engines of the trucks started up and they grumbled their way back to the gate. There was another surge as the aviators tried to follow the trucks, but there were too many Kims. Many of the civvies could not look back at their former comrades, but there were a few who were trying to yell back as well, telling the POWs that they wouldn't be forgotten, that they would be set free too.

But Harper remembered one civvie all too well. The first one to decline reenlistment, the one who had started it all, Wesson. He sat at the rear of one of the trucks, a triumphant grin on his face, holding up the middle fingers of both of his hands to the watching crowd.

Later that night, Harper stood alone, blanket over his shoulders, looking out to the dim lights of the administrative compound. He shivered every time the wind shifted and came over him, causing snow to drift across his feet. He looked up at the night sky, barely made out a star or two. Even after all these years they still weren't certain which part of the Soviet empire—okay, the Russian Federation or whatever the hell they were calling it this week—they were being held in. He looked again at the warning wire, about two feet tall, running on both sides in front of him. So easy to step over and walk the handful of paces to the first electrified fence. A quick grasp and a jolt of pain—probably a hell of a lot less pain than he had put up with from the various Ivans and from Frogger back in North Vietnam, and then . . .

Well, he'd be gone from this place, that's for sure.

'Hey, Cap,' came a voice. 'What are you doing?'

'Thinking.'

'About what?'

Grissom came up next to him, little steam clouds forming about his mouth. Like Harper, he also had a blanket over his shoulders. Harper looked to his EWO and said, 'I've just been watching the compound over there, ever since the civvies left.'

'Unh-hunh.'

'How many went over in the trucks?'

'Twenty-eight.'

'Okay. What then?'

Grissom said, 'What do you mean?'

He gestured to the compound. 'That's where we arrived. We know what kind of place is over there. Runway, aircraft hangar, barracks for the Kims and the Ivans, a few support buildings. That's it. You bring the civvies over there . . . you'd think they'd be going somewhere, right?'

'Yeah.'

Harper said, 'I've been here all afternoon, right up until now. Lamontagne, he went back inside and got me my blanket. There's been no aircraft leaving that compound. Not a one. And they've been over there almost twelve hours.'

'Hell, Cap, this is Russia. Things are late, things break down, all the time. Doesn't mean anything.'

'Yeah, but does it make sense to split up your guard force, to watch two separate groups? I don't think so.'

Grissom stamped his feet. 'What are you driving at, Cap?'

'Like I said, I've been here ever since they left. And about the only thing I've noticed going on over there is a chimney, working overtime, over there on the west side of the compound. Smoke going up in the air all afternoon long. Look, you can still make out the sparks.'

'Cap . . .'

'Yeah, Tom. The chimney for their little crematorium. It's been working overtime, ever since the civvies went over there. That's what I'm saying.'

'The bastards,' Grissom whispered.

'Yeah. Maybe they got tired of dealing with the civvies. Maybe they got pressure to cut expenses and decided to get rid of those who weren't military any more. Who knows. Lots of questions.'

Harper coughed, moved the blanket around. 'But it does tell me one thing, though. I'm pretty sure the Sixth Allied POW Wing is going to be maintaining a one hundred percent reenlistment rate, at least for the near future.'

Grissom stood with him for a while, as a few more sparks could be seen traveling up into the night sky. Then he cleared his throat and said, 'Speaking about the future, Cap . . .'

'Yeah. What's on your mind?'

Grissom spoke slowly, like a boy on his first date, slowly exploring the buttons on his companion's blouse. 'It's like this, Cap. With the civvies having left and all, well, there's plenty of empty cells back there . . . Some guys who've been bunking, well, they're seeing this as an opportunity to have their own space . . . and I'm in no rush or anything, but if you wanted to do something, well, I mean . . . I could understand, it's been a long time and . . .'

In the cold night, Harper smiled. 'Relax, Tom. If you're good, I'm good. I have no intentions of moving.'

Grissom seemed relieved. 'Thanks. Me neither.'

And they stayed out there in the yard in silence, until the whistle signaled that it was time to return to their cells.

The interrogations started up again, and Harper stared at his questioner—Ivan VII—with disbelief.

'What the hell is the point?' Harper asked. 'I mean, please tell me. What the hell is the point?'

This Ivan was portly, with black hair teased up forward in some sort of pompadour. He had on blue jeans and a heavy white Irish sweater. 'The point is, Captain Harper, that while the Soviet Union is no longer, your home country is very much alive and vigorous. You are strutting across the world stage, bumbling here and there, pretending we don't matter, we don't exist. There's even talk of expanding NATO further eastward, so those ungrateful Poles and Hungarians . . . I lost two uncles fighting those Nazi bastards during the war so the stores in Warsaw and Budapest can sell Sonys . . . and if you think Mother Russia is going to sit back and do nothing, well, you're wrong.'

'But there's no longer a cold war!'

Ivan frowned. 'Says who, as you'd say? We're in a time of peace, of reconstruction, of trying to stay alive. And our armed forces are still in need of intelligence, are still in need of knowing how to confront the almighty Uncle Sam. So. Shall we begin?'

Harper rubbed his hand across his face. 'Damn you, it's been almost thirty years.'

Ivan's face brightened. 'Yes, it has, hasn't it? And your Air Force is still flying your B-52 bomber, even now. So. Let's begin by discussing the area around your base called Nellis . . .'

The interrogations continued. So did the suicides, which sometimes occurred in clusters. The food improved a bit, as did the clothing. Sometimes the GRU would bring in a television with a VCR, which allowed movies to be shown. But when the movies were finished, the televisions were quickly removed. The musicals, the plays, the lectures, all that finally faded away. Life now consisted of reading, talking, watching television, doing some exercise, and sometimes drifting through an interrogation. Those stir crazy stayed at a constant level—much to everyone's surprise—but the suicides and deaths from no medical care continued to whittle down the number of POWs, including their SRO, Major Cooper, who died of an apparent heart attack.

Then, one day, when the number of POWs was at forty, the trucks returned.

No illusions.

That was the byword.

No illusions. Everyone knew the probable fate of the civvies taken away two years earlier.

Their current senior reporting officer—Navy Commander Walter Gibson, from Boston—lined them up and shook everyone's hand before they got on the trucks. Harper found that tears were just rolling down his cheeks, as he looked at the surviving members of the Sixth Allied POW Wing. Gibson stood in front of them, saluted, and they all saluted in return. This time, for whatever reason, the Kims and the Ivans were patient.

'Gentlemen,' Gibson said, 'it's been a privilege serving with you.'

They started going into the trucks, one by one, and Harper made a point of helping Grissom up so that he sat next to him. Two Kims were in the truck with them, and all thoughts of grabbing a weapon and making a last stand just drifted away. He took a breath. Soon it would be over. However it ended, it would be over. The man on the other side, named Hanks, grabbed his hand, and Harper in turn grabbed Grissom's hand. Someone started reciting the Lord's Prayer, and others joined in. The truck ride was mercifully brief, and Harper looked out the rear, surprised at last to see the prison from the outside. The road was bumpy and pockmarked, and the trucks went into the hangar, the same hangar where they had first landed in this accursed place, nearly thirty years earlier. They got out and then the trucks left, leaving behind the stench of poorly made diesel, and more Kims closed the hangar doors. The other doors were locked. Two darkened windows looked down on the open hangar floor.

They were alone.

Commander Gibson looked around and said, 'If we're going to wait for whatever's waiting for us, then we're going to wait as military men. Fall in.'

They lined up on the concrete floor, standing still. Harper was in the last row and looked around, taking it all in. Nearby was one of the darkened windows, and then a light came on from the other side. He stared at the window and then moved his head, so he was looking from out of the corner of his eye. There was movement behind the window, and he could make out figures in there. Then the light inside grew brighter. The forms took shape. Harper almost laughed. The glass looked like it was supposed to be one-way, but in the fine tradition of the old Soviet economy, it wasn't working so well. There were two men, well fed and well clothed. He could easily make out their faces. They looked in, and then it seemed an argument was taking place. But he could not make out a single word. The talking seemed to go on for a while, and then the men left the room and the light went off.

The minutes turned into hours. Long hours. Permission was asked and granted by some to sit on the floor, but Commander Gibson gently urged them back on their feet when they felt better.

Then the door opened up. Four Kims came out, followed by Ivan VII. He was in dress uniform and had a clipboard in his hand. 'Francis, Robert L. Please come forward.'

Some murmurs and whispers, and Lt. Robert L. Francis, USAF, went forward and through the door, which was closed behind him. More prayers were being said. A few tears. But no one was shouting, no one was whining. They stood in formation, and Harper was never so proud of his fellow POWs.

The process continued. Open door, a name announced, and one by one the members of the Sixth Allied POW Wing were being sent to their fate.

Ivan VII came out. 'Harper, Roy E.'

He moved forward automatically. Hands brushed his back and arms as he went through, and the voices stayed with him. 'Go with God, Roy.'

'Chin up, pal.'

'We'll all be together soon, just you see.'

'Cap, you give 'em hell.'

He turned at the voice of Grissom, who gave him a thumbs-up. He returned the gesture and took a deep breath and went through the door, into a small room. There was a chair and a table and bright lights, and after a voice in the darkness said, 'Please sit down' and he did just that, something cold and sharp was pressed against the back of his neck.

Cold. Jesus, it was cold. He blinked his eyes, rubbed at the crusts that had formed at the corners. The ground seemed to sway and move and then settle down. He opened his eyes. He was in a room with a low ceiling, with beds stretching off to the distance. There were dim lights and shapes moving about. Someone came to him with a glass, and he drank the water greedily.

'Tom?'

'No,' came the voice. 'It's Francis. Lieutenant Bob Francis.'

Harper remembered the name. 'Yeah. The first one to leave, back at the hangar.'

'Yep. And the first one up, I believe. Here. Take another swallow. It helps. I know.'

Harper did just that. It left a bitter metallic aftertaste in his mouth. He gave the empty glass back and sat up, then touched the back of his neck. There was a raised welt there, a welt that was sore. He rubbed at his eyes again.

'Drugged, am I right?'

'That you are, Captain. And to answer your first question, I don't know for how long. And if you can hold on for a bit, I've got some other guys to assist. If you feel like it, give me a hand when you can.'

Harper looked around. The building was rough-hewn, made out of logs, it looked like. The ceiling was low, made of split wood. It looked like there were windows in the walls, but the shades were drawn. He got up, wavered back and forth as his sense of balance came back, and almost tripped as he started away from the bed. He looked down at the ground. A gray travel bag, stenciled HARPER. How thoughtful of the little bastards, he thought, and then started walking, a twinge of guilt following him. He knew he should have been helping Lieutenant Francis with the others but . . . shit, he needed to know what was going on.

A door led outside. He took a quick breath as he went out in the dusk, and then looked around, knowing his mouth was open in amazement. There were tiny clusters of POWs, talking among themselves, pointing and staring. He had to rub at his eyes again. There was no more flat landscape, no more frozen steppes. All about them were jagged and exposed peaks, mountains punching up into the darkening sky, their summits covered with snow. The ground was rough dirt and gravel, with some sort of scrub brush growing about. There was a wire fence about a hundred yards away, and there were other buildings as well, small and made in the same rough-hewn style.

He went up to the first group, murmured his greetings, rubbed at his arms. A Navy officer named O'Halloran said, 'The Urals. That's where we are. The fucking Urals. I'll bet you they got intelligence that we were about to be discovered, so the fuckers moved us. That's what happened.'

'Nah, those mountains are too sharp,' another said. 'Somewhere in the south. Kazakhstan. That's where.'

Somebody said, 'Anybody see any Ivans? Or Kims?'

'No, not at all.'

'It's getting dark.'

'Where are the lights? Where are the fucking lights?'

Harper suddenly realized what the last question meant. Where were the lights? At the Siberian Sheraton, the lights were bright and were on the moment the sun touched the horizon. For security, no doubt, but also to prevent the POWs from seeing the night sky. But as it grew darker, only smaller lights illuminated the fence area. Somebody came up to

Harper, squeezed his shoulder. 'Good to see you, Cap.'

'Tom,' he said. He felt guilty he had left the barracks without checking up on him, grateful that his EWO was once again at his side.

'I've checked out the fence,' Grissom said, his voice tinged with excitement. 'Nothing like the Siberian Sheraton. No electrical insulators, and it's a single fence. And look at this dirt.' He kicked at it with his foot. 'Good digging dirt. I tell you, Cap, there're possibilities here. There are definitely good possibilities here.'

'Yeah,' Harper said, 'but where the hell is here?'

'If everybody would just shut up, I'll let you know,' came a new voice, and the group moved about as a lean man came nearby, on crutches. It was Armstrong, a B-52 pilot from the Ozarks, a hunter, trapper, and amateur astronomer. Harper had learned that during the first escape attempt, when Townsend had frozen to death out there on the steppes, Armstrong had fought and argued and demanded to try out on his own. But none of the SROs would let him go. He was too valuable for his knowledge of the stars, and because of a hasty ejection from his burning bomber north of Haiphong, he had lost his right leg below the knee. Yet Armstrong said that wouldn't have slowed him down, and, most days, Harper believed him.

The crowd around Armstrong waited, expectantly, as the night sky grew darker. Stars began to appear, and Harper craned his neck back, hardly breathing, as he saw stars for the first time in decades. Yet he stayed silent, waiting, as the others stood still. Armstrong moved his head back and forth, and then said, 'The date. Who's got a good idea of the date.'

'September second,' somebody said.

'Okay. That's what I thought. Well.' Armstrong let out a deep sigh.

'Well?' came a demanding voice from the darkness. 'Where in hell are we? Where did they dump us?'

It was like Armstrong was hesitating, and he said, 'Anybody else think it's not September second? Do they? Could the Ivans have put us under for a while?'

'Jesus, Armstrong, tell us, will you? We were under a day, maybe two. What's the deal?'

Armstrong said, his strong voice now shaking, 'You're not going to believe me.'

SIXTEEN

For the second time in as many days, Clay Goodwin was back at Sloan Woodbury's home on Brattle Street, and if Sloan had any questions about the disposal earlier that day of Annie from South Boston, he kept them to himself. Clay opened the stainless-steel refrigerator, found a leftover piece of steak, which he chopped up and made into a sandwich with cheese and onion slices and horseradish. He ate over the sink in Woodbury's kitchen as Woodbury sat at the big kitchen table, a glass of port or sherry or some other fag wine in front of him. Clay thought he was being pretty fucking gracious, eating his dinner over the sink so there were no dishes to clean up, but Woodbury sure didn't seem to appreciate the gesture. Clay swallowed some Sam Adams beer and said, 'I've got a message of sorts from Mister Pickering.'

'I'm sure you do,' Woodbury said quietly.

'Yeah, well, it's one of those messages that's kinda direct, you know what I mean?'

Woodbury's voice was chilly. 'I've dealt with Mister Pickering for a number of years. I know exactly what kind of messages he sends. And what do you think was on his mind?'

268

Clay shrugged. 'I think before the night is out, something has to happen.'

Woodbury nodded, picked up his wineglass. 'All right. So there are no illusions. Before midnight, all right?'

Clay looked up at the clock. It was just past ten P.M. 'Why?'

'Why not?'

Clay said, 'I think Mister Pickering would want something earlier.'

'And I'm telling you midnight, that's why. It'll be a good time back there at the facility, that's why. And that's the way it's going to happen.'

Clay picked up the cold bottle of beer, eyed the fat old man in the chair, and it was like the damn guy was picking through his mind, for Woodbury said, 'I know what you're thinking. You want to wrap this up now, and you're trying to figure out if you can squeeze out the protocol information from me over the next few minutes. Well, Clay, think about this. There are hidden alarm systems throughout the house. Come anywhere near me, and they'll be triggered. You may be fast, but I don't think you're that fast. And even if you do get to me, you have to get the protocol information out of me. That will take time. Maybe two hours' worth. So why bother? Stand there and drink your beer and wash your face and hands, and before you know it, it'll be done.'

Clay grinned, went to the refrigerator, and pulled out another Sam Adams. Damn, this guy was good, and he figured, sure, he certainly had to be, to negotiate with the Russians and Chinese and North Koreans and French, and walk away with his shorts still on. Sure, the man was good, and if he wanted to sit on his ass for a couple of hours, why the hell not? Any shitstorm that would fly would bypass one Clay Goodwin, and if Woodbury got in trouble with Pickering, so what. Pickering signed the checks and this former secretary of state didn't. Clay popped open the beer and yawned. Sure had been a long day, hadn't it?

Woodbury said, 'Let's go to my office upstairs, and we'll wait it out.'

'Sure,' Clay said, and followed the man as he waddled his bulk upstairs and down a hallway to the office. Lights were switched on, and Woodbury sat in his leather chair. Clay found a nice comfortable matching couch across from the desk. On the wall were a variety of photos and plaques and certificates, and Clay paid them no mind. Stuff like that was for weaklings, guys who needed their egos massaged at every turn. Clay knew what he was good at, knew what he could accomplish, and he didn't need a photo or a piece of paper to tell him any different. And he also held on to his beer and remembered what that little teen whore had said, about Woodbury's unusual tastes. He wondered if Pickering knew the ins and outs of that particular piece of news, and decided to save it for a future time, when he need a favor or something.

Woodbury toyed with his glass of port or sherry or wine and said, 'I was hoping this night would never come, you know? Years and years . . . I never really thought it would happen.'

Clay fought back a yawn, took another swallow, thought that the long day and no sleep and alcohol were becoming dangerous, but screw it. In a couple of hours it would be over and he could crash at the Parker House or Copley Place or anyplace except here, and get some serious z's in. But Woodbury seemed to be in a talkative mood, and after the fat man took a sip, he said, 'But you know what, it's almost liberating, to talk about the protocols and how they were established. As they say, Clay, you now have a need to know. Would you like to hear that?'

270

Hell, no, was his first thought, but he figured if Woodbury kept on talking, at least the time would pass quicker. 'Sure. Go right ahead,' and he settled himself deeper into the couch, shifting some so that his waist holster didn't dig into him too much.

Sloan Woodbury looked over at the slumped position of Clay Goodwin, who was trying desperately to keep his eyes open, and wondered why he just didn't undo the combination lock and get it over with. And he knew why: stubbornness. He hated the thought of being at the beck and call of Pickering and his bloody errand boy. All right, so he couldn't say no. It would have to happen. But damn it, it would happen on his say-so, and it would happen at midnight. Not a second or minute earlier.

He also wondered what twisted god or fate had brought this man into his office. Over the years Woodbury had thought about who he might have finally unburdened his soul to: a Senate committee, a journalist on *Meet the Press*, or a sentencing judge in the federal court system. But this creature, this man-ape who thought with the reptile part of his brain and had so much blood on his hands? This would be the man who would finally hear it all from Sloan Woodbury's lips? It was so frightfully absurd as to be amusing.

'Well,' Clay said, 'are you going to talk or what?'

'Sure,' Woodbury said. 'I'm going to talk.'

And he started telling the tale, and where it started. In Vladivostok.

SEVENTEEN

Vladivostok, the Russian Federation

When the phone rang, Secretary of State Sloan Woodbury sat up in an unfamiliar bed, wondering where the damn noise was coming from. He looked over at a night table where the briefcase with the communications gear from the Signal Corps officer had been set up. But the damn thing was quiet, unlit. The sound came again, and he saw that it was the phone from the hotel. The actual hotel phone! He switched on a light, saw that it was one A.M. local time, and picked up the receiver.

'Woodbury,' he said.

'Ah, Mister Secretary,' came a man's voice, slightly accented. 'Please hold for Minister Filipov, will you?'

Woodbury rubbed at his face, swiveled around in bed so he could rest his feet on the carpeted floor, grimaced when he felt the bits of dirt on his feet. This was supposed to be the grandest hotel in all of Vladivostok, the Maxim Gorky, and based on the food, water pressure, and rug, Woodbury doubted the damn place would pass as a Holiday Inn in Omaha.

And what the hell was the foreign minister calling about, damn it? Woodbury had just wrapped up a late night dinner with Mikhail Filipov not more than two hours ago, and all he wanted was a good night's rest and a quick flight back to Tokyo, and then to the States.

A click on the phone line. 'Mister Secretary. So sorry to disturb you at this hour. But a matter has come up that requires the attention of both of us.'

'Jesus, Mikhail, what is it that can't wait?'

'I'm sorry, Mister Secretary. Perhaps I was not clear. This is a matter of the utmost urgency. For both our countries.'

There. In diplomacy speak 'utmost urgency' always meant haul your ass to where it has to be, because something serious has just happened, or is about to happen. Woodbury wiped again at his face. 'Okay,' he said, 'give me ten minutes. Do you want to come to my room, or shall I go to yours?'

'Actually,' Filipov replied, 'I would appreciate your joining a member of my staff. He will be outside your door. He will take you where you have to be.'

'Then we're meeting outside of the hotel?'

'Yes, I cannot say any more. You know why.'

Of course. Who knew how many intelligence agencies had the phone lines in this hotel tapped. 'All right, then. Let me get my staff together.'

'Alone,' Filipov said. 'I must see you alone.'

Now it was getting interesting. Woodbury shifted the phone to the other ear. 'Alone? That's quite . . . extraordinary. I'm afraid I'm going to need more information from you, Mister Foreign Minister, before I agree to accompany you anywhere alone.'

'Ten minutes,' Filipov said. 'Then you will learn why it is necessary.'

Woodbury hung up and got dressed, taking his time. Ten minutes or no, he wanted to run through what in hell was going on. So far the summit had gone off without a hitch, with the usual press conferences where he and Filipov went through their little dances of amusement and goodwill, to let the dwindling press corps report that yes, the new relationship between the United States and Russia was proceeding along as planned, though still fairly slowly.

Still, he thought, shrugging on a suitcoat, it sure would have been fun, back in the days of real negotiations, real diplomacy, real power politics. Back in the days of Dulles and Ball and Kissinger. When the only relationship that counted was between the United States and the Soviet Union. Everything else—South Africa, Central America, the Mideast, Europe, the Koreas, China—all flowed from that great conflict. Jesus, what a time to be in the State Department, back when things mattered. During those great struggles he had been a student at Harvard and then an intern at the White House and later the State Department, learning those first lessons. And now? Shit, another secret that was rarely reported on, was that the State Department—in many ways—was part and parcel of the Commerce Department. In the good old days, a hotel like this would be stuffed with pundits, think-tank members, and even network anchors. Now, it was hard for any network—even the twenty-four-hour cable ones—to work up the interest to come here, to Vladivostok, the easternmost city of the crumbling Russian empire.

But that didn't mean the hotel was empty. No, sir. Because in all the rooms around him were CEOs and CFOs of some of the major American companies—from computers to network systems to old brick-and-mortar concerns such as mining and timber—all drooling at the thought of coming in to play in a somewhat fair and somewhat regulated emerging market economy. They hadn't gotten everything they wanted, but some progress had been made, another tiny step in bringing Russia

274

into the world of capitalism, a place where profits could be made and—more important—profits could be taken out of the country.

He looked in the mirror, was again distressed at how pudgy his face was getting, and went to the door thinking that he would probably be taken to some dacha somewhere, where Mikhail would offer pepper vodka and they'd sweat in some sauna, and maybe arrange an understanding or something about the ABM treaty or NATO expansion. But Jesus . . . what a late hour.

He opened the door, recognized the face of the man standing there, a flunky of the foreign minister. Polished and subservient, he beckoned Sloan Woodbury to follow him, which Woodbury did. There were two unsmiling members of the Secret Service who made to follow him, but Woodbury raised his hand and said, 'Fellas, I won't be gone long. I'm off to see Filipov. You just stay here.'

And the last thing he saw of the two men, one was speaking urgently into his shirt cuff.

Fifteen minutes later, in the rear of a luxurious and armored Mercedes Benz—only the fading Communist apparatchiks bothered with the Zils anymore—Woodbury was taken through the dark streets of Vladivostok, heading to God knows where, with a motorcycle escort up forward, blue lights flashing. The flunky from the Foreign Ministry was helpful and courteous, except when Woodbury wanted a direct answer, and the driver just grunted and stared straight ahead as he did his job. Even in the interior of the Mercedes Benz, Woodbury could make out the smell of salt air and diesel fuel, out there in the harbor. Some harbor, filled with rusting trawlers and abandoned military vessels and rotting nets. Just across the sea was the modern, functioning nation of Japan, a short distance really, but when he looked at the crumbling concrete blocks of apartment buildings as they sped through the night, Japan could have been on the far side of the moon.

They were now on a bumpy highway—did any other type of highway exist in this country?—and suddenly took a left, down an unmarked lane. More bumps and Woodbury had to hold on to a leather strap by the rear window, and then it smoothed out. They blew past an open gate and were on a runway. A military base, well lit, and the armored car pulled up to a small passenger jet. A Tupolev something or another, and a little knot of fear started burbling around in his gut. This was not good. This was outside the realm of normalcy. He peered through the thick glass and saw Mikhail Filipov come down the short stairway of the aircraft. He came over and opened the door and extended his hand. 'My dear Sloan, thank you so much for coming. Please. I apologize for not being clearer in my conversation.'

Woodbury got out on to the damp pavement, still a bit foggy from lack of sleep, gave Filipov's hand a quick grasp and let go. 'Really, Mikhail, this is highly irregular. Very irregular.'

'Of course it is, which is why you are here at such an unseemly hour. Because it is so highly irregular. Please join me.'

Woodbury was struck at the absurdity of it all, being alone on the tarmac with the Russian foreign minister. What would Filipov do if he went back into the Mercedes Benz? Have him arrested? Deported? Threaten the new trade understanding between the two countries?

He shrugged. 'Very well. So long as it will not be a waste of time.'

Filipov smiled, the lights from the runway making his skin

look waxy. 'Many things may happen this evening, Mister Secretary, but I guarantee a waste of time will not be one of them. Please. My private aircraft. Do join me.'

Woodbury followed the foreign minister up the mobile stairway, thinking, all right, no sauna but maybe pepper vodka in his private jet, maybe something so sensitive that he didn't trust any room at the hotel, not trusting the FSB, the KGB successor, which would be amusing since Filipov had spent enough time in their ranks before bouncing over to the Foreign Ministry. Filipov snapped something in Russian to a pilot up forward, and Woodbury turned as the cabin door swung in and was shut. The door to the cockpit was shut as well, and he hardly had time to look at the interior: couches, swivel chairs, and a work area with a desk. There was a whine of engines racing up at speed and Filipov went to one of the thick leather chairs, sat down, and fastened a seatbelt. Woodbury swayed as the jet began moving, and said, 'Minister Filipov, really, I must protest. What is the meaning of this?'

'Please, Sloan. Sloan, my friend. Please do sit down, for I do not want the American secretary of state to be injured in my own private jet. It would be quite distressing to me. Please sit down.'

'Minister Filipov,' he said, grabbing on to the side of a bulkhead for support. 'Until you tell me—'

'Mister Secretary,' Filipov said, no trace of warmth left in his voice at all. 'If you get injured, it may cause me distress, but will not prevent this aircraft from departing. Please sit.'

Woodbury looked at the lean face of Filipov, recalled all of the intelligence briefings he had received on him, his ruthlessness, his taste in music and women and wine, and his determination to still fight for Russia and her place in the world, even when the place was becoming a drunken third world laughing stock. That little knot of fear returned. Woodbury said nothing, sat down, and buckled up. The jet accelerated, and very shortly they were airborne.

When a cruising altitude had apparently been reached, Filipov got out of his seat and went to a galley in the rear. He came back with a steaming cup of coffee, in white china with the double-eagle mark of the czar on the side, and Woodbury took the offering. Filipov sat across from him with his own cup of coffee, and nodded. 'My apologies, Mister Secretary.'

'Apologies will not serve,' Woodbury said sharply. 'Right now there is chaos erupting back at the Maxim Gorky, and I think it would serve both our interests if this aircraft was turned around immediately and brought back to that military base.'

Filipov looked thoughtful as he raised his cup of coffee. 'In the buckle of your belt is a transmitting device, so that your State Department or CIA will always know of your whereabouts. When you were in the Mercedes, it was disabled by a concentrated microwave emission. Don't ask me to go into any details, that's what we hire the Japanese for. In any event, it is no longer working. But a duplicate is working, which indicates that you are currently in an office building at the airbase. And in that office building, a gentleman who sounds very much like me and a gentleman who sounds very much like you—and even looks like you, from a slight distance—are having a friendly yet detailed discussion on whether your country will assist us with our dispute with the EU over our Beluga sturgeon caviar export limits.'

Filipov puffed a breath of air across his cup and took a sip. Woodbury followed suit, even though his stomach was doing some slow rolls and dips. When he put the cup down in his lap, he said, 'You have kidnapped the secretary of state of the United States of America.'

'I have done no such thing,' Filipov replied. 'I have merely requested his cooperation over the next two hours to bear with me, as his country and mine reach a new understanding, a new agreement.'

The rolls and dips in his stomach started slowing. Woodbury felt just a bit better. Now they were edging back into diplomacy. Let Filipov play his old KGB games. So what?

'All right,' he said, allowing himself to smile slightly. 'You've gotten my attention. What's to be discussed, Minister Filipov?'

Filipov said, 'If you will allow me . . . When I was a cadet at the Frunze Military Academy, one bit of knowledge I brought from there was the notion of preparing the field of battle. To know the terrain, know the placement of your weapons and those of the enemy. You and I are not preparing to battle, but the field of our discussion . . . it must be prepared. Do you understand?'

'Yes, I do.'

'Fine.' Filipov made a movement with his hand and the interior of the cabin darkened. His voice was softer. 'Take a look out the windows, just for a moment. Tell me what you see.'

Woodbury moved the chair around, looked out, squinted his eyes. Darkness. Save for the stars in the sky, the land below them—snow, mountains, ice, frozen tundra—seemed to go on forever, with no cities, no villages, no lights, no signs of humanity at all. He shivered involuntarily, wondering what would happen if this little metal cocoon of warmth and light were suddenly to fall from the sky. How long would any of them live out in this wilderness?

279

'I don't see much,' he said, rotating his chair back.

'*Da*,' Filipov said, as the lights came back up. 'Not very much. But they are out there, nonetheless, waiting.'

'Who?' Woodbury asked, though he was pretty sure he knew the answer.

Filipov took a small sip from his coffee cup. 'The Chinese, Mister Secretary. Who else? Beyond that horizon, beyond where we can see, they are there. Waiting. Working. Breeding. More than a billion of them, Mister Secretary. More than a billion, growing each year, more and more. Soon they will run out of land. They will run out of resources. To the south they have the Koreas, Vietnam, Burma, and India. Crowded places all. But to the north? What will they see? They will see an empty land, populated sparsely by a people whose birthrate is plummeting, year after year after year. An empty land full of timber, oil, uranium, coal, thorium. Soon, Mister Secretary, soon enough, the Middle Kingdom will bestir itself and start to move north. And they will move, Mister Secretary. That, as you say, will be a lead-pipe cinch.'

Filipov paused and looked out the window. 'We cannot allow that to happen. Russia must survive, will survive. And we will need your friendship, your assistance, even a formal alliance, to see that this survival happens.'

Woodbury felt a thrill race through him, thinking, now, this was an agreement, an understanding he could sink his teeth into. Oh, the other agreements and treaties were fine, but they nibbled around the edges, around the peripheries of what was possible. Increased trade, increased diplomatic ties, maybe an understanding that NATO expansion and missile defense would proceed without too much fuss in the future. But here and now, he could not believe what Filipov was offering: what seemed to be a formal alliance between Russia and the United States to keep the Chinese in their home territory! Imagine the possibilities, the headlines, the interviews, the legacy he would be establishing . . .

'Well, Minister Filipov, that is an interesting proposal, one that I will have to take back and—'

Filipov raised his free hand. 'Sloan. Please. Do not insult me. You and I, we are men of the world. We do not need our staffs, our Duma, our Congress, our fellow diplomats to work this out. We do not need even our respective presidents. Do you not agree?'

Woodbury kept his mouth shut and let his eyes glance about the cabin, where they were supposedly alone. Filipov noted the look and said, 'You worry about electronic surveillance. That this is some trick to make you speak freely and to have these words used against you later, perhaps by some FSB plot. That is what you are thinking, am I correct?'

Woodbury looked at the man, wondered what was going on behind those light blue eyes. Son of a diplomat in the old Soviet Union, Red Army officer, KGB member and then foreign minister. Rising up that ladder of success, not unlike what Sloan had done, except in this notorious country sometimes losing your place on the ladder also meant losing your head.

'It was a thought,' he said.

'Of course. Then let me continue to be frank with you, Sloan. And this is how I will start. In two years, perhaps one, I will become president of Russia.'

'Isn't there an election that has to take place?' Woodbury asked dryly.

Filipov motioned with his hand, as if a buzzing mosquito were bothering him. 'A formality. Those who matter, the oligarchs, the *mafiya*, the media . . . they are in my corner. I will be elected. And do you know what I need most, once I am elected?'

Woodbury thought for a moment. 'Time.'

'*Da!*' Filipov said, slapping Woodbury's knee. 'Time. I need time, or the Russia you know and the Russia I love will no longer exist. The Chinese will start small, with provocations, with little thrusts and parries. And we do not have what it takes to resist them. And you too, my friend. You and your nation need time as well. Am I not right? You need time to put gentle restraints on our friends in Beijing. To protect Taiwan, Korea, Japan, even Vietnam. To let the Chinese government mature into something that will not get your New York *Times* and Washington *Post* all upset in their editorial pages. We both need time, Sloan, and we both need each other.'

Woodbury looked at the man again, now feeling as if he were back at Phillips Exeter Academy, learning to skate on a neighborhood pond, feeling his way out on the slickness and hearing the sickening creak of thin ice under his blades. Inches away from disaster. Aloud, he said, 'Granted, we do need each other. And what are you proposing, Minister Filipov?'

The foreign minister smiled. 'After I have bared my soul, you are still quite formal, Sloan. Must be that prep school and Harvard upbringing, am I right?'

'You wouldn't be the first to say it.'

'Well. Let us look at what we have here, on the ground. Like the lessons I learned at Frunze. You have the military might, and, I hope, the will, to prevent the Chinese from breaking out from beyond their borders. If possible, either formally or informally, we can assist with our diplomacy, our own military resources.'

'Your military resources, from what I've seen,' Woodbury shot back, 'are either rusting on runways or sinking dockside in your harbors.'

There. Filipov flinched a bit, and Woodbury enjoyed the sight. The foreign minister said, 'That was a very impolite statement.'

Woodbury said, 'As you suggested, Mikhail, I was baring my soul.'

A nod. 'All right. I grant you that. Our military resources are no longer a match for you, or the Chinese, or even the Chechens. But they can be part of the equation. You see, Sloan, we need you to hold the Chinese back. Our future is with you. But I am a realist. I know there will be no growth, no real investment in my country, so long as there are no rules, so long as the old Communists in the Duma prevent private land ownership, so long as our tax system lets billions of dollars in wealth flow out to Switzerland and the Cayman Islands. I do not need lectures on who we are and where we are going. I know too well the low birthrates, the high death rates, the fact that our economy is the size of Holland's. Holland's!'

Woodbury saw how Filipov's hand was holding the coffee cup in a tight grip, and the foreign minister said, 'This I plan to change. I plan to make Russia a nation again, and not, like one of your journalists has said, a broken-down Congo with nuclear weapons. So I will need your assistance, Sloan, you and your nation's.'

'You said your future is with us. Why not go west? Aren't they closer, more in tune with your needs?'

Filipov smiled, but it wasn't a very friendly sight. 'You know the answer, Sloan. The Europeans are squabbling children. They waste their time complaining about the Turks, about

French cheese, about British beef. What do they know about realpolitik, eh?'

Woodbury sat silent for a while, listening to the subdued whine of the jet engines, and then decided to let it all out. 'Very well,' he said. 'I think we can come to some sort of arrangement. An alliance of sorts, both working toward containing the People's Republic of China. It will take time, it will take some serious pressure from me and the president and certain members of Congress, but it can be done.

Filipov's face showed no emotion. 'All right.'

Woodbury said, 'You know my next question, don't you?'

'Of course. What's in it for you?'

Woodbury nodded. 'True. Expanding our reach out this far is an expensive proposition, and in some quarters, an alliance with you—either formally or informally—will be very unpopular, politically.'

Filipov shrugged. 'We understand the expenses. We have all of Siberia to offer you and your companies. Oil, timber, natural gas, uranium . . . I know of those corporations who are generous contributors to your president and your party. Equally generous trading concessions should ease some of that burden of expenses, don't you think?'

Woodbury thought of the CEOs resting comfortably back at the Maxim Gorky Hotel. Wait until this news came out! In their gratitude, the corporate donations would flow in by the millions, tens of millions, hell, hundreds of millions! Both houses of Congress safely in one party's hand for years to come . . . This was quickly turning into a summit that would leave even Kissinger slack-jawed in astonishment. And envy. Always envy.

'There is still the political price,' Woodbury said. 'Money alone won't clear the way.'

'Understood,' Filipov said. 'What do you propose?'

Woodbury felt like he was at one of those television game shows and had just emerged as the winner and was able to pick any number of prizes, just lying there on a table, waiting to be picked up.

'Cam Ranh Bay,' he said. 'The Vietnamese are offering us your old Pacific Fleet port facilities. Any objection?'

'None.'

'NATO expansion,' Woodbury added. 'We don't want any resistance to the former Warsaw Pact countries joining up. Including the Baltic states.'

'Will you humiliate us in doing so?'

'It can be done quietly and with a minimum of fuss.'

A mild shrug. 'Is there a possibility of us joining NATO, in the future, as a full or associate member?'

'Of course.'

'Then, no objections. Oh, some will wail and gnash their teeth, but you can count on the Kremlin, Sloan. You can play with your NATO.'

'Missile defense,' Woodbury said.

Now Filipov laughed. 'You and your Defense Department, you helped bring down Gorbachev and the Soviet Union by outspending us, over and over again, for that fantasy. Go ahead. Spend all you want. Deploy all you want. As before, you will get the usual shocked statements from some in the Duma and our media, but develop, deploy, and be damned. We will not be along for this game. We have better things to worry about, better things to spend our money on. There will be no response from our side.'

Privately, Woodbury knew that Filipov was dead-on, and had better sense about the matter than his own president. But politics were politics, and if he could bring this package to the

Man with a guarantee that the Russians wouldn't do something crazy if missile defense continued, well, all the better.

'Very good,' Woodbury said. 'Human rights.'

Filipov looked bored. 'So?'

'You have to improve your human rights record,' Woodbury said, bringing out the same phrases that had been said over and over again. 'The harassment of the media outlets that don't agree with you, the treatment of civilians in Chechnya, your support for the separatists in Georgia. It has to stop.'

Filipov finished his coffee, and Woodbury suddenly realized that the cup in his hands had gone cold.

'No.'

'Look, Mikhail, I—'

'No, look here, Mister Secretary. There is an expression here, a rude one, which I'll now pass along. Fuck you and your mother. I have given you plenty. Don't be greedy. Or this aircraft will turn around and head back, and there will be no deal. Understood? No deal.'

Now it was Woodbury's turn to remain silent, looking at the foreign minister. Filipov seemed to sigh. He put his cup and saucer down on a counter near the chair and said, 'I tell you this. You can complain all you want, make all the speeches you care before the UN and Harvard, and I promise that I will pretend very strongly to care. And in exchange, I won't criticize you about your Los Angeles Police Department and how they treat the Negroes, and I won't point out how your civilized and forward-looking nation still sentences teenage boys to death. How is that?'

Woodbury said, 'I had to try.'

'Of course. But who gives a shit, eh? Human rights? Please. I mean, you were an intern once, during Dr. Kissinger's tenure for Mr. Nixon. Am I correct?'

'Quite correct.'

Filipov smiled. 'Then I would think you would have learned something from the master.'

Woodbury smiled back. 'I learned a lot.'

'Good. Have we a deal, then?'

Woodbury hesitated, and said, 'Yes, we have a deal. But I do need to know one more thing.'

'Yes?'

'Why are we here, in your aircraft? Couldn't we have gone someplace else, without all this fuss?'

Filipov seemed to wait, just a moment, then said, 'I am taking you somewhere special, Sloan. Someplace special where the deal will be, ah, finalized. That's where we are going.'

'And where is that?'

'You will find out,' Filipov said, leaning over to pick up Woodbury's coffee cup. 'You will soon find out.'

For a while they flew on in the night in silence, and Woodbury reflected on what had just happened. Single-handedly, he had come up with a deal that would be a legacy for him for generations to come. Kissinger and his Nobel Peace Prize for that Vietnam fiasco. Bah. What Woodbury had just pulled off in this cabin would be written about in books for the next hundred years. Preventing a war between China and Russia. Helping save Russia so that it would survive and become a peaceful member of the European community. Working with Russia to keep China in bounds, until its paranoid and expansive Communist government evolved into something that could work with its neighbors. And last, and definitely not least, finally opening up this vast market, this vast mother lode of natural riches and resources, to the corporations and companies that had helped put this president in the White House and had secured a majority in both houses.

Not bad for a night's work!

He shifted in his seat and looked out into the darkness. Damn it, though, why was he still bothered? There was still something here that wasn't right: this mysterious trip to some-place to seal the deal. What in hell was going on with that?

And then the plane shifted and the engine tone softened, and Filipov said, 'Prepare for landing, Sloan. Quite soon now.'

Woodbury fastened his seatbelt, looked out the window, and flinched as the landing lights were switched on. But there was nothing there. Just an unyielding blanket of snow, moving beneath them, as the plane's altitude lowered. Snow and ice and snow and ice and damn it, was the pilot drunk? He grabbed on to the armrests of his chair and was going to shout a warning, that they were about to crash into the tundra, when an airstrip appeared and the plane landed with an audible thump.

The engines slowed and he felt himself pushed back into his seat, as the aircraft brought its speed down quickly. Now they taxied for a distance, before going into a well-lit hangar, and when the engines shut down, a mobile stairway maneuvered by two uniformed soldiers came up to the cabin door, which was quickly opened. Filipov was on his feet. 'Come along, Sloan. This shouldn't take too long.'

Woodbury followed Filipov down the gangway, shivered in the cold, even though he saw heaters lining the walls of the hangar. 'What is this place?' he asked.

'One of the more remote outposts of our country, I'm afraid, and a place I learned about only a short time ago. Remember that later, won't you. Here. This way.'

He walked with Filipov as they went through a series of doors and corridors. Filipov kept up a running commentary as they went deeper into the facility. 'I was once in Thailand, but I'm sure you know that.' They entered a small room, with a large window with glass on one side. Filipov said, 'When I was there, I heard the interesting legend of the white elephant. Perhaps you have heard of it?'

Woodbury said, 'Yes, I have. White elephants were the sole property of the royal family. And sometimes, to destroy or burden an enemy, the king would give that person a white elephant. Caring and protecting for it would bankrupt him.'

'How true,' Filipov said, standing next to him in the darkened room. 'I have always loved that story. Sloan, my friend, the old Soviet Union is dead, and those of us coming to power in its wreckage have to thrive despite its poisonous legacy. Unfortunately, some of this legacy cannot be ignored. Like a white elephant.'

In the darkness Sloan could sense the man turning to him. 'Sloan, we have reached a deal, you and I, that can change the world. But I need to ensure that there is something between us, some sort of extraordinary understanding, to ensure this deal is never reversed.'

'Minister Filipov . . .'

Then the window was slowly lit up to reveal the interior of an airplane hangar. And standing in the hangar, in short rows, were a number of men. They were thin and haggard and wore old clothes, and something about their faces, their attitude, made Woodbury's feet seem like they had just been hammered to the floor. His fists clenched and he stared ahead, not daring to move his eyes, not daring to say a word. He wished now he could turn and walk away, take everything back, demand to go back to his hotel room, demand that this entire episode had never taken place, for he realized with a sick twist to his gut what was about to happen.

'As a gift, and as a gesture of my good will, I present these men to you, Mister Secretary,' Filipov said formally. 'These are aviators from your Vietnam war, POWs that were brought here many years ago, and continuously interrogated for their knowledge of certain strategy, tactics, and weapons systems, among other intelligence matters. My apologies, Mister Secretary, that my government has been keeping them all these years. It should not have happened. And my apologies, as well, for another set of POWs that we were keeping from the Korean conflict. It appears that they have all died. Yet, in the spirit of our new agreement, Mister Secretary, I set these men free in your custody.'

Woodbury looked on in horror, and said the first thing that came to his mind: 'Mikhail, we don't want them.'

EIGHTEEN

As she drove in the darkness, Patty Harper was glad that Paul had fallen asleep, as she looked for a pay phone, any pay phone. The motel they had stayed in had one, but it was out of order. And on this stretch of road there was nothing but trees and brush as she drove south in the darkness. Yet she knew this isolation wouldn't last forever. She would find a pay phone, she'd call the Berwick Police Department or the Maine State Police, and if Jason's criminal brother had a problem with that, too fucking bad.

Beside her Paul stirred and said softly, 'Mommy, are we gonna see Daddy?'

With her free hand she gently rubbed her boy's head. 'Soon, babe, real soon.'

Steve Josephs of the New Hampshire State Police went downstairs for a drink of water, and when he came back upstairs, there was a noise from his boy Michael's bedroom. He softly stepped in and saw the little guy was folded over, face peering at the nightlight. Michael looked up and said, 'Dad, I had a bad dream.'

Steve went in and sat on the bed, kissed his cheek. 'It's okay. It happens sometimes. You just go back to sleep and everything will be fine.'

Mike yawned and rolled over. 'Did you catch any bad guys today?'

'No, I didn't,' he said.

'Oh. Was it a fun day?'

He thought about that van back in Brentwood, burnt out and with bodies in the front seat. He hoped the poor bastards had been dead before the van caught fire. Even in his boy's room, he could still smell what it had been like back there.

'Sure, pal,' he said. 'It was a fun day.'

Mike yawned again. 'Your daddy. He caught bad guys, too, didn't he?'

'Yes, he did.'

'And did he shoot any of them?'

Steve said quietly, 'Maybe a few. Why do you want to know that?'

Mike's voice seemed sad. 'All my friends have two grand-dads. I'd like to have two granddads, too.'

Steve bent down to kiss his boy again, and then he rubbed his bristles against Mike's cheek. 'Me too,' he said.

Frank Burnett of Channel 21 rolled over in his bed, trying to get comfortable. Beside him Carol sighed and breathed as she slept deeply, and he envied her ability to fall asleep in about thirty seconds. He could never get to sleep quickly after a workday, and especially after a day like this. Every news program was like balancing on a tightrope, waiting for something to go wrong: a missed cue, a frozen teleprompter, a dead mike. And decompressing after a busy day usually meant an hour or so of tossing and turning and staring at the ceiling. But today . . . He had gotten a phone call from Tom Strafford, the general manager, who was out in Los Angeles, meeting with the corporate masters. Tom and others down there had seen the satellite feeds of the six P.M. and eleven P.M. newscasts, and were wondering why in hell a New Hampshire television station was so goddamn interested in a Maine story.

And of course, once Tom got ranting, he didn't particularly care what kind of excuse Frank came up with. All that mattered was what he said, just before hanging up the phone, out there in L.A.: 'Something like your Maine coverage raises a lot of questions here, Frank, a lot of questions about the news judgment of our news director.'

Sure. Questions. And while there might be a lot of questions, the answer was usually the same. Tossed out on your ass and then spending the next month or so scouring the want ads in *Editor and Publisher* magazine, while the wife and children looked at you with anger and barely disguised contempt, knowing they would have to move away from friends, family, and school, all because Daddy Screwed Up.

A cough. He strained his ears, trying to listen. Another hacking cough. Either Mary or Megan. Hard to tell. He rolled over, silently apologized to his buddy Jason, wherever the hell he was, whatever the hell he was doing. This story was now officially killed, and he would have to wait to see its resolution, either by the wire services or another television station. But not from Channel 21.

Jason Harper was now finding it hard to keep up with Roy, and lots more questions were rolling through his mind. Earlier his brother had been up to answering most of them, but when they reached a certain street in Cambridge, Roy kicked his walking pace into overdrive and went back to his usual quiet self, only saying, 'We are so close, brother, we are so close I can practically smell it.'

Maybe so, but the only thing he could smell was the exhaust from the cars and trucks and buses grumbling by, and the occasional whiff of grease or fat being cooked at a local restaurant. His stomach was making its emptiness quite known, he was also thirsty, and his feet were throbbing. Yet Roy looked to be in worse shape, and he kept pressing on.

They were going down a residential street with large Victorian-style homes with porches and gazebos and stained glass and surrounded by wrought-iron fencing, nice even sidewalks and overhanging trees, but in Jason's mind, all he could see was his own tiny home.

Back in Berwick, where two men and a dog had been killed, and windows shattered and doors blown open, and his wife Patty gone with their son Paul, and Patty had left and Jason realized even if she did come back tomorrow, God, the fissure that was between them was the size of the Grand Canyon.

And for what? For what reason? Damn it, even through the hours of talking, hours of unburdening his soul, there were still a shitload of questions left, and now Roy was moving quickly, very quickly.

'Hey!' Jason called out. 'Roy, wait up!'

A couple of college-age women trundled by, knapsacks on their backs, grins on their faces, and Jason was humiliated at how much he sounded like a little boy, chasing after his older brother. He took a breath, finally caught up with Roy, grabbed his arm and spun him around, the duffel bag bumping into his chest.

'Hey, Roy,' he said, 'hold on.'

Roy pulled his arm free. 'Sorry. No time. We're almost there.'

'Yeah, that's what you've been saying, and I've had enough.

294

Damn it, where the hell did you escape from? And where are we going?'

'Jason, I—'

'No,' he said. 'Right now. Before we go any further. I want those two answers. Right now.'

His brother stood there, cheeks gaunt, his chest heaving, duffel bag now in his gnarled hands.

'All right,' he said. 'Right now.'

Clay Goodwin stirred himself, yawned. God, that nap had felt good. He rubbed at the crust in his eyes, found that he was still holding on to a half-full Sam Adams. Not bad, falling asleep like that, not even spilling a drop.

'Clay.'

He sat up straighter. 'Hunh?'

Like some overweight toad, staring at him with round eyes, Sloan Woodbury was there across from him, empty glass held in his chubby hands. Woodbury said, 'You fell asleep.'

'No, not really,' he said, taking a healthy sip from the Sam Adams, noticing it was now quite warm. 'I was just resting my eyes.'

'Bullshit.'

Clay said, 'Prove it otherwise.' He looked up at the wall clock, noticed the hands' position, even in the dim light. 'Getting on toward midnight, Mister Woodbury.'

The old man looked up as well. 'True. But it's not midnight yet.'

Clay finished off the beer. 'Can't figure out what you're doing, why you're dragging it out like this.'

'Haven't you heard that confession is good for the soul?'

Clay laughed. 'Man, you are certainly confessing to the wrong guy.'

295

'I guess I have to work with what I have.'

'True,' Clay said, thinking which of Sloan's fingers he would break first, if he didn't pull through at midnight. 'We all do.'

Sloan Woodbury sighed, thinking about this day, the longest and dreariest of his life, which had started out fairly well, paying for a night of pleasure—well, his kind of pleasure—and ending up in his office, ready to kill thirty-seven men he had never met. Oh, he knew decisions he had made and agreements he had reached before had resulted in the deaths of thousands across the globe. But those decisions had not been his alone. They had come as a result of meetings, briefings, hearings, and the ultimate decision had been made by whatever individual happened to be occupying the Oval Office. But now . . . He glanced down at the combination lock on the desk drawer. Now it was so personal as to be frightening, so frightening that the creature sitting across from him caused him hardly any anxiety at all.

But the decision would be made. The phone call would take place. And it would be his, and his alone, and damn it, before it happened, he was going to clear his soul.

Even if it meant clearing it with the Devil's representative himself.

'So,' Woodbury said, 'let me continue the tale.'

NINETEEN

GRU Internment Facility 12

For a man who had spent a lot of time with the duplicitious, double-dealing, and murderous KGB, Filipov seemed amused by Woodbury's exclamation.

'I am sorry, Sloan. What do you mean by what you just said?'

Woodbury felt trapped, double-crossed, thinking, damn this man, he knew exactly what he was doing! He played me well and brought me right here, every step of the way!

'You know what I mean,' he shot back, refusing to look out through the glass, to the open hangar where the Americans were standing. My God, a part of him thought, all those rumors, all those dismissed reports, those crazed family members, still believing, year after year . . . All true. A brief flash came to him, a memory of when he had been an intern at the White House, two months after the Paris Peace Accords, when he had overheard two of Kissinger's closest advisers talking something over in the men's room, for God's sake. One had said, 'Henry should watch what he says in public. He knows all the POWs haven't come back. So he should just shut up.' And the other guy had laughed:

'You try shutting up Henry, you see what happens to your career.'

So it had been true. All true. And years later, he, Secretary of State Sloan Woodbury, was the lucky son of a bitch who was there when it came up and bit him in the ass.

Filipov looked like he was playing the dummy, and playing it well. 'I'm sorry, Sloan. I thought you would be pleased to have your Air Force and Navy officers returned to you. After all, it has been a mystery all these years. The congressional hearings. The investigations. The amateur Rambos going into the Laotian jungle. Now the mystery is solved.'

'Solved? Sure, solved, but at what cost?' Woodbury glared at the impassive foreign minister. 'You set me up.'

Filipov's face didn't budge. 'I do not understand.'

Woodbury waved his finger in the man's face. 'You've offered the deal of a lifetime, a deal that will change everything, a deal that guarantees peace, security—'

'Profits,' Filipov interjected.

'—for both our countries, for this part of the world, and then you toss this stink bomb into the middle of it.' Woodbury took a breath. 'You fool, what kind of deal do you think I'll be able to get through the Congress if I come back with these men? Do you think Capitol Hill will be in a mood to celebrate a new understanding between Moscow and Washington? The hell they will! Even if I were to take them back home, like some damn conquering hero or something, they'll be howling for blood and a break in diplomatic relations! That's what's going to happen.'

Woodbury looked out at the row of men standing there, and one of them turned and looked at him, and he had the creepiest feeling that the man could actually see through the glass. Woodbury clenched his fists again. 'These men have been declared dead. Their friends, their family, their nation, have moved on. We can't afford to bring them back.'

Filipov stayed silent for a moment, and then said, 'And we cannot afford to keep them.'

'You sure as hell have been doing a pretty good job of it, all these years!'

'Previous regimes, perhaps. But not the one I will be heading in a year or two. Sloan, I will not have this Damocles sword hanging over me when I become president. You perhaps do not know what it is like.' Filipov stepped in closer and lowered his voice. 'We know many things about you, Mister Secretary. We know that you have reached the limit of your political career. You have no interest in being a congressman, a senator, or even president. And we know why.'

'And how's that?' Woodbury said.

Filipov smiled slightly. 'Let us say your private life would not survive a close examination. Am I right?'

Woodbury felt sweat starting to trickle down his spine. 'I have nothing to say about that.'

'Da. Very good. But know this, Sloan.' Then Filipov's voice became quiet, almost pleading. 'I will become president in a year or two, and I will not have this time bomb here, ready to go off and destroy our agreement, just as we're making progress against the Chinese. It has been a miracle that the news has not come out these past years. Some rumors have, here and there, and it was in both our interests to see these rumors ignored. But we cannot ignore these men anymore. Eventually the truth will come out. It will not happen when I am president. Sloan, we need each other, and we need your help.'

'Help? What kind of help?'

'Take these men away from here. Remove them, make

arrangements, a secret trial in your military. I do not care. But their deaths will not be on my conscience.'

Woodbury said, 'That's impossible.'

Filipov shrugged. 'I thought with Americans anything was possible, eh? Sloan, these men are no longer guests of the Russian Republic. They will be leaving within a few hours, either with your cooperation or without it.'

Woodbury said desperately, 'It can't be done!'

'Of course it can,' Filipov said, smiling, looking at him. 'We know what you want, what you need. Your legacy, to secure your place in history, to secure peace in this part of the world. And we need your assistance as well. These men are part of the price. So either they go with you, or perhaps we will dump them in Vladivostok in the morning.'

Vladivostok. What few news media that were there . . . a Pulitzer Prize, worldwide fame, ready to be picked up for the asking. And for the businessmen? Jesus, what would they think?

The businessmen. Woodbury cleared his throat. 'You are offering these men to us, correct?'

'Yes.'

'Then you don't care what happens to them once they depart.'

Filipov was now looking out through the glass. 'They must live. That's all I care about. I will not be a party to you . . . arranging an accident for these men. If it ever comes out about how they ended up in my country—perhaps from one of your reporters stumbling over an old hidden archive—I will have clean hands, saying they were given over to you.'

Clean hands, hah, Woodbury thought. And just suppose they did end up dead? Then Filipov could blackmail him later, maybe start chipping away at some of the concessions they had just reached. But if they could be kept alive, until nature and old age took care of the problem ... Woodbury found himself thinking furiously of who was back there, at the Maxim Gorky, who would do it, who would be a party to it, who could work something out.

'Time. Give me some time.'

Filipov said, 'How much?'

'Enough time to get back to Vladivostok, set something up with somebody.'

'A member of your staff?'

'No,' Woodbury said, his eyes drawn back to those lonely and gaunt men. His countrymen, sacrificed once for their nation, and destined to be sacrificed once again. 'A capitalist.'

The flight back seemed much quicker than the flight out, and he spent the time staring out at the dark, thinking through options, factors, how and where it could be done. He tried to keep it all focused on that, and not on those men, lined up, standing in an empty hangar in the middle of nowhere. When he was brought back to the Maxim Gorky, a pinkish line of light was beginning to appear on the eastern horizon, and smoke and steam were rising up from the factories and old apartment buildings. He went through the service entrance, got what he needed from the same Foreign Ministry flunky who had escorted him earlier, and then he was on the tenth floor, banging on it. A bleary-eyed and cranky Hiram Pickering answered, a white terry-cloth robe slung about his skinny frame. He eyed Woodbury and said, 'Trouble?'

'Yeah.'

'Come on in, then. And don't worry none about ears in the room. It's been swept clean.'

So the next hour was spent in the man's room, sitting on uncomfortable furniture, hearing the sounds of traffic increase as Vladivostok bestirred itself to whatever life it had. Woodbury was surprised—then again, maybe not—by the reaction from Pickering after he explained all that had gone on, all that was now in the balance. Pickering nodded and picked up a room service menu, and looked over.

"Kay, I'll do it, but there's gonna be compensation involved,' he said.

'Guaranteed.'

'And I don't care what that Russkie told you. There's gotta be some sort of protocol in place to . . . to eliminate the problem if it looks like it's gonna go public down the road. Can't afford the scandal.'

Woodbury sighed, knowing the old man was right. 'Agreed.'

'We'll call the protocol Nolan,' Pickering said. 'After that story about the man without a country. Philip Nolan.'

'Whatever works.'

Pickering put the menu down on his lap and said, 'Those boys, how did they look?'

Woodbury said carefully, 'I really couldn't tell.'

'Good. That's for the best then, ain't it?'

Woodbury thought of what was ahead, the two choices. One led to increased trade, an increased chance of peace, a new American century in the Pacific and Asia. And the other . . . months of conflict, charges and countercharges, every newspaper, magazine, and network news show all clambering around this story, all rooting around the bones and decay of a war nearly three decades gone, while the real job in front of this administration, of managing both Russia and China, was ignored.

'Yes,' he said, 'it's for the best.'

TWENTY

Jason Harper looked at his older brother in disbelief, not quite believing what he had just said. 'Nevada?' he asked.

Roy had shrugged off his knapsack, started unzipping it. 'Yeah. Nevada. Pretty funny, isn't it? All those groups, all those people looking for us over in Asia, in Vietnam or Laos or Cambodia. First they miss us because we're in Siberia, and then they really miss us because we're in Nevada. America's last surviving POWs from the Vietnam War, the last surviving missing in action, the focus of fundraising and parades and those funny black and white flags and bumper stickers . . . and we're right in the United States. Like I said, pretty fucking funny, don't you think?'

'How . . . who was keeping you prisoner? How did they do that?'

'Sorry, bro, I answered your first question, about where I was being held. And now I'm going to answer your second question. We're about to visit someone very famous, very special. In that house resides the very man who put us in Nevada. One Sloan Woodbury.'

'The secretary of state?' Jason said, and a man and woman strolled by in the darkness along the sidewalk, giving them a wide berth, the man muttering something about goddamn

303

tourists getting in the way. Jason said, 'How do you know he's responsible?'

Roy was on his knees, going through his belongings, and again Jason was reminded of a medieval knight, back from the Crusades, slightly mad, searching for a relic. Roy said, 'Because I saw the son of a bitch, right before we were transferred out. I saw him talking to somebody in the darkness. I saw his face and I recognized it, recognized him as Mister Secretary of State Sloan Woodbury. Then me and my guys, we were disabled and taken someplace else. That someplace else being the American West. What do you think? That Woodbury saw us and that was it? He was in it all the way!'

Jason tried to keep up with Roy, tried to think it through. 'What do you mean, we're going to visit him?'

Roy stood up, breathing hard, something in his hand, and Jason recognized it as a weapon of sorts, crude and homemade no doubt, but it had the shape of a pistol. 'We're going in there and we're going to grab him. And then we're going to bring him someplace where he can—'

'Hold on,' Jason said, looking around, trying to see if anybody was paying attention to what was going on, what his older brother was saying. 'You're talking about kidnapping him?'

'I'm talking about saving my buddies, guys I've bled with and cried with for the past thirty years, Jason, and we don't have time anymore for debate.'

'Damn it, why didn't you tell me this back at the beginning?'

Roy started walking along the fence, his head tilted back, like he was looking for something. 'Oh, sure. You would have believed that right from the start. Missing brother turns up alive after nearly thirty years, and says hey, I'm here and I came from Nevada, of all places, and it was the government's fault. Would you have believed me back there?'

Jason couldn't help himself. 'I'm finding it hard to believe you right now.'

Roy was looking up at the utility poles, wondering if Dunbar in Nevada had been wrong, Dunbar who had been so specific in briefing him about this part of the task. He then heard what Jason said and turned to him. 'Excuse me?'

They were near a streetlight, making his younger brother's face look even more troubled. 'I said, I'm having trouble believing you right now. And I can't believe you're asking for my help in kidnapping a former secretary of state!'

That's it. This far and no further. He clenched the home-made zip gun tight in his hand and leaned into Jason, grabbed his shoulder. 'Tell me, little one, what did you do?'

Jason tried to pull free, but Roy was pretty damn strong, all those years bulking up and building his strength, all designed for this moment in time. 'What . . . what do you mean, what did I do?'

'Come on, Jason. I went down when you were what, twelve, thirteen? What did you do when you got older, hunh? When you were twenty, thirty, thirty-five? Did you ever look for me, did you? Did you?'

'I . . . I . . . wrote some letters, I was in contact with our congressman, I . . . I . . .'

Roy felt it all blow through him, all the years of waiting, of desperation, of seeing each day slide turgidly into another, all those wasted hours and decades. 'You did shit, didn't you? You big small-town newspaper editor, writing all those snotty and pretentious editorials about right and wrong, about the evils of the military, and you were so safe and so stupid that you bought the story, didn't you? Missing in action. So what did you do to find me, Jason? Hunh? Did you go to Vietnam? Did you go to Russia? Did you contact any other family members who lost their brothers or sons or husbands over North Vietnam? What did you or anybody else do to get us out? I'll tell you what. Absolutely fucking nothing.'

Roy pushed him back, saw him fall against the wrought-iron fence and land on his butt on the sidewalk. Roy said, 'I don't need your help, I don't want your help. Just leave me the fuck alone, and I'll take care of it myself. Like I always should have.'

He turned around, and there it was, right there, just like Dunbar said it would be. He kept his back to his brother and then pulled himself up and over the wrought-iron fence, landing in a bed of shrubbery, and then he waited, breathing hard.

'Bonny 02,' he whispered to the house. 'Target in sight.'

There! Patty Harper saw a Mobil station with a pay phone, off to the left, and she gently braked the Volvo and drove right up to it. She looked over at young Paul, sleeping still, and did her best to bring the Volvo to a halt without a bump. She let the engine run as she got out and went over to the pay phone, which was mounted on a lightpole just outside the darkened Mobil station.

She punched in the numbers, and the phone started ringing. It was picked up on the third ring, and a male voice said, 'Berwick Police Department.'

Patty could make out some chatter in the background, other voices, radio noise. It didn't sound like anyone at the Berwick Police Department, and then she remembered. It was in the middle of the night, right? Time for the local yokels to be in their bed, sleeping . . .

'This is the York County dispatch center, am I right?' she asked.

'Yes, ma'am,' the dispatcher said. 'This is the line for the Berwick Police Department. Is this an emergency?'

'I need to talk to the police chief in Berwick. Jed Malone.'

'Ma'am, if this isn't an emergency, then the normal officer hours for the Berwick Police Department begin at eight A.M. You should call back then.'

She moved the receiver to her other ear. There was a slight tapping noise and she looked up and saw all sorts of flying insects and bugs banging against the overhead light. 'Tell you what,' she said. 'This is Patty Harper calling. I'm the co-owner of the Berwick *Banner*, which burned down yesterday, and where a worker of mine got killed. I know the chief wants to talk to me, and I don't think he wants to wait until fucking eight A.M. What do you think?'

Dead air for a moment, except for the radio traffic and chatter in the background. The voice sounded a bit strained. 'Hold on, please.'

Jason paced along in a fury, his back and butt hurting where he had fallen against the fence and the sidewalk. Roy had no right to do that, no matter what had gone on, no matter what kind of crazy mission he was on to kidnap the secretary of state. And the story! Somewhere along the line, it just went off the rails. When Roy had jumped into his life, Jesus, about twenty-four hours ago, it had seemed so wonderful, like a life-time's worth of Christmas and birthday gifts dumped in his lap. The story at first had seemed plausible enough, especially with the two armed men who had broken in and killed Caleb and sent them all scurrying away. But then the paranoia, the refusal to let him go to some major news outlet like a Boston television station or the *Globe* or the *Herald*, and now a one-man crusade to kidnap the secretary of state. Jesus!

He stopped at a street corner, realizing he had no idea where he was. Someplace in Cambridge, that's all. No money, nothing. He turned the corner and started walking, hands in his empty pockets, walking along, looking for a phone, looking for help.

There. Two blocks ahead. A Store 24. He hurried the pace, wincing at the pain in his back, humiliated and hurt again at the thought of his brother tossing him to the ground like that. What in hell did Roy expect? Did he expect Jason to keep on going along on this crazy mission, without having his questions answered? Good God, his house was trashed, his family almost killed, and here he was, tagging along with Roy, helping him out as best he could, and all he wanted was some questions answered. That's all. Was that too much to ask?

At the Store 24 it was crowded in the parking lot, and a couple of college-age kids cut him off and pulled up in a rust-red Toyota Camry.

He looked outside for the phone, didn't see one. Maybe inside. He went inside and someone jostled him, yelling out, 'Hey, Henry! Don't forget my smokes!' and a bald kid with earrings pushed him aside, laughing, the stench of marijuana on his clothes. There. By the counter. A pay phone. He didn't have any cash but he did have a phone card. So. Who to call? He sure as hell didn't know where to find Patty, but he was sure he could get a hold of Jack Schweitzer all right. It was late enough and the guy would bitch and moan—especially since he and Patty had abandoned him to be practically by himself earlier that day—but Jason was sure this story would make up for it. Give Jack an hour or so to get down here, and he'd be back on the road, heading north, for a quick meeting with Chief Malone and—

There. On the counter, by the Sikh seriously holding court behind the cash register. At his side, a small television set. Tuned to CNN. A burned-out building, firefighters in Berwick Fire Department turnout gear, wetting down . . .

Oh my God.

He stood still, not hearing anything, anything at all, just looking at the images flashing before his eyes on the television screen. His newspaper. Destroyed. And . . . pictures of Patty and himself, for Christ's sake, with a caption underneath saying MISSING. And . . . Jack Schweitzer. Poor-ass picture, from his driver's license it looked like, and the caption there . . .

MURDERED.

Jack Schweitzer, full-time reporter and sometime assistant editor.

MURDERED.

At the back of the store, 'Told ya! Told ya you'd forget my smokes, you stupid shit!'

Roy stayed still, waiting to see if anything would happen. Dunbar had told him this would be the diciest moment—if the house had a security system that could detect someone walking on the grounds. Before becoming a radar-navigator for a B-52, Dunbar had worked with his dad in a security firm in Oklahoma and had managed to keep a bit updated with the latest security measures by careful reading of the newspapers and magazines allowed in Russia and Nevada.

But no lights went on, no horns or sirens let loose. So it seemed clear. He looked up to where he had spotted what he wanted, up there on the utility pole, but waited a moment. He went over on hands and knees to something he had seen just a moment ago. A brick walkway, heading to the front door.

How bloody cute. His hands went over the surfaces until he found a brick that was loose. He worked it back and forth, back and forth, until it came free in his hand.

He took a breath. At least Jason was gone, at least he wasn't on the other side of the fence, face peering through, whining about something or another. With the brick in one hand and his knapsack in the other, he decided on a quick reconnoiter, to go around the house. It was large and rambling, but at least the grounds were fairly clear of stuff like hedges and picnic tables and kids' bikes, anything he could trip over. The lawn was well kept, and there was a large flagstone patio at the rear, and he imagined a tent erected over this patio, summer parties into the evening, soft music and waitresses passing around drinks and fancy snacks, all while Sloan Woodbury held court for the well-paid and well-heeled people of Brookline and Cambridge and other intellectual hotspots. He imagined impassioned discussions among the trees by the fence, talk about treaties and the military and the future of peacekeeping, of decisions made and decisions ignored, the conversants all the while feeling confident of their education, their superiority, their knowledge of what would be right for America.

And meanwhile, he and the others had shivered in barely heated cabins in the high country of Nevada, eating cold bologna sandwiches and wondering again, day after day, whether anybody remembered them.

There. Up on the second floor, some lights. A couple of raised voices. So the secretary of state had a visitor. Security? Or somebody else with the landed gentry, discussing what must be done to protect our place in the world, blah blah blah. He hefted the brick in his hand, found himself now back in front of the house, near where he had come over the fence.

310

'Time to target,' he whispered, as he pulled out the zip gun that was made for him just before he left Nevada. 'Seconds.'

With his back to the house, he raised the pistol and aimed and fired.

'Well,' Clay Goodwin said. 'That's all well and good, Mister Secretary, but do take a look at the time.'

Woodbury noted that it was indeed midnight, and for just a miraculous moment it seemed that the pressure at the back of his head and chest had eased. The decision had been made. That's all. Just unlock the drawer and make the phone call and say the code word, and it would be over, and this evil man with the grin and thick mustache and nearly shaved head would finally leave him alone. Then Woodbury would leave this house tomorrow and go on a trip. Where, he didn't know and didn't particularly care. Maybe France. Yes, Provence would be nice, and the French were always courteous to him now that he was out of office. In office was another matter— they were insufferable and put on the attitude that they were the true repository of western civilization—but out of office they seemed to enjoy being in his presence, as if they were appreciative of his realpolitik views and decisions.

'All right,' he said. 'I can tell the time as well as anybody else.'

He moved the chair back, grunted some as he bent over to undo the combination lock. Just as he reached down, he thought he heard a noise from outside, a popping sound, and just as he noticed the sound, the room went dark.

Clay thought that when the fat man got done here, it would be time for another Sam Adams and then to head out. He was tired. It had been a long day, and he knew that tomorrow he'd have to start hunting down what in hell had really happened to the Ebony Three crew, but not now. The chair squeaked, and then Woodbury moved down to where the secure phone was located, and—

Darkness.

Clay sat up, dropping the beer on the floor, hands free.

'What did you just do?' he said.

'Nothing,' Woodbury said back. 'The damn house just lost power. Hold on—'

'No,' Clay said, turning in the couch, ears now tingling, a free hand reaching behind him to the waist holster. 'Just sit and wait. Hold it right there.'

Before the lights had gone out, Clay had heard a noise. He was sure of it. He looked out the window behind Woodbury, saw the glow of lights. Not a city-wide blackout. Specific to the house. His pistol—a 9-mm Browning—was now in his hand and he said, 'Can you get to the phone in the drawer?'

'No, I can't. The combination lock . . . How in hell can I see? Do you have a flashlight? Matches?'

'Not so you'd notice,' Clay said, standing up, pistol now in both hands, looking around again, gauging what was going on, what might be happening. He got to the door, gingerly opened it up, listened. Nothing. 'The phone on your desk. Pick it up.'

There was a clattering noise, and now Clay's eyes were adjusting. He could make out the bulk of Woodbury, sitting there, a slight movement. 'Yes, there's a dial tone.'

'Good. It's too dark to try nine-one-one. Dial the operator. Middle key in the bottom row. Tell her there's an attempted burglary in progress at your house, you need the police. Do it now.'

'But we just lost power, that's all.'

'You're the former secretary of state, you have the right to be paranoid. Make the damn call.'

He stood by the door, thinking of all the rooms down there. Lots of places to hide. He heard Woodbury make the call but tried to ignore what he was saying. He was trying to see and hear what might be going on out there, in the darkness. Clay was good and he was fearless, but he was also no fool. Right now his priority was keeping this fat guy safe and secure until he could open up that drawer and make the call. In a few minutes, the Cambridge police would be crawling around this joint, and if a fuse in the basement had blown out, so what. Apologies all around and maybe a nice letter to the chief, but in any event, back up to the office they'd go and Woodbury would make that damn call.

Then he would—

Something smashed through the front door, shattering glass. Clay raised his pistol, balanced what he had heard, decided to go for it. He sprang from the office, went to the stairs. The ambient light was better down here and he could see the hole in the fancy-pants glass, and he moved quickly down the stairs, keeping to the side so that the stairs wouldn't creak. He took a series of deep breaths, looked at the opening in the glass, saw where it was. Sure. Broken glass and then the hand would reach in, try to undo the deadbolt, and when Clay saw movement like that in the next few seconds he would ventilate whoever was standing on the other side of the doorway. It sure as hell wasn't Girl Scouts, and it sure as hell wasn't a grad student of Woodbury's coming in for a conference, and even in Cambridge Clay was sure he'd get away with a justifiable shooting.

He got to the bottom of the stairs. Waited. Nothing. He thought about yelling up to Woodbury but decided no, keep quiet. Let's see who tries to come through the front door.

He waited.

Nothing.

Well, funk this, he thought, and he stepped closer to the door, and closer, and his alarm bells were jangling, were ringing really hard, and he wondered why that was happening, and why he was expecting some noise, something as he was walking toward the broken glass—

His feet on the polished wood were hardly making a sound.

There was no broken glass there.

And as he turned, something smashed into the back of his head.

Woodbury hung up the phone and waited. He thought about calling down to Clay, to find out what the hell was going on, when there was a thudding noise from downstairs. Then some rustling. He tried hard to listen, to sense what was going on.

'Clay?' he called out. He was ashamed of how weak his voice sounded.

Then, feet racing up the stairway, a bobbing light illuminating the outside of his office. Woodbury heard the far-off sound of a siren, coming toward his house, and that made him feel even better. Clay was coming back up, having found a flashlight from downstairs. That's all. And the police, well, he'd apologize to the police and then—

The light came into the room. The room was lit up by the reflecting light. And Clay wasn't standing there, no, sir. It was an older man with a beard and weathered skin and dirty clothes and a duffel bag slung over his shoulder. In one hand he held a flashlight, and in the other it looked like a knife. A knife. And in a flash of terror as quick as a bolt of lightning, Woodbury knew who this man was and why he was there.

And sure enough, he was right.

The man strode right into his office like he owned the

314

place, a very happy grin on his face, and said, 'Mister Secretary, permit me to introduce myself. Roy Harper. Captain, United States Air Force. And I'm damn glad to make your acquaintance.'

Then the man plunged the knife into him, and Woodbury screamed.

Through the fog of the throbbing at the base of his skull, Clay heard a noise, a noise that made him open his eyes. It sounded like somebody in pain, somebody not doing well at all.

Like me, he thought, like poor fucking me. He tried to move and couldn't. Arms and knees bound together, he was on his side in the living room, just to the side of the entrance-way. He shifted his weight, found that the guy who had clocked him hadn't used ropes or plastic tie-downs. Nope, it felt like . . . shit, it felt like dish towels. How about that? The great and mighty Clay Goodwin, tied up by an amateur using dish towels. He forced himself to relax and then gently tested the bonds. Legs pretty tight but there was wiggle room in the arms, and he started working at it, gently pushing and tugging.

Amateur hour maybe, he thought, but the guy was good. He had snuck into the house without sound or fury—probably through the kitchen—and then tossed a rock or brick through the front door from inside, just to see who might come down, all armed up and ready, to check what was going on. And the son of a bitch—and Clay was pretty sure his last name was Harper—had been waiting for him.

Another tug, another gentle movement. Well, pal, I'm gonna be free in about sixty seconds or thereabouts, and then I'll show you the breadth and depth of talents that a true professional can bring to a dance like this.

*

Damn, that was easy, Roy thought, and he pulled the knife free and then got to work from his knapsack, his magic bag of tricks. Man, this had worked well, shooting a bullet at the utility pole, where a step-down transformer pumped power into the house. One round was all it took, just as Dunbar had said, and the house was dark and he got in with no problem, and now, he thought, now we are cooking.

He took out a rag, stuffed it into Woodbury's mouth, and then slapped a couple of lengths of duct tape about his face. He leaned in and pulled on an ear, and said, 'You're not going to die. Not for a while, at least. I just pricked you a bit, to get your attention, to make you feel pain. Pain is a great motivator, and I want to make sure there is not a single doubt in your mind, Mister Secretary, that I am capable and quite enthusiastic about causing you pain. I'm sure you can understand why, correct? And right now, you and I are leaving this house, and you will accompany me without any difficulty, any dragging around, and if I even sense you're trying to slow me down, the next part of your body my knife will visit will be in the testicular region. There. Have I got your attention? Please nod.'

The man nodded, eyes welling with tears. Roy gently tapped him on the top of his head. 'There. That was good. Let's get going, all right?'

Another nod. Roy was feeling so fine, so righteous, and he helped the older man up to his feet and said, 'You know, this was so easy, and so much fun. Maybe I should have joined the diplomatic corps, instead of the Air Force.'

Woodbury found himself groaning against the rag as the madman pulled him out of his safe and warm and secure office and dragged him out into the hallway. The light in Harper's hands made crazy shadows and movements against the wall.

Woodbury's left shoulder was burning and was wet from where the pilot had hurt him, and his legs were shaking as they came to the stairs. Where was Clay? What had happened to him? The police . . . he was sure he had heard sirens. Why weren't they here yet?

Harper held on to his left arm and led him down the stairs, and his legs almost collapsed underneath him and probably would have, except for something pointy and sharp digging into his ribs. Damn it, where was Clay?

At the bottom of the stairs, Woodbury groaned again. Clay Goodwin, a disciple of the devil for sure, but a man who was trying to protect him, was on his side in the living room, tied up somehow and motionless.

'Come along,' the pilot said. 'We've got places to go.'

They headed to the door.

Clay moved, thankful he had stayed still. He was close, pretty damn close, to getting the dish towels free from his arms, and he didn't want that bastard to think he was doing anything. He wanted him to think he was out of it, 'cause it would have been easy for him to come over and finish the job, especially since the dumb shit had left Clay's pistol on the floor, just six or seven feet away. Hell, that's what he would have done if the roles had been reversed. The door slammed shut and Clay tugged again, and again, and there . . .

Damn it, yes!

He pushed himself up off the floor, got his legs undone in just seconds, and then he was free. He scurried across the floor—no use getting up and presenting yourself as a target—and got his weapon, and immediately felt a hundred percent better. Now it was time to get some serious shit done, and he was looking forward to it.

Clay reached up and opened the door, and saw the two of them, at the end of the walkway.

Roy came up to the wrought-iron fence and a gate. Woodbury was breathing hard and whimpering, and Roy loved hearing those sounds, loved the fact that the man responsible for everything was right by his side, and was hurting. If he'd had time, Roy would have spun him around and started yelling at him, yelling right into his ear: How does it feel to hurt? How does it feel to be helpless? How does it feel to be a prisoner?

But of course there was no time. There was just the gate, and it popped open—damn thing had a battery backup to control the lock, as Dunbar had predicted it might—and then it was time to grab another car and get the hell out of here. So close, so damn close, and he wished somehow he could send a quickie message to the boys back in Nevada, saying everything was moving just fine.

But as he got out on to the sidewalk, he quickly changed his mind.

There were no cars nearby. None. Just the sound of a police siren, approaching from a nearby street. And around him were beautiful homes and wrought-iron fencing, and not a hiding place anywhere.

They were trapped.

Clay got off the steps, now moving fast, going down the brick walkway, his head throbbing, but that was okay, this fucking thing was going to get wrapped up in about ten seconds, 'cause he could still make out the forms of Harper and Woodbury, standing there on the sidewalk, barely visible through the shrubbery and fencing. In just a few seconds more he'd be out on the sidewalk and he'd tell Harper to let Woodbury go, and

318

if he didn't do that in a butterfly's heartbeat, he'd spill his brains and blood all over this fine Cambridge sidewalk.

Woodbury looked at the man holding him, surprised at the anger and the fear in the man's eyes. Something's gone wrong! His plan to get me out of here isn't working, something's wrong, and listen to that siren grow louder and louder. This was going to work out all right, just fine, and maybe there'd be some strange tales to tell when this madman was in jail, but it was still survivable, still doable, and now, no doubt whatsoever, he'd get to his secure phone and make that call to Nevada. This man had hurt him, had taken him away from his home, and it was time for him and his comrades to disappear.

Roy took a deep breath, looked up and down the nearly empty street. The car he had stolen, way back when in Michigan—that had taken him nearly fifteen minutes of delicate work in a Wal-Mart parking lot to achieve. But here? In this crowded place?

Woodbury started tugging away. The siren was louder. Roy could even make out the reflected blue light from the cruiser's strobes a street or two away. He turned, saw Woodbury, and then saw furtive movement along the walkway from the house. Damn security guy was out and free. Well, he had done a quick and dirty job in securing him, and obviously not a good one.

What now?

The only thing that could be done. He started apologizing under his breath to the survivors of the Sixth Allied POW Wing and brought the knife up, just as—

A squeal of brakes, as tires screeched next to them. He

319

turned quickly, saw a rust-red car pull up, the passenger door popping open, and leaning over was—

Jason. Who was screaming, 'Get in, get in, get in!'

Which was just what Roy did. He opened the rear door and tossed Woodbury in the back and tumbled himself in front, and Jason threw it into reverse, backed it up, just as the police cruiser turned the corner at the other end of the street, just as a man with a gun came through the open gate to Woodbury's house.

Jason was yelling and the engine was racing and Woodbury was groaning, and Roy just sat there, smiling. Bonny 02 was now ready for her final mission.

TWENTY-ONE

Through the wildness of driving through the crowded and quite berserk streets of Cambridge, a yammering voice was bouncing around in the back of his mind, saying over and over again: You stole a car, you stole a car, you stole a car.

And another voice was saying, Yeah, and it was pretty damn easy, wasn't it? Just stepping out quickly from the Store 24 and jumping into the front seat and putting it into reverse, and thank God he could find his way back to Woodbury's house. Now it was one hell of a confusing jumble of moans, shouts, and the sound of the engine racing. Roy was on his knees, leaning over the rear of the seat, flailing around at Sloan Woodbury, pushing him on his side, and in a quick glance Jason saw that Roy was tying the older man's wrists together.

'There,' Roy said, breathing hard. 'Got you, got you good.'

They were at a stoplight. Jason looked to the left and right, and hissed, 'Roy, get your ass down. There're still people out on the streets. You might be spotted. C'mon.'

Roy flipped around, sat down in the seat, picked up his duffel bag, and rummaged around inside it, grinning. 'You came back,' he said.

'You just figured that out?'

'What happened?'

The light turned green. He accelerated, turned left. Time to get on a highway, get the hell out of here. Cambridge had too many twisting and turning streets, and once the police got the word out, it wouldn't take long for roadblocks to be thrown up. 'I saw something.'

'Saw what?'

He found that by keeping his eyes straight on the road, he could talk without choking up. 'I was at a Store 24. Was getting ready to make a phone call. Saw some footage on the television. CNN.'

Roy asked, 'CNN, that's the cable news channel, right?'

His poor Rip Van Winkle brother. 'Yeah, that's right. They had footage from Berwick, Maine. It . . . it . . .' He took a breath, saw a sign up ahead for Route 3, quickly checked his memory. Sure. Route 3 north would bump into Route 128, and from there . . . Well, where in hell would they go? New Hampshire? Vermont? Maine? Canada? What in hell did Roy have planned anyway? And how far could they go with a kidnapped secretary of state in the backseat of a stolen car?

Another red light. Another stop.

'Jason. What did the footage show?'

He kept his eyes forward. 'It showed my newspaper, Roy. Burned to the ground. And Jack . . . Jack Schweitzer, a guy that worked there . . . a really good guy. He had apparently been murdered. Murdered! Who murdered him, Roy?'

His brother made a motion to the rear seat. 'Ask him.'

Jason turned, saw the familiar face of the former secretary of state, saw his tousled hair, his eyes bulging in fear, his cheeks red, the gray duct tape tight against his face, nostrils flaring, and something wet and red spreading against the white shirt he was wearing, about his left shoulder—

322

'Roy, he's bleeding.'

'Really?'

'Yeah, he's bleeding from his shoulder. What happened?'

Roy moved again, a wad of white gauze in his hand. 'I guess that a bitter veteran of the Vietnam War stabbed him, Jason, to get his attention. That's what I guess.'

Woodbury groaned as Roy worked on him, opening up his shirt and putting the bandage on the wound. Jason's foot on the brake started trembling. The interior of the car smelled of tobacco, stale beer, and fear, lots of fear. From both Woodbury and himself, Jason thought, but Roy? Roy didn't seem afraid, not at all. It was like . . . it was like this had all been thought through, anticipated, planned. That's what. And Jason suddenly realized he was seeing his brother as he must have been when piloting a B-52 bomber over hostile territory.

Roy sat back down. 'Jason?'

'Yeah.'

'Jason, the light's turned green.'

Oh. He accelerated, saw the exit ramp up ahead, offering both Route 3 North and Route 3 South, and he said, 'Roy, where are we going?'

'North.'

'Why?'

'To see a friend of yours, that's why. A friend you offered to me earlier, but a friend I really want to see now, with our cargo back there.'

He tried to think of what Roy meant, and then remembered, back in New Hampshire, just as they were heading south to Massachusetts. 'Frank? You want to see Frank Burnett, from Channel 21?'

'Yep.'

He bore right, got on to Route 3. Woodbury was moaning

323

again, and Jason said, 'But . . . Shit. The story of the century. That's what you've got planned, right? The story of the century.'

Roy folded his arms, looking mighty pleased with himself. 'That is correct, young man. And I hope you don't mind sharing it with television. Do you? Because that's the only way we're going to get my buddies free. To have Sloan Woodbury himself, on live television, telling the world what went on with him and the Russians in Siberia, and to tell the world where the prison camp is, in Nevada. We do that, we prevent the same thing happening to my buddies that happened to your newspaper guy. That kind of national publicity is going to be the only thing that saves them. Nothing else will.'

Jason accelerated again, but made sure to keep the speed just a few miles above the limit. There was no doubt that this crate would never have a chance of outrunning a Massachusetts State Police cruiser, and he didn't want to offer the car up as a target. 'Roy, what makes you think Frank will put Woodbury on the air?'

'That's where you come in, Jason. You're going to convince him.'

'Unh-hunh.' The road ahead looked clear. 'And what makes you think Woodbury will say anything?'

The grin on Roy's face was still there. 'That's why I stabbed him, Jason. To put him into the proper frame of mind.'

Woodbury felt the burning in his shoulder go on and on, and no matter how he moved around, the pain was still there. Through the haze of the burning sensation, he could make out bits of conversation from the two men up forward. One was the escapee—and how many times had he had nightmares about this very moment, that an escapee or a family member would turn up at his doorstep, or in a lecture hall, armed with a weapon to kill him?—and the other seemed to be his brother. There was some discussion of going on air, and he shuddered as the car went over a pothole, jarring his shoulder. On the air. A broadcast. Something about the truth. Earlier he had wondered at what point in his life the truth would come out, and what would be the avenue: a Senate investigation, *Meet the Press*, or a sentencing judge. It seemed like the two men up front had their own ideas about where he was going, who he'd be talking to. A small-town television station? Was that going to be it?

He moved again, more gingerly, and still the pain shot through his shoulder. He was ashamed as the tears started forming in his eyes. Another secret revealed. Sloan Woodbury, arbiter of American diplomacy, settler of fates for millions, was and is and always will be a physical coward. He hated physical exertion, hated the forceful touch of another human being, and he still remembered, with blow-by-blow detail, the last time he had been in a fight, as a freshman in that horrid high school in the Bronx, when Jimmy Dillon wanted his lunch money. He had attempted to put up a fight and had been stomped in an alleyway near the school. Father wasn't much help, but Grandfather, who owned a drugstore and soda fountain, could and did help. With a few free ice cream sundaes, Sloan had bought himself a couple of allies, allies who had returned the favor—with interest!—to young Jimmy Dillon. And ever since that day, one way or another, either formally or informally, Sloan had always depended on others for his physical protection.

Clay. How in hell did this character up forward disable Clay Goodwin and get him out of the house? How in the world did that happen?

The pilot turned in his seat, looked back and patted

Woodbury on his legs. He moved away from the man's touch. The pilot said, 'Relax, Mister Secretary. We've got some time ahead of us. And then you're going to be making the speech of your career, one that historians will be writing about for decades to come.'

Woodbury closed his eyes. The flimsy structure he had built all these years, the emerging alliance between the United States and Russia, based on the foundation of these lost men being hidden and kept secret forever, was starting to teeter dangerously. He had no doubt what the pilot wanted, and why he had been kidnapped.

But he couldn't do it. When the time came, he could not do it, could not allow the secret to be revealed.

Yet his shoulder burned again, and he wondered how in God's name he would be able to resist.

Clay had to step out of the house, to clear the air from his head, for the whole place was filled with friggin' cops, and while he loved cops and what they did, there were too many questions being tossed his way, too many questions that he couldn't answer. The first unit on the scene pulled up right after Harper had bailed out with Woodbury, and the first few minutes—precious minutes, where they could have gotten a description out of the vehicle that was being driven, no doubt, by the pilot's brother—were spent interrogating him and asking why he was holding a pistol. The two Cambridge cops had seemed a hell of a lot more interested in that than anything else, and they wouldn't let up on him until he retrieved his wallet and showed his carry license for the state of Massachusetts.

After everything proper had been taken care of, the two cops next rolled into what had just happened, since they were responding to a burglary call, and then they realized—only after the fifth or tenth time Clay had told them—that former Secretary of State Sloan Woodbury had been kidnapped. Clay had earlier thought about it for about three or four seconds, whether he should tell them what had happened, and then decided that the truth should be told, for maybe the first time in his professional career. His resources were limited, and right now, getting Woodbury and the POW and his brother under wraps was a priority. Oh, a certain phone call had to be made out to Nevada, but that could wait. Getting Woodbury and company in a secure facility was what counted. And for that he had turned to the Cambridge cops.

By then a sergeant had arrived, and then a hell of a lot of brass, and then—barricaded at both ends of the street—those professional jackals showed up, the news media. Clay could make out the bright lights of the TV lighting, as correspondents from the Boston stations were out doing their stand-ups. He had a healthy hatred of the news media—the only thing they produced were headlines and heartache—but at least at this hour in the morning they could be helpful, putting out the information about Woodbury and the vehicle that the newspaper editor, Jason Harper, had been driving. It had been a red four-door, maybe a Camry, and he was sure that they would be scooped off the streets in an hour or so if the cops did a half-decent job.

He stood in the rear yard, listening to the chatter of police radios, the murmurs of officers scouring the grounds, looking for evidence, the *whap-whap* of the news choppers overhead, showing off nothing except an aerial view of the neighborhood, and the dedication of the Boston television channels to outspend each other in worthless coverage. His head ached and his wrists occasionally tingled, as if they were mocking him for being ambushed and secured by an amateur, an old guy who had been kept prisoner for years. There were a number of Clay's acquaintances—and a few enemies—who would have gotten a hearty laugh at seeing how he had fouled this one up.

Well, as they say, he thought, payback can indeed be a bitch. When Woodbury was eventually safe and secure, then that left the two brothers, and he now had a personal interest in ensuring that they never saw another sunrise or sunset. That they could count on. But right now, even with the Cambridge cops and the Brookline cops and the Massachusetts State Police on the case, he was going to need some additional firepower in his corner. He was under no illusions. Clay knew he had Fucked Up, and that sometimes meant a death sentence in his business.

Near him was the gravel driveway, and parked there was his Excursion. He paused, looked around. Nobody, for the moment at least, seemed to be paying him any attention. Clay went to the Excursion, unlocked it, and within a moment had his cell phone with the encrypted transmitter. There was a number to call, only in an emergency, and what had just happened sure in hell had made it to that level. He dialed the number and waited. He didn't have to wait long.

'Pickering,' came the familiar voice. My God, did the old man ever sleep? His voice sounded as crisp and confident as it had in the man's private jet earlier in the day.

'Sir, this is Clay Goodwin.' He paused, and Pickering said, 'Go on, boy, I don't have all night. What's wrong?'

'Sir, Sloan Woodbury has been seized. I believe it was done by—'

Pickering said, 'I don't want to know any more about the circumstances. Just answer my questions. Have the police been notified?'

'Yes.'

'Have you told them who you think done it?'

Clay saw a police sergeant emerge from the kitchen, start walking over to him. 'No, I haven't. I didn't think it would be prudent.'

'Well, you're the man on the ground, as they say . . . Why this call?'

The sergeant stepped closer, looking determined. He'd have to make this quick. Clay said, 'If Woodbury and his kidnappers are retrieved by the authorities, it's going to take some delicate work on my part to ensure that we keep it controlled. I'm going to need support.'

'What kind?'

'A pretense. I need to be something else.'

'You got something in mind?'

'Something that's worked before. Remember the Seattle matter, last year?'

The police sergeant was now standing in front of him, looking pretty impatient. Clay held up a finger, listened to Pickering's breath on the line. 'All right,' Pickering said slowly. 'I wish I could forget Seattle, but results are what counts. Okay, you've got it, but make it worth the effort, son. It's not the kind of thing we can pull off every week.'

'Only if I need it, sir,' Clay said.

Pickering clicked off. Clay did the same. The police sergeant said, 'You're Goodwin, right?'

'Yep.'

'I'm going to need you to come in and talk to my supervisor,' he said, breathing hard. 'He's got some more questions to ask you.'

Clay said, 'I've already told my story three times. Why do I need to talk to the supervisor?'

''Cause I'm telling you, that's why.'

329

Clay stepped forward and said in a quiet voice, 'Tell me, Sergeant, and I'm not going to raise a fuss. It's just that I need to know this. The supervisor just wants to ask questions so it looks like he's doing something constructive, while you guys are doing the real work. Am I right?'

The sergeant tried unsuccessfully to hide a smile. 'Not bad. But I'm still going to need you to come in.'

Clay said, 'Sure.' He held up his cell phone. 'Look, let me put this away in my Ford, let it charge up some. Then I'll be right in.'

The sergeant made to say something, but someone yelled out from the kitchen, 'Hey, Cooper! The lieutenant wants you!' He nodded at Clay and said, 'Fine. Put your phone away and then haul ass into the house.'

'Sure,' Clay said, and he walked over to the driver's side, opened the door, and reached in with the cell phone, to hook it right up like he said. Just as he started coming out of the Ford, his pager started vibrating. He looked at the screen and suddenly smiled. He looked up to the kitchen door. The sergeant had gone inside. He looked to the street. The gate to the driveway was open. A Cambridge police cruiser was parked at the entrance, but if he was careful and deliberate . . . He got in and turned on the ignition, and slowly backed out, seeing he had at least a couple of inches' clearance on both sides. When he got to the street, he pulled back and then quickly accelerated, heading to the end of Brattle Street. He couldn't believe his luck. Up ahead was the police barricade and he reached a hand into the glove compartment, pulled out a thin leather wallet.

At the barricade a uniformed Cambridge cop came over and Clay lowered the window, flashed the leather wallet to the officer. 'I'm off to Ten Ten Commonwealth,' he said by way of explanation, and the cop nodded and motioned to another officer, who pulled open a blue wooden sawhorse. Unbelievable.

Could it really be that easy? Flash a bit of tin and mention the headquarters address of the Massachusetts State Police?

He moved the Excursion through the opening, and then slowed down as the press started pushing in around him. There were lights, microphones thrust into his face, and shouted voices. One insistent cameraman was right at his left fender, preventing him from moving, and now there was a young woman reporter-type, blond hair and makeup and long fingernails. Her handheld microphone bore a logo, matching the station logo on the side of the camera. Clay grinned and said, 'Help you with something?'

'Jamie Kiley, with *Eyewitness News*,' she said. 'Can you tell us what happened at Mister Woodbury's residence? Has there been a shooting? Is he all right? What happened?'

Other reporters were elbowing in around her, but she had a glint in her eyes and a smile on her face, proud that she was the one scoring the interview. Clay spoke up so that her microphone could pick it up, as well as her competitors'. 'Sorry, kitten, I can't tell you what happened back there. But I sure can tell you what's going to happen next.'

'Certainly, sir. And what's that?'

Clay pasted on his very best smile. 'You tell your fucking camera guy to get out of my way, or I'm going to run him over and then come back and strangle your pretty fucking throat with your microphone. Got it?'

Her face seemed to turn white, and then Clay remembered something. 'Oh. I forgot one more thing. Please?'

There was a motion with her hand, the cameraman moved back, and Clay saw daylight—or nightlight, if you had to be picky—and got the hell out of there, feeling pretty good for the first time in a while.

*

Roy Harper turned again and looked at Sloan Woodbury, lying there, slumped in the rear seat of the small car. Woodbury stared back at him, quite visible from the highway streetlights as the car made its way north. He knew he should have felt something stronger about seeing the man again for the first time in years. Some sort of rage, some sort of anger. Yet there was only the sense of satisfaction of seeing him there, bound and helpless. Jason was concentrating on his driving, so Roy moved about in the seat, facing back to the former secretary of state. He remembered back in Guam reading stories in *Stars and Stripes* about the negotiations, about Kissinger and Rogers and all the other diplomats. Those men had been so far up the food chain that it was like they existed in another universe and sent out their orders and directives through some long-distance telegraph. He looked again at that pudgy face, knowing that the thoughts that went on behind those wide and fearful eyes had sent him and his brothers over the hostile airspace of North Vietnam, had killed and injured thousands of Vietnamese, and had sentenced a certain number of POWs to lifelong imprisonment.

He reached back, nudged a leg, and Woodbury tried to move away. Jason looked over quickly. 'Something wrong?'

'No,' Roy said. 'Just sharing a moment with Mister Woodbury.' He took a breath. 'Do you have any idea, Mister Secretary, what it's been like for us these past years? Do you?'

The old man turned his head away, shifted his weight again.

'Maybe you don't,' Roy said, 'but I'm going to tell you, just the same. Not looking at me won't make it go away, Mister Woodbury.'

TWENTY-TWO

**Tract Twelve, Lot Fourteen, Tomopac Military
Reservation, Nevada**

While most of the POWs were trying to understand what in
hell Armstrong had been saying about their location, the
lights along the fencing and on the outside buildings came up
brighter and a procession came through a main gate, heading
toward them. Other aviators came out of the main building,
huddled together, low voices and questions being raised and
no answers given, and somebody near Roy Harper whispered,
'Kims. Look. They have Kims here. Here, of all places!'

Harper looked over at Tom, who shook his head. The Kims
were armed as before, but they had on blue jeans and parkas
with fur-trimmed collars. An older man stepped forward,
began speaking in a loud voice. 'My name is Ilyich Sergevich
Malenkov. Most of you already know me, I'm sure.'

Roy could not believe it. The man was Ivan V. Ivan looked
around, his face and eyes hard, and said, 'I am no longer in the
employ of the Russian government. I am now, as you say, free-
lance. My paymaster is different, but my role remains the
same. And so, my friends, your role also remains the same. You
are to remain prisoners here forever.'

He gestured to the armed North Koreans. 'These men also have the same orders, the same discipline. The only thing different is where they are and the amount of pay they receive. The only thing different for you, gentlemen, is where you are located, and the fact that as of today, the interrogations have ceased. I am sure you have already determined you are no longer in my country. I am also certain you will find out eventually where in your own country you are located. The temptation to escape, I am sure, will become intolerable. Yet I am sure you will resist this temptation.'

Malenkov said something in Russian, and another North Korean came forward, holding a cardboard box. Malenkov took the box and dropped it on the ground. 'In this box are forty files, gentlemen, one for each of you, describing in great detail your families and how and where they are residing. We know where they are at every moment of the day. There are other people in our employ out there, keeping them all under surveillance. If any of you escape, please know that within the day, everyone in your family will be dead. And to ensure that the temptation to escape is quite put to rest, also know that in addition we will kill the family of one other prisoner. So. One escapee, two dead families, your own and that of your comrade. Gentlemen, like my former country and its relationship with the United States, each and every one of you is linked to each other in a MAD embrace: Mutual Assured Destruction.'

Harper felt his legs starting to shake. Malenkov said, 'You will have a comfortable and safe life here. You will have plenty to eat, plenty to read, movies and television shows, and no more questioning. You can have an easy life here . . . if you choose.'

Another command was barked out, and two of the North Koreans came into the group, pushing and shoving until they found someone in particular, a Navy F-4 pilot named Stewart, from Key West. 'Hey!' Stewart said, as he was dragged out. 'Hey, hey, what's going—'

One of the North Koreans struck him in the back of the head. He fell to his knees, gasping, and then the other North Korean raised his automatic rifle and in a stuttering burst of fire, Stewart jackknifed and fell flat on the ground. A foot trembled, and the surrounding hills echoed and reechoed the sounds of the shots. Harper just closed his eyes. A bad dream, he thought. This is all just a bad dream. I was drugged and this is the effect of the drugs. To think I am back home in America, somewhere in the West, and I am still being held prisoner by Russians and North Koreans. Malenkov spoke up, almost apologetically. 'I am sorry for that man's death. I am sure he was quite brave, to have lived through so much and this long. But Lieutenant Stewart was a threat. It was his misfortune to have been an orphan, with no wife, no children. He had no immediate family. The urge for him to escape would be too great, so we had to eliminate the threat.'

Malenkov looked about the group, as if trying to stare at each and every one of them. 'And in doing so, we want to ensure you know just how serious we are.'

With that, he went back through the gate, followed by the North Koreans, including four who were carrying the body of an American aviator, home at last on his native soil.

By the end of the week, a consensus had been reached: Nevada. And another consensus had been reached: their new home was Camp Betrayed.

Besides the main building, there were five other wooden cabins around it, with individual rooms. Without even discussing it, Harper and Grissom took up residence again as roommates, as did many others. It was odd, Harper thought, to see how quickly they fell back into the same old routine.

After two weeks Armstrong gave a talk to the assembled survivors of the Sixth Allied POW Wing, out in a flat portion of land, near the south fence. 'Yeah. So like I said, that's where it looks like they dumped us.'

'Won't somebody notice us?' someone called out from the rear of the crowd. 'Overflights, tourists, hikers . . .'

Armstrong scratched at an ear. 'Well, I dunno about that. Nevada's a pretty big fucking place, and the government owns most of it. Gunnery ranges, bombing ranges, nuclear weapons sites, aircraft testing facilities. Wouldn't be hard to dump forty guys in a corner of some mountains. Lots of places here have restricted airspace, no roads, no trails. We could be in the corner of some restricted area . . . might not be civilians or military within a hundred miles or so. Like I said, wouldn't be too hard to keep us hidden.'

'So we're fucked,' another voice said.

Armstrong cackled. 'Henry, we've been fucked for so long, we're almost whores.'

After another week, paper and pencils came forth from Malenkov, so the POWs could request newspapers or magazines or periodicals, and after some reflection Harper asked for the hometown newspapers from his part of the state, in addition to the newspaper that Jason was now running, the grandly named Berwick *Banner*. Others refused to have anything to do with anything that reminded them of home: Harper, however, had an almost insatiable hunger to learn what was going on back home, thousands of miles and almost thirty years away.

But sometimes the knowledge wasn't worth it. The papers got passed around, and soon it became clear that his younger brother had a decidedly leftist bent when it came to editorials: when it came to military pay, military benefits, and the military budget, they could never be small enough. And the military itself came in for sharp criticism as well: the terms *warmongers* and *paid killers* were often sprinkled through his brother's editorials. Harper steeled himself for the sharp comments from his comrades, but he was surprised when they never came.

Grissom explained it during a lunch of soup and bread. 'Cap, he's out there, and we're in here. Nothing he's doing is going to change anything. And besides, you think people here don't mind seeing the ones who sent them over Hanoi get beaten up a bit in print?'

'Still, it's my brother. You'd think he'd . . . well, you'd think he'd have some respect.'

'For you? Cap, don't take it personally, but to him and everyone else in your family, you are no longer part of the equation. None of us are.' Grissom spooned up some more of the watery soup. 'None of us exist.'

After about two months in their new prison, Harper was sitting on a rock near the west fence, staring out at the sunset. In so many ways Camp Betrayed was so much worse than the Siberian Sheraton. There, at least, there was something to do, in resisting and getting through the interrogations. There were no interrogations here. Nothing to focus one's attention, one's hate. Here, there was just being a consumer, a drone, a nothing. An epidemic of stir-crazy sickness had broken out and Harper could feel himself struggling against the darkness in his soul. His EWO came up and sat next to him. 'Hey, Cap.'

'Hey, yourself.'

'Pull up a rock?'

'Sure. Knock yourself out.'

Grissom sat down and Harper stayed quiet, just watching the sun settle into the mountains. Sometimes at this hour of the day he could see little faint sparkles of light, as the setting sun reflected off an airliner, flying off safe and secure in the distance, filled with happy Americans. Fuck 'em all. He picked up a pebble, tossed it. Grissom did the same and said, 'Things are going on.'

'Do tell.'

'The escape committee is up and running.'

'Goody for them.' He picked up and tossed another pebble to the distance. 'What have they been doing?'

'Staging escapes the past couple of weeks, that's what.'

Roy picked up another pebble, bounced it in his hand. 'Getting stir crazy, Tom?'

'No, Cap. I'm not.'

'If they've been staging escapes, how come the head count every morning and afternoon and night is the same?'

Grissom scuffed at the ground with his foot. 'Because they come back, that's why. They've been going out on reconnaissance missions, Cap. This place is a joke. You can get out of the compound without breaking a sweat. Trick is, of course, to make sure you're here when the Kims do the head counts. Thing is, if there's ever an escape, we've got to know what's out there beyond the mountains.'

'Unh-hunh.'

'There's also been a couple of break-ins at the other compound, where Iran and the Kims live. Quiet stuff, just gathering intelligence, going into the office area. Trying to find out who put us here, and why. Shit like that.'

Harper thought for a moment. There. Little glint of light. A free aircraft filled with free people, flying over this wonderful free country. 'Tell you what, Lieutenant. You sign me up with the escape committee, you give me first crack at getting out of this shithole, then I'll tell you who put us here. I already know that.'

That got his EWO's attention. 'No fooling?'

'No fooling.'

Grissom said, 'Okay. It's a deal.'

Harper looked over at the serious face of his crewman. 'Just like that?'

'Yeah. Just like that.'

Harper rubbed at his jaw, said, 'All right. One more thing, though. Why the wait? How come I've never been asked to join the escape committee before?'

Grissom said, 'We've been saving you, that's why.'

'Say what?'

Grissom looked out at the wire fence. 'There are a certain number of men who are considered particularly trustworthy. We need to bring them in when they are needed, one at a time. You've always been held in reserve, Cap, right to the point when we'd need you most. Like right now. Okay, it's a deal. You'll be part of the breakout crew.'

'Crew?'

'Yeah. We're working on different contingencies, Cap. We figure there's going to be one chance, and one chance only. We've got to make it work.'

A breeze came up, and Harper hugged himself and said, 'Okay. I've got a few ideas of my own about that. It'll probably take a lot of time.'

'Time is what we've got plenty of.'

'Yeah. Okay. The guy who sent us here is Sloan Woodbury, secretary of state.'

Grissom sighed. 'Figured it was somebody in the government. All right. How do you know it was Woodbury?'

Harper turned to his EWO. 'Because I saw the son of a bitch, back in Siberia.'

The months slipped by, just like before, into years. But this time, Harper started training, jogging around the compound, watching what he ate, trying to lose some of the fat he had gained from just sitting on his ass for months. The food was plain but plentiful: U.S. military-style rations, how frigging ironic. A routine of sorts was settled into by the members of the Sixth Allied POW Wing, but Harper noticed there was a parallel routine: the day-to-day life of getting by, exercising and eating and reading and watching videos; and the little sessions, little meetings, with the escape committee, gathering intelligence, working on devising maps of the area. Harper wasn't too surprised to find out that Grissom headed the committee. Besides the physical training, there was other training as well. How to pick locks. How to steal a car. How to knock out power to a residence. Another surprise was the collapse of the Senior Reporting Officer system: they had survived too long, had gone through too much, to bother much now with a formal line-of-command reporting system, though all considered themselves active-duty military.

Except for the head counts, the Kims and Malenkov left them pretty much alone, except every month or so, when the Kims ran something called a fire drill. Bells would be rung and whistles would be blown, and the prisoners would be forced to stand together in a group in the center of the compound. A North Korean would go through each building, to ensure there was nobody left behind. When everybody was out, the North Koreans on the ground would step away, to the gate, and wait. And after a minute or two, a horn would blow, and the prisoners would be allowed to disperse.

There were rumors about what the fire drill was for— including one that it was really just that, a fire drill to get them out in case one of the buildings was set ablaze—but a POW named Barnes took care of that theory.

'Found it out during one of our office visits last night,' he whispered to a meeting of the escape committee. 'There's some sort of agreement, some sort of protocol, in case security is severely breached. Ol' Malenkov gets a code word, a phrase, and a few minutes later we're all dead men. That's what the fire drill is for. To get us out in the open so we can get machine-gunned that much more easily.'

'How fucking thoughtful,' Grissom said.

It happened when Harper was lifting weights behind the mess hall. A Navy navigator named Tyson found him and said, 'Hey, Harper. When you have a chance, Grissom wants to see you, in cabin four. Something about a cribbage game starting up.'

Harper dropped the weights on the ground. 'What did you say? Cribbage?'

'Yeah, cribbage.'

Something heavy and wonderful seemed to want to burst right out of his chest. 'Hey, thanks.'

He took his time, walking slowly to cabin four. It was early in the morning and the Kims were up in their guard posts, keeping an eye on them in the exercise yard. The morning head count had matched the evening head count and everything was fine, and when he got to cabin four, two aviators were there at the door, with homemade knives. They nodded at him and let him into the rear, where there was a toilet and shower, and Grissom and two other Air Force guys, Holman and Bolger, were standing around a shape on the ground. Harper got closer, saw it was a man on his back, breathing fast, breathing shallow. Grissom backed away and Harper looked down and then up at the impassive faces of the three men.

He looked down again and it was like the whole cabin had been quietly struck by lightning, for he could actually feel the hair rise up on the back of his neck. A duffel bag lay on the concrete floor next to the man. The man had on jeans and a light down coat and heavy boots and he wore a beard, and he could have been any one of the members of the Sixth Allied POW Wing, except for one thing: he looked to be about twenty years old.

'Tom, who the hell is this?'

Grissom said, 'This might be our ticket out of here, Cap. That's what he is.'

Holman, with a long red beard—the rules against hair and beards and mustaches had long been ignored—said, 'Found him this morning. Poor kid had made it through the south fence line without being spotted by the Kims. Looks like a lost hiker. God knows how long he's been out there, or where he's come from. But he's been through a lot. Exposure and dehydration. I think he's dying.'

Bolger, whose own beard and hair were black, spoke up. 'And I don't think he is. Get him warmed up, get some fluids in him, and I think he'll make it. I really do.'

Harper looked down at the face of the young man, his eyes

mercifully closed. He could not think of what to say. Holman said, 'So? What do you want to do? Take him over to the gate, show the Kims and Malenkov that a civvie from the world has made it through?'

Bolger said, 'It's a thought. The kid could survive. Why not give him a chance?'

Holman shot right back, 'Are you fucked? We give this kid over to the Kims or Malenkov, two things are going to happen: either he gets killed or he gets a life sentence, right here with us. And that's if he makes it, and I don't think he will. He's dying. Right, Harper, Grissom? He's dying. And if he's dying . . .'

Harper felt a tingling beginning at his hands and feet. 'If he's dying . . .'

Grissom completed the thought. 'Then it's go time, Cap. You ready?'

Harper didn't say anything. He looked back at the young man—hell, just a boy—whose face was raw and sunburnt, whose lips were swollen and chapped, whose hands were cracked and bleeding. His thin chest rose up and down, up and down, and the rasping noise grew louder. Holman said, 'Frig this, I'm not going to wait forever.' He walked out of the bathroom. Bolger said, 'You know what he wants to do.'

'So?' Grissom said.

Bolger turned to Harper, his face pleading. 'Harper . . . Roy . . . Is this what we've become? Is it? Have we become as bad as those fucks keeping us here?'

Holman came back with a pillow. Bolger said, 'Screw this. I'm outta here.'

Grissom stepped in front of him. 'No, Paul. We're all in this, all of us. There can't be any dissension. Not at all.'

The rasping noise grew louder. Holman held the pillow in both of his hands. 'Listen to that, guys. Listen. The guy's dying. Can't you hear that? He's dying.'

There was no answer. Holman looked at each and every one of them. Harper stared right back at him, not flinching a bit. Holman just nodded, bent over, and placed the pillow over the young man's mouth and nose. He pressed down. Harper closed his eyes. The rasping noise faded, slowed, and then stopped. Holman remained in place, remained there until Bolger snapped, 'Oh, for Christ's sake, the poor kid's dead. Give it a rest.'

Holman lifted up the pillow. The boy's chest wasn't moving. His skin color was fading to gray. There was now a thick odor in the bathroom and Grissom said quietly, 'You want anything from your room?'

Harper said, 'No. Nothing. I go out with what he brought in here, nothing else.'

Holman dropped the pillow. 'You lucked out. Looks like the kid's about your size.'

'Yeah, luck,' Harper said. He started unbuttoning his shirt. 'Let's get going.'

'Sure,' Grissom said, and then Harper stopped for a moment, knelt down by the boy's side, looked at his quiet face. He bent over and kissed the kid's dry forehead.

'Thank you,' he said, his eyes suddenly filling up. 'Thank you.'

Three days later, dawn breaking out. Harper looked out to the east, at the pink line growing up beyond the line of hills. His shoulders were sore where the knapsack had rubbed against him, and his feet hurt, and there was about a swallow of water left in the canteen. His eyes were crusted as were his lips, and in the third day of his journey, little random thoughts of hysterics started trooping through his mind at odd times, that the clothes he was wearing—belonging to one Barry Young, of Spokane, Washington—would again be host to a dying man.

The route out of the camp had only been roughly approximated, and after a number of hours Harper knew that the emphasis was on rough. Twice he had hiked out a few miles, only to end in a cul-de-sac of rock and soil, dead ends. Once he had followed a dry streambed, remembering his survival and evasion training, that stream and river beds, when followed, would eventually lead to a village or a town. But this particular streambed had dribbled out against a rock wall. Nothing. A day earlier he had hiked through the remnants of a bombing range, and he had stepped carefully around the craters and scraps of metal. It would be hysterically funny if, in this daring escape attempt, he should be blown up by a piece of ordinance from his own young comrades in the Air Force.

Now dawn was coming, and he knew he'd have to find a place to rest, to try to sleep. But there was this rise coming up, and he wanted to see what was over that ridgeline. If it was a long view of blankness, of rocks and deserts and peaks, he would just shake his head and find a hole to crawl into. There was nothing else he could do, for even with a bit of water left, he was not going to give up. Not at all. And if his body was found, the clothes and the identification would tag the dried-out corpse as one Barry Young. But there was a note in the duffel bag, a note describing what was out there, in the dark hills, where the survivors of the Sixth Allied POW Wing still lived.

There. Top of the ridgeline. His heart was thumping. Sure enough. Rocks, desert, peaks in the distance.

And right there. A paved road. A crossroads. And a clump of buildings. Electric lights. A tractor trailer rumbling by.

'Jesus,' he whispered. 'Sweet Jesus.'

The crossroads boasted a motel, a convenience store, service station, café, and—in another bit of twisted humor—an Army-Navy surplus store. When Harper eventually stepped into the café, his heart was racing so hard and fast he thought his arteries would burst, like an old garden hose finally giving way. The floor was old planks and there were booths along one wall, and a counter with stools, and truckers and ranchers looked up at him and then looked away. He forced his legs to carry him across the floor, and he sat down on a stool, dropping the heavy duffel bag by his feet. A chubby waitress with dyed blond hair and acne scars on both cheeks came over and poured him a cup of coffee. She smiled and he smiled back. He thought she was the most beautiful woman he had ever seen.

'Breakfast?' she asked.

'God, yes,' he said, and he opened up the menu and felt a shock. The prices! The money that Barry Young had in his wallet, he had hoped it would take him a long way, but now . . .

The smells from the kitchen began assaulting his senses, and saliva was pooling in his mouth. He swallowed and said, 'Two eggs, over easy please. And bacon. And toast.'

'Sure.' She nodded, and walked over to an opening in the wall that led to the grill. He slowly looked around the room, at the Old West prints hanging on the wall, the calendar, the truckers hunched over their breakfast dishes, the ranchers with cowboy hats, dusty blue jeans. Somebody laughed, and Harper found it the purest and best sound he had listened to in years. The laughter of a free man, living in a free country.

The breakfast came and he ate it so quickly, he wished he had all the time in the world to eat another one. The little hysterias started coming through again, and he had to fight against an urge to stand up and start talking, start talking in a great flood to tell these men and women what had happened to him and the others, what was hidden back up there in the mountains, to tell and tell and tell.

He shook his head, clenched his fists. All it would take was a hint that something was going on, a hint to Malenkov and the people out there who supported the prison, and in a few minutes all those men and friends and brothers up there would be dead. He had to follow the plan. Had to see it through. Had to complete the mission.

He left a two-dollar tip (and he still couldn't believe the prices!) and went over to the counter to pay. The same waitress took the money and he noticed a Greyhound sticker on the side of the cash register. 'Excuse me?'

'Yeah?' she said, counting out the change in his dirty and callused hand.

'The Greyhound bus. Does it come through here?'

'Which way are you going, west or east?'

'East.'

'Well, there's one stopping here in thirty minutes. Can sell you a ticket if you'd like.'

He looked at the money in his hand, and then dug out the remaining bills that Barry Young had been carrying with him. He passed the money over to her and said, 'How far can this take me?'

She counted out the bills, looked at a schedule taped to the greasy counter. She slid three dollar bills back and said, 'What you got here, mister, can get you to Lansing, Michigan. That good enough?'

A good start. A very good start. 'Sure.'

She nodded and opened up a ticket book. 'Going any place particular?'

He couldn't believe he was able to get the words out to her. 'Home,' he said. 'I'm going home.'

TWENTY-THREE

Chief Jed Malone of the Berwick Police Department was in his late fifties, overweight, and with a gray mustache. He had a soothing, grandfatherly presence that Patty Harper found so wonderful at this hour, two A.M., in his basement office in the town hall. He yawned a lot as she told him the story of what had happened in the past twenty-four hours, and the story came out in long stretches of monologue, as she told about the events that had begun with the ringing of the doorbell that night in her home, when all she had to worry about was keeping advertisers happy at the paper, their son safe at home, and her husband happy both at the paper and at home.

One doorbell ring. She was sure she would have given up a year of her life to make everything go away from that point in time, to prevent that damn man from coming to her door and crushing everything in her life.

She paused in her talking to look over at the small couch in the corner of the office where Paul was curled up, sleeping. The office was plain, with light green cinder-block walls, filing cabinets, a desk and some chairs, and the couch, and framed certificates and photographs on the wall. Malone kept on writing and she wiped at her eyes. She had broken down twice during her monologue: once when she described how poor Caleb had been shot, and again when she told the chief what had gone through her mind when she saw that Jack Schweitzer had been killed.

Malone looked up. 'I'm sorry, Patty, but you should have come to us from the very start. This . . . I don't know. You should get a good lawyer, Patty, because the AG's office might want to come after you and Jason for obstructing justice, at least. I mean . . . Well, we're still dredging the Salmon Falls River for those two gunmen. That man who said he was Jason's brother will be in a world of hurt when we catch up to him.'

Patty rubbed at the sides of her head. 'What do you mean, the man who said he was Jason's brother?'

Malone started to get up from his desk. 'I'm sorry, Patty, but this investigation has been taken out of my hands. The Department of Justice has intervened, and in a couple of minutes a special investigator from their Portland office will come talk to you.'

Patty said, 'You mean I have to say this all over again?'

Malone shook his head. 'No, he's looking for specific information about the man claiming to be Roy Harper. Patty, look, let him ask the questions, and then I'll put you and Paul up at my house. I'll make sure you're informed of everything that's going on.'

As the chief ambled his way out of the small office, he patted her shoulder and she reached up and touched his rough hand. This was the way it should be. Safe and secure in the police station. She should never have listened to Jason or that crazy man—now the chief was saying he wasn't even Jason's brother—and should have come to the police from the very first moment.

She sighed, looked over at Paul, sleeping there peacefully. God bless you, boy. She felt a sharp pang remembering how she had left things with Jason, the last time she had seen him at their home, just before she drove off. She had threatened him, she had said awful things about the future of their marriage, and she shouldn't have done that. She had been angry, but God, where was poor Jason now, where was he, and what was he doing?

The door to the office opened up and she heard somebody come in. 'Mrs. Harper, I apologize for having to ask you some of the same questions, but I promise I'll make it as quick and as painless as possible.'

The man went by, wearing dark gray slacks, blue suitcoat, and blue Oxford shirt with no necktie. He smiled at her, his face sharp and angular, with a thick mustache and closely shaved head, and damn it to hell, why was she recognizing him, why did he look familiar, why—

There. He had been outside of the Berwick *Banner* office yesterday morning, when Jack had been killed and the place had been torched, and she had seen him leaning against the fender of his vehicle, looking at photographs, looking like he was waiting for somebody special to come by.

Like her and Jason.

She cleared her throat. 'Um, I think I need to see Chief Malone, just for a second.'

The man kept on smiling, dropped a file folder on the chief's desk. 'Oh, I don't think so.'

'Yes,' she said, knowing her voice was sounding faint. 'I really do.'

He maneuvered around the desk, opened up his suitcoat slightly, exposing a waist holster and some type of weapon. 'Mrs. Harper, I think you're going to stay here and answer my questions. I think that's what you're going to do.'

'But . . . I mean—'

'I know what you're thinking,' he said calmly. 'You have the police chief out there, a couple of cops and some detectives from the Maine State Police. How in the world can I force you to do anything? And I'll let you know how: if you scream, make a noise, do anything untoward, I'll take my pistol out and I'll blow the head off that little boy sleeping over there on the couch.'

She groaned, both fists against her face. He went on. 'I'll tell a little lie. I'll say that the pistol went off accidentally. You'll say something else.' The man shrugged. 'Maybe they'll believe you. Maybe they'll believe me. Whatever. But the results will be the same. You will be alive and that little boy will be dead.' He leaned over and spoke right to her face. 'And it will be all your fault. Do I have your attention?'

'Yes.'

His smile was wider. 'Good. Let's get talking now, shall we?'

And he sat down in the police chief's chair.

Jason Harper yawned, looked at the dashboard clock of the stolen Camry. It was two-thirty in the morning. Roy was next to him, fists clenched in his lap. The former secretary of state was behind him, breathing hard. They were now in New Hampshire, heading north, going through Nashua, the state's southernmost city.

'The body,' Jason said.

'Hunh?' Roy asked.

'What happened to the body of the hiker? What did they do with it? I mean, even the North Koreans might be suspicious of seeing a young guy instead of you, dead in your bunk.'

Roy said, 'You're a smart guy. You figure it out.'

Jason thought for a couple of miles.

'Suicide,' he said. 'After you got out of the compound, your death would be staged so that the Kims wouldn't think anything out of the ordinary had occurred . . . but hanging wouldn't do it, and you couldn't slit the wrists of a dead man . . .'

Jason felt a chill at the back of his throat, spared a glance to his brother. 'He was burned, right? Self-immolation.'

'Bingo,' Roy said. 'There were kerosene lamps for the outlying buildings. Some of the kerosene was stolen and used. That I know about. I mean, I wasn't around there to find out. Yeah, that's what happened, Jason. This poor guy was dressed out in my clothes and in an isolated corner of the compound . . . there you go.'

'Pretty cold,' Jason said.

'He was already dead. One of these days I'll look up his family and thank them. In the meantime, let's keep on making tracks.'

Jason looked at the dashboard clock again. Two-thirty-five in the morning. Why wasn't he tired? Nerves and adrenalin, he thought. That's what's driving us. Nerves and adrenalin. There was going to be a major crash of his body in the next few hours, and he wasn't looking forward to it.

'Speaking of tracks,' Jason said, 'I think we need to cover ours better. We've been on the road for more than an hour. All it's going to take is some sharp state trooper to pull us over and run those plates and find out they're stolen. And then there will be a major shitstorm when he sees who's in the backseat.'

Roy seemed to ponder that and said, 'How much longer to where your TV guy lives?'

'Probably twenty minutes or so.'

Roy sighed. 'Yeah, okay. That makes sense. Any place off this road that might have some vehicles parked? Like a mall or hotel or something?'

Up ahead was a series of exits, and Jason said, 'Good timing. There's a couple of hotels up here on the left. We'll probably find something we can use. Okay, big brother, once we get new wheels, what next?'

Roy said, 'What do you mean? I've already told you, at least three times. We go get your TV guy.'

'Yeah, and then what?' He switched on the directional, carefully slowed down to match the off-ramp speed. 'Let's say Frank is home and we convince him that this is the biggest story of the century. Let's say it's four A.M. or thereabouts. What then?'

Roy sounded irritable. 'Jesus, it's pretty apparent, isn't it? He takes us back to the television studio and puts Woodbury and me on the air. That's what happens next.'

Jason shook his head as he came to a set of traffic lights. 'Nope. That's going to be a big mistake.'

'Why?'

Jason made a left-hand turn. He couldn't believe he was going to say it, but he had to. He gave another glance to Roy. 'You're a smart guy. You figure it out.'

'What?'

He felt a childish glee at the tone of Roy's voice. 'You heard me. You're a smart guy. You figure it out. Roy, I've been with you for the past twenty-four hours. I don't have to tell you what shit I've gone through to stay with you. And what I'm telling you is that we're now on my turf. Okay? And I'm also telling you that going to Frank right away is a big mistake. Figure it out.'

Another set of traffic lights. Lots of stores, office buildings,

354

motels. Nashua was a strange part of New Hampshire, a city that was more Massachusetts than parts of Massachusetts, with traffic problems, strip malls, a large immigrant population, and a sense sometimes that the whole place was bursting apart at the seams.

'Well?' he asked.

Roy said, 'The time of day. Right? Getting us on the air. Shit, I guess I see it now.'

'Yeah. Let's say we get to Frank and he's convinced, and we're at Channel 21 at, say, four-thirty in the morning. Okay. What then? Go on the air and preempt some game show or Hollywood tabloid show. Total impact . . . a few thousand insomniacs in New Hampshire and parts of Maine and Massachusetts. Maybe a wire story or two, right before the cops come in and raid the studio. No, we want to go on at the time of maximum impact.'

'What time would that be?'

'Seven A.M. or thereabouts. Channel 21's the ABC affiliate. You could have them preempt *Good Morning America*. Hell, maybe Frank could convince them to break into their morning show.'

Roy said, slightly embarrassed, 'I'm sorry. What's *Good Morning America*? Is it a news show?'

Jason nodded, saw the lights of a Marriott up ahead. 'Sort of. News, interviews, some weather, and stuff. There's one on every national network, and they're quite popular. You get your story out at that hour, Roy, and I can guarantee you a hell of an impact. Better than doing it quick and right off the bat.'

'So why not go get Frank now? And get to the newsroom early?'

Another set of lights. Damn it, didn't any of these traffic

lights ever go to blinking yellow? 'Because that'll give us too much time. Time for Frank to reconsider. Time for Frank's bosses to intervene and pull the plug. Time for somebody in the newsroom who calls a friend who calls a friend who calls a friend, and there's a bunch of cops coming in to get Woodbury and arrest you and me. No, we've got to schedule it right, Roy. Schedule it so there's enough room for Frank to figure out what's going on, time enough for him to get us into the studio without having half the cops in New England on our tail. Plus . . . well, it sure would be nice just to stop driving for a while. You know what I mean?'

Roy nodded. 'Fair enough. Okay, we're on your turf now.'

'Okay.' Green light and he made a left. The hotel's parking lot was full of cars and pickup trucks and SUVs. There sure as hell didn't seem to be any security around, which was great. All he cared about was that Roy should be as good as he said he was at stealing vehicles. He took a breath. Okay. One more thing and we'll see where that takes us. He slowed the Camry as he made a right into another almost-full parking lot. He put the car in park and moved in his seat so he was looking right at his brother.

'Roy?'

'Yeah?'

'We've got to clear up one more thing before we go any further, okay?'

Roy didn't look happy, his skin sallow under the harsh light of the streetlights. 'All right, but make it quick.'

'Good. I will. How in hell did you know I was friends with Frank Burnett?'

The answer was too quick. 'You must have told me.'

Jason shook his head. 'No. I've gone over what we've talked about this past day, and mostly it's been you talking and me listening. I know a lot about what happened to you. You know very little about me and what happened to me after you were shot down. You know the basics, but I guarantee you that I've not said one word about Frank and Channel 21.'

'Back in Berwick, just as we were leaving—'

Jason shook his head again. 'Nope. I told you that we should see a friend of mine, a friend who could help you publicize what happened to you. I didn't mention a name, or where he worked.'

The sounds now were of the out-of-tune engine rumbling and the strained breathing of Woodbury in the rear. Jason said, 'How did you know? Research, even in prison?'

Roy said, 'Yeah, research. Even in prison. We were allowed newspapers, magazines, some books. When I gave the word that Sloan Woodbury had seen us back in Russia, and when we found out that he had retired and was teaching at Harvard . . . well, there was just me and two other guys from that part of New England. And I had a brother who was a newspaper editor, and in getting the paper I saw a piece that Frank had published in your paper. An op-ed on the New Hampshire primary or something, and later I saw in another issue a picture of the two of you at some UNH alumni function, and the caption said something about the two of you going to college together. That's what happened.'

Jason rubbed at the steering wheel. 'This whole thing . . . this whole thing in coming out and seeing me . . . it's all been a plan? Right? To use me and my connections. You weren't coming home to see your younger brother, to see your family. You were just coming here to use me and who I know. Right?'

Roy didn't even pause. 'Right.'

Jason put the Camry back in drive, surprised that he wasn't angry, surprised that he wasn't much of anything. Maybe he was finally starting to crash from all this exertion. 'Okay. Now that we've gotten that cleared up, let's go steal us a vehicle.'

Sloan Woodbury was resting, thinking, evaluating. The pain in his shoulder had lessened, and if he kept his movements to a minimum, the searing sensation was at least tolerable. The two men hadn't stopped yapping since they got out of Cambridge, and Woodbury had to put up with a lecture from the POW about the rough life his buddies were enduring in Nevada. Well, tough titty. They were all aviators, they all volunteered to serve their country, and where was it written that keeping their fate secret wasn't in the best service of their country? Somehow, he knew that if he could get this damn gag off, he could start talking and start doing something. He knew he was physically weak, knew that ever since he had been a child, but one thing he did have was the power of his voice, the power of persuasion.

The young man stopped the car in a parking lot at some hotel in godforsaken New Hampshire. He thought a bit about what Clay must be doing, what the police in Massachusetts must be doing, but gave up on that. This was now his mission, to get out without playing a part in this madman's show, without appearing on television and explaining all about what had happened in Russia and Nevada. Right now, he thought, right at this moment, Mikhail was on an Aeroflot aircraft, heading into Dulles Airport to reach an agreement—an understanding that started all those years ago in Mikhail's own private jet—and sign a treaty, a treaty that would establish peace and prosperity in the Pacific for another hundred years.

And all that was to be given up for a handful of ghosts?

The madman got out and went to a dark green van. He had something in his hands, jimmied something about, and then crawled inside. Woodbury could make out a light inside the van, flashing about. Then the van roared into life and the side door opened up, and the driver—Jason, that was it, right?—got out and was joined by his brother, and both of them reached back into the Camry and manhandled him out. The pain came back and he screamed against the gag as he lurched out on to the asphalt. 'Hurry up, hurry up,' one of the two murmured, and then he was tossed into the rear of the van, thankfully landing on his good shoulder. There was other movement, and then the door slid shut.

He sat up, using his feet. His wrists were aching, but it felt better when he leaned against the van's wall. From the outside light he made out an upholstered floor, a padded bench along the other wall. Children's toys and a diaper bag and other debris from some suburban soccer-mom. The van drove on for a while, making some turns, and he gave up trying to figure out what the driver was doing. There was more conversation up front, but he couldn't make out what was being said. But that was all right. He needed a little time—which it seemed he was going to get—and just a little luck.

The van stopped. He looked up to the front, seeing some trees through the windshield. The van backed up, and then made another turn, and then backed up some more. Tree branches scraped against the outside of the van. Then it stopped. The engine shut off. He waited to see what was going to happen next. A bit more movement up forward, some talking, and then one of the two men got up and came to the rear.

Just a bit of luck, he thought. Just a bit of luck.

Roy Harper rubbed at his eyes, yawned some, and then saw

Jason switch off the engine. They were adjacent to a dirt parking lot, partly illuminated by a solitary street lamp at the lot's entrance, and the van had been backed in among some trees and brush.

'There,' his younger brother said. 'Last summer Patty and I went canoeing down the Merrimack River from here, parked our car back here. Nice place to spend a couple of hours, maybe even catch up on some sleep.'

'Not too much sleep,' Roy said.

'Enough, though,' he said. 'Enough to take the edge off.'

Roy looked out into the dark woods about them, thought he could actually smell the scent of the water rolling by. He rubbed at his face again and said, 'Jason, look, what I said back there—'

'You don't have to say anything more,' his brother said flatly.

'Yeah, I do,' he said, feeling the words rise up in his throat. 'All the years behind bars, what kept me going was knowing that you were safe, that you were doing all right, that at least you were living and breathing and raising a family. That's what kept me alive. Seeing you a day ago, happy in your house . . . I almost turned around and left you, Jason. You know why? Because you looked so happy, so at peace, and I felt like such a shit, thinking I was going to come in and turn everything upside down.'

Roy knew his tone was getting plaintive, and didn't care. 'But I had that four-letter word driving me. Duty. I had more than thirty guys back there in Nevada depending on me, depending on me to get them free. And I'm sorry I had to use you and your family and expose them to danger, but I had no choice. You understand? I had no choice. I had to do it. Had to.'

Jason kept silent for a moment, just reached over and squeezed his hand. 'Okay. It's really okay. Look, why don't you crawl back there, get some sleep.'

Roy yawned. 'Sleep sounds good but there's no way I'm sleeping back there with that sack of shit. I'll stretch out here, Jason. Why don't you go back there and keep an eye on your guest.'

'All right,' Jason said, and he started to climb out of the seat.

'Oh,' Roy said, looking back at the shape that was Sloan Woodbury, out there in the rear. 'Watch yourself back there.'

Jason said, 'I can handle myself. Don't you worry.'

Luck is mine, Woodbury thought gleefully. Finally, a bit of good fortune, having the younger of the two come back in the rear. Up front the madman was stretched out across both seats and instantly began snoring, and the younger man, Jason, yes, Jason, was now sitting across from him. Such luck! If the madman had come back here, Woodbury knew he wouldn't have had a chance, but now . . . One of the first rules of negotiation is to know your opponent, and Woodbury had a fairly good idea of what this lad was about. He was the weaker of the two, the civilian, the one whose life had been changed dramatically by having this wraith appear at his doorstep. The past day or so had been one long, unending nightmare, and now it was Woodbury's turn to offer a safe haven, a way out.

His opponent was a fortyish American, no doubt frightened and confused, and the polished table was the dirty rear of a stolen van. Woodbury started breathing heavily through his nose, reached over, and tapped Jason with his left foot. Jason moved away, but then Woodbury started whimpering, panting for effect. He could feel the snot running out his nose, the tears forming in his eyes. The man seemed to move around and try to ignore him, and Woodbury struck him again with his foot, harder.

Jason whispered, 'Roy? You awake?'

Snores in reply. Woodbury started moaning, shaking his head, back and forth, back and forth. Jason clambered over and whispered again, 'What's wrong?'

Woodbury panted some more, and Jason said, 'You having a problem breathing?'

He nodded up and down, furiously, grunted some more. Jason seemed to ponder that and said, 'All right. I'll take the gag off, you don't try anything funny. All right? I'm taking it off so you can breathe better. That's all.'

Another group of nods, and Woodbury felt the fumbling of the young man's fingers against his skin, and keened some in pain as the duct tape was pulled free from his face. Even with the pain, the air felt cool and wonderful on his skin. Next Jason tugged—with some disgust on his face—on the rag in Woodbury's mouth, and he helped spit it free.

'Oh,' Woodbury whispered. 'Oh, you have no idea how good . . . oh . . . please, can I have some water?'

Jason scuttled back to his place on the floor. 'Sorry. We don't have any.'

Even in the faint light, Woodbury tried his best smile, hoping that smiling in such a way would affect his words, his tone. 'That's fine. Honest, it is. Please, I don't know your name. What is it?'

'Jason. Jason Harper.'

He moved a bit, nodded again. 'And I'm sure you know who I am.'

'I know.' The voice was flat, no emotion. This was going to be a toughy.

362

'Well,' Woodbury replied, trying to put some worldly cheer in his voice. 'Well, Jason, we sure are in a situation, aren't we?'

'I don't know what you mean by we.'

'You. Me. That man up forward who says he's your brother.'

Jason said sharply, 'He certainly is my brother!'

'My apologies,' Woodbury said, trying the soothing tone. 'Of course he's your brother. Tell me, Jason, where are you from?'

'Berwick, up in Maine.'

Woodbury said, 'Ah, I know the place.'

'The hell you do.'

'North Berwick. Next town up. Home of the great nineteenth-century author Sarah Orne Jewett. Am I correct?'

'Yeah, you are.'

Another bit of useless trivia, kept in his mind's memory bank for situations such as these. He pressed on. 'Jason, what do you do in Berwick?'

'I'm a newspaper editor. A small paper. Called the *Banner*.'

Oh, this was too good, too good to be true. 'A newspaperman. Jason, if I may . . . Your brother has told you a fantastic tale, has he not?'

Jason's voice was raised again. 'He's told me what happened to him and other guys who were reported missing in action during the Vietnam War, that's what he's told me.'

'Of course, of course,' Woodbury said. 'And you're his brother. And of course you're going to believe him when he tells you these things. What brother wouldn't? But you're a newspaperman, Jason. I know newsmen and newswomen quite well. And no matter the story, the background, there is a bedrock quality to them and their work. Am I correct?'

'I don't know what you're driving at.'

'What I'm driving at, Jason, is that all newsmen and newswomen strive to seek the truth, correct? And in doing so, they talk to various sources. In fact, they try to get both sides of the story. Isn't that right?'

Jason was quiet, and Woodbury wondered if he had pushed too hard, too quick. He was trying to think of his next approach when Jason made the choice for him. 'So. That's what you're saying, hunh? You want to tell me the other side of the story?'

'Exactly right,' Woodbury said, hoping the glee wasn't showing in his voice. 'You're exactly right. Don't you think it's fair? After all, I was at home until just a few hours ago, when my house was broken into, I was assaulted, stabbed and then kidnapped. Don't I deserve to tell you at least my side of the story, of what might have happened to your brother and his . . . friends.'

Another pause from Jason. Woodbury's mouth was dry and his face was sore and his shoulder was still throbbing over there, but this . . . this could be it.

Jason whispered, 'Roy?'

The snoring went on.

Woodbury said, 'All I want to do is talk.'

The young man thought again. 'All right. Talk. But don't try anything funny.'

Woodbury grinned. 'That's the furthest thought from my mind.'

TWENTY-FOUR

Considering everything she had no doubt gone through in the past day, Patty Harper wasn't that bad looking. Still, Clay Goodwin thought, she might look even better in the next hour or three, if things worked out and he had some play time. In the meanwhile, it was focus time, and that stretch of time was tiny indeed. He had gotten here just at the right moment, had jived his way past the local cops without any problems whatsoever, and if he was lucky, he had the key to solving one major problem right before him.

Patty glanced over at her boy, over at Clay, and then back to the sleeping boy again. 'Who are you?'

Clay said, 'I'm a problem solver, that's what I am.'

Now she was looking back at him. 'But the police . . . they think you're from the Department of Justice.'

'Yeah, ain't that a hoot.'

'How did you do that?'

'Simple, really,' Clay said, looking about the tiny and depressing office. Jesus, imagine being at the top of your game, a police chief in small-town Maine, and this is your reward? Clay was under no illusions about how he would end up, that it would occur in a hail of bullets or an explosive device, but at least he would end as a warrior, not some flunky in a sweaty polyester uniform.

He said, 'You come in and you have a knowledge of the case, of the people involved. You show an official ID. If they have a question, they can call the Department of Justice and they can get someone on the other end of the line who'll verify that, yes, I am who I say I am. Of course, that someone has just been paid a lot of money to say something like that, and maybe somebody with a knowledge of computers and phone lines has done some trickery so that a phone line going into the Department of Justice doesn't exactly ring out at the Department of Justice, but that's too technical for my little head.'

'But I don't—'

Clay held up his hand. 'Sorry, ma'am. Your question time is over. My question time is about to begin. And the answers you provide will go a long way to determining whether your young boy over there grows up. Do I make myself clear?'

Her face was pale. 'You're a monster.'

'No doubt I am,' he replied cheerfully, 'but you know what? Sometimes this world needs monsters like me. Trust me, I get paid and I get treated very well for my work. Now. Question time. Where are they?'

He looked at her eyes, saw the struggle there for a moment, wondered if she was going to stall through Plan A ('I don't know what you're talking about') or Plan B ('I don't know').

The pretty Mrs. Harper went straight to Plan B, which was a good sign of progress. She said, 'I don't know.'

Clay made a show of sighing, to put a bit of fear into her, and she said quickly, 'Honest to God, I don't know. You have to believe me! They left yesterday morning. All I know is that they were leaving to see someone, someone that Jason's brother just had to see.'

366

'Did they say who this was?'

'No.'

Clay toyed with a pen for a moment. 'Mrs. Harper, I'm not going to waste time here, so listen carefully. Your husband and his brother, just a few hours ago, assaulted and kidnapped Sloan Woodbury, the former secretary of state. They are now missing. What I need from you is some idea of where they might have taken him. What do you have?'

She was silent, eyes filling with tears, and he sharpened his voice. 'Come on, Mrs. Harper! Where would they take him? Does your husband have friends in the military, in politics, anybody influential, anybody at all?'

He stood up and placed both hands on the desk, just as the little guy on the bench rolled over and yawned and said, 'Mommy, can we go home now?' My, what a wonderful little gift that was. The boy was looking over at him and his mother's eyes were flowing, and Clay lowered his voice and said, 'I'll make this complex so the offspring doesn't understand, but if you don't want to see brain matter from the offspring on that awful cement wall in sixty seconds, you'll tell me where you think they might be going.'

She shuddered. 'Frank. I think they'd be seeing Frank. I'm sorry, that's the best I can come up with. Please don't hurt . . . please don't hurt the offspring.'

'And who is this Frank fellow?'

'He's the news director for Channel 21. Over in Manchester.'

Oh, Mother of God and all the saints preserve us, he thought. A television guy. Which made sense. Would you take your brother and his outrageous story and the secretary of state to the Boston *Globe*, or the New York *Times*, where there would be delays and questions asked, and time stretching out so that the danger of being found out increased with every minute? Or do you go to an acquaintance, someone who practically runs a fucking television station? Jesus! If that word got out . . .

'You know where he lives?'

'Yes. In Bedford. Next to Manchester.'

'How long from here to there?'

'About an hour and a half.'

He looked at his watch. It was two-thirty in the morning. If they left right now, they could be at the TV guy's house by four A.M. All right. That's where they were headed, hell, that's where they might be right now. Time for a quick intelligence check.

'The number.'

'What?'

Clay said, 'The number for your Frank guy. Give it to me, right now.'

'I . . . I need to look in my purse.'

'Go ahead. Make it snappy.'

Clay watched as she put a small leather purse in her lap, started pawing through all the contents that broads seemed to need to carry around with them, and pulled out a small date-book. Nervously she read off the number. Clay picked up the chief's phone, dialed it. It rang ten times before a sleepy male voice said, 'H'lo?' and Clay said, 'Sorry, wrong number,' and hung up.

'Okay. It doesn't look like your hubby's quite there. Come along, let's go for a ride.'

He got up from behind the desk, and Mrs. Harper said quickly, 'Take me, please. Leave Paul here. Take me . . . and . . . you can do anything you want. Anything. But please . . . leave Paul here.'

Clay smiled, made a tiny bow in her direction. 'Ma'am, that is certainly a gallant offer, and the best one I've received in days, but I'm afraid I must decline it. We will all travel as a happy group, all the way to Bedford.'

And he showed her his holstered weapon, one more time. 'Just a reminder, as we go out past the police. Nothing unusual, nothing hysterical, nothing at all except smiling and good-natured cooperation, or something bloody splatters against the rear of that nice blouse you're wearing. Okay?'

She nodded. Clay said, 'I really must insist on hearing an answer, Mrs. Harper.'

'Yes,' she said sullenly. 'I'll do whatever you want. You bastard.'

Another bow. 'My birth certificate says otherwise, but I'll let that be. Come along, it's time for us to go.'

Jason Harper listened again to the snores of his brother, and then turned to Sloan Woodbury, still finding it hard to believe that this man he had seen on the television shows, whose face had been on the cover of *Time* and *Newsweek*, was sharing the rear of a stolen van with him. 'All right, talk. But keep your voice down. I don't want you to wake up my brother.'

Woodbury nodded and said, 'Very good. First, Jason—may I call you Jason?—first, I must offer my sincere apologies to you and your family for what you have been put through. Please believe me when I say we had no choice in what we did.'

Jason struggled to keep his voice down. 'Fuck you, your apologies, and your choices.'

Woodbury said in the semidarkness of the van, 'Your anger is quite understandable, as a brother and a family member. But as a newspaperman and a citizen, please, hear me out. My predecessors and I, we did the best we could, under difficult circumstances.'

'You and your predecessors, you betrayed them. All of them. More than a hundred POWs. All of you knew that they were in Russia. Right?'

The former secretary of state sighed. 'We didn't know. I admit we had suspicions. Of course we did. And it was no secret, was it? There were rumors, half-truths, in books and newspaper articles. And publicly and privately we approached the Soviets, and they denied it. What then? Break off diplomatic relations? Engage in a new arms race? Bomb Moscow on the off chance that perhaps they were holding some of our POWs?'

Jason was tired, God he was tired, and he didn't want to spend time arguing with this creature, but Roy was sleeping, so let him sleep. He said, 'But there's no more Soviet Union.'

'Yes, of course,' the older man replied. 'On the surface, all seems free and democratic in the new Russia. But what is beneath the surface is the old Communist leaders, the old party apparatus. Of what value would it be to those men to have old, embarrassing secrets unearthed? So the silence remained, until a few years ago. As your brother no doubt told you.'

'Then what? What happened then?'

Even in the semidarkness he could see Woodbury shrug. 'A change in government, a change in policy. Suddenly, officially, these men were located. And then they were turned over to our custody. From there . . . well, you know just part of the story, I am sure.'

Jason got on his knees, got close up to Woodbury so he could speak in the smug man's face. 'Part of the story? Part of the story? Yeah, I guess you're right. The part I know about is being drugged and dumped into Nevada. The part I know about is that the surviving MIAs aren't in Russia or Vietnam or Laos. They're in the United fucking States, and you and your buddies have put them there, have threatened to kill them and their families. That's the part I know about. Any other parts you got in there you want to tell me about?'

The man seemed unflappable. 'Yes. There are.'

'Well, here're a few more,' Jason said, hoping his raised voice wouldn't wake his brother. 'My family was threatened, not more than a day ago, by goons hired by you or whoever to keep watch on us to see if anybody managed to get out of Nevada and get home. And my newspaper was burned to the ground and a man who worked for me—' Jason swallowed— 'a good man, was killed. All because of you.'

'No, I deny that.'

'You deny that it happened?'

'No, but I deny I had anything to do with it. Look, I don't know the particulars of what happened in your home or your place of business. I do know that stringent security was put in place, for obvious reasons. If these things happened to you and your family and your newspaper and this poor gentleman . . . I apologize. I promise that those responsible will be punished. But Jason. There are still a few facts you haven't considered, facts your brother hasn't told you.'

'Such as what?'

'Such as the fact that when he and his friends were offered to us by the Russians, everyone had moved on. Vietnam was forgotten except for the occasional documentary or movie. The lives of their families and their loved ones had settled down. Former wives had married. Sons and daughters had grown up with new fathers. Wouldn't their lives have been torn apart by having men they presumed dead back alive? Can you tell me that the man up front there, the one who stabbed me, hasn't disrupted your life?'

Jason kept quiet, thinking of Patty and Paul, God knows where, but safe. At least they were safe. Woodbury said, 'Then there is our nation. You're a newspaperman. I don't have to point out certain facts, that times have changed. For better or worse, Asia is changing, and we have an ally in Asia, an ally whose home address is Moscow. With their help, there is a chance to avoid war, to avoid the deaths of millions to come. Can you imagine how this new, barely breathing relationship would survive if these former prisoners were put in front of the television? Can you?'

Jason found that his fists were clenched. 'Who said you could play God?'

'You did,' he simply said. 'By voting, you told us which party you wanted in the White House. By not voting, you told us you didn't care. Either way, a choice was made. Jason, time is running out for another choice. What you're going to do.'

Now the back of his head seemed as tightly clenched as his fists. 'What do you mean, what I'm going to do?'

Woodbury said, his tone still polite and soothing, 'Your brother is not well. He and the others . . . well, another part of the tale. They have been prisoners so long, they have gone mad. They believe in plots against them. Keeping them safe and fed and medicated and isolated was merciful. And you saw what happened once he got out. He broke into my house, kidnapped me, and assaulted me. All serious crimes. Now, I've heard the two of you talk. I know he has some grand illusion of getting me on television, and getting me to confess. But it's not going to happen. You're an intelligent man. You know the police, the FBI, right now, are looking for me. This will not end well, and it's going to end on the road between here and wherever you're taking me, with a police chase, a pullover, and a bullet to your brother's head. And even if by some miracle you get me to that television station, I will not say a word about anything. I mean, what are the two of you planning? To torture me with a knife again, in a studio? No, I will keep quiet, and again, Jason, the police will be out there. Unless you make the right choice, Roy will be dead in a matter of hours.'

Jason closed his eyes. 'So what's the choice?'

More simple words. 'Come over here, undo my arms. Let me out quietly and I'll walk away. I'll make some phone calls. First, I'll let the Cambridge police know I'm alive and well. Second . . . Well, it's time for a change in the status of your brother's friends. After this upcoming summit is over, it might be time to let the world know what really happened to those MIAs. It would take some time, with news leaks and commentary, to plant the seed in people's minds, but there's no reason not to think that by the end of the summer they could all be reunited with their families. Peacefully, without violence or threat of violence.'

Jason turned to where his brother lay, sleeping and snoring, his body stretched out, his haggard face looking almost peaceful in the dim light. My God, just to cross this country on some stolen money, a bus ticket, and a stolen car. To come this far, this close . . .

'What about my brother?' he asked.

'Excuse me?' Woodbury said.

'What about my brother? Like you said, there are serious charges against him. Breaking and entering. Assault. Kidnapping. What will happen to him?'

'Oh, I have some influence in these matters,' Woodbury said. 'I can see all the charges being dropped.'

'And would he have to go anywhere? Back to Nevada?'

'Of course not. He could stay with you. Just so long as the both of you stay quiet, not go to the news media, while you allow us to work out an equitable situation with his friends.'

Jason still looked at his brother. Woodbury's voice now had a plaintive tone to it. 'You know it's a good deal, Jason. For your brother and his friends. It's the best deal possible.'

He turned. 'Okay. What next?'

'Come over here and undo my arms. That's it.'

Jason thought. 'All right. I'm coming over.'

In his years Woodbury had again and again fed desires that he knew prevented him from ever being married, from ever entering elective politics, but as much pleasure as he got from satisfying those desires, it paled in comparison to sealing a deal like this. The young man moved over to him and Woodbury kept his face blandly neutral, knowing that to show pleasure or excitement at this point would be dangerous. Just get his arms free and get the hell out, and sure enough, he would be making phone calls, just as he promised.

But while a signed treaty was one thing, a promise was another.

The first phone call would be to Nevada, to eliminate, once and for all, that damn threat that he had been living with all these years. Enough was enough, and if Mikhail Filipov had a problem with those men's deaths, well, too bad.

And the second and third and fourth phone calls would be to every law enforcement agency he could think of, and he knew that if he worded things right with the correct contacts, within a few hours this van would be on the side of a highway or roadway in this miserable little state, pocked full of bullet holes, and the two men inside would not live to see another sunset.

374

There. Jason was right next to him and Woodbury shifted his weight expectantly.

Roy Harper slept fitfully, wondering why his back was aching so, and thinking he could hear voices out there in the distance. But he was tired, oh so tired, and he kept his eyes closed.

Next to the former secretary of state, Jason could really smell the stench of sweat and fear on the large man. Woodbury graciously moved to allow easy access to his arms, and Jason moved in closer. Woodbury said quietly, 'This is for the best, you know.'

'You're right,' Jason said. 'I do know.'

Woodbury was trying to think of who he should call right after Nevada when pain exploded in his wrists, and the gag was slapped back on his mouth, stifling his scream. The pain was a twisting, tearing sensation, and as he howled into the gag he sensed that Jason was there, winding the tape around his wrists, digging into the flesh. Then the sensation stopped, and he flopped to the floor of the van, barely listening as the man came close to his ear.

'You forgot a few things there, Mister Secretary, in your nice little lecture,' Jason's voice whispered to him. 'Like the little demonstration I just gave you. That was something my brother went through, in Vietnam and in Russia. Called weightlifting. Torture sessions like you just experienced would go on for hours. I just gave you a little taste. The men who went through torture like that came from all across the country. What you and your friends call flyover country. Am I right? Places you ignore. Well, you said something earlier about choices. But there's something I have no choice over, and that's my brother. He's my brother, and I'm going to help him and follow his lead and do everything I can to make it right for him. So take your nice words and offers and shove them up your fat ass.'

Jason got up, wiped his hands on the carpeting of the van. Roy was now sitting up, looking over at him. Roy said, 'Things okay?'

Jason moved up and sat down in the passenger's seat, the fabric still warm from where his brother had been sleeping. 'Things are great.'

'Good.' Roy yawned and started the engine. The little digital clock over the radio said it was four A.M. Jason saw that and said, 'Good. We can be to Frank's place in about a half-hour.'

Roy started easing the van out of its hiding place. 'I figure that's going to be one big surprise, when the two of us show up.'

Jason folded his arms. 'It'll be a night he won't forget.'

Patty idly stroked the hair of her little boy, fast asleep across her lap. He had been fussy and whiny when they had made that walk through the police station and outside into this Ford Excursion. Some questioning looks had been cast their way, but she had forced a smile as the man led her out, spinning confident lies about taking her someplace for something to eat and some rest. Even Chief Malone had bought the lies, and when he looked at her, she couldn't look at him. She didn't want him to see any fear there, didn't want the march out of the police station to be delayed at all, for she was so frightened about what this man—God, she didn't even know his name!—could do to Paul.

376

She cleared her throat. 'What's your name?' Patty then looked to see if he would respond. She didn't particularly give a shit whether his name was Dave or Doug or Trigger, but she remembered once seeing a PBS show on self-defense, and the instructor said one of the most important things for a victim to do was to establish a bond with the captor. Too often, the instructor had said, the captor saw his abductee as a thing, an object. Establish a bond, talk, show the captor that you were a human being, and your chances of survival would increase.

Or so the instructor said. Right now she wondered if the confident self-defense instructor she had seen on television had ever tried to establish a bond with a killer while wearing soiled underpants.

He whistled low as he drove, some tune she couldn't name. 'Clay. You don't need to know any more.'

'Clay . . . why is this happening? Why?'

He said, 'Why? Because your brother-in-law didn't have enough sense to stay put, that's why. And guys like me have to be called out to clean up the mess he made, before it gets any bigger.'

'You burned down our newspaper, didn't you?' She couldn't bring herself to ask him about poor Jack.

'Yep.'

'Why?'

'Because it worked, that's why. Got you stirred up and in the open, where you made a phone call. Here's a news flash for you, if your paper ever gets rebuilt. This world of ours is wired tight. Phone calls, faxes, e-mail, cell phones. If somebody wants you, they can find you.'

Patty said, 'Are you Russian?'

The man laughed. 'Hell, no, why would you think that?'

Paul stirred some under her touch. 'Because the men who

377

broke into our house yesterday, and killed our dog, and almost killed us . . . Roy told us they were Russian.'

'Sure they were. But they were mercenaries. Just like me. Paid to do the dark work in the shadows that nobody wants to know about, but that needs to get done.'

Patty looked out at the silent homes as they sped through the night, most of them dark and safe and secure, with quiet families slumbering in peace, and she thought of Jason and the desire to have him here, to have him say everything was going to be all right, and the desire was so strong that it made her chest ache.

Patty touched Paul's cheek, marveled at its smoothness. 'It's not right.'

'Oh, spare me,' Clay said, starting to slow the Ford down. 'What do you know about it?'

'I know it's not right, that's what I know!'

Clay said, 'Honey, you're a pretty good-looking woman. Okay? But that doesn't mean you should get on a jet someday and fly to Saudi Arabia and decide to visit Mecca while wearing a thong bikini. Okay? You'll be out of your element, out of where you belong. Just like now. The big guys have decided that your brother-in-law and his buds are to be missing in action. Forever. Understand? Forever. And my job right now is to make sure that happens.'

He turned on the directional. 'And my other job is to gas up before we get any further. I don't want to be on fumes while we pay a visit to your friend in Bedford.'

Clay turned into a twenty-four-hour service station and convenience store on Route 202 in Rochester, outside of the Lilac Mall, and Patty recognized it right away. My God, she thought, looking at the lights of the store, how many times had she gassed up the Volvo right here among these pumps, and now she was back, in the company of a madman, a madman who could kill her and her boy without even breathing hard.

He reached down and popped open the gas cap with a side lever by the seat, and stepped out. 'Now, don't anybody move, okay?'

And before he went to the fuel pump, he turned, as if remembering something. 'Oh, and another thing, dear. Our conversation these past few minutes has been wonderful, and I think you're a lovely woman and probably a great mom and great in the sack, but that's not going to change a thing. If I have to do what must be done to take care of business, I will. No matter what lovely bond exists between us. Okay?'

Patty bit her lip, watched as he went to the rear of the Excursion and started up the pump. Gassing up a vehicle. Such a boring, mundane, everyday task, and again she couldn't believe the terror rampaging through her while sitting in this safe city in this safe state. She stroked her boy's face again and whispered, 'Paul, Paul,' then jerked with fear when the door opened up again.

'Okay, time to pay, and time for your little guy to come join me.'

She tightened her grip on her son. 'Why?'

'Because I'm not paying at the pump with a credit card, I'm going to pay inside the store with cash, and I want your boy with me when I do it.'

'No,' she said. 'Take me. Please.'

He shook his head. 'Nope. And have you make a fuss in there, with your boy safe out here? Honey, negotiating time is over.' He leaned in and said, 'Hey, guy, come on, get up!'

The tears started flowing again as Paul woke up, murmuring, 'What? Mommy, is Daddy here?'

'No, no Daddy,' Clay said, gently picking up the boy, Patty looking on, thinking, I will go crazy, in a matter of seconds, I will go insane and do something awful here, because my boy is in this killer's hands. 'How about some ice cream?'

Paul started sobbing. 'I don't want ice cream. I want to go home.'

Clay hoisted him up on his hip, gently closed the door, as Patty heard him say, 'Sorry, sport, we all have things we want and can't have.'

She sat in the Excursion, trembling, her hands shaking. She forced her purse open and reached in for some tissue, weeping and thinking and hating what she had become. A weak, sniveling woman who couldn't even protect her own son. And her hand closed around something soft.

Inside the convenience store, a yawning young man with orange-dyed hair looked over the counter as Clay and the boy approached, passing displays of soda and chips. 'Sure is late for your boy to be out,' the guy said.

Clay looked out to the pumps, saw the Excursion and the shape of Patty Harper there, sitting still and pretty on the passenger's side. 'Well,' he said, 'poor guy was fussy and wanted to come in for an ice cream.'

'No, I didn't,' the boy said, with Clay holding on to his sweaty little hand. 'I want to go home.'

'Shhh, bud,' Clay whispered down to him. 'We'll be home real soon. Just you see.'

'Still, it is pretty late, don't you think?' the young guy said. The nametag on his blue smock said KARL. Clay smiled as he handed over a twenty and a ten, thinking that one of these days he might come back and pay Karl a visit. Teach him some manners, and if that failed, well, pump a couple of

380

rounds into that pimply face with the ridiculous hair. Improve the breeding stock of the species or something.

'You know, I think you're absolutely right,' Clay said, smiling widely. 'Thanks for the advice.'

Maybe it was the time of night or Clay's expression, but the young man called Karl kept his mouth shut as he passed the change back. Clay took the money and said, 'C'mon, guy, it's time to see your mom.'

Outside, he gauged that gassing up had taken about four minutes, which still made him on schedule to get into Bedford by four A.M. As he stepped out into the parking lot, Clay froze, just looking at his vehicle. The young boy started whimpering again. 'My hand! You're squeezing too tight! It hurts.'

Clay said nothing, just looked.

His Ford Excursion was empty.

TWENTY-FIVE

In Bedford, New Hampshire, Frank Burnett rolled over again and tried to get back to sleep. The phone call a few minutes earlier had jangled him out of a deep sleep, and now he was having a pisser of a time trying to calm down and relax. It wasn't the wrong number that was keeping him awake, but the threats last night from the station manager, now on a red-eye from Los Angeles, heading up to Manchester airport and then to a late-morning meeting to ream out his ass.

Frank rolled over again. Okay, maybe—just maybe—he had let the personal impact on the professional. How could it possibly be anything else? To see the newspaper that Jason and Patty had worked on, had put together, to see it charred and burnt, and with their guy Jack Schweitzer dead in the ruins . . . well, sorry.

He sighed. Sorry wasn't going to cut it in a few hours, of that he was damn sure. He looked at the bedside clock, at the blood-red numerals. Four-oh-five in the goddamn morning. Thanks, mystery caller, you will have robbed me of something I was so looking forward to, a peaceful night and a quiet morning.

He closed his eyes.

*

In Raymond, New Hampshire, Steve Josephs woke with a start, thinking someone was in the bedroom, someone who had reached down and . . . well, okay, it must have been a dream. Had to have been a dream, because he had been certain that somebody had been in his room and had rubbed bristles across his face.

Just like Dad used to do.

Dad.

Once, just once, he thought, staring up into the night, listening to Jill sleep next to him. Why can't I dream about you, Dad, and see your face? Would that be too much to ask? Just this once?

In New York City, on the second floor of a building on the corner of West 44th Street and Broadway, Gary Keegan sipped at his third cup of coffee of the morning in one of the dimly lit control rooms of ABC. Just below him and visible through the glass was the studio, being prepped for an upcoming edition of *Good Morning America*, ready to go on the air in just over three hours. In his headset he could make out the chatter of other producers and sound technicians. He let his eyes flit over the dozens and dozens of television screens before him, showing different satellite feeds, blank screens, test patterns, other network shows, and affiliate programming. He saw a half-dozen or so anchor types from all across the world giving out news reports. He saw footage of a typhoon hitting Hong Kong, a small jet airliner crashing in Durban, and the latest in a series of gun battles between the Israeli Defense Force and Palestinians. He smiled to himself, enjoying the pictures flickering around the screens. One of his most deeply kept secrets was that he was a science fiction fan, collected pulp magazines from the 1930s and 1940s, and one of his favorite tales was about a future society where everything and anything was recorded and broadcasted for people's amusement. Terribly self-absorbed and pretentious, he knew, but he enjoyed being in this comfortable chair in this comfortable city, drinking hot coffee, and watching the miseries of the world unfold before his very eyes. It was real and it was live and, best of all, it was safe.

In the darkness he heard: 'Sue?'

'Yes?' another bodyless voice replied.

'Lead-off still Sloan Woodbury missing?'

'Unless they find him.'

Another voice: 'Any idea who might have done it?'

Somebody giggled: 'War crimes tribunal at the Hague?'

Another chuckle: 'If you couldn't get Kissinger, I guess Woodbury's second best.'

Gary cleared his throat. 'All right, a little less chatter, folks. Let's have a nice, normal, quiet broadcast, okay?'

Another voice: 'Sure thing, boss.'

He leaned back in his chair. 'Good.' A nice, quiet broadcast would be wonderful for a change.

In Washington, D.C., at the Watergate complex, Brandt Cummings sat in his office, glumly staring at the phone. He was an assistant attorney general in the Justice Department, had earlier been attorney general for the State of Oklahoma, and right now was hating the very thought that he was in this cesspool of a town. But when the current administration had roared into office, he had taken the job as a favor for one particular gentleman, who—as he so quaintly put it—wanted 'one of my own to keep an eye on that stupid bitch who got herself appointed AG.' So here he had been doing the work of the department, but also being the eyes and ears and occasionally, though he hated to admit it, an enabler whenever this particular gentleman needed a favor.

He shuddered, remembering an event in Seattle last year. A fugitive arms dealer from Iran had been captured at the border crossing into Canada, and there was great speculation in the news media about what secrets he could reveal during his trial. But the fat bastard never got to trial. A man claiming to be from the Justice Department took him briefly into custody, and he was never seen again.

And pieces of the Iranian arms dealer washed up a week later in Puget Sound.

Cummings shuddered again, opened up a lower desk drawer, saw the nice little bottle of Smirnoff vodka sitting there. The drink of choice for aspiring alcoholics. There had been one holy hell of an investigation after that fiasco, about who that guy was and how the Iranian had been set up. Cummings knew the whole story, knew it quite well, and those months of investigation had been pure, nail-biting torture, waiting to see if it would come back to bite him, as it should.

Yet the investigation finally petered out. He was safe.

But now the phone had rung again, another favor had been demanded, and Cummings knew he had to say yes. For Hiram Pickering had a long memory, had many resources, and knew lots of things about people—like Cummings's hobby of video-taping preteen-age girls at the beach—and he knew he could not, and would not, refuse his request.

He picked up the smooth glass bottle. Damn this fucking town.

And as he poured his drink, in kitchens and bedrooms and offices in Georgetown, Arlington, and McLean, men recently appointed to prominent positions in the Department of Defense, the Federal Communications Commission and certain congressional, Senate and White House staff were having similar thoughts, and were uttering similar curses.

Clay Goodwin tugged at the boy's hand again, furious thoughts racing through his mind, looking around the empty parking lot and deserted road, wondering how in God's name the bitch got away. Didn't she know what he could do, was able to do?

He took a breath. There she was, head coming up from inside the front of the Excursion. She had ducked down. That's all. But why? He went around to the driver's side of the vehicle, popped open the door, and almost tossed the brat in. 'Where were you?' he asked. 'Doing something funny with the wiring or something?'

'No, not at all,' she said, grabbing the boy and bringing him down to her lap. 'I was getting a tissue out of my purse. I dropped my house keys on the floor. That's what I was doing.'

Clay had a pretty good bullshit detector and had a feeling she was pulling something off, but when he put the keys into the ignition and turned it, the engine started right up. She was now looking away from him and was again holding the child, and he felt a flash of anger and envy so strong that it actually startled him. He knew he would never have anything like this, a woman to love and be with him, an offspring he could call his own. All the women he had in his life were either paid for, coerced, or were otherwise temporary in nature. Long ago he knew marriage and home life was not for him: his mind and personality were not hardwired for it. Long ago, too, he thought he had come to an acceptance of it, but seeing this woman and the natural way she held her child, well, it made him want to smash something.

And just then, the engine died.

*

Patty tried hard not to look triumphant, tried hard not to squeeze young Paul, as the Excursion's engine sputtered and coughed, and the vehicle drifted to the right and stopped. The road was now quite deserted, in farm country on the outskirts of Rochester, and Clay's face seemed to line itself with anger.

'Okay, hon, what the fuck did you do?' he said, speaking low and clear.

'Nothing,' she said. 'What could I have possibly done?'

She was terrified of the look on the man's face, but also fascinated by what she was seeing. It seemed like he was struggling to restrain himself from doing or saying a host of things, and then the look in his face seemed to calm down. 'Okay. Your choice. Just remember this. It was your choice. Time to find another ride.'

Then Clay switched on the hazard lights, stepped out, and started unloading plastic suitcases and soft duffel bags from the rear of the Excursion. Paul whimpered, and Patty stroked him, and a voice inside her said, you did it girl! Talk about girl power! You really did it!

Well, she thought, me and Playtex. It had been a close-run thing, pulling out the four backup tampons she always carried in her purse, sliding out of the Excursion on the driver's side, popping them into the gas tank, and getting back into her seat without being spotted. Well, she had been spotted, after crawling back into her seat and closing the door, but only barely. Thank God he hadn't seen the door open and shut!

But now Clay seemed to be talking to himself, as he worked out there in the rear. She looked around at the countryside. Maybe she could make a run for it, bring Paul along, and hide in the woods or brush out there on the roadside. She tensed up her legs, reached down for the door handle, and—

'Time to get to work, hon,' Clay said, opening up her door and startling her. 'C'mon, out, out, out. You and the brat.'

Patty took Paul and stepped outside onto the gravel. 'What do you want?'

'Want? I want you to look nice and pretty and scared. Like you are right now. C'mon, to the rear of the car. March.'

She moved with Paul, carrying him, his head buried in her shoulder, and followed Clay as he led her to the rear of the Excursion. The man reached into a coat pocket, pulled out a knife, and Patty felt her breath catch. No, not here, not this! But Clay knelt on the pavement, shoved the knife into the left rear tire, and there was a sigh and wheeze of air as the Excursion settled down. Then he stood up, put the knife away, and brushed the dirt off his knees.

'You stand right there, honey. Just look worried. And I'll take care of everything else.'

Patty saw him fade into the shadows of the side of the road, and then turned to face the dark road stretching out before her. She had bought her husband and his brother some time. How much, she didn't know. But she had also bought herself a chance, the first real chance since they had left Berwick. Maybe nobody would come. Maybe a cop would come. Maybe nothing would happen and the sun would rise and the evil out there in the shadows would go away.

Maybe.

Andy Powell was listening to a syndicated radio show out of Las Vegas that focused on UFOs and alien abductions, yawning and looking forward to crawling into bed with his bride of less than nine months in just a little while, when he spotted the flashing hazard lights up ahead. About a half-hour ago he had gotten off-shift at the Wentworth-Douglass Hospital in

Dover, where he was an emergency room nurse. The night had been a quiet one and he had caught up on some paperwork in a quiet corner of the ER, and was looking forward to two days off and some serious playtime with Kathy, who wanted to get pregnant and who was doing her best to drain him two or three times a week. Which was just fine. Kathy was a legal aide for a firm in Dover, they were both doing well and had enough money socked away to start house hunting in the fall, and he couldn't believe how lucky he was.

Luck. Lucky for this disabled driver he had come along. He got closer to the car, saw it was one of those Ford SUVs, and smiled at seeing the woman at the rear, holding a kid and looking scared. Not to worry, ma'am, he thought, pulling over. Your troubles are over.

He stopped, and as he put his own Honda CRV—a lavish wedding present from Kathy's parents, and he certainly hadn't been too proud to turn them down!—in park, his door flew open and he looked up to see a large man standing there.

Patty had read plenty of novels where something terrible was happening to the heroine, and the heroine always mentioned dumbly that everything seemed to happen in slow motion, which certainly wasn't the case here. The headlights down at the end of the road seemed to appear too quickly after they had pulled over, and the 4 × 4 slowed down and a young man inside smiled at her as he pulled in front of the disabled Excursion. She turned and then everything seemed speeded up, like a VCR tape in fast-forward. Clay seemed to leap from the shadows, open the driver's door of the other car, lean in and—

Flash! of light and *boom! Flash!* of light and *boom!* The figure in the driver's seat of the car jerked and fell and Patty refused to scream, refused to move, refused to do anything, as Clay dragged the man out of the car and pulled him into the brush.

Lack of time often meant a lack of niceties, so when Clay popped the door open, he knew he wasn't going to do the peaceful route and just grab the guy out, or the negotiation route and try to talk him out of it. Clay pulled out his 9-mm Beretta and popped him twice in the chest, then dragged him out of the driver's seat before he got a chance to get blood everywhere. A head shot would have been better, but Clay hated being around brain tissue. As he dragged the guy out, his wallet popped free, and after he dumped the body in the brush, he picked up the wallet and tossed it into the car. Better if the guy was not ID'd for a while, keep the trail colder. His own plates would, of course, trace back to the Hartford office of J.P. Security Services, but a quickie phone call would hopefully get it towed out before somebody found this guy's body decaying in the underbrush.

He moved quickly and efficiently, putting his gear into the rear of the CRV, and then he went over to Patty and her boy and gently pushed them along to the vehicle, its engine still running. Patty didn't say a word as he opened the passenger door and helped them in.

'Just remember,' he said, before going over to his own side. 'You get any more bright ideas, there's a man over there who's dead because of you. Just remember that.'

Clay walked around the rear of the CRV, got in, and put the vehicle in drive.

Time to make tracks.

They were now in Bedford, New Hampshire, and Roy was

following Jason's directions quickly and efficiently. In the rear of the van there was an occasional moan from Sloan Woodbury, but nothing else. Jason still felt wired after what he had done to the man. He could not recall the last time he had actually caused physical pain to someone—perhaps once in grammar school, in a schoolyard fight over a stolen Ring Ding from a lunch bag—and yet there had been a burst of guilty pleasure at causing Woodbury to moan under his touch. There was little traffic, and each time he saw an approaching set of headlights, Jason's hands started sweating some, as he imagined the lights belonged to state or local police, out on the hunt, looking for them. But none of the lights seemed interested in them, and now they were in a residential development in the town, traveling slowly down Duncan Street.

Roy said, 'I can't believe how much this place has grown up. God, I remember when this was all farmland.'

'Me too,' Jason said. 'Lots of open land is gone now, Roy. Plowed up and planted with homes. Fortunately or unfortunately, this is one of the fastest growing states in the East. Lots of changes to get caught up on.'

'Yeah, I guess.'

'Okay. Up here, at Piper, take a left.'

Roy made the left, and said, 'Frank. A good guy?'

'Oh, sure.'

'And you met him in college?'

'Yep. Worked on the college newspaper with him. Drank a lot of beers together, planned out our futures. Start out in journalism, write a half-dozen or so books by the time we were thirty.'

That made his brother smile. Roy said, 'So you're closing in on forty. How many books have you done?'

Ouch. That one stung. 'None. Dreams sometimes get deferred.'

'Yeah, but didn't somebody say a dream deferred is a dream dead?'

'Maybe,' Jason said, looking up the dark lane at the good-sized homes set away on each side. 'I've tried my hand at fiction once or twice, but nothing came out right. It's like the characters . . . it was like they were made out of clay or something, and every time I tried to make them talk or move or do something, they just crumbled in my hands.'

'Then try nonfiction.'

It may have been odd to be having a literary conversation with his brother at this hour of the morning, with a kidnapped American government official in the back of a stolen van, but Jason found he was enjoying it. 'I have, you know. I've done research on a book about the U.S. military and its effects on local communities. You know, problems with bases being built, the economic pressures, the environmental issues, land-ownership debates. I've done a lot of research but nothing's really jelled. Okay. Up there. The brown house, there on the left.'

Roy pulled the van over and switched off the engine. 'No offense, Jason, but maybe that book hasn't come together because the idea is so dull.'

'Maybe so,' he said, hating to admit that Roy was right. 'Maybe so.'

'Still,' Roy said, opening the door, 'if there isn't a book in what we've done the past twenty-four hours, then I must be pretty thick. You think that's an idea?'

Jason got out and shivered in the June air. 'Sure. A great book idea. Thing is, I don't know what the ending is going to be.'

Roy said, 'A happy ending. That's what it's got to be. A happy ending.'

Jason nodded. 'Okay. I agree.'

'Good,' Roy said. 'Let's go wake your friend up and start researching the next chapter.'

Jason fell in next to his brother as they strode across the dew-damp lawn, heading up to the two-story house, everything dark except a pale orange circle of light on the front door, marking the doorbell. The street was empty as well, except for their own van and, parked up a ways, an SUV of sorts that Jason couldn't identify in the darkness.

Carol nudged him, once, and then twice, harder. Frank Burnett rolled over and said, 'What? What?'

'Downstairs,' she whispered. 'Can't you hear it? The damn doorbell's ringing!'

He sat up, and then the noise came back, a noise he thought was part of a dream, as the doorbell downstairs gonged. 'Shit, hold on.' He rolled out of bed, picked up a thin robe, and Carol muttered something and said, 'I'll go check on the twins. Don't do anything stupid, like letting in whoever's out there.'

Frank yawned and scratched the back of his head as he went out the bedroom and down the stairway. The doorbell gonged again, and he went through the dark living room, stepping on a doll and cursing the goddamn Mattel company. As he got closer to the door, he realized just what a stupid thing he was doing. Who the hell could be on the other side of the door that he was so eager to open? He detoured to the fireplace, picked up a black iron poker and then pocketed a portable phone from the kitchen counter. He made it back to the door just as the doorbell rang again, and Carol called down, 'Could you please make that racket stop?'

'Sure,' he said, 'why not.' He held the poker and portable phone in one hand, and then placed his thumb against the speed dial that would call up 911. By the door, he flicked on the outdoor lamp, and then peered through a side window. A familiar shape was there, waving at him, and Frank said with wonder, 'I'll be dipped in shit.'

He dropped the phone and the poker on the floor, opened up the door, and said, 'Jason! Are you okay? Jesus Christ, where in hell have you been!'

Jason smiled at him, nervously shifting from one foot to the other, and beside him was one of the scrawniest and most worn-out men Frank had ever seen. The older man had a gray-white beard, and his face was wrinkled, like he had been outdoors a lot. Jason grasped Frank's hand and squeezed it, and damn it, there were tears in his eyes. Another hand grabbed his shoulder and Jason took a deep, shuddering breath and said, 'Frank, I've been through hell and back, and I need your help.'

Without hesitation, 'You've got it.'

Jason pulled his hand away, and then put an arm around the older man, gave him a squeeze. 'Frank, you're not going to believe this. But trust me, you've got to trust me.'

Something about the older man's eyes was now disturbing Frank. They had the gaunt, feverished look of a biblical holy man. He suddenly wished he hadn't been so quick in dropping the fireplace poker, but then the man smiled and Jason gave him another squeeze on the shoulder, and that made Frank feel better. Jason trusted this man, whoever the hell he was, and Frank said, 'Okay, I trust you.' He glanced at his watch. It was just past four-thirty in the morning.

Another deep breath from Jason. 'Frank, I'd like you to meet my brother. Captain Roy Harper, United States Air Force.'

From upstairs Carol was calling to him, but Frank couldn't

394

hear a thing. He was staring at the older man's face, remembered the very few times in college when Jason had mentioned anything about his older brother. Frank said, 'Jason, hold on. Say that again?'

Jason was beaming. 'My brother. Roy Harper. Alive.'

'But . . . hell, he's been missing in action for, shit, almost thirty years!'

The man smiled again. 'Oh, I haven't been that missing. I've always been around. Just far away.'

Frank looked to Jason. 'This is true? No shit?'

'No shit,' Jason said. 'He came to my house night before last.'

A breeze was dancing around Frank's bare legs, and he didn't care. 'Vietnam. Captain Harper, did you escape from Vietnam?'

'No,' he said. 'Nevada.'

'Nevada!' Another call from Carol, and Frank yelled back, 'Hold on, just a sec.' He looked back at his visitors, stared at Jason and then the older man, and there, buried under the wrinkles and the beard and the weariness about the eyes, he could make out the family resemblance. 'You two should come in. We've got to talk.'

'Sorry,' Roy said. 'We don't have time.'

Jason said, 'Frank, I know what happened to the *Banner*. And I know what happened to Jack Schweitzer. And it's all connected to my brother escaping from a facility in Nevada. He came to my house, and in less than twelve hours Patty and me and Paul were almost killed, our newspaper was burnt down, and Jack was murdered. Frank, we need your help. There are more POWs being kept in Nevada. We know where they are and how to get there. We've got to do something before they all get killed.'

Frank pulled the robe tighter around him, his heart starting to race away in his chest, the scent of a raw-meat story now wafting through his nostrils. 'You want me to go on the air with this?'

'Yes. This morning. It has to be this morning. The people who burned down the *Banner* and killed Jack, they're after me and Roy.'

Frank looked at the older brother and said, 'No offense, and truly, I mean this, no offense, but how do I know this story is true?'

Jason said, 'Two reasons. One is, you've got to trust me. Roy's told me everything that happened to him, being shot down over North Vietnam, held prisoner there, transferred to a Soviet military intelligence camp in Siberia, and then, a few years ago, taken to a prison on government land in Nevada. They started out with about a hundred survivors. Now there're only thirty-six.'

'Why Nevada?'

Jason seemed impatient, but Frank, while still detecting one hell of a goddamn story, was also hearing the ringing alarm bells of trouble. A hell of a story was a very close relative to a hell of a hoax—remember cold fusion, anybody, where a couple of scientists claimed years ago that they could create nuclear fusion on a lab tabletop, and nobody else could duplicate their results?—and he wasn't about to jeopardize his job for some crazy story, not with his wife and sickly twins upstairs.

'Think it through, Frank. Washington is entering into a new relationship with Moscow. What would a story about Vietnam POWs being held in Russia do to that new relationship? They had to be hidden, they were, and now we don't have much time. Frank, you've got to trust me on this.'

Roy kept staring at him, and Frank could feel something

coming from him, like the subsonic hum of an electrical generator. Frank said, 'Okay. Trust is good, Jason, but I've got a hell of a responsibility to the station and to our license before putting something like this out on the air. Okay. What was the second reason I should believe this story?'

Now it seemed to be Roy's turn. 'Do you know who Sloan Woodbury is?'

'Sure. Secretary of state.'

The older man nodded. 'Secretary of State Sloan Woodbury was the man responsible for keeping our existence secret. He's also the man responsible for bringing us over to Nevada, and keeping us prisoner there. If Woodbury were to confirm this story, would you put it on the air?'

Frank wasn't sure where Jason and his brother were taking this, but having Woodbury in the mix changed everything. He said to them both, 'You better believe I'd put it on the air.'

Jason grinned. 'Good. He's in that van over there, waiting for us.'

Frank looked at them, looked over at the van.

'No fooling?'

'No fooling,' Jason said. 'We'll tell you how he got there, but only if we get going.'

My God, what a story, Frank thought. Right here. In his lap.

'You hold on,' he said. 'I'm getting dressed, and then we're heading for Manchester.'

Roy was now grinning. 'Best news I've heard in a while.'

TWENTY-SIX

In the newsroom of Channel 21 in Manchester, New Hampshire, Troy Stanton was going over the morning copy for *Daybreak New Hampshire*, the morning program that ran from 6 A.M. to 7 A.M., just before the network came on the air with *Good Morning America*. The newsroom was fairly deserted, the computer screens and telephones quiet, with the only constant sound being a couple of police scanners on the assignment desk. Just beyond the assignment desk was the equally empty studio, which had the set for the news broadcasts, the soft interviews with the fake fireplace, and the kitchen off to the left for the cooking segments. At the assignment desk was George Shay, the assignment editor, who was on the phone with somebody, frantically scribbling notes, his short blond ponytail hanging on his shoulder.

Besides a couple of national stories of interest, a live shot from their bureau in Meredith in the Lakes District—reporting on a missing canoeist on Squam Lake—it was pretty thin. Troy was the morning anchor and did all the news and sports, while Paula Chase did the weather. It was 5:05 A.M. and Troy felt rested and refreshed, while poor Paula—checking over printouts from the National Weather Service at the next desk—looked like she had spent the previous night clubbing in Nashua. He knew that hardly anybody else in the organization envied his morning shift, and he didn't care. He liked getting up early in the morning, liked driving on the empty roads coming in here, and liked being in the empty newsroom before everybody started trooping in, from the sales staff to management to the engineers. Too many people. He liked the solitude and, most of all, liked getting out after lunchtime and having the rest of the day to himself.

George hung up the phone, called over to him. 'Hey.'

'Hey, yourself.'

'Man, that was the damnedest strange phone call I've ever received.'

Troy picked up another page of copy. 'How's that?'

'That was Frank. He's coming in.'

Troy stopped looking at the piece of paper. 'Now? What for? He never comes in 'till eleven.'

George shook his head. 'Something's up, that's all I know. He said he's coming in, he told me to make sure the phones were working between here and New York, and he wanted me to get hold of CNN, reserve some satellite time, from now 'till eight A.M.'

'What for?'

'Wouldn't say.'

'You're right, that is strange.'

George shook his head again. 'That's not the strange part.'

'Oh?'

George picked up the phone. 'The strange part is, he told me that after I made the calls, to make sure the newsroom is locked tight and secure. And not to let anybody in that we didn't know. No matter who they were. Including cops.'

Something started tickling the back of Troy's hands. 'You're right. That was strange.'

But George didn't reply, now talking to someone on the ABC news assignment desk, just checking in, and Troy went back to looking at the morning copy, which now seemed painfully insignificant.

In the rear of the van Sloan Woodbury kept his face calm, while this new person—whom he figured was the television companion of the younger brother—was now loudly arguing with the two of them.

'Jesus fucking Christ, Jason, you didn't tell me that you two kidnapped him! Jesus Christ!' Frank was sitting in the passenger's seat of the van, while Jason drove and his older brother sat in the rear on the floor, right across from Woodbury, who kept looking up front. 'I would never have agreed to even talk to you if I knew you had done this. Hell, I would have called the Bedford cops on the both of you if I knew you had him tied up in the van.'

Jason shot back, 'We didn't do this on a whim. He was involved in everything we said, about bringing the American POWs back to Nevada and keeping it secret. He's the one who knows it all. What we did was a small crime to expose a bigger one, Frank. That's what it is.'

'Crime? You sure as hell are right about that. What the hell is going on with you? Have you lost your mind?'

'No, I haven't lost my mind. Have you lost your taste for news?'

Part of Woodbury was appreciating what was going on. He knew his chances of getting out of this van and this state without saying a word on television were going to depend on who was roped in, and he was feeling much better. As much as he hated and despised the news media, when it came to having their cherished ethics called into question, they were

400

getting more and more defensive. And this one was doing a fine job.

'No, Jason, I haven't lost my taste for news. But I sure as hell haven't lost my sense of decency. I mean it, my God, that's Sloan Woodbury back there. Sloan Woodbury! And you're expecting me to go along with this kidnapping, to air nothing more than a hostage tape. Is that what you want me to do?'

'No, I want you to broadcast the news. That Sloan Woodbury entered into an agreement on his own with the Russian government to remove American prisoners of war from the Soviet Union and to set them up in a prison in Nevada. And that not only were these prisoners kept captive in their own country, arrangements were made to kill them and their families if they ever escaped. That's the story, Frank. It's not a hostage tape.'

Woodbury watched as the man called Frank looked back at him, probably struggling inside to do whatever he thought was right, which was a pretty stretchy word under certain circumstances. Like one's definition of adultery.

Frank said, 'I can't put him on the air like that. He looks like a kidnap victim, which he is.'

'Small crime for a bigger one. Remember the Pentagon Papers, Frank? The smaller crime was publishing the secrets of how we got into the Vietnam War. The bigger crime was the lying and duplicity and idiocy that got us into that war in the first place. It's the same thing.'

Again, that tortured look on the newsman's face. Quite interesting. Woodbury grunted and tried to catch the man's attention, and it worked. Frank said, 'I've got to talk to him.'

'I don't know if that's—'

'Jason, it's nonnegotiable. I've got to talk to him, or it's over. Right now.'

Roy spoke up. 'Okay,' he said. The other two men seemed as surprised as Woodbury, as Roy came over and gently pulled the tape off his mouth. Woodbury spat and spat again, and worked his mouth and tried to get some saliva moving around.

The newsman turned around in his seat and said, 'Mister Woodbury.'

'Yes.'

'Is what I've been told true? That this gentleman was held captive after the Vietnam War, with other prisoners? That they were held in Russia? And were later brought to Nevada after your intervention? Your own arrangement, on your own? Is it true?'

Woodbury looked at all three of them, thinking, fools, I've outnegotiated men who murdered their political opponents and raped their wives. He caught a glance of the time. Five-thirty A.M.

'No,' Woodbury said. 'Not a single word of it is true.'

Patty Harper jumped a bit in the seat of the stolen car when Clay shoved his cellular phone under her face and then pulled the Honda over to the side of the road. 'Here,' he said. 'We're about thirty minutes out of Bedford. Call your friend Frank and see if he's there. Punch in the number and hit send. If Frank answers, tell him to sit still, that you're coming over to see him. And then hang up. If you want to see your offspring keep on breathing.'

She started to punch in the numbers, said to him, 'What if his wife answers? What if he's gone?'

'Then, honey, find out where in hell he's gone to, and if your husband and brother-in-law are with them.'

Paul moved around a bit on her aching lap as she dialed the number, held up the unfamiliar phone to her ear. She shuddered as Clay moved in his seat, putting his head next to hers, to listen in. The phone was answered on the fourth ring: 'Jesus . . . who is this?'

'Carol?'

'Yes?'

'Carol, it's me . . . Patty Harper.'

'Patty. Oh God, Patty, are you all right? Where are you?'

She clenched her eyes tight. 'Carol, is Frank there?'

'Frank? No, um, he's gone.'

'Did he go to the station? Did he?'

Carol paused, started talking, stopped, then resumed. 'Patty, he told me not to say anything. Please. Are you all right?'

She kept her eyes shut, not wanting to see the face of the man sitting next to her, the man who had earlier killed the driver of this Honda as easily as crushing an ant. 'Carol, was Jason with Frank when he left? And was there another man there?'

'Patty, what kind of trouble are you in?'

'Carol, please, just answer the question. Please. Is Frank gone, and did Jason and another man go with him?'

'Yes, he did. He's on his way to the station. Look, I can—'

Clay snatched the phone out of her hand, snapped the cover shut. He didn't look happy and he said, 'Remember that blood that got spilt, earlier? Well, honey, whatever new blood gets spilt in the next hour or so, it all belongs to you. So just remember that.'

He put the Honda in drive and made a screeching U-turn. Off to the east the sky was brightening to a light pink as the sun began to rise. It was 5:45 A.M.

In the rear of the van, Roy crossed his legs and listened to his

403

brother and his brother's friend duke it out over the niceties of putting him and Sloan Woodbury on the air. Roy was tempted to whack Frank over the head, tape him up and dump him next to the secretary of state, but even in these last hours, he found a patience he hadn't even known he possessed. They were heading in to the television station, and with a sense of satisfaction he remembered what he had been doing about thirty-six hours ago, as he snuck into the yard of his brother and his family. He had called that one in a series of early steps to right a terrible wrong, and now there were just a handful of steps left. Just a handful, and he felt an old memory tug at him, of flying Bonny 02 back to Anderson at Guam, getting the main runway beacon nice and clear, all engines running fine, plenty of fuel left, bomb racks empty.

'Bonny 02,' he whispered. 'Have runway in sight.'

The two men up forward didn't hear him, but Woodbury seemed to take notice, though Roy had long given up trying to read what was going on behind those piggy little eyes. He turned his attention to what was going on up forward.

'I'm sorry, Jason,' Frank said, waving his hands around for emphasis. 'This is too crazy a story to depend on just you and your brother, especially with a kidnapped secretary of state back there who says you're lying.'

Woodbury piped up, 'Which he is, sir.'

Frank went on. 'Look. Let's be reasonable. You've thrown a lot at me in a very short time. And time is what I need. Pull over, let Mister Woodbury free. Then, well, go wherever you have to so you don't get captured. And let me track down the story. I can get it together in a couple of days. Find out if this place in Nevada exists. Find out if there really are POWs being kept there.'

Jason shot back, 'Time? That's our problem. We don't have

enough time. Look, Frank, Jack Schweitzer is dead. Get that? Dead because Roy managed to escape and get out, dead because somebody wants to keep the truth muzzled. My newspaper got burned down. All right? These people are playing for keeps, they're playing for high stakes. I swear to you, Frank, if we don't get this story out now, get ahead of them, then by the time you and a film crew arrive in Nevada, all you're going to find are some burnt holes in the ground. And me and my brother will be dead in a car accident somewhere.'

Woodbury said to Frank, 'Sir, if you attempt to put me or this poor crazed man on the air, then I promise you that by the end of the day you will be out of a job and your television station will lose its license.'

Roy smiled. 'Why do you care?'

The van slowed down as Jason made a left-hand turn. Roy now had everyone's attention, and he liked the feeling. 'Like I said, Woodbury, why do you care?'

Woodbury remained quiet. Frank said, 'I'm not sure what you mean.'

'What I mean is this,' Roy said. 'Why does he care what happens or doesn't happen in a little television station in New Hampshire? He didn't ask you to jump out at a stoplight and go find a cop. He didn't ask you to convince your friend Jason here to let you go. No. He just threatened you with losing your job and your license if this proceeds. Why does he care? He cares because what Jason and I have told you is the truth.'

'It certainly is not,' Woodbury said. 'This is all fine, sir, but if—'

Roy interrupted with, 'Frank, don't you worry about a thing. You get us in the studio and he'll corroborate everything I've told you. Everything.'

'How?' Frank asked.

Roy felt his smile get wider. 'I'll appeal to his better nature, whatever's left of it.'

Woodbury said, 'He'll torture me, that's what he'll do.' He shifted his bulk, lifted up his shoulder, and winced. 'See? This madman stabbed me just before he kidnapped me, back in Cambridge. Is that what you want on air, sir? A kidnap victim, a hostage, being tortured on air?'

Frank said, 'Is that true, did you stab him?'

Roy said, 'Only in self-defense.'

'This is outrageous!' Woodbury said. 'The man broke into my house, brutally stabbed me in the shoulder, and dragged me here, for no good reason. He's lying. Self-defense, my ass. Look, you're about to make a career decision here. Are you going to let these two get away with it? Are you?'

Roy saw the look in Frank's face and said, 'Here's the deal, Frank. I promise you that when we get to the television station, Mister Woodbury will calmly and forthrightly tell you the truth, will tell you what happened in Russia, will tell you where the rest of the POWs are being held. I promise you that. If the time comes when Woodbury is sitting in your studio and he refuses to say one word, then I'll sit in a corner, nice and pretty, while you call the cops. How does that sound?'

Frank still looked torn. Woodbury was now glaring over at him. Jason made another turn. 'We're here, Frank.'

He looked out the windshield, sighed. 'All right. Go up to the front door, first visitor space.'

Jason said, 'Are we going ahead? Are we? Because if you're not, I'll drop you off and go somewhere else.'

Frank looked at him, his face troubled but his eyes bright and alive. 'The hell you will. This is now my story, and I'm going to make it count.'

Roy looked at the bright blue numbers on the dashboard clock. It was 6 A.M.

Clay made calls on his cell phone, explaining, threatening, cajoling. He realized that the poor woman next to him must be terrified, knowing that with every phone call he was making her future was getting dimmer and dimmer. Which was true. There was no way he was going to let her and her boy walk and breathe later today, and the only reason they were here next to him and not in a drainage ditch somewhere was that they had something he could use: a connection to Jason Harper and his brother Roy. The minute their value was gone, well, they'd be gone as well.

He checked the speed. Seventy miles an hour in a sixty-five zone. Not bad. No chance for an embarrassing police pullover.

'Hey,' he said. 'How far are we away from the television station?'

'About fifteen, twenty minutes,' she said, her voice weak.

'Hunh. Not good.'

He paused, running options through his mind, knowing that when this was done and gone, he'd have to go far, far away. If everything worked well, which was still a doubtful proposition, he couldn't be seen in public for a very long time. Pickering Industries had been loyal to him and would probably find him a position somewhere out in the Pacific or Asia, which was fine. He knew he could adapt in any environment, and the opportunities for work and fun in some of those countries tearing each other up—like Indonesia or Sri Lanka, for example—gave him a chill of excitement, just thinking about it. Still, he sure would miss the good ol' States.

Oh well. Time for one more phone call. This situation was about to spiral right out of control, and the only way he could bring it under control was to use the local resources. The resources no doubt would be good, well trained, and independent, and suspicious of outsiders like himself, but resources were resources just the same and, with the right applied pressure and flattery, could be made to dance to whichever tune he requested.

He looked down, scrolled through the local directory of phone numbers, found the one in Manchester. He speed-dialed it with a press of the thumb, brought it back up to his ear.

'Manchester Police, Officer Wrenn speaking,' came the male voice.

'This is Clay Goodwin, Department of Justice,' he said slowly. 'I have information on the whereabouts of Secretary of State Sloan Woodbury. He's being held hostage at a television facility in your city.'

He paused, listened to the stammer of the officer's voice, and then gave Patty Harper a quick smile. 'Hold for your shift commander? Of course I'll hold, son.'

He looked at his watch. It was 6:10 A.M.

Jason felt his breathing quicken as they got out of the van, Roy helping out Woodbury, knapsack bouncing over his shoulder, Frank moving ahead deliberately with a keycard in his hand. Roy hesitated for a moment, and then tore away the duct tape binding Woodbury's arms. Woodbury glared at him but said nothing as he rubbed at his wrists. Before them was the two-story brick building that housed Channel 21, and Jason recalled the first time he had toured the place, back when Frank had actually been the six P.M. anchor. The building had been built right up against the edge of the Merrimack River— on the south side of the parking lot, the river was visible as it roared toward Massachusetts—and had housed one of the smaller mill buildings in the great Amoskeag complex that had processed cotton and leather over a century ago.

All of the windows on the ground floor had been bricked over, and only the windows on the second floor—belonging to the managers, sales staff, and administrative staff of the station—were glazed and open. The parking lot was nearly empty at this hour of the morning, and surrounding the television station were other old brick buildings, except for a rise two blocks to the north, which boasted the city's convention center. Jason hurried up to be with Frank, his brother, and Woodbury— being firmly escorted into the station by Roy—and when they stepped into the dark and cool lobby, he remembered the better times he had spent here, touring the studios and offices with Frank, and felt a pang of anguish, recalling last fall, having dinner with Frank and his family. They had come here right after the six P.M. news had wrapped up, and Paul got to sit in the anchor chair, while Frank had one of the cameramen zoom in and out on the boy's face. My God, he thought, Patty must be frantic, wondering what in hell was going on.

They took a right to a short hallway, and again Frank used his keycard to let them in. A man sitting at the assignment desk looked up, his eyes filled with questions, and Jason could hear the murmur of the morning anchor going through the day's news. Well, my friend, Jason thought, the morning newscast is going to get a hell of a lot more interesting.

Frank turned and said, 'Green Room. We're going to put you there while I set things up. Roy.'

'Yes?'

'My goal is to get you on'—he looked up at a large digital clock—'in just over an hour. That's when I'm going to get on the horn with New York and tell them what we have going on

409

up here. I won't give them any warning. If I'm right, then we're going to preempt *Good Morning America* and about thirty million people are going to see you live. Roy, I need you ready, and more importantly, Secretary Woodbury . . . well, you understand.'

Woodbury said, 'I don't care what any of you say now. You're all liable, you're all criminals. I'm not going to say one word in front of any camera. You can believe that.'

Roy said, 'You're not going to get any trouble from me. But you need to know that the bad guys are out there. The police might be roaring through that door any second.'

Frank said, 'You let me worry about that. I just want the story, and I want it right . . . in just fifty-nine minutes.'

Jason felt his hands start tingling as he saw the confident look on his brother's face. What in the world did he have planned?

'In fifty-nine minutes, Frank,' his brother said, 'we're going to make history. You can count on it.'

On the assignment desk a man with a ponytail answered a ringing phone. His face seemed to turn pale. He said, 'Frank?'

'Yes, George?' he answered.

'I've got Chief Gibbons here, Manchester Police,' George said. 'For you.'

'I'll take it in my office,' Frank said. 'Jason, you remember where the Green Room is?'

'Yes, I do,' he said.

'Then take your brother and Mister Woodbury there, and let's get started.'

Jason moved ahead, Roy behind him, holding on to the secretary of state's elbow, gently propelling him along.

Steve Josephs answered the phone right after the first ring

shot him out of a deep sleep. He wasn't sure if he had been dreaming, but the phone call—certainly not good news, no good news was ever phoned in at this hour of the morning—had dumped him into reality, which now sucked. He had been looking forward to some quiet hours with Jill and Michael, and now . . .

'Hello,' he said, wiping at the crust around his eyes with his free hand.

'Steve? Dispatcher Conrad, Concord. We have a SWAT team call-out.'

'Hold on.' He got out of bed, swung his legs to the floor, looked at the time. It was 6:20 A.M. On the nightstand was a small pad of paper and a Bic pen. 'Go ahead.'

'It's at the television station in Manchester. Channel 21, right off Exit Nine. It's a hostage situation.'

'Unh-hunh,' he said as he scribbled automatically. 'Where's the command post?'

'South end of the parking lot across the street. Cole Business Complex.'

'Okay. On my way.'

He hung up the phone and walked across to the far closet. Jill rolled over and said, 'What's up, hon?'

'SWAT team call-out.'

'Oh.'

Steve sensed about a ton of worry, concern, and displeasure in that single word. Jill was a wonderful wife and he knew he was lucky to have her and Michael, but she had never really liked it when he had joined up with the state police's SWAT team. Bad enough, she would often say, trying to arrange a life around a trooper's schedule, but it was worse whenever the phone call or pager alert came in. For being on the SWAT team meant you were always on call, twenty-four hours a day, unless you were deathly ill or out of state. The call-outs usually came about eight times a year, which didn't sound like much, but it sure as hell could cause havoc on family get-togethers, birthday parties, or stolen quiet times at a vacation cottage up north in the Lakes District. As the unit commander once said, 'If one of us goes, we all go.'

From the closet he pulled down his BDUs—battle dress utilities—which were a dark green-and-brown camo pattern. As he got dressed in the early morning light, Jill got up from the bed and said, 'I'll get you some coffee for the road. Where are you going?'

'Manchester.'

'What's up?'

He reached up to the lockbox, undid the cover, and pulled out his service pistol, and then grabbed his utility belt. 'Hostage situation. Don't worry, babe. It's probably nothing, be over by the time we get there. You know Mark Murdoch, he's the negotiator. He can talk anybody out of anything. I'm sure he'll be there before me.'

She didn't say a word, just went downstairs dressed in a long T-shirt from the North Hampshire Police Academy. Steve went back to the bed, sat down, and pulled on his boots, already feeling the adrenalin surging through his body, forcing himself to calm down, breathe nice and slow, and just go through it like it was a training session. That's all. Just another training session. He put his boots on, snapped on the utility belt, listened to Jill moving around in the kitchen downstairs. He refused to let his mind wander as to what might be waiting for him. Just get to the site. That's all. Steve walked out of the bedroom, thought about going into Mike's room, and decided not to. The poor guy was a light sleeper and if he kissed him goodbye, there was a good chance he'd wake up. And Mike was not a morning person. Steve didn't want to add to Jill's troubles by saddling her with a whiny and cranky boy, as much as they both loved him.

At the bottom of the stairs Jill met him holding a travel mug with instant coffee and a little paper bag. 'I made you an English muffin,' she said. 'Eat it on the way.'

The little touch of love from her almost made him choke up. He took the coffee and the simple breakfast and said, 'Thanks. Don't worry. It'll be fine.'

She tried to smile. 'I always worry. Be careful.'

'I will.'

He got out into the cool morning air, saw with amusement that other commuters were starting off to their vehicles. Well, he thought, getting behind the wheel of his cruiser, my commute is sure as hell going to be quicker and more interesting. He started up the powerful V-8 engine and flicked on the overhead lights. By the time he got to Route 101, he had the siren on and was pumping it up to a buck-ten in speed, the commuters pulling off to the left and right like nice little civilians, and as he carefully sipped the coffee and ate the English muffin, he realized with a cold sense of dismay that he had forgotten his morning ritual as he left, to touch the photos of his loved ones and to promise them that he'd come back home.

TWENTY-SEVEN

In his glass-walled office adjacent to the Channel 21 newsroom, Frank Burnett spared a quick glance to the studio, where he could see the back of Troy Stanton's head as he continued with the morning news show. Next to him was the weather reporter, Paula Chase, and he could make out the looping wires coming out of their right ears, making them both look like little robots. He turned on the light, looked at the relatively small trophy wall on one side, near the credenza, showing him with a variety of presidential candidates, who trooped through the state every four years for a chance to move into 1600 Pennsylvania Avenue.

He looked down at the phone, noted the blinking light. This was going to be rough. He punched the incoming-call button, picked up the phone. 'Frank Burnett.'

'Frank, Chief Gibbons. Are you all right?'

He took a breath. 'Yes, I'm fine.'

'Are you able to talk?'

Okay, first lie of the morning. 'No, not really.'

The chief said, 'We've received word that Secretary of State Woodbury is being held at your station. Is that true?'

'If you say so,' Frank said, hating to put the chief through these hoops, but he didn't feel like he had any choice. He and the chief had known each other since the chief had been a lieutenant with the department, and he a weekend correspondent. While Frank had never lied to him about any previous story, he had also never had any story like this one.

'Frank, how many are there with you?'

'The usual crew. Plus others.'

'You just hold tight,' he said. 'Is it true that a guy named Roy Harper is holding the secretary hostage?'

'That I can't say,' Frank said, looking around the studio again. Precious minutes were slipping away. 'Look, my position is . . . precarious. I've got to get off the phone.'

'Frank, don't worry. We'll get you out of there.'

Frank said, 'Chief, please take your time. Please. We really are okay. We're not in any danger. Believe me. Don't rush into anything. I'm sure it can be resolved peacefully in just a while.'

And he hung up and went out to the studio. Maybe when this was all over, the chief would forgive him.

Maybe so. But he wasn't going to count on it.

'George,' he said, walking up to the assignment editor. 'No more phone calls for me. Or for the station, for that matter.'

'Frank, what the hell is going on?' George asked, his eyes drifting for a second to the corridor leading to the Green Room.

Frank said, 'You and your wife . . . Corinna. Just had a baby girl, right?'

'Yeah,' he said, not sure why he was being asked the question. 'Justine. She'll be six months old next week.'

'What's going on,' Frank said, 'is a story that Justine's going to read about in her high school history textbooks. We've got work to do.'

The first news bulletin moved at 6:35 A.M., from the Concord, New Hampshire, bureau of the Associated Press, after an alert reporter heard radio traffic coming from the police scanners in the office. Two follow-up phone calls later, the story moved across the regional and national wires:

URGENT

MANCHESTER—(AP) Manchester and N.H. State Police are responding to the television studios of Channel 21, where they believe former Secretary of State Sloan Woodbury is being held hostage, according to police sources.

Secretary Woodbury was apparently kidnapped from his Cambridge, Massachusetts, home at about midnight last night.

It is not known who is holding Secretary Woodbury hostage, or why, police said.

Phone calls to Channel 21, the ABC affiliate for the state, have gone unanswered. The 'Daybreak New Hampshire' program is continuing to be broadcast, uninterrupted, by the morning anchors Troy Stanton and Paula Chase.

Manchester Police Officer Laura Gibson, a spokesman for the department, confirmed the response of units from Manchester and the State Police, but declined to say what information led police to believe that Secretary Woodbury is being held at Channel 21.

0635

In the control room for *Good Morning America* in Manhattan, Gary Keegan was looking again at the schedule for the morning broadcast—now less than a half-hour away—when the ringing phone at his elbow made him curse silently. Why couldn't things just be quiet for a change, so close to broadcast time? He picked up the phone.

'Gary?' came the familiar voice of one of his junior assistants.

'Yeah, Ruth. Go ahead.'

'Gary, Associated Press out of Concord, New Hampshire, is reporting that Woodbury has been found,' Ruth said, her voice trembling just a bit.

'Alive or dead?'

'Supposedly alive. AP is reporting he's being held hostage at one of our affiliates, Channel 21 in Manchester.'

A few other voices from control-room personnel chimed in with appropriate expressions and obscenities, and Gary cut them off: 'Stop the chatter. Ruth, what's the follow-up?'

'I called Channel 21. No answer. I called the police in Manchester. They've confirmed that they believe Woodbury is being held there and that they're responding to the scene. A Department of Justice source told them. No answer at Justice here or in D.C.'

Gary looked at the banks of televisions. 'Which one is the feed for Channel 21?'

'Screen B-4.'

'Tyler, cut in the audio please.'

He looked at the screen, saw the typical fresh-faced young newscasters, and then heard, '. . . and Paula will be giving us one last look at the day's forecast, and it's going to be a good one, right?'

'You bet, Troy, especially since you have that charity golf tournament this afternoon at the Wentworth—'

'Tyler, switch off, please.'

Silence. He could sense everyone looking at him, listening. He said, 'Brian?'

'Right here, Gary.'

'Woodbury's already the lead for the newscast. Change it to reflect what AP is reporting, also that the Channel 21 affiliate is not reporting anything amiss. And Ruth, you keep dialing up those New Hampshire clowns until your fingers bleed, all right?'

Brian and Ruth murmured their replies, and he looked up at the closest digital clock. It was 6:41 A.M.

Within a minute of the AP bulletin being issued, chaos erupted in a number of newsrooms in New England, including the five television stations in Boston, the New England Cable News Channel, and the four television stations in and around Portland, Maine. All of them dispatched film crews and satellite trucks to Channel 21 in Manchester. They were shortly joined by reporters from a dozen or so radio stations and newspapers, including the largest regional papers, such as the Boston *Herald*, Boston *Globe*, the Concord *Monitor*, the Lawrence *Eagle-Tribune*, and the *Union-Leader* from Manchester.

But other phone calls were being made as well.

Within two minutes of the bulletin being issued, the Associated Press bureau that had started everything received a phone call from a former New Hampshire senator who was now an assistant secretary of defense. The revised story moved about ninety seconds later:

URGENT

MANCHESTER—(AP) A Department of Defense source has told the Associated Press that former Secretary of State Sloan Woodbury is being held

418

hostage at a television station by a Vietnam veteran with mental problems.

Secretary Woodbury was allegedly kidnapped from his Cambridge, Massachusetts, home by Roy Harper, 56, a former Air Force pilot who escaped from a mental health facility operated by the Veterans Administration in California a week ago.

Harper, originally from Dover, New Hampshire, was a B-52 pilot in the U.S. Air Force who was shot down over North Vietnam in 1972. Soon after his rescue, Harper was hospitalized in a number of veterans' hospitals over the years.

Manchester and N.H. State Police are responding to the studio of Channel 21 in Manchester, where Harper brought Secretary Woodbury, according to the source. It is not known what demands—if any—are being made by Harper.

Phone calls to Channel 21, the ABC affiliate for the state, continue to go unanswered. Since word was received by Manchester police that Secretary Woodbury was being held hostage, the 'Daybreak New Hampshire' program is continuing to be broadcast, uninterrupted, by the morning anchors Troy Stanton and Paula Chase.

0642

Sloan Woodbury looked around the small room in distaste. In his life he had spent a lot of wasted minutes in such rooms, called Green Rooms for some odd reason going back to the days of theater, and this one was small, with a couch and two chairs, and a table with copies of *Newsweek* and *Time*. The *Time* magazine had a picture of an older and grayer Mikhail

Filipov on the cover, and the headline said, 'A New Partnership?'

Question mark. How appropriate. It should be an exclamation point, to demonstrate just how unusual and wonderful it was that Russia and America were finally finding their place on the world stage, a stage prepared by him only a few years ago, a stage now threatened by the two brothers sitting across from him. He tried to ease his breathing. The pain in his shoulder was now a dull ache, and even moving slightly didn't hurt as much. A tiny advance. How wonderful. Let's try for another.

Woodbury said, 'This isn't going to work, you know.'

The younger brother's left leg was jumping up and down, but the older brother, with his knapsack in his lap, seemed reasonably calm. 'Don't you worry, Mister Woodbury,' Roy Harper said. 'Don't you worry about a thing.'

'You're the one who should be worrying, Mister Harper,' Woodbury said. 'First of all, I'm not going to say a word on camera. Not a word. And if you plan to use your knife on me again . . . well, I doubt very much that any television station will broadcast that, and if they do, I also doubt that anyone will pay attention to what I might say.'

The man's little smile was infuriating. Woodbury said, 'And besides that, do you think the police are going to sit by and let you play your little drama? Do you? I wouldn't be surprised to see police coming through that door any minute. You, sir, are fooling yourself.'

Roy shook his head. 'Nope. You're fooling yourself, Mister Secretary. See, your problem is you don't have any faith in the people anymore. You expect them to be little sheep, sent here and there, keeping their heads down while you and yours do your treaties, seal your deals, and keep secrets hidden away in remote mountain valleys. You don't have faith in the people to do the right thing, to handle unpleasant news. You live up in your lovely, decorated, and quite safe tower, casting down your decisions and choices to the unwashed peasants below. Well, that's about to end in just a few minutes.'

'Don't bet on it,' Woodbury said.

'Bet? I wouldn't think you'd be stupid enough to bet against survivors like me and my buddies.' Roy got up and said to his brother, 'Any idea where there's a bathroom in this place?'

Jason said, 'Go out the door, take your first right. It'll be right there.'

Roy said, 'Can I trust you alone with him?'

Jason stared right over at Woodbury, and Woodbury felt cold for a moment, remembering how the younger brother had tortured him briefly back there, in the rear of the van.

'Yeah,' Jason said. 'You can trust me.'

Patty looked about her at the familiar skyline of Manchester, called the Queen City, for God knows what reason. Clay handled the Honda with sure ease, seemingly not even bothered by the fact that it was stolen and that its driver was slowly getting colder and colder in a ditch about sixty miles back. They took an exit off Route 293, and Clay said, 'Behind you. Red knapsack. There's a black wool blanket in there. Take it out.'

She moved and young Paul murmured, 'Mommy, I'm hungry . . . I'm really hungry . . .'

'I know, babe, I know. You just hold on and be a brave boy.' She moved awkwardly around in her seat and unzipped the knapsack. She took out the thin wool blanket, and Clay said, 'Here's the drill. There's no argument. No discussion. The next few minutes are critical, and you need to do the right thing for you and your boy. Okay?'

421

'Yes, yes,' she said, the scratchy wool blanket in her hands. 'Okay.'

'Good.'

The vehicle started slowing behind another line of vehicles. Up ahead, she could see the flashing blue lights of police cruisers, parked across Elm Street, which led off to the right and went almost directly to Channel 21. Only yards away were police officers, armed and ready to rescue her son and her if she could just say a word, make some sort of signal, but it couldn't happen. Not with this madman beside her.

Clay said, 'I want the offspring on the floor in front of you. Put the blanket over him. Impress him to keep his mouth quiet. We're going to be passing through a checkpoint or three, and I don't want to hear a word from him or from you. Understand? Just look pleasant and slightly bored. Got it?'

She refused to give him the satisfaction of hearing a reply, so she bent down to Paul and said, 'Hon?'

'Yes, Mommy?'

'We're going to play a game, just for a minute or two. Hide and go seek. Okay?'

'But I don't want to play a game! I'm hungry! I want to go home! I want to see Daddy!'

Clay said, 'Hush him up, or you know what's going to happen. Hush him up.'

The line of cars moved slowly, as each vehicle in front of them was waved off to the left. Hysteria was starting to gurgle at the back of her throat, hearing the threatening tone in Clay's voice, and she brought Paul up to her and squeezed him and said, 'Just one little game, please. For Mommy? Okay? Just one little game, and later today we can do anything you want.'

Paul was sniffling. 'Can we go home and see Daddy? Please?'

A voice from the past, her old drunk father, screaming at her mother in the kitchen: Don't make promises you can't keep. Unnerstand? Don't make promises you can't keep.

'Of course, Paul. Of course. Now, please, let's play the little game. Get down on the floor here and . . .'

Paul went to the floor of the Honda and she draped the blanket over him. 'This better not take long,' she said. 'It's too hot for him.'

Clay switched on the air conditioning and said, 'No more talking. Just sit back and keep your trap shut. Unless you want something bad to happen.'

They were now at the intersection. A cruiser was blocking most of the road, except for one lane blocked off by orange traffic cones. She sat back, folded her arms, felt her heart thump hard at seeing the Manchester police officer come up to them, scowling. 'No,' she said. 'I don't want something bad to happen.'

When the door to the Green Room shut behind Roy, Jason looked over at Woodbury, who made to speak.

'No,' Jason said.

'No? What do you mean, no?'

'I don't want to hear you talking, so keep quiet,' Jason said. 'The only time I want to hear you speak is when you're out in the studio.'

'Not going to happen,' Woodbury said.

'We'll see,' Jason said. 'My brother's gone this far. You and everybody else should stop underestimating him.'

'It's still not going to happen.'

Jason said, 'Oh, for God's sake, shut up, or I'll go over there and see how that knife wound is doing.'

Woodbury's face reddened and he kept quiet. Jason looked

to the door of the Green Room. Jesus, Roy, he thought. How long does it take for you to go to the bathroom?

Clay toggled the switch that lowered the window as the cop approached. He opened up a leather wallet and the cop took it from his hand. 'Clay Goodwin, Department of Justice. I need to get through the perimeter and to the command post. I have my assistant with me as well.'

'Hold on,' the cop said, going back to his cruiser. Clay tapped his fingers together and glanced over at Patty Harper and the shape on the floor that marked her son. Part of him was wondering if he should have just taken care of business back there when he had gotten this Honda. Dumping her and the boy next to the idiot driver—yet another example of how no good deed goes unpunished—would have reduced the tension of trying to get to the television station. But she and the boy had value, if he could contact Jason Harper and convince him to release Woodbury in exchange for their safety.

Of course, such an exchange meant a whole 'nother series of problems, but at least that was an option, an option that wouldn't exist if he had popped the two of them back there at that deserted road.

The cop strolled back, his face no longer scowling. 'You're cleared right through, Mister Goodwin. Take a right, and then another right. Offices at the south end of the Cole Business Complex is where the command post is set up. The bottom floor.'

'Thank you kindly,' Clay said, and he put the wallet away and put the Honda into drive. He rolled up the window and said, 'Nicely done, Mrs. Harper.'

'I can't believe how they let you right through,' she said.

'Cops are cops everywhere, Mrs. Harper,' he said, eyeing a

state police cruiser up ahead that was blocking another intersection. 'My bona fides have been established by his superior officer. His superior officer has no doubt contacted the Department of Justice and has received numerous assurances of who I am and what kind of authority I have. The police chief here has no reason to doubt me, and if that's the case, neither do any of his officers.'

He made another right, went down a two-lane road bordered on the right by a canal filled with murky water, and to the left by a two-story brick building that looked to be a twin of the television station, barely visible for a moment as he made the turn. Police cruisers of all colors and departments were lined up along the road, two helicopters were overhead, television satellite trucks and radio news vans and crowds of the curious were holed up behind yellow crime-scene tape and blue wooden police sawhorses. A bit of pride seeped into him, that he had caused all of this, though the pride was tempered by the thought that Hiram Pickering was probably shitting bricks while watching the whole circus unfold on Fox News or CNN. But what other choice did he have? Go in Rambo style and try to do everything by himself? Sure, and find himself in whatever passed for a jail in this city, while the POW pilot got Woodbury in front of a television camera and screwed up billions of dollars worth of deals. No, it made sense to use the tools that were out there, the professionals. They had a hostage situation and they were under pressure to get it resolved quickly, and his job was to make sure it was done properly.

He turned left, into a parking lot that was being kept clear for the higher-ranking officers. He found a space toward the very end and he backed the Honda into it. He put it in park, switched off the engine. Across the way the parking lot bordered the street, and he could make out the nearly empty parking lot of Channel 21, and just the south end of the building. There was yellow tape lined up there as well. He took the keys and put them in his jacket, then turned to Patty Harper and pulled out his cell phone.

'All right,' he said. 'You stay here, nice and comfortable. In the red knapsack, in the bottom, there is some bottled water and some energy bars. Best I can do under the circumstances. See this?' He waved the phone under her nose and she turned away, and with his other hand he grabbed her shoulder, hard, and she winced.

'Yes, I see it!' she said, her voice sharp. 'So what?'

He found his breathing had quickened. What was it with this woman that tormented him so? 'Look. It's more than just a cell phone. It also contains a transmitter. See all this gear back here, all the plastic cases and storage bags? Those contain the tools of my trade, my bags of tricks. And snuck in there, hidden so well that nobody can find it, is an explosive charge.' He grabbed her face, turned her so she was watching the amused expression on his face. 'You see, a long time ago I decided I wanted the best antitheft unit for my vehicles, and this one tickled me. If my truck or car or van was ever stolen, all it would take would be a phone call on this little phone to send out a transmission, and in a matter of seconds drivers on a highway would be using their wipers to clean off the blood and guts from the former car thief in front of them.'

Her eyes were tearing up, a sight he usually enjoyed but this time didn't. He released her face and said, 'Just so there is no misunderstanding. I'm leaving you and your boy for a while. I'm going to be in that building over there. I'll be keeping watch. You make for the door, you try to get out, you try to do anything that brings you attention at all, there won't be enough of you and your offspring to fill a milk jug. Clear?'

426

She was weeping without making any sounds. She nodded. He said, 'Again, just to clear everything up. If I even suspect you're doing something in here, I'll set you off. Got it?'

Patty nodded, and even with the tears coming down, spoke clearly: 'I'd like to sit on the driver's side. Please. I want to give Paul some room.'

'Sure,' Clay said, opening the door. 'But make sure you keep his head down. I see that guy sitting up with you, boom! Two senseless and tragic deaths, for no good reason.'

He got out and closed the door behind him. He took a deep breath. Two helicopters were still circling overhead. Groups of police in SWAT gear—helmets, goggles, vests, camouflaged uniforms, MP5 submachine guns and large bulletproof shields—were forming in one part of the parking lot, talking among themselves, checking each other's gear. Regular uniformed cops—both Manchester and state police—were also moving up and down the sidewalk. On the other side of the street, the cameras from the television stations were starting to line up. Out on Route 293, traffic was hardly moving, as the morning commuters took in the amazing sight just a couple of hundred yards away. What an incredible scene, what incredible chaos.

But Clay wasn't afraid. Chaos meant things happening for no good reason, meant confusion, meant people shot and killed who should be captured alive, meant a lot of things.

For his purposes, chaos was good.

He checked his watch. It was seven A.M. Time to do some real work, and he headed up to the steps that led to the office building.

With the morning newscast done and Channel 21 through-out this part of New England now transmitting the cheery

427

opening music for *Good Morning America*, Frank gathered the skeleton morning crew of Channel 21 and explained what was going on. Besides the on-air talent and George, the assignment editor, there was a producer, soundman, and two cameramen. They were all young, they were all eager, and right now, most of them were frightened and confused. He gave them a quick rundown of the situation, the story of American POWs being held at a secret location in Nevada, and how one of them had escaped, and how he was now here, with his brother and the former secretary of state, who was responsible for all that had happened. As he talked, the phones in the newsroom rang and rang and rang, as if punctuating his remarks.

'What we have here is a huge story, possibly the biggest one that has ever been broadcast from an affiliate like us,' Frank said, looking at each and every one of their faces. 'With a story so huge comes equally huge risks. The police are right now surrounding this building. They may come in at any moment. In the confusion, there may be some gunfire. Somebody may get hurt.'

The looks, the stares, the constant ringing of the telephones. He squeezed his hands together, behind his back. 'In a little while we're going to start broadcasting this story live. We're going to break into the national feed, and if we're lucky, New York will see what we have and go national. But I can't force any of you to stay here. With a little fancy footwork, I'll probably be able to do it by myself, from setting up the sound and camera to doing the actual on-air interview.'

'Frank,' Troy said, 'cut to the fucking chase, will you?'

'Okay, here's the deal. I'm going to ask all of you to leave. If you take the south corridor, past the archive rooms, there's a fire escape door there. Go out and make sure the door locks

428

behind you. But I suggest you leave right now. There might not be any time later.'

And young Troy looked at the equally young Paula and George and everyone else on the morning shift of Channel 21, and he said, 'Maybe I'm just speaking for myself, Frank, but screw it. We're in the news business, and I'm not bugging out.'

'Me neither,' said Paula.

'Me neither,' said George.

The rest of the crew said the same thing. Frank found he had to wipe at his eyes. 'Great. Okay. Look. Let's get things set up. I want the interview set. Three chairs. I want them all miked. We don't have much time.'

Frank turned and headed to the Green Room. Time. That was one fucking big joke, because right now he had to get assurances that Secretary Woodbury was going to go live in about ten minutes and corroborate this story, or Roy and Jason Harper would be heading to jail, the television station's license would be headed to a shredder, and he would no doubt be heading to divorce court and the unemployment office. Simultaneously, if possible.

Jason looked at the clock in the Green Room. It was 7:05 A.M. What in hell was going on? And where in hell was Roy? Woodbury was sitting there, his fat sides pushing against the arms of his chair, looking pretty satisfied, though he was unshaven and his clothes were a mess. But Woodbury looked like he had everything under control, everything to gain, and right then, Jason couldn't dispute that. Frank was gone, Roy was gone, and for all he knew, he and Woodbury were now in an empty television studio.

Woodbury said, 'Things aren't going so well, are they?'

Jason glared at him, looked up at the closed door.

Where was Roy?

'Looks like your brother ran into a bit of trouble, doesn't it.'

Jason said, 'Shut up, will you?'

Woodbury smiled. 'Things are falling apart, aren't they? It's just you and me. That's it.'

All right, Jason thought. Let's get up and go to the door. Just poke our head out, see if Roy is coming back, because, Christ, how long can a man spend in the bathroom?

Where was Roy?

Woodbury said, 'Still a chance to give it all up. Surrender peacefully, Jason. It can still happen.'

Jason didn't want to waste his breath on the old man. He got up and went across the small room, and then the door quickly opened up, and he stepped back, as if struck, for coming into the room was a stranger in uniform.

TWENTY-EIGHT

The command post was in a suite of offices that looked as though they had once belonged to a failed dot-com or something, but Steve Josephs at the moment could have given a shit. Metal desks had been pushed to one side of the room, phones that had their connecting wires wrapped around them were piled in one corner, and in moving some of the crap around, somebody had dropped a computer monitor on the floor, where it cracked open with a spectacular display of glass and dust. Voice messages crackled out from police radios, and the thrumming of the two helicopters overhead sometimes caused the windows to vibrate. Now State Police Sgt. Hank Griffin—the immediate supervisor of the SWAT team—was in front of a white board that he was using to sketch out what was known about the floor plan for the building that held Channel 21. Steve stood with the other two snipers from the state police—Russ Pridham and Tom Coffey—and three snipers from the Manchester Police Department's Special Response Team. He and his fellow snipers were in green-and-brown camouflage, while the Manchester team was dressed all in black, the difference between a relatively rural police force—the Staties—and an urban police force—Manchester. Still, they were good shots, good guys, all of them, and Steve

431

was glad to be there. One thing he wasn't glad about, however, was the lack of good intelligence. The Manchester guys were good, and like most departments they had floor plans and interior photographs of schools, hospitals, and public buildings in the city in the event of a hostage taking, but a television station?

Hank pressed ahead, sketching with a black marker. He was bald except for a close-trimmed fringe of gray hair around his scalp, and the top of his head glistened with sweat. 'Right now, this is what we know. The first floor has an open lobby here, and the studios are to the south end of the place, while some of the transmission and editing facilities are here, to the north. There are no open windows on the first floor. There are four entrances, one on each side of the building, with the main lobby here, on the west side.'

Then he went to the other side of the board, sketched a large square with a question mark in the center. 'The second floor. Offices. Management types, sales people, administrative staff. No idea how many offices are up there or how they are laid out.'

'Number of people inside?' one of the Manchester cops asked.

'Nothing firm, but you can figure on about six or seven for the usual morning shift. We know from the Manchester chief that the news director is there. Add in Secretary Woodbury and his two captors, and we're right around ten.'

'Negotiations?'

'Dead in the water. Nobody's answering the phone over there. We've tried bullhorns, we've even tried e-mail to the Channel 21 system. Nothing. And that's adding to the pressure that the guys next door are facing. The FBI Hostage Rescue Team is en route, but that's going to take a couple of hours. In the meantime, this site belongs to the Manchester PD, with our assistance.'

Even with the noise and the confusion, Steve felt a sense of calm come over him. On the high-speed run over here, thoughts had tripped along in his mind, about what might be waiting for him when he got here, but as before, being here with his team, with his brothers, calmed him right down. The job was at hand, and he would do his job. Simple as that. He asked, 'What do we know about the two guys who are holding the secretary hostage?'

Hank jiggled the marker in his hand. 'Two brothers. Jason Harper, a newspaper editor from Maine, and his brother, Roy. Supposedly Roy is a Vietnam vet with a history of mental problems. Word I'm hearing is that he has some grudge against the secretary, wants to force him to conduct some sort of broadcast from the station sometime this morning. There's planning going on right now next door on the entry team and what they're going to do and when they're going to do it. What I'm going to work through right now is a strategy for using the snipers to our best—'

The door leading to the main corridor outside opened up, and an older man, wearing green chino workpants and shirt, with thick glasses hanging around his neck by a thin chain, came in, eyes blinking quite hard. Hank looked over and said, 'Excuse me, how did you—'

'No, you can excuse yourself,' he said. 'The name is Norm Poulton, and I'm one of the janitors for Channel 21. I was told to come here and talk to a Sergeant Griffin about what that damn building looks like from the inside. Here I am. Do I stay or do I go?'

Hank smiled, and so did Steve and every other sniper in

the room. 'Sir,' Hank said, going over to shake Poulton's hand. 'You most certainly can stay.'

And stay he did. In the next five minutes they learned more than they had in the previous fifty. Poulton worked with Hank, putting together a detailed floor plan, and the snipers crowded around, noting window areas and possible points of entry. Hank also made Poulton promise to go next door and repeat the same briefing to the planners putting together the entry teams.

While this was going on, Steve perked up when the janitor mentioned a crawl space above the second floor. 'How big is this crawl space?'

'Hunh?'

'The crawl space,' Steve said. 'Where is it, and how big is it?'

Poulton took the marker from Hank's hand and made another sketch, this one thinner than the others. 'That there building was part of the mill system here, years and years ago. When they gutted it and turned it into a television station, they put in a ground floor and a second floor. But the dimensions were all off when they started the reconstruction. Too much headroom upstairs. So they closed off the second floor, with a four- or five-foot space between the ceiling and the roof.'

'Is it accessible?' Hank asked.

'Shit, yes, but hardly anybody's gone up there.' Poulton tapped the marker against the other two floor plans. 'On the north end, there's a set of stairs inside, for a fire escape. Goes up two floors and then there's a ladder to a hatchway. Pop that open and there's a catwalk, maybe four feet wide. Got boxes of shit up there, when the damn station started running out of storage.'

Steve was beginning to feel better about the situation. Snipers only worked when there was a possibility of acquiring a target. Based on what they had seen so far, it had looked hopeless: bottom floor locked down, no windows, no way of seeing the hostage taker. But now an opportunity was there.

One of the Manchester snipers beat him to it. 'This catwalk. Where does it end?'

The janitor shrugged. 'Right in front of the studio, where they hang all their lights and crap from metal frames and such.'

Steve said, 'So you can see the studio from that location, and whoever might be sitting there.'

Poulton frowned. 'Shit, yes,' he said. He rummaged around in his pocket, pulled out a fistful of keys. 'Any one of you young fellas want to take a look?'

Steve looked to Hank, caught the tiny nod. Hank said, 'Yes, I believe we do.'

Up on the clock it was 7:07 A.M.

Roy Harper enjoyed the confused look on the faces of his brother and the secretary when he went back into the Green Room, knapsack now lighter in his hands. He stopped and said, 'Hey, how do I look?' He rubbed at his bare face, enjoying the sensation of clean skin for the first time in years. The uniform was mildewy and thin at the rear and the shoes didn't quite fit, nor did the uniform cap, but at least the rank was correct, as were most of the service ribbons. He came to attention and saluted his image in a mirror on the wall. He saw an old man with weathered skin, who should have at least been a brigadier general if he had never been captured and stayed in the service. If he lived through this day, maybe the Air Force could make some amends.

Jason looked confused. 'Roy, what in hell are you doing?'

Roy said, 'In a matter of minutes, little brother, I plan to be out in that studio, being interviewed by your friend. What kind of impression would I make if I still looked like a desert rat who's been under a rock for thirty years?' He brushed some dust off the front of the coat. 'This makes much more sense.'

His brother said, 'Where in hell did you get it?'

'An Army-Navy surplus store in Nevada, that's where.'

The door opened and Frank came in, gave Roy a look. 'What's going on? And why the uniform?'

'Never mind the uniform,' Roy said, conscious of the time pressing in against him. 'Are you ready?'

Frank shook his head. 'Question is, are you ready? And the secretary?'

Woodbury kept silent. Roy felt a sense of joy and accomplishment that he hadn't felt since graduating from flight training. He thought about his brothers, waking up out there in Nevada. Your last morning in captivity, he thought. Your very last morning. 'Give me two more minutes, Frank, and we'll be ready to go on the air.'

'No offense, but no, you won't,' Frank said. 'I need assurance that everything is going to be all right, before I call up ABC in New York and tell them what I'm doing. You give that to me, and a couple of minutes after that we'll be ready to go on the air.'

Roy nodded, moved his knapsack from one hand to the other. 'I can guarantee that.'

'Good. I've got some work to get done, so come out when you're ready.'

When Frank left, Roy went over and sat down next to Woodbury. 'Mister Secretary, it's time you and I had what's politely known as a "Come to Jesus" meeting.'

436

'I have nothing, and will have nothing, to say to you or anybody else,' Woodbury said, staring right over at him. 'Not a word.'

Roy reached into the knapsack, past everything else, to what was lying there on the bottom, which had traveled with him all those long miles. 'Okay. I'll make a bet with you. It's now seven-ten in the morning. By the time it's seven-twelve, you and me and my brother will be heading out to the studio, ready to talk. How does that sound?'

'You're crazy,' Woodbury said.

'Maybe so,' Roy said, his fingers finally reaching the prize. 'But you must admit, I look pretty damn good in an Air Force uniform.'

And so it was clear.

Clay Goodwin sipped from his second cup of coffee in the office that had been taken over as the main command post. White boards had been filled with scribbled diagrams, empty doughnut boxes were on a table, next to another table set up with radio gear, and men in SWAT gear were huddled in little groups, going over plans and scenarios on the pale gray carpet. One officer was in a corner, dialing and redialing a phone, trying to reach somebody in the television station's newsroom. Once he thought he had gotten through, but the person in the studio had hung up on him. Before him was the chief of police for Manchester, as well as a major in the New Hampshire State Police. The chief was on a phone and the major was listening in. Both were good men, with years of experience and training, with the self-confidence that in this state, at this time, they were at the top of their game and the masters of all they surveyed, and this room, by all accounts and procedures, should have belonged to them.

It made Clay almost sad to turn their world around.

There had been phone calls, threats, shouts, curses, table pounding, finger waving, more phone calls, and pressure on the two men from all parts of the country and the state, and all it boiled down to at 7:11 A.M. to be exact, was that this crime scene and hostage taking was now under the direction of Clay Goodwin, Department of Justice. Ol' man Pickering had worked wonders, but Clay knew with a tinge of sorrow that he would probably have to leave his lovely nation for many, many years once this puppy got wrapped up. Too much publicity, too many news cameras, too big a story for him to wave bye-bye and disappear. When it came out—probably later today, maybe early tomorrow morning at the latest—that in fact there was no Clay Goodwin working in any capacity for the Department of Justice . . . well, he was certain that if the good major and the good chief ever caught up with him, Clay would be shot while trying to escape.

On a nearby table somebody had set up a portable television showing the broadcast from Channel 21, which was still using the ABC footage of *Good Morning America*. That was a damn fine thing to see, for it meant that if something was going on inside that studio, it hadn't happened yet. In a matter of minutes that studio was going to be breached and Woodbury was going to be rescued and those two damn Harper brothers would be taken away and disappeared. Kept locked up and incommunicado overnight, Clay was sure that he could arrange for both of them to hang themselves in their cells in remorse for what had occurred. Why not? Had happened lots of times before, no problem in making it happen again. All it took was enough money and squeeze, and nobody was safe in any kind of prison.

Well before that happened, Clay would also make sure that

Woodbury got on the phone and said whatever words had to be said to a remote place in Nevada, to make sure this shit-ass problem never happened again.

The chief got off the phone and said, 'Public Service of New Hampshire has cut power to the studio, but their diesel generators kicked right in. Looks like they're still operating on their own power.'

Clay nodded.

The state police major said, 'We've gone up to the building with our sound surveillance equipment. The place is still buttoned up tight, but it looks like everyone's grouped in and around the studio. We can't hear too well, but all the voices are in that one location.'

Another nod. Clay could tell that the two men were barely holding in their anger over being overridden, and sometime—maybe in a year or so—he'd send them an apologetic note for trampling all over their turf. But in the meantime the job had to be done.

'Very good. I understand you have a sniper team that's going to be entering the building?'

'Yes,' the chief said. 'A state police sniper and a spotter from my department. They'll be going in on the north side of the building. We're also going to have snipers on top of four area buildings, keeping watch on the entrances and the second-floor windows.'

'The sniper who's going inside,' Clay asked. 'What are his rules of engagement?'

The major said, 'So long as he abides by New Hampshire state statutes and our own procedures, he can react if, in his best judgment, he can end it without harm to the hostages. He's also to fire if it appears the hostages are in immediate danger.'

'Good. What happens after he's in place?'

The chief said, 'Then we move in the entry team. Coordinated entry through the main lobby and south entrance. We can have the studio secured in a minute or two, if we're lucky, after they're in place and a go order is issued.'

There was a commotion outside, and Clay saw a line of men troop by, rifles in their hands. Sniper teams, it looked like, heading out. The other SWAT team members looked up, and the major and the chief exchanged glances.

'Fine,' Clay said, looking out a large window to the parking lot below, where he could make out the solitary form of Patty Harper, staying put like a good girl in the SUV, parked on the far side of the lot. Once the entry was complete, she and her son would be taken care of as well with one call from his cell phone. As he once learned, there was no problem in the world that couldn't be solved with a well-placed explosive.

'Luck is what we're all about. Gentlemen, once your snipers and entry teams are in place, you're going to receive your go order.'

After drinking the warm water and eating the chewy snack bars, Paul calmed down some and was stretched out on the seat of the stolen Honda, his head in her lap. She watched as police officers trooped in and out of the building, as cruisers entered and exited the parking lot, and helicopters flew noisily overhead, and she couldn't understand why none of them—none of them!—had any curiosity about her sitting here all alone. A few minutes earlier she had gotten a brief taste of excitement, of the possibility that this damn nightmare was going to end, when two police officers on the side of the parking lot facing the television station started unrolling yellow tape, to set off another perimeter or some damn thing.

One of the cops had looked over at her, and just when she got up the courage to wave frantically at him, he turned around to keep watch on the street.

Damn it! And there he and his buddy stood, arms folded, guarding an empty street.

Paul started gently snoring, a nasal little tone that even in this moment made her smile. She touched her lips with her fingers and kindly traced them on his smooth cheek. Her little man, and this poor little man's father and uncle were holed up over there, while it seemed like a hundred or so cops—no doubt lied to by that slick monster Clay—were preparing to go in and kill them.

And here she was, sitting on her increasingly sore and uncomfortable ass. Sure, maybe she could pop open the door and make a run for it, but suppose she was spotted by Clay? Even at ten or twenty feet away, metal from the blast could still cut her boy down . . .

She moved her left leg, felt it bump up against something. She gently kicked it again, and then—without waking up Paul—she leaned down and picked it up.

A wallet. Black. She opened it up and removed the driver's license, and she saw a smiling man's face and the name, Andrew Powell, and she had to put the license back quickly, because she couldn't stand looking at the face of a man she had helped kill earlier this morning, dead because all he wanted to do was to help out, and in helping out had crossed the path of a creature who killed as easily as others breathed.

When she shoved the license back into the wallet, her finger struck something sharp. 'Ouch, damn it,' she said, looking at the little bead of blood on her finger. She sucked the fingertip and then put her finger back in, easier this time. A piece of metal, all right. She snagged it and dragged it free, and then looked at it, heart thumping.

A spare key to the Honda.

Sloan Woodbury kept still, listening to the man in uniform go on, while every now and then hearing the low roar of a helicopter overhead. Very good, he thought, the police are here. While Woodbury was under no illusion about his relative importance to the current administration, he was sure that the police would be roaring in rather quickly. That would be something to see, but if Roy was concerned, he certainly didn't show it. He was now sitting next to him, close enough so Woodbury could make out the odor of mothballs from that uniform, and his dirty gray knapsack was in his lap.

'You see, Mister Secretary, when we were in Russia, security was extremely tight, even though we were in the middle of a snowy and icy desert,' Roy said, and even Woodbury had to admit that there was a certain kind of doomed nobility about this man who was still determined to wear the uniform of an Air Force captain. 'Things changed when we got to Nevada. Oh, security was still tight, but it was mostly a self-imposed security. Our families were kept under constant surveillance, and we were told if any of us escaped . . . well, I don't need to tell you that. You know why my brother and his family were almost murdered.'

Woodbury snapped, 'If you have a point to this little speech, do get to it. I'm getting bored.'

Roy said, 'While in Nevada, security was also tight, but the concern was on us escaping from the compound. Some of our more enterprising prisoners found that on certain occasions we could escape at night and spend time in the office area of Malenkov and his guard force. The locks in there were

442

a joke, Mister Woodbury, and we found out a lot of information about where we were located, how we were supplied, and what kind of procedures were put in place for a host of different scenarios. We also learned about Hiram Pickering's involvement in the whole matter, as well as your own, Mister Secretary.'

The sound of the helicopters faded away. Jason was keeping still, and Woodbury found that he was now hanging on to every word from Roy.

'You see, Malenkov, the camp commander, was highly paranoid about his own existence, and for good reason,' Roy continued. 'If plans were there to eliminate us, no doubt there were plans out there to eliminate him and the North Koreans if the circumstances warranted it. So. The best we could figure, Malenkov was in contact with some of his former GRU pals from Mother Russia, and he wanted an insurance policy to make sure that if something bad were to come down on the camp, nothing bad was going to happen to him.'

Woodbury felt something foul-tasting, like old pennies, begin to coat his mouth. He swallowed, found the taste grew stronger. Roy took out a nine-by-twelve manila envelope and said to his brother, 'Jason, please, just for a moment, don't look over here. Okay? I'll explain it all later.'

'All right,' Jason said, sounding confused but listening to his older brother.

Woodbury thought the helicopters were back, then realized that the buzzing sound was coming from his own head. Roy undid the clasp of the envelope and Woodbury wanted to yell, wanted to shout, wanted to flee the room, but he had no strength, none, as the buzzing in his head grew louder and louder, as first one, and then another, and then another, black-and-white photograph was slipped out of the envelope and

443

fanned before him. He gave the photos a glance—ah, Melissa, that was her name—and turned away, suddenly afraid that he was about to vomit all over the floor. Ruin, absolute and total and utter ruin. All those years of disgust and shame and secrecy at his special needs, his special fetish, all exposed. The moment he had always dreaded, finally here, from this ghost of a man.

Roy said, 'This was his insurance policy, Mister Secretary. I'm not sure that he ever told you he had them, but this was what he had, for his last line of defense. And this policy now belongs to me. Sir, you are going out there and you are going to tell the truth about us and Siberia and Nevada, and if you don't . . . well, I guess you can imagine what will happen to these photos.'

The damnable photos were put back in the envelope. The top was closed. Jason said, 'Can I look now?'

'Sure,' Roy said. 'Mister Secretary? Sir?'

Woodbury could not look at him, the humiliation burning through him was so great. Nausea was battling with shame for control of his guts, and his mouth was filled with saliva.

Roy said, 'If you can't speak, will you at least nod?'

Woodbury nodded.

Roy said, 'You're not bored anymore, are you?'

Hating himself, Roy Harper, and the world, Sloan Woodbury nodded again.

Steve climbed into the back of a van with the other snipers and with the Manchester cops who were going to help him get into Channel 21. He sat on the metal floor, his Remington Model 700P .308 rifle with mounted scope balanced in his hands. He was trying to shut out the nervous talk from the other cops, the chatter of the radios, tried to focus on what was ahead of him, but something was bothering him. Something was bothering him something awful. For when he and the others had finally left the Cole building, he had quickly glanced into the main command post room and seen the chief and Major Carlucci of his own state police, and he had recognized the third man in there as well. A stocky guy with a thick mustache, close-cropped hair, and he instantly recalled where he had seen him before.

On that traffic stop on Route 125, the day before. Where the guy had claimed to be a security consultant, heading home to Connecticut. A cool customer who had even offered him a job.

So what in hell was he doing here?

Next to him was his spotter and escort, a Manchester cop named Ross Nelson. Steve looked at him and said, 'You hooked up to your CP?'

Ross was about his age, wearing the standard vest, web gear, Kevlar helmet, and radio mike suspended in front of his face. His eyes were light blue and quite wide. 'Yeah, what do you need?'

'Find out who that guy was, talking to your chief and my major back there. The guy with the mustache.'

'You fucking with me?' Ross asked.

'No, I'm not. Find out. It's important.'

So Nelson moved his head, murmured into the mike, and murmured again, as the van made its way up the street, hitting a pothole once, Steve holding on to the rifle with his gloved hands. Didn't make sense. Then Nelson said, 'Guy's from the Department of Justice. Goodwin. Believe it or not, he's running this fucking show.'

'Really?'

'Yeah, really.'

Steve closed his eyes, remembered again that traffic stop

yesterday, also remembered how hinky the whole thing seemed. All right. Maybe he wasn't a security consultant. Maybe he was with the Department of Justice, working undercover. Possible. But why would he be here, at this hostage scene? What could the connection be? And what should he do about it? The damn guy must have checked out, for the chief and his major were listening to him. Those were two sharp cops, and he couldn't believe anything could be put past them. And what should happen? Ask the chief and the major to hold everything up so they could run a credit check on that character?

The van halted, the door popped open, and he moved automatically. Time to focus on your job, pal, and to do it well, he thought. That other shit is way above your pay grade. Steve and Nelson and two other members of the Manchester SRT came out, and the van kept on moving, reversing course to go back down the street. They were on the north end of the building, luckily behind some shrubbery, for out there were dozens of television cameras, broadcasting everything that was going on, and you could be damn sure that there were people inside the studio watching the other stations.

They moved in a crouch to the plain gray metal door that had KEEP OUT stenciled on its top. One of the Manchester cops used a key to slowly unlock the door, and then he popped it open and he and another cop muscled their way in, Heckler & Koch MP5s in their hands. One tipped his head back to Steve and Nelson and whispered, 'Clear!'

Steve followed Nelson in, carrying his Remington rifle at port arms. They were in a small room, stairs of concrete rising up to their left. Before them was another gray metal door, also locked, and two empty metal trash barrels. CHANNEL 21/NO TRESPASSING was on a sign in the center. One of the SRT guys nodded and knelt down in a corner, keeping an eye on the door. 'Twelve in position,' he whispered into his mike.

'Okay, let's get moving,' Steve said, and they quietly went up the stairs, with the other Manchester SRT member up in front. Another locked metal door. The SRT guy knelt down, identical to his colleague below him, and whispered, 'Number Ten in position.'

Nelson looked to Steve and he nodded in reply. From the concrete and steel landing, there was a metal ladder, about five feet tall, that went up to a square access panel, which was locked. Nelson went up the ladder with the master key from the janitor and opened the lock. He put the key away in a pocket and raised up the panel, holding out his 10-mm Glock in front of him. The SRT officer on the landing followed his progression, also aiming his pistol up to the panel. Nelson wormed his way up, and in a matter of a few heartbeats he poked his head back through.

'Clear,' he whispered. Steve nodded, slung his rifle over his back, and started climbing up the ladder, utterly forgetting the problem of the mysterious man back at the command post.

Jason joined Roy as they shepherded Sloan Woodbury back out to the studio. He noted the time and said, 'Sorry, Mister Secretary. It's seven-thirteen. My brother was off by a minute. What do you think about that?'

Whatever Woodbury thought, he kept to himself. Jason wondered what in hell Roy had shown the old man to cause him to fold up like that in a matter of seconds, but whatever mojo Roy was playing with this morning, it sure as hell was working.

Frank Burnett came toward them, past the empty anchor desk. 'Well?'

Roy had the manila envelope and something else in his hand, but with his free hand he gently touched Woodbury's good shoulder, the one that wasn't bleeding. 'Mister Secretary, if you please.'

The studio seemed to fall quiet, except for the incessant ringing of the phones. Frank and Jason and Roy and even some of the Channel 21 people—all were staring at the man who at one time was one of the most powerful and influential statesmen in the world.

He seemed to sag, like a Thanksgiving Day parade balloon with a leak. 'Yes,' Woodbury said.

'Yes, what?' Frank demanded.

'Yes,' he said, his voice almost croaking. 'What these two men have said is true, about the POWs in Russia and in Nevada. There are still more than thirty of these men being held captive on American soil. It's all true.'

Frank's eyes seemed to light up. 'And you'll say that in a few minutes, live, on air?'

Woodbury nodded. 'I will.'

Jason felt like shouting or singing or dancing or doing something, for his brother had won, Roy had made it, and in just a little while the evidence would be out there, his friends would be freed, and—

'Okay,' Frank said, 'that's good and all, but we've got two little problems. The first one is that all the outside phone lines have been cut, save for one, which is picked up by a cop.'

Woodbury's face seemed to come alive, like a bit of hope had been tossed his way, and Roy said quietly, 'What does that mean?'

'It means that when we go live, it might take a few minutes before New York sees what we're doing over the satellite channel we've rented, and before they decide to break in on their morning show. I'm guessing they will, once they see what's going on. But I sure wish I could have made that call to clear things up.'

Jason said, 'What's the second problem?'

Frank pointed to a bank of television screens behind the anchor desk, and Jason suddenly felt topsy-turvy, as most of the screens were showing the exterior of Channel 21, as well as a fair number of police in SWAT gear moving across the parking lot to the building's doors.

'We might not have more than a couple of minutes before we get shut down, and I'm going to need time to set up the secretary and Roy and get them miked up, and—'

Jason interrupted. 'I'll take care of it.'

'What?' Roy asked.

'I said, I'll take care of it. I'll pick up the phone and start talking to one of the negotiators. Stall for time. Make them promise not to do anything rash. You go ahead and take care of things, Frank. I'll handle the cops.'

And as he headed to the nearest ringing phone, he saw the smiling face of his older brother, for the first time looking like he was proud of him.

The catwalk was narrow and crowded with cardboard boxes of files and videotapes. It was slow going, for it was only wide enough for one of them. Nelson went ahead, on hands and knees, and Steve followed. The air was dusty and the light was dim, but at least they were able to move without making any loud noise. Steve followed Nelson, kept watch on the man's boots, his rifle secure on his back. Then Nelson slowed as the catwalk opened up to a wide area, not quite as crowded with boxes and tapes. Bright lights were shining at them and he could make out sounds from down below. Nelson turned to him smiling, pointing down. Jesus, Steve thought, that janitor was right. Everything before them was open and clear, and he quickly realized that the lights glaring down worked to his advantage. The people on the floor would be blinded if they looked up, and with all these boxes and other crap up here, well, this was a damn fine place.

The studio seemed about fifty or sixty yards away, about the upper limit for using his scope, but it was manageable. Nelson moved to the left and set up a spotting scope and extra magazines for his pistol, and Steve slowly undid the rifle, loosened the bipod up forward, and lay down on the floor, his elbow and knee pads lessening the strain. Nelson moved up close to him and whispered, 'Ready?'

'Just a sec,' Steve whispered back, adjusting the bone mike. The mike took a while to get used to and sounded strange to the novice, but it worked by picking up sound vibrations from the bone and could hardly be heard only a few feet away. He moved around, felt something dig in his hip. With his right hand he reached down and pulled out the offending item. A small cardboard box with a bright red sword being pulled from a stone. Excalibur Arms, and unbidden, the voice of the salesman came back to him: 'A real special round with special qualities, gentlemen, if you want to blow your opponent into next Tuesday!'

He gently put the cardboard box down, shifted his position again, put his eye up to the telescopic sight. The blur of the studio quickly snapped into focus, and he quietly moved about until he saw a man come into view, a man wearing an Air Force uniform. Next to him was another man whom he instantly recognized as the secretary of state, Sloan Woodbury. A third man was placing tiny microphones on their chests, and when he moved away Steve saw that he had the secretary and the crazy vet sitting together on a couch. He moved again, centered the crosshairs on the chest of the Vietnam vet. He raised his head a bit, caught Nelson's eye, nodded. Nelson whispered into the microphone, 'Sniper team A is in position.'

Steve waited a moment. The Manchester police and the state police SWAT team operated on different radio frequencies, and he didn't want to have both he and Nelson broadcasting at the same time. Then he spoke into the bone mike, to his sergeant back at the command post: 'This is Steve. I'm in position. Target acquired.'

TWENTY-NINE

The spare Honda key seemed to be made of a precious alloy. Patty quickly inserted it into the ignition, and waited. Her legs and hands were trembling. What now? She looked over to the office building and saw a shape there looking over at her. Could be Clay. Maybe, maybe not. Would she risk her boy on the off chance that he might not be looking in their direction?

My God, she thought. What can I do? She looked over the parking lot, at the two Manchester cops standing sentinel there by the police tape, and then she turned on the engine. It started right up, and she almost thought about switching it off—perhaps Clay could actually hear the engine running—but then a state police helicopter roared overhead and she felt better. He wouldn't hear a thing.

Her hand went down to the headlight switch. She turned the headlights on and off, quickly, three times. Then she paused, and did it again, this time letting the lights stay on just a second more, and then she repeated the quick pattern, over and over again. Dit-dit-dit. Dash-dash-dash. Dit-dit-dit.

SOS.

'C'mon, c'mon,' she whispered. 'Look over here, guys. Look over here!'

And on the AM radio station, now playing, the announcer

was excitedly going on about a hostage crisis taking place not more than a hundred yards away from her.

Roy sat back against the couch, feeling comfortable, feeling good. The lights were bright, and it was amazing to see what a television studio looked like from the inside. All the small sets, the chairs, the large cameras. All the props to make illusions. But not this morning. No, sir. The props here would be making history, in a very few minutes.

He could smell the stench of fear from Woodbury next to him, and he almost pitied the poor bastard. The photographs were enough to turn his stomach but they had been a powerful weapon—much more powerful than the special packages he had trained with on his long dead and gone Bonny 02!—and when this morning was over, he planned to give them back to Woodbury. To hell with it. Maybe the son of a bitch would put them in his next book or something, with certain parts blurred out.

He moved his other hand, which held something metallic and familiar, and nudged Woodbury in the side. 'Mister Secretary?'

'Yes?' The solitary word bore no emotion.

'Just so we're in complete understanding, besides the envelope, I'm also holding the knife that I used on you a few hours ago.'

No reply. People were moving around in the studio, and his younger brother—his brave, loyal younger brother—was speaking to somebody on the phone. Roy said, 'If you decide at the very last minute not to keep your part of the bargain, I plan to slit your throat, on live TV. Just so you know.'

Woodbury sighed. 'The knife won't be necessary. Not at all.'

'Good.' Roy tried to catch his brother's eye but failed. Damn it, so this was what it had been like to feel good, to feel at peace with the world. Frank came over and started going through the kinds of questions he was going to ask, and the kinds of answers that would work, and Roy just nodded in all the right places and kept looking at his brother.

The chief and the major had left the command post for a moment to take care of some problem involving the governor or some damn foolish thing, when the state police negotiator in the corner sat up quickly and said, 'Hello? Who's this? Can we talk? Please? Can we talk?'

Clay dropped his coffee cup and strode over to the negotiator, who was writing down something on a legal pad of paper. The negotiator said, 'Who's this? Jason? Look, Jason, can you tell me how many—'

'Give me the phone,' Clay said.

'Jason, please, hold on, just for a moment.' The negotiator, a hard-eyed smaller man with steel-rimmed glasses, looked up at Clay and said, 'What the fuck do you think you're doing, screwing around like this?'

Clay smiled. 'I'm not screwing and I'm not fucking. What I'm doing is my job, and you'd better let me do it if you want your career to exist past noon today, pal. You've heard everything that's gone on in this room, right? You know who's running this playground, and it's me. Hand over the phone.'

Clay felt sorry for the state police officer, who was just doing his job and probably hated Clay with every fiber of his being, and who could blame him? The negotiator's face turned red, and he held the phone up and said, 'Fuck you and whatever it is you're going to do. I'm sure as hell not going to be part of it.'

With that, the negotiator strode out. Except for a couple of officers manning the communications gear, Clay had the place to himself. 'Thanks,' he called out to the negotiator, and he put the phone up to his ear.

'C'mon, c'mon,' Patty said, flicking the headlights off and on, off and on. 'Can't you at least turn your back, just for a moment?'

Paul was quiet, too quiet, and Patty felt sick at what was going on with her boy. She knew he should be fussing or crying or doing something, but it was like he had given up, which sickened her. But all she could do was to keep up with the headlights, flashing the SOS to anybody out there who might see her.

'Please,' she murmured. 'Please, somebody, see me.'

From out of the corner of his eye, Jason saw the activity at the other end of the studio, where Woodbury and his brother were seated on the couch, and Frank was fussing around with the microphones or whatnot. Jason had started talking to a cop on the other end of the line. He knew enough to know that it was a negotiator and he was counting on that, to buy them some time, to ensure that Roy and the secretary got the story out on the air.

But something went wrong, quite quickly. The officer on the other end had seemed concerned about what was going on, in the few seconds he had talked with him, but then there was a noise, like the phone was being passed from one hand to another, and then silence.

He looked around the studio, wondered if this was the moment that the cops were coming in, that the negotiator was giving up, when a different voice came on the line. 'Jason?' it asked.

'Yeah, that's right, and I'm telling you right now, if you want this to end peacefully, pull those cops back, all right?' Jason said, hoping his voice wasn't trembling too much. 'You hear me? Pull the cops back and nobody gets hurt, and this can end peacefully, in just a little while.'

'Unh-hunh,' the man said. 'Tell you what, Jason. Are you up to a counteroffer?'

'Sure,' he said, looking up again at the bank of televisions, seeing all of the police cruisers and uniformed cops and SWAT team members, moving in closer to the building. 'What's your counteroffer?'

The man said, 'Here it is. You and your brother and Secretary Woodbury come out of the building, right now, and I won't kill your wife and son. How's that for a fucking counteroffer?'

It felt like the whole building was coming in on him, closing in, making it hard to breathe. 'What?' he asked, and now he knew his voice was trembling.

'You heard me,' the man said. 'You get out of there in thirty seconds, you and your brother and Woodbury, and I won't kill Patty or Paul. There. Is that clear?'

'Who the hell is this?' he asked, ashamed at how weak his voice sounded.

The man chuckled. 'Let's just say I'm a person with an intense interest in seeing this situation settled in the correct way. And pal, the correct way is the three of you walking out. Right now. Before Patty and Paul are dead.'

Jason took a breath, tried to ease the hammering in his chest. 'You're bluffing.'

'Am I? Let's look at the facts. Your wife is wearing blue jeans and a light blue Oxford shirt, sleeves rolled up. There's a mole just behind her left ear. On her right hand, there is a scar, maybe from a kitchen accident. Your son Paul, he's wearing Oshkosh-B'gosh overalls, a Winnie-the-Pooh T-shirt, and—'

Jason said, 'Shut up, damn it, shut up!' He looked over at Roy and Woodbury, the secretary of state staring straight ahead, his brother sitting there smiling, looking so sharp and clean in his Air Force uniform. 'Please don't hurt them. Please.'

Another chuckle. 'Then we're almost there, Jason. Just walk on out and I won't touch them, not at all.'

Jason took another breath. 'I can't do that.'

'Oh yes you can. You're doing this for somebody you haven't seen in nearly thirty years. Are you willing to risk your family for him? For friends of his, that everyone has forgotten about? That everybody thinks are dead? Are you willing to risk your wife and son for men who've been dead all these years?'

Roy caught his eye, gave him a wave. Jason waved back. Another breath. He remembered everything the two of them had gone through the past thirty-six hours, the tales his brother had told him, of the solitude, the hardship, the death, the despair, and how he had practically walked across the country, barely surviving, to make it all right. To help his brethren. To fulfill his duty.

'Yes,' Jason whispered. 'God help me, I'm willing to do that.'

And he hung up the phone.

Officer Sal Cloutier was a seven-month veteran of the Manchester Police Department, and he was glad to be on the perimeter with Officer Fred Roth, a five-year veteran. This was the biggest call he had ever been on in his short time with the department, and as he stood there, he repeated the unofficial cop's prayer: Dear God, please don't let me screw up.

In front of them was yellow police tape, Currier Road, and the nearly empty parking lot that belonged to Channel 21. Near the building he could see the state police and Manchester SWAT teams slowly moving into position, and while he thought they looked cool in their boots, combat clothing, helmets, goggles, and protective vests, he was seriously rethinking his earlier interest in joining the SRT. Man, this was some heavy shit, to go into a place where hostages were being held, when there was a pretty good chance of gunplay. It was one thing to respond to a domestic or to pull over a pickup truck weaving across a solid yellow line, but to actually insert yourself into a dangerous situation like this, well, he wasn't sure if he'd ever have the stones for that.

He turned to look at Fred, who was standing there chewing a piece of gum, when something caught his eye. He turned and saw the headlights of a Honda, on the far end of the parking lot, turn themselves off. Hunh. He waited, wondering why the lights had just gone on like that.

'Hey, rook,' Fred said.

'Yeah?' He turned back.

'What are you looking at?'

'There's a Honda back there. I thought I saw the headlights come on or something.'

Fred said, 'You remember what the sergeant said when he put us here?'

Sal felt his face get red. 'Stay put and keep an eye on the road.'

Fred folded his arms. 'So here's a word to the wise, rook. The sergeant tells you to hop like a bunny, hop like a goddamn bunny. The sergeant tells you to keep eyes up front, don't be scratching your ass and looking in the wrong direction. Got it?'

Sal was going to say that he hadn't been scratching his ass, but let it slide. 'Yeah, Fred. I got it.'

'Good.'

Patty froze, wondering if she had been caught. Just as she had switched off the headlights, she had seen movement over at the office complex. In the window, no doubt about it, was Clay Goodwin, looking right in her direction. She felt like a small furry animal being faced by the cold eyes of a rattlesnake. She could hardly move, and when Clay raised his hand and gave her a slight wave, she bit her lower lip, not wanting Paul to hear her sob.

Steve Josephs felt himself slip into the zone. His breathing, his heart rate, everything seemed to slow down. All that really existed was the universe in his telescopic sight, and the whisper of voices in his earphone. Part of him admired the radio discipline that was exhibited over the special SWAT frequency. There was no chatter, no idle talk, just clipped, professional voices, talking to Hank, the SWAT team supervisor.

'Cooper's in position.'

'Barry's on the roof, sighted in.'

'Hank, entry team about five meters away from the main entrance.'

And as he waited, the crosshairs firm on the chest of the man in the Air Force uniform, he remembered the hours and days and weeks of training, the countless rounds shot out of this very same rifle, the booming echo over the test range, getting the shot right at fifty yards, seventy-five yards, and a hundred yards. About six to eight times a year he and the other SWAT members had been called out, but never to anything this huge. Usually it was a drunk who barricaded himself in a trailer, deep in the forest up in the Great North Woods, or some fugitive on the lam from Massachusetts or New York, holed up in a motel room in the Lakes District.

But nothing like this. Not for a moment.

Voices. He raised his head up from the scope for a moment. A man's voice, coming from up forward, and he turned his head to the left, to check with Nelson, his spotter. Nelson looked over at him, pointed down to the studio. The man's voice became clearer, and he could see him moving around the couch where the Air Force vet—who didn't look particularly crazy but who did look pretty worn and tired—and the secretary of state were sitting. A trick of acoustics, that was all, and the man's booming voice could actually be heard up here, in bits and pieces:

'. . . so when I'm done, Roy, I'll go to you first . . .'

'. . . we'll start with how you and the other personnel listed as missing in action . . .'

'. . . how long you were kept captive in the Soviet Union . . .'

'. . . how many of you died in Russia . . .'

'. . . State Woodbury and how he learned of your fate over three years ago . . .'

'. . . the survivors who are still there . . .'

'. . . how you escaped . . .'

Steve swallowed, rubbed at his face. Bristles were there, where he hadn't shaved this morning. Nelson was now looking right at him, his eyes showing surprise, and he silently mouthed two words: Holy shit. Steve shook his head, placed his eye back at the telescopic sight. The view was slightly blurry, and he couldn't understand why, until he pulled back some and saw that his hands were trembling. He was out of the zone, that's all. Time to go back. He moved and then his elbow struck the cardboard box that contained the special ammunition. It tilted and he thought the damn thing would tip and fall over. Make some noise. He looked over to Nelson, who was now back in his own zone, head down at the spotting scope.

With his right hand, he moved the box closer to him, where it belonged.

Head back on the sight. Breathe in, breathe out. Crosshairs back on the vet's chest. The view was no longer blurry.

He was back in the zone.

His right hand went up to the bolt action of the rifle.

Clay found himself smiling as he hung up the phone. Jesus, that son of a bitch had balls. You had to give him that. Having never been married or had children or any other particular relationship that actually mattered, he thought that appealing to somebody like Jason about the life of his wife and son would have worked some magic. But no, the newspaper editor—an editor!—had hung up on him. He walked over to the window and looked out at the parking lot. Patty Harper seemed to be looking over at him, and he put his hand on his cell phone, thought about ending it right now.

Why not?

Because, he thought. Focus on what was important, and what was important was getting Woodbury and company out of there before the television station got its act together, and making that phone call to Nevada. If he lit off the Honda right now, then that would definitely screw up this nice little train as it was heading to the station. He couldn't imagine the cops rushing into the TV studio right after a car bomb blew up in their laps. So. Just for the hell of it, he waved at Patty, sitting up straight in the Honda. Feel good, hon, he thought. You've got at least some more minutes to live. Make 'em worthwhile.

Movement, behind him. The chief and the major came in, accompanied by the negotiator, and it had been a very long time since Clay had ever seen such a pissed-off trio. Clay spoke quickly, saying, 'I apologize. I took control of the negotiations from this officer here, and I shouldn't have.'

The chief said, 'Who were you talking with?'

'The brother of the vet.'

The major said, 'And what was the upshot?'

Clay looked out the window again. Patty Harper was sitting there, pretty as a little doll. He said, 'Not much. He sounded as crazy as his older brother. Talking about Vietnam and plots and conspiracies. He said something about stopping the radio waves going into his head, and then he hung up.'

'That's bullshit,' the negotiator said. 'I started a dialogue and he was clear and coherent. Until you got on the phone.'

Clay said, 'Be that as it may, what's the status of the entry teams?'

The major looked to the chief, who said, 'They'll be ready to go in two minutes.'

'Good,' Clay said, feeling better that he was just seconds away from closing this situation up. 'You'll get your go order then.'

The chief said, 'No, we're going to try negotiations again. That's what we're going to do. And we're going to try negotiations even if it takes all morning.'

Clay took a moment, just a second to hold on to everything, and said, 'Gentlemen, I'll remind you that being from the Department of Justice, and this matter involving a kidnapping and a former government official, I'm controlling this hostage scene. And when your entry teams report they are ready to go in, they're going in.'

'Buddy,' the chief said, coming to him, face red, fists clenched. 'You are so way out of line, I'm getting your ass tossed out of here in about one minute.'

Oh, this was going to be some fun, Clay thought, as the chief plowed his way toward him, and just as he started closing in, one of the cops manning the communications console said, 'Sir, take a look!'

They all stopped, looked to where the cop was pointing. The television set that had been showing the studios of *Good Morning America* down there a few hundred miles southwest in New York City was now showing a blank screen, with the Channel 21 logo.

'Something's going on,' the chief said.

'Chief,' Clay said, 'you are so right.'

Automatically, he checked his watch. It was 7:24 A.M.

'Gentlemen,' he said. 'It's time for your entry teams to go in and end it.'

Frank stepped out of his office, adjusting his necktie. It had been a couple of years since he had sat in front of a camera, and he was surprised at the sparrows rumbling around in his belly. He smiled at the memory. Other times, other people had complained about the butterflies in their stomachs, and he had said, butterflies? I'd kill for butterflies, 'cause I got sparrows with sharp beaks and claws bouncing around down there. In his career at Channel 21, he had interviewed lots of people, from Hell's Angels heading up to Laconia for the annual Motorcycle Weekend, to three different presidents of the United States making courtesy and political calls to the home of the first-in-the-nation primary.

But for this interview, the sparrows in his gut had turned into eagles.

He went back into the newsroom, looked up at the clock. It was 7:21 A.M. George came to him, shaking his head, holding a cell phone in his hand. 'Sorry, Frank. I've tried three cell phones and not one of them was able to get through to New York. Maybe the cops are running interference, maybe they disabled the local cell towers. All I know is that I got blanked out. We're just lucky the cops haven't killed our satellite uplink.'

Frank said, 'Don't worry about the phones. We're going on in two minutes, and it's going to be up to New York to see what we're doing and break in. Just hope our satellite dish is still in one piece by then.'

George grabbed his arm as he went around the assignment desk. 'Frank . . . this story? Is it the real deal?'

'Yeah, it's the real deal.'

'Are you certain?'

Frank said, 'As certain as I'm going to be, and if I'm wrong, well, I'll be in the unemployment line tomorrow.'

George shook his head. 'You and me and everybody else in here. Okay, Frank. Your call.'

'Yes,' he said. 'My call.'

He stepped out into the bright lights of the studio, sat down in his chair, picked up the mike and fixed it to the lapel of his suit jacket. He took a breath. Beside him was Roy, looking pretty impressive in his Air Force uniform, and next to him the secretary of state, looking disheveled and about sixty seconds away from a heart attack. Right about this moment, Frank thought, the station manager would be landing at Manchester, right from a red-eye in Los Angeles. With any luck, he'd catch this little broadcast in about sixty seconds.

464

Before him were the two cameras, the bright lights, and a little huddle of Channel 21 personnel, waiting to see whether history was being made or the craziest dumb mistake a news director had ever made since old Philo Farnsworth invented TV.

'Sixty seconds, Frank,' George said.

He nodded. Up on the banks of television screens, he saw *Good Morning America* flicker out, to be replaced by a slide with the Channel 21 call sign, which stayed up for about ten seconds before it was replaced by the animation that showed A CHANNEL 21 SPECIAL REPORT.

He took another deep breath and picked up his notes. Damn eagles were now the size of condors.

Jason stood there, about ten feet away from the studio, eyes tearing up, so full of pride and fear that he wasn't sure how he was going to make it through this broadcast. He was afraid of what he had just heard, the threats against Patty and Paul, and all he could hope, all he could think about, was that this man—whoever he was—was somehow among a bunch of cops and that they wouldn't allow him to hurt his family, if possible. And the pride . . . there he was, his long-lost and presumed-dead brother, back home alive, who was about to change the world and save his fellow POWs and set everything right. Everything. And when this was over, well, it would be time to fly to Florida, to see Mom and Dad, and he wondered how in God's name they were going to respond.

A movement. Roy was motioning to him to come over, and he knew that it was close, very close, but he quickly walked over and Roy grabbed his hand and brought him down, and Jason was surprised at the kiss he got on his cheek from his older brother.

'Forgive me,' Roy said, 'for losing my temper with you, and for taking advantage of you. I couldn't have done this without you, Jason. I'm proud of you, kid, real proud of you. I love you, bro.'

Jason opened his mouth, but Frank hissed, 'Jason, get the fuck out of the shot, will you?'

He nodded, tears now rolling down his cheeks, and took his place back with the small crowd of station personnel.

Roy was surprised at how calm he felt, how right everything was. He had done it, he had really done it, and in a matter of hours, maybe even minutes, his boys would be rescued, would finally be set free, and tonight, for the first time in decades, he would really fall asleep as a free man. My God, he had done it. He had really done it. All those years of despair, of treachery, of loneliness, of planning and replanning, figuring out every scenario, every angle, every possibility, were finally coming to a close.

'Bonny 02,' he whispered. 'Mission accomplished.'

In front of him, he saw a cameraman hold out his hand to Frank, showing five fingers, then four, then three, two, and a little wave. Beside him, Frank said, 'Good morning. I'm Frank Burnett, Channel 21 news director, and this is a Channel 21 special report.'

THIRTY

In the control room of *Good Morning America*, Gary Keegan sat up as somebody said loudly, 'Gary, look at monitor B-4! That Manchester affiliate just broke in, and they're interviewing Secretary Woodbury!'

He looked over at the monitors, saw the familiar face of Secretary of State Woodbury, sitting on a couch, looking damn uncomfortable but looking alive. Some news guy seemed to be running the interview—he looked familiar, Gary had probably met him at some affiliate convention or something—and there was another guy in an Air Force uniform. Something was going on, something newsworthy, damn it, and while Woodbury might have been a reported kidnap victim, Gary didn't see any gun being held to his head. Earlier in the news segment they had done a quick piece about the supposed hostage situation, complete with video from their Boston affiliate, but this one belonged to him, just him. The adrenalin was pumping through him like a firehose, and he toggled a switch and listened to the audio:

'. . . have an exclusive story that will clear up one of the most enduring mysteries of the Vietnam War: the fate of a hundred aviators reported missing in action, some of whom are still alive. This story will be verified by one of those pilots, missing for almost thirty years, Air Force Captain Roy Harper, and former Secretary of State Sloan Woodbury . . .'

Gary toggled another switch so fast that he sprained his thumb, speaking urgently to one of the cohosts of *Good Morning America*, sitting in the studio below him: 'Charlie, in ten seconds we're dumping you and going to our Manchester, New Hampshire, affiliate. Sloan Woodbury is there, and he's about to make a public statement about MIAs from Vietnam. Some of them are still alive!'

Across the United States and some portions of the world that were viewing the morning show through a satellite channel, approximately twenty million people saw the male cohost of *Good Morning America* raise a hand to his ear and say, 'Ladies and gentlemen, we are now switching over to our affiliate in Manchester, New Hampshire, Channel 21. Secretary of State Sloan Woodbury, reported kidnapped not more than eight hours ago, is apparently going to be making a statement concerning the whereabouts of American servicemen reported missing in action in Vietnam, and who are reportedly still alive.'

At Blair House in Washington, D.C., the door to an elaborately decorated suite was thrown open, and a man in a dark blue suit said, 'Sir! You really must see this. Please!'

The man who was being spoken to rose from his breakfast table, wearing a white terry-cloth robe, and walked into the adjoining room. Some of his staff were clustered around a television set, and they pulled away as he came closer. With a

468

shock he recognized one of the men on the television, and then saw another old man sitting next to him, dressed in a U.S. Air Force uniform.

'Oh, Sloan,' said the President of Russia, 'this is not good.'

'. . . Harper was shot down over North Vietnam in December 1972 during the Linebacker II air raids. For almost three decades, his fate—and the fate of more than two thousand others like him—was unknown. Officially, he was listed as missing in action. Unofficially, there were rumors. Rumors that some of these prisoners were still alive. Rumors that some were taken to the Soviet Union. Rumors that are apparently true . . .'

At military facilities across the United States, personnel having their breakfast stopped eating. Those who were watching other networks received urgent phone calls telling them to switch over to the ABC affiliate. At Nellis Air Force Base in Nevada, one young officer, part of an airborne special forces unit conducting training at one of the many bombing ranges nearby, sat by himself in a chair, fists clenched in rage. 'I knew, I knew it, I always knew it.'

'. . . for nearly thirty years, Harper and his fellow officers were tortured, interrogated and kept prisoner by the GRU, the Soviet Union's military intelligence agency. They were forced to reveal secrets about United States military planning, nuclear weapons policy, and strategy and tactics used by the United States Air Force . . .'

In Nevada, Tom Grissom spooned up some of his watery and cold oatmeal, looking over at the expectant faces of his fellow

469

POWs, seeing the hope and anger in their eyes. He ate mechanically, not wanting to see their expressions, and somebody elbowed him and leaned in to whisper in his ear: 'Another fucking day in paradise. How many more? Hunh? How many more?'

Tom kept silent, looking at the empty chair next to him that had been occupied by his captain and dear friend all those long years.

'. . . unfortunately, during these years of captivity, there were deaths. Executions by the GRU and their guards. Suicides by prisoners, despondent over their fate. Diseases that were untreated by the Soviet captors. The number of about a hundred began to dwindle . . .'

Phone calls were placed, promises were made, exorbitant fees guaranteed, and first one, and then another, and quite shortly all the major networks in the United States were carrying the feed from Channel 21 in Manchester.

'. . . then, a few years ago, the surviving members, who called themselves the Sixth Allied POW Wing, received a visit from then Secretary of State Sloan Woodbury and then Foreign Minister and now Russian President Mikhail Filipov. The Russians were prepared to turn over the forty surviving POWs. But they encountered a problem. Namely, a representative of our own government . . .'

In his office in Dallas, Hiram Pickering sat before his desk, looking at the television set in a wooden cabinet next to his mini bar. Three of his closest associates were there, watching, keeping quiet. Hiram sighed, said, 'Howie, I know it's early and all that, but how about fixing me a drink?'

One of his boys got up and went to the bar, past a Frederic Remington sculpture of a cowboy on a horse, and Hiram turned to another man and said, 'Henry, I know you're enjoying the fucking show and everything, but start making some phone calls. I want my jet fired up and ready to leave. I'm gettin' out of Dodge for a while.'

'Where to, sir?'

Hiram grimaced and sipped at the drink when Howie passed it over. 'Anywhere but here, fellas. Anywhere but here.'

'. . . through means and methods which are still not known, the surviving POWs were taken from Russia and were placed in a secret facility in the far reaches of a testing range in the Nevada mountains. Those survivors are still there. Their lives are in danger . . .'

In the command post Clay could not believe what he was seeing, could not believe how in God's name these people were just sitting here, when he had said three times, 'Give them the go signal, gentlemen. Your entry teams. Give them a go signal.'

But he was ignored as the state police and the Manchester officers gathered around the television set, and Clay was going to say it again, because he could just imagine what in the world was going on with Mister Pickering. Then, it was as if God Himself was listening to him, because when the camera shot went over to Roy Harper, sitting there with an envelope in his hand, it was quite clear to see what he was holding in his other.

Clay said, 'Get your people in there! Give the go order!

471

Look, he's holding a knife! He's threatening Woodbury! Tell that sniper to take him out!'

The chief and the major looked up at him from their television viewing, faces troubled, and Clay knew right then and there he had won.

'. . . it is our fervent hope that in broadcasting this story from Air Force Captain Roy Harper and Secretary of State Sloan Woodbury, the lives of the men still being held captive in Nevada will be spared, and this whole story will get the attention it deserves . . .'

At the Glynn Assisted Living Facility in Longboat Key, Florida, a man slowly buttered a piece of toast, half listening to the television set in the next room, where his wife sat watching the morning news. In the past few years his wife had found it hard sleeping through the night, and most mornings he found her in her favorite chair, dozing with an afghan she had made ten years ago tossed across her lap. Those mornings he would just turn down the television and make her breakfast and gently wake her up. It was a comfortable routine.

One that was about to end.

'Dear!' she called out. 'Hurry up, come here, you've got to see this!'

He put the toast and the butter knife down, walked into the next room, saw with horror that his wife was on the floor, leaning up against the television. She turned to him, weeping, her wrinkled hands on the screen.

'It's Roy, it's Roy, he's alive, he's alive, look!'

And Tom Harper knelt down with his wife, as in prayer, and touched the television screen again, as his son, his missing son, oh, my dear boy, smiled and prepared to talk.

His wife, weeping, said, 'I always knew it. Always. I always knew it.'

'Now, speaking about what happened to him since his shoot-down nearly thirty years ago, Air Force Captain Roy Harper. Captain Harper . . .'

The trick acoustics were still working, and Steve Josephs had heard the entire statement from the man who called himself the news director down there in the studio, and through it all he had kept his breathing nice and even, nice and smooth, the crosshairs still centered on the chest of the man he now knew as Captain Roy Harper. Beside him Nelson had only once said something, another repeat of 'Holy shit,' but Steve hadn't moved. He had just lain there, listening but staying in the zone.

A voice, in his earphone. 'Steve, this is Hank. You have a go for a shot.'

He waited.

'Steve, acknowledge.'

He waited.

'Steve, the target is holding a knife near the hostage. You have a go.'

Next to him Nelson whispered, 'Steve, you've got the go. Take the shot.'

His finger was firm on the trigger.

Jason folded his arms tight, suddenly remembered what it had been like when he had been twelve years old, hugging himself and knowing that he would never see his brother again, never, and he rocked back and forth on his heels, so happy that he was wrong. His brother had made it, was right

473

before him, and when this was over he would never be alone, ever again.

He turned his head. He thought he heard voices from up beyond the lights.

Nelson said louder, 'Steve, take the fucking shot.'

Breathe in, breathe out.

'Steve!'

Breathe in, let a half-breath out.

And, God forgive me, pull the trigger, work the bolt, pull the trigger, work the bolt.

Air Force Captain Roy Harper, feeling the smile spread over his face like the touch of the morning sun, had opened his mouth to speak when the hammer blow struck him in the chest.

THIRTY-ONE

For millions of viewers, the next thirty or so seconds of videotape were loud, confusing, and upsetting, and for the rest of the day this particular piece of videotape was shown, reshown, and examined, frame by frame, by news organizations all across the world.

Viewers saw the man identified as an Air Force officer from Vietnam thrown back violently in the couch, grab at his chest, and then fall to the floor. The camera spun to the left, then the right, at the faces of the interviewer and the former secretary of state. A man came into view, right toward the Air Force man on the ground, and then there was a shuddering to the videotape, as if an earthquake had struck, and clouds of smoke and loud explosions, and then the camera tilted up, to the overhead framework of support beams and lights.

Then there was a high-pitched sound, a rainbow graphic of different colors, and back to the studio of *Good Morning America*, where the cohosts—for probably the first time in their professional careers—were speechless on live television.

Frank Burnett flinched at the sound of the gunshot, heard

Roy grunt, and saw Woodbury drop to the ground. Another shot pounded at his ears, and as he turned to see Roy slump to the floor, there were hollow-sounding *booms* ringing out from both ends of the studio. Smoke suddenly went billowing in the studio's direction, and there was a clanging noise, like a small bell being struck, as metal objects flew through the air and fell to the floor. From out of the corner of his eye, he could see Jason running over, face frantic.

He half-remembered seeing a television report on SWAT team procedures, and was recalling seeing a demonstration of what were called flash-bang grenades when he went blind and deaf from the explosion.

From the command post Clay watched with satisfaction the studio of Channel 21 quickly becoming a mass of smoke, flash-bang grenades going off, and the beautiful sight of Roy Harper being shot and falling to the floor. He knew what kind of fire-power snipers had: a .308 round like that punched a hole into somebody you could wave through, and Roy was no doubt dead before he hit the ground.

The command post was practically roaring with the sounds of radio chatter, orders being given, and he smiled and decided it was time to take a close-up look and make sure Woodbury was fine and could make the phone call, and that the surviving brother was taken into his custody, where he could join his wife and son for a hell of a reunion.

Man, what a perfect end to the day that would be.

On the television screen, the footage was now coming from the ABC affiliate out of Boston, which had a crew and satellite truck nearby, and Clay watched for just a moment as the screen showed the lines of SWAT personnel flowing into the building.

Good job, boys, he thought, remembering how much he loved cops.

Then he left the room.

When the first shot seemed to explode from up and behind him, Jason flinched and then screamed, 'No!' as he saw his brother grab at a red spot on his chest, his face grimacing with pain. He raced to his brother, his feet feeling like they were wading through sodden concrete, another shot exploding again from up and behind, and Roy, his brother Roy, now crumpled on the floor. There were screams and shouts and yells and Woodbury fell to the floor, covering his head with his hands, and Frank was turning, his mouth open in shock, his skin now pasty white under the bright lights. It seemed to take hours to cross the few feet, and as Jason fell to his knees on the concrete floor, other explosions roared in the distance. He rolled his brother over on his back, the hat gone from Roy's head, his eyes staring up, blood streaming out from his mouth, the once-proud Air Force uniform torn and sodden up front.

'Roy!' Jason's face was wet and he knew tears were flowing, and he didn't care, placing both hands underneath his older brother's shoulders, trying to lift him up. 'Roy, Jesus, don't you go! Don't you dare leave me again! You hold on, damn it! You hear me! Hold on!'

Shouts, out there on both sides of the studio: 'Police! Hands up! Hands up!'

He pulled his brother closer to him, the dead weight straining at his arms. 'Oh, Roy, Roy,' he said, now bawling. 'God, I've missed you so much. Don't leave me, please. God, we've got so much to do. You hang on!'

Something metallic clanked near his feet. He turned and saw something hissing from a metal cylinder, recognized it as

477

an explosive and turned his head, yelped when the *boom* tore at his back, his ears now ringing, and Roy, Roy was looking at him. Smiling. Lips moving. But Jason's ears were ringing from the explosion, he couldn't hear a thing. He brought his head further down, trying to hear what Roy was saying, and hands tore at him, pulling him back. All about him were police in SWAT gear, fatigues and helmets and face masks, smoke in the studio, more shouts and yells, and he yelped as he was thrown to the floor, a knee now pressing down on his neck, and he tried to yell, tried to say, 'My brother, you've got to let me talk to my brother! I didn't tell him everything! I didn't do enough!' but his face was pushed down on the floor, and his wrists seared with pain as handcuffs were snapped on.

Roy looked up at his brother right after the loud explosion, sounding like a grenade, went off behind Jason's back. But Jason stayed with him, and he had to give him that. There were shouts and more loud bangs, and men in commando gear roaring through, and his chest hurt real bad, worse even than the time old Bonny 02 got hit over North Vietnam, so many eons ago. Jason was crying, great weeping sobs, and Roy started whispering up to him, not to worry, he had done a good job, the very best, and that he was proud to call him his brother. They had gone through it together, these past thirty-six hours, and if it was going to end now, well, at least they were together.

He wasn't sure Jason had heard him. The poor kid was coming closer, trying to say something but Roy couldn't make out the sounds, and then the commandos were on Jason, pulling him away, and damn it, he was so tired, he had done so much.

He closed his eyes to the darkness.

Woodbury raised his head, saw a cluster of people over by the couch, saw the uniform pants leg of Roy Harper turned at an odd angle. Loud voices, smoke in the air, and then he was lifted up by two of the cops and half dragged, half carried through the smoke and the chaos. The small group of men and women who worked at the television station were being herded in front of him, like misbehaving sheep, their hands held high. Woodbury coughed as he went through the lobby and then outside, and he found his voice, saying, 'I can walk, damn it, I can walk!'

He leaned over, trying to catch his breath, outside on the sidewalk. Two Emergency Medical Technicians were upon him, and he waved them off, and other cops came up to him, and he turned on them. 'Leave me alone for just a moment, all right? Leave me alone!'

Another coughing fit overtook him, and he walked out into the parking lot of the television station, amazed at what was going on all around him. At the far end of the lot, near the street, police were lined up behind barricades, and behind those barricades was a crowd of people and television crews and satellite trucks and reporters with notebooks and microphones. Nearby the errant staff of Channel 21 were lying on the pavement, hands on their heads, as SWAT team members went up and down, checking for weapons, searching for God knows what. He winced as a helicopter went overhead, and then another. More police came up to him and he waved them off. He coughed again. That had been close. Very close indeed.

There. Clay Goodwin was approaching, a grin on his face, a cell phone in his hand. Woodbury took out a handkerchief, wiped at his face, felt the throbbing now really return from the stab wound in his shoulder. He wondered where the EMTs were. He would like to have his shoulder looked at and then talk to Clay. Time to start salvaging this whole damn fiasco, beginning with that phone call to Nevada.

Two SWAT members came out of the smoke-filled lobby, looking over at him. There was something odd about the look on their faces. He was expecting pride or curiosity or concern for his condition, but all he got from them was disgust. Utter and complete disgust.

And then he saw the open envelope in one of the cop's hands, an envelope that had been in the possession of Roy Harper.

From her spot in the Honda, Patty caught most of what went on. Even from inside the SUV, she could hear *thumps* as explosions were set off, and she could even see the cops in full battle gear race into the lobby of Channel 21. From the radio station she could hear the excited voice of the announcer, 'It looks like police are now storming the building! We have reports of shots being fired from inside the building. It appears that one of the men taking Secretary of State Woodbury hostage has been shot!'

The blabbering went on. She didn't think that she had any tears left after the past thirty-six hours, that her eyes and tear ducts would have just given up, but she had to wipe at her face, again and again, the saltiness even running into her mouth. She wept for herself and her husband and her husband's brother—a lost soul whom she had insulted and tormented when he had appeared on their doorstep two nights ago—and most of all she wept for her quiet boy next to her, whose childhood had been stolen from him. The door to the office building flew open and Clay Goodwin ran out. She moaned in fear, until she saw him run to the police line, show a badge or something, and be allowed under the tape and across the street, into the now quite busy parking lot.

And just before he reached the parking lot, he looked back at her and waved, pointedly raising the hand holding a cell phone.

Steve said into his bone mike, 'This is Steve. Standing down.'

Next to him, Nelson tapped him on the shoulder. 'Good shooting.'

He said nothing. His right shoulder ached from the kick of the weapon. He started picking up his gear, refusing to think of what had happened and what was probably going to happen. And he decided that if Nelson said one more word, he would break his fucking nose, as much as he liked him.

Frank Burnett was on the hard surface of the parking lot, hands cuffed behind him, part of him wondering whether his station manager had seen this little cluster-fuck unfold after he had flown in from Los Angeles. Nice going, he thought. You get the story of a career and spend so much time blabbing about it, introducing the two key witnesses who could prove the story, you run out of time. Oh, no doubt the storming of Channel 21 would be the lead in every single newscast tonight and on the front page of all the newspapers tomorrow, but to what end? The story hadn't gotten out. All that had gotten out was his own personal opinion of what he had heard.

Roy was back there in the studio, shot, on his back, and Woodbury had been rescued. And would the story now be told?

No. Not at all. Excuses and explanations and the mighty God Spin would be brought in to clean up the mess.

He raised his head, to see how his crew was doing, and something hard tapped against the back of his skull.

481

'Move again and you'll be in real fucking trouble. Sir.'

He put his head down and closed his eyes.

Clay got up to Woodbury and now the helicopters were right overhead, making it hard for him to make himself heard, but he grabbed the fat man's arm and pulled his ear close and said, 'The number, Woodbury! Give me the number for the Nevada facility!'

Woodbury looked awful, like all of his blood had been drained and replaced with embalming fluid, and he weaved back and forth like he had just come off a weekend drunk. He gazed up at Clay, eyes wide and red, lips shiny with drool, and Clay squeezed the man's arm again, hard, for emphasis.

'The number! What's the number?'

And that seemed to stir a random brain cell or three, for Woodbury rattled off seven digits, seven glorious numbers, and with each number uttered, Clay punched it into his cell phone. But before pushing that sweet SEND button, he needed one more thing.

'The code phrase, Woodbury. What is it?'

Again, that moist, dumb look about his eyes, like a cow being led into a slaughterhouse and not quite sure what kind of bad thing was about to happen, only knowing that the bad thing was nearby and quite bloody. He squeezed the man's arm and yelled, 'What the hell is the goddamn code phrase?'

Woodbury whispered something and Clay almost screamed, 'Louder, you damn fool!'

'"Ashes, ashes, we all fall down."'

Clay said, 'Say again?'

Woodbury's voice was louder: '"Ashes, ashes, we all fall down."'

482

Clay grinned, and now there were cops and a couple of EMTs around, and it was like that damn helicopter overhead was trying to blow them away, so he walked off a few dozen yards, to the southern end of the parking lot, and hit the SEND button. He pushed a finger in his other ear and hunched over the phone, and it rang and rang and rang, and was picked up on the fourth ring.

'Yes?' came the voice, Russian-accented.

'I have a coded message for you. Are you ready to receive?'

'Yes.'

'Message follows: Ashes, ashes, we all fall down. Repeat: Ashes, ashes, we all fall down. Do you copy?'

Silence. More cops were coming out of the studio, and it looked like one Jason Harper was being carried, handcuffed and hog-tied, out the front of the lobby.

'Say again, do you copy?'

The man on the other phone said, 'Yes. I copy. It will take some time.'

'That's okay. Just get it done.'

It seemed like the man sighed. 'It has been a very long time.'

'You're fucking telling me, pal,' Clay said, hanging up on him.

In a condo unit on Longboat Key, Florida, an elderly man and his wife hugged each other, kneeling on the carpeted floor, weeping and wondering why God could be so cruel as to take their boy away for three decades and bring him back for just a few moments only to take him away again.

Jason was dumped on the ground, his face and nose scraping against the concrete, his eyes burning from the tears and the smoke, his ears still ringing. Gloved hands poked and prodded him. 'Any weapons?'

'No.'

'If you're lying, we'll strip you down, right here. Your choice. Any weapons?'

'No.'

One of the cops rolled him over on his side, so he could look up at the fierce face, with the goggles and helmet and bulletproof vest. 'You got anything to say?'

'I didn't have enough time,' Jason said.

'What?'

His chest was so tight, he wondered if he was having a heart attack. 'That was my brother back there. Just before he was shot, he told me that he loved me.'

The tears came back. 'I didn't have time to tell him the same thing.'

The cop shrugged, rolled him back on his face. 'We've all got problems today, sir.'

Woodbury was alone now, just for a moment, as he pushed away the cops and EMTs and the brass of the Manchester police and the New Hampshire State Police. He looked over at Clay, making that phone call, and then to another clump of SWAT team members, who seemed to be passing the photos around, the photos that Roy Harper had threatened him with only a few minutes earlier. He thought he had been safe with the agreement, safe in knowing that when he was done with the television broadcast, as distasteful as it was, the photos would be in his possession.

Everything else could be salvaged, but if those photos had gotten out? Utter ruin.

Well, he thought, they are certainly out now, and what could he do? Go over and ask for them back? Ask those rough cops who had just saved his ass if he could have the photographic evidence of his perversity back in his sweaty old hands?

There. See? They were looking at him. And when this day was over, what would be the story, what would be in people's minds when they heard the name Sloan Woodbury? Would they recall his years of service, all of the treaties and agreements and understandings that had been reached, all for the benefit of his nation and its people?

No. When this day was over, all anyone would think of would be Sloan Woodbury, depraved pervert.

He wiped at his face with a coat sleeve.

But there was something he could do. Something that would outshine, that would overwhelm and drown out whatever photos existed of his dark desires. Something he could do, right now, to change the story that was going to be reported today.

Woodbury started walking to the line of the news media, pressing against the police line like some hungry, insatiable beast, and he knew exactly what he was going to do.

Clay snapped the cover of his cell phone shut with satisfaction and looked over to the Honda. Problem one solved. Problem two was in the hands of the police. And problem three was about to join problem one on the solved list.

He opened up the cover, and just as he was going to dial a certain number, he looked over to where Woodbury had been standing with the cops and—

The damn fool was walking right to the news media! Jesus!

Clay started running, yelling at Woodbury, 'Hold on, don't you dare!'

To be this close and to have it snatched away. He would not allow it.

*

Patty saw Clay standing by himself, talking into the cell phone, speaking loudly and quickly it looked like, and then the call was complete. Clay turned around and was now facing her. She reached over and squeezed Paul's hand, hoping it would come quick, it would come very quick.

Then something caught Clay's eye, and he started running, the cell phone now at his side.

And Patty took her hand away from her boy, threw the Honda into drive, and pounded the accelerator to the floor. The CRV seemed to leap out of the parking spot like it had a jet engine in its ass, and she kept it floored, going past two Manchester cops, right through the plastic barrier tape which got stuck on the windshield, over the curbing and into Channel 21's parking lot. Paul started screaming and she pushed him to the floor of the CRV, and kept the accelerator right flat to the surface.

Clay yelled out again to Woodbury, as the damn fool reached the press line, and then something loud caught his ear, like the damn helicopter was going to land on him, and he glanced up and saw nothing, and then looked to his left, at the approaching grill and hood and body of a Honda CRV.

He spun and held up the cell phone like a weapon, started pressing numbers frantically, and he reached the third numeral just as he saw the determined look on Patty Harper's face.

'Shit,' Clay said. He knew the odds had always been against him, that it would end bloodily some day. But now? To a fucking woman in a car?

It wasn't fair.

She didn't flinch, she didn't duck, she didn't close her eyes. She kept the accelerator right where it was, right up to when there was an almighty *thump* as the Honda struck Clay. She was expecting to run over him or drag him or a number of things, but she didn't expect to see the son of a bitch fly up like that, right to the edge of the rocks that marked the end of the parking lot. She hit the brakes and skidded to a halt. Clay fell across the rocks, bloody and clothes torn, and it was amazing, it looked like he was trying to get up, and she put the Honda in reverse, hit the brakes again, put it back in drive and headed right to the rocks.

He was hurt, no doubt about it, he was seriously fucked up, and with his good arm he reached down and behind, trying to get at his weapon, and then the Honda was on him again, and this time he didn't bother to say a word. What was the point?

This time, the *thump* was followed by a sickening crunch, as the Honda plowed into the rocks, and even went over the edge of the parking lot for a few feet. She lost sight of Clay, and then there he was, in the flowing Merrimack River, about a dozen feet away. He wasn't moving, not at all, and then he was pressed against a boulder in the water. The engine was grumbling something awful and Paul was talking to himself and there was pounding on the passenger's side door, but she kept watch, kept watch until she saw the lifeless body of Clay Goodwin slowly roll over, the head underneath the water, only the legs and feet visible.

Paul said, 'Mommy, can I come up?'

'Oh, yes, love, please, do come up.'

Paul came up, lips trembling, and she hugged and hugged him, kissed and kissed the top of his sweet head, and he said, 'Were we in an accident, Mommy?'

'Yes, Paul, yes, we were.'

Paul pulled his head away, face full of concern. 'Was it a bad accident?'

She couldn't help herself. She kissed his forehead. 'No, dear. It was a good accident. A very good accident.'

Something was going on at the other end of the parking lot, and Woodbury didn't care. He pushed away the officers of the Manchester Police Department and the New Hampshire State Police and went up to the reporters, all of whom started shouting. He raised his hand, and when there was some semblance of quiet, he began.

'My name is Sloan Woodbury, and I have a statement to make.'

In Nevada Tom Grissom was doing his morning walk around the exercise yard, and for once his fellow members of the Sixth Allied POW Wing were leaving him alone. It had been long days since Roy had gone out over the fence, and now, well, maybe it was time for the planning to begin. Yet again. And the wait, oh God, the terrible wait . . . that would start up again. Could anything be worse than those long days and weeks and months and years of waiting, just waiting?

Could there be anything worse?

The inner gate opened, and a line of Kims came trooping in, whistles blowing, AK-47s now in their hands, and the other POWs stared and looked at each other. A fire drill, of course, but this didn't look like a drill. Not at all.

Tom had just gotten his answer.

The statement from Sloan Woodbury was carried live on every network in the United States, and on several other networks around the world, and it was later estimated that nearly a hundred million people heard the words of former Secretary of State Sloan Woodbury, speaking from a parking lot of a relatively obscure television station in New Hampshire, describing in great detail what had happened to one hundred American MIAs. Certain men made certain decisions after they heard what they heard from the secretary of state, including those who worked for one Hiram Pickering, who suddenly found himself without a flight crew when he arrived at his private jet.

Tom Grissom felt the fear ripple through his fellow POWs as the Kims shouted at them and pressed them together. Some of the prisoners were cursing, fists clenched in rage, while others seemed dumbfounded that it was all coming to an end, right now, in this isolated corner of their home country. He felt sick at knowing what must have happened, that Roy must have been captured and the news had gotten out somehow, leading to this, the Malmédy solution.

Holman, who had helped him prep Harper the day that kid had stumbled into camp, was next to him. 'The fucks were lucky,' he said. 'Lot of us had knives and shanks back in the barracks. We were going to take some of 'em with us if it ever came to that. Shit, it looks like our shit-ass luck has finally gone away.'

'Sure has,' Tom said, feeling like he was in a mass of sheep as the yelling Kims pushed and shoved them against the wall of the nearest building, and Tom knew why: so that the two closest guard towers would have a clear field of fire, without worrying about the prisoners making for the wire.

Holman slapped him on the back. 'Well, we did our best. Right?'

Tom nodded. 'We sure did.'

'Well, screw the Navy.'

Tom found himself smiling, in spite of it all. 'Yeah, screw the Navy.'

The Kims on the ground moved back, now holding their AK-47s in front of themselves, and the moving and the shifting of the prisoners stopped. Somebody started singing something, 'Amazing Grace,' it seemed like, but Tom kept silent. There was nothing amazing or graceful about what was going to happen.

The Kims worked the actions on their rifles. Holman said, 'Here we go.'

Then there was a noise.

A noise that made the Kims stop and look up.

A noise that quieted every single one of the POWs.

It grew louder, deeper, and then the thrumming noise was recognized by one of their crew: 'Helicopters! We got helicopters inbound!'

Everyone was looking around, looking up at the sky, and by God, there they were, four of them, popping right up over a ridgeline, and they came in low, looking sleek and black and ugly, so fast and smooth, and there were yells from the prisoners, their hands started waving, and one of the Kims by the fence made the mistake of firing at the lead helicopter. The short stutter of gunfire was immediately drowned out by return fire from the first two helicopters, lights flickering and flaring from weapons pods slung under the fuselage. Tom dropped to the ground, as did everybody else.

More gunfire, and then explosions. Tom raised his head. The other compound was burning, as one of the helicopters fired rocket after rocket into the buildings that had housed Malenkov and the North Koreans. The guard towers were all burning as well, and from one of them a Kim whose clothes were ablaze fell to the ground.

'Hose those bastards!' somebody screamed. 'Kill 'em all! Kill 'em all!'

The Kims fired back and then broke and ran, but none of them ran far, as accurate and deadly gunfire rained down from the helicopters. Their bodies tumbled and crumpled and Tom was surprised at how sweet the revenge tasted. He started yelling, too, though he didn't know what in God's name he was saying. It was just so good to see their guards, their tormentors, their overseers, run away and die.

'Look, look, they're landing! They're landing!' Tom turned his head, his eyes gritty from the dust and dirt being kicked up by two helicopters that had landed at the other side of the compound. Soldiers dived out and ran away from the spinning blades, weapons held at the ready, but there was no return fire. All of the Kims were dead, wounded, or were standing still, arms held straight up. The two helicopters that had dropped off the troops rose up again, and the noise started lessening. Tom and then the others slowly stood up as the soldiers approached, dressed in black fatigues, wearing helmets and goggles, American flag patches on their shoulders.

'Dress it up,' Tom said suddenly. 'Let's dress it up.'

Which is what they did, much to his surprise. The prisoners lined up in neat rows, standing straight and proud. As the soldiers came closer, they could all see the tears streaming down the prisoners' faces. Someone yelled out, 'Sixth Allied POW Wing, atten-*tion*!'

The heels snapped together, but the rescuing soldiers were quicker off the mark. They stopped before the group, and as one raised their hands in salute. Tom and his brethren saluted in return, and he could not believe the joy and pride racing through him. They had done it. Roy had made it. It was going to be all right. Finally, after so very long a wait, it was going to be all right.

The salutes were completed. Both groups of men stood there in silence, staring at each other.

At Tom's side, Holman broke free and stood in front of the former prisoners, looking at the young and strong and confident soldiers. Then he said loudly, 'Jesus, what took you so fucking long?'

And he was smiling, and then everyone was smiling and laughing and then talking and hugging each other, free men all.

EPILOGUE

Two weeks after the police raid on Channel 21, Jason Harper sat in the back yard of his home in Berwick, Maine, a new laptop on the picnic table before him. He had tilted the screen around so that the sun wouldn't obscure it, but even then, it was hard to get the words out. He had always prided himself on being a quick and efficient writer, but these past few days, the words had come out as slow as old motor oil on a February morning. He looked over at the slow-moving Salmon Falls River, shuddered as he remembered what he and his brother had dumped in there that first night. Both bodies had been recovered last week by the Berwick Police and the Maine State Police, and if they wanted to come talk to him about it, they sure as hell knew where he lived. Berwick was certainly never going to be the same, and in a few short days, if they were lucky, the reborn Berwick *Banner* would be reporting on it.

There was giggling, over by the maple tree, and he looked over at Paul, playing with a puppy who seemed intent on chewing a green tennis ball to death. The dog's name was Mulligan and it was a springer spaniel—they all thought that getting another Labrador retriever would hurt just too much—and by the maple tree Patty had planted some flowers, in memory of dear brave Caleb. Just as Roy had suggested, they had honored their pet for trying to save all of them, especially young Paul, who after a couple of nights of nightmares seemed to be doing all right.

The side screen door slammed shut and his wife came out carrying a glass of lemonade, and she bent down and kissed him, and he kissed her back, and she rubbed the cold glass against his forehead, making him smile. 'You doing okay?' she asked.

He sipped from the lemonade. 'Writing a book is so damn different from doing newspaper stories, I don't have to tell you that. It's going slow.'

She sat down and grabbed his hand. 'That's all right. So long as it keeps on going. You just write about everything, Jason. Everything that happened.'

He squeezed her hand. Even now he would look at her from the corner of his eye, remembering that she had killed a man. His own bride had taken another man's life. He had tried to talk to her about it just the other night, and she had sweetly cut him off with a kiss and a hug, saying, 'Dear heart, I'll never talk about that. Ever. Except to say this. He was going to kill me and Paul, and I got to him first, and that makes me very happy.'

Me too, he thought. Very happy indeed.

Jason said, 'That's what I'm trying to do, to get everything down. But there's a lot of ground to cover.'

'I'm sure there is, and I know you'll cover it well. I have no doubt.' She leaned in and said, 'There's somebody here to see you.'

'Oh? And how did he get past the cruiser at the end of the driveway?'

'He asked politely, that's how. Look, here he comes now. You need a break anyway.'

Jason stood up, saw the man walk hesitantly toward him. He seemed about his own age but was lean and muscular, with close-cropped hair, wearing a red polo shirt and blue jeans. He came forward and held out his hand. 'Mister Harper?'

'Yes,' Jason said, giving it a quick shake.

'Um . . .' The man stood there, embarrassed, his eyes looking like they were starting to tear up. 'I . . .'

Patty slipped her arm through her husband's. 'Go ahead. It'll be all right. I promise.'

The man nodded, bit his lower lip. 'Okay. The name is Steve Josephs. I'm with the New Hampshire State Police . . . I was, um, I was the sniper who shot your brother. I wanted to come here and tell you personally just how sorry I am that I did that. Honest to God, I haven't slept a good night since then. I'm so very sorry for what I did.'

Jason looked at the expression on the man's face, at the tears in his eyes, the trembling now taking place in his lower lip, and he said quietly, 'That's all well and good, but why don't you apologize to him yourself?'

And from the kitchen door, his brother Roy came out.

Roy came down the steps and out into the bright sunshine, still having to force himself to move ahead, to get things done, for he was sorely tempted each and every day just to sit and watch everything. That's all. Just sit and watch his brother and his sister-in-law and his nephew, and their new dog, and just taste the good food and cold drink, and feel the free air upon his skin and soul. The past days had been a blur, highlighted one afternoon by a long and wonderful phone call with his EWO, Tom, who said that even now there was talk of a reunion for the freed prisoners. A reunion, after spending almost thirty years together! That had caused some good belly laughs for a very long time, which made up for the hours of debriefs, with everyone from the CIA to the FBI to his very own Air Force, who didn't seem in a particular hurry to get rid of him. While his rank was in question, he was still in the service, though a long leave had been granted.

About the only R & R had taken place last week when they had all made a brief and lovely trip to Florida, and the hot sun and sands and being with Mom and Dad actually made him sluggish and slow, as if he couldn't process everything. Seeing the two of them had been sweet indeed, but the bright light and heat was too much, and he was glad when they came back to the cool air of Maine. His parents would be up next week, but right now it was a beautiful day out here in the backyard, and every other day ahead was going to be beautiful as well.

There was a man with his brother and Patty. He went over and Jason said, 'Roy, this is Trooper Steve Josephs, from the New Hampshire State Police. He has something to say to you.'

Steve stood there, the strong young man looking like he was ready to bawl, and then he said, 'I was the sniper, back at the TV station. I'm sorry you were shot like that. But I had to do it.'

Roy rubbed at his chest, felt the tenderness there, just now getting better. 'Sure. Orders and all that. But son, what in hell did you shoot me with? It felt like a mule kick.'

The trooper smiled, pulled something out of his pocket and tossed it over to Roy. He caught it and examined what looked like a regular rifle cartridge, except the bullet was almost soft to the touch. 'This was it?'

Steve said, 'An experimental round that we've been testing. Some salesman gave us all samples a couple of weeks ago. It has a special paraffin-and-rubber tipped round that's designed to disable and hurt. Not to kill. That's what hit you.'

Roy tossed the cartridge back to the trooper, who caught it easily. 'It sure as hell disabled me, that's for certain. It was like I couldn't breathe, for the longest time.'

Jason said, 'You said it's experimental?'

'Yes.'

'Then why did you use it?' he asked. 'I mean, shouldn't you have used your regular round?'

Steve nodded, his eyes welling up again. Paul was with the puppy and was laughing, and Steve said, 'I should have, and it's still up in the air what's going to happen to me when all of the hearings and investigations are over. You see, sir—'

'Roy,' he said.

'Roy, you see, just before we were put into position, I noticed something. The lead guy from Justice who was running the show, I had seen him the day before, on a traffic stop. But back then he said he worked for a security company in Connecticut. That sort of rattled me.'

Jason said, 'Considering who he was and what he did, I can see why.'

Steve's voice got stronger. 'So I went in there, not liking what was going on. And when we got into position, up where we were, we could hear everything that was being said down in the studio. I heard that TV guy talking to you before going on air, and when you went on air, well, I heard the whole thing, about you being taken to Russia and kept there for years, and then being sent to Nevada. That really struck me, Roy, it really did. And you didn't look violent, not at all, so I prepared my rifle, just in case I got the go order. You see, I didn't want you to get hurt. I had to know.'

Roy knew where this was going, but said it anyway. 'Had to know what?'

Steve's head bobbed, and the tears were really coming

down his cheeks. 'Had to know if you knew my father, Roy. You see, when I was a kid he was in the state police, but he was also in the Marine Reserves. He got called up when I was real little, back in 1968. He was in a firefight near Hue and was reported missing in action. I . . . I never really knew my dad, and I thought, well, maybe you had heard of him, or had seen him, or . . . Well, you know.'

Roy reached over, squeezed the young man's shoulder. 'Sure, I know. And I'm sorry, Steve. I truly am. All of us there were aviators. There were no Marines or Army personnel. I'm sorry I didn't know him.'

Steve folded his arms, nodded, and Roy saw that even Patty was fighting back tears, as was his brother. My God, the damn war's been over for thirty years, for thirty damn years, and we're still fighting it and remembering it and mourning it, especially all those lost men, all those lost men with families still out there, living and hoping and praying.

He pulled in Jason and put his arm around him. 'Steve, talk to my brother here. He's a writer, you know? And he's going to write the damnedest book ever about POWs and MIAs from Vietnam, starting with the old stories and lies, and going right up to what happened in Manchester. You see, I was in the Air Force and he's just a civvie, but we have one thing in common.'

Roy looked at his family, and at Steve Josephs, and squeezed his brother's shoulder once again. 'We're going to bring them home. All of them, even if it means just recovering their remains. And you'll see, we'll get your dad home. That I promise you.'

Steve wiped at his eyes. 'Thanks, Roy.'

Roy touched him again with his free hand. 'No, thank you, son. For always remembering. And never forgetting. Not ever.'